INTO THE LABYRINTH

INTO THE LABYRINTH

Q Christina Byrnes Wampler

Q Christina Byrnes Wampler Author

TO ELENA AND SADIE

FOR THE READER, THIS GRIMDARK WORLD WILL MAKE
YOU LAUGH, CRY, FALL IN LOVE, RAGE, AND PONDER.

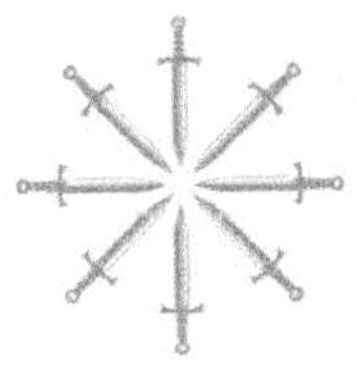

This book contains the following themes and depictions, presented without mitigation:

Graphic violence and gore

Psychological distress and trauma

Sensory deprivation and isolation

Segregation and enforced hierarchies between species

Sexual content and sexualized illustrations

Boundary-pushing attempts at seduction

BDSM

This book is written and edited in British English

Honor Roll:

Name	Element
All Unnamed Beta Readers	Air
Assassin Designs Official	Electricity
Brea Redmayne	Metal
Elena Arroway	Ice
Josy Stokes	Venom
Miss Rage Tattoos	Venom
Prose Without Thorns	Fire
Sandra Griffin	Illusion
Scarlett Stokes	Water
Siena Kacary	Metal
You the reader <3	...

PROLOGUE: NYX

The Beginning of the End

The ruling family holds many special privileges, but their true power comes from their sway over the nobility.

-Politics and Dengar by King Blackthorn, written 15 AT

Nyx walked into the ballroom, feet padding softly across the slowly swirling miasma of colour that was the floor. It had been infused with Theos when the castle had been created. Theos was the Elemental magic that Aervel used to have access to in the Age of Theos.

Nyx tilted her head back to look at the stained glass, where the Elemental Runes were depicted in mosaics, circling the sky above. Warm sun shone down through the simple symbols, painting the floor in a colourful medley.

The top Rune was two hexagons overlapping slightly. The Rune for Illusion, and the God of Illusion, Marvos. Next to it was Axios's Rune, Electricity, *my Element*. A mighty lightning bolt was the Rune for Electricity. Six more Runes made up the rest of the circle. A swirl for Air, a four-pointed star for Venom, a square for Metal, a single flame for Fire, a droplet for Water, and finally a triangle for Ice. Nyx smiled, continuing on towards her room. She loved the stained glass, and could look at it for hours.

Her father's deep voice stopped her in her tracks. *It's coming from the throne room; today is Dad's day off.*

Nyx crept to the edge of the door, listening in.

I wonder who he could be talking to.

Peeking around the door frame, she saw her father on his throne. His wings were twitching in agitation. Silver eyes bore into his visitor. "You said we have how many years?" Her father's voice cracked slightly.

That's not like Father. He's never scared.

Nyx's heartbeat quickened, and she could feel her eyes prickle with tears that threatened to fall. Her father ran a hand over his bald head. His fine ring, featuring a square which was the Elemental Rune for Metal, shone in the light.

Maybe I shouldn't be listening to this.

Nyx's feet stayed planted.

The male held out a Theometer, showing the king.

"This will be our last year to complete the trials. The food has been measured for Theos."

Nyx looked to the device. Aervel Venom-Element healers had used them before the fall of Theos to measure Theos-derived diseases.

Aren't they supposed to light up?

"There's barely any left in the crops. Theos deficiency is on the rise. If the Theos isn't revived, the kingdom will die out within the year." The visitor said, his red wings signifying that his Element was Fire. He was in full plate armour, likely coming straight from the front lines at the Hell Portal.

The Gods had blessed the Aervel species with Theos, then mysteriously took it away two decades before a portal to Hell had opened.

Thousands of Minotaur had been released through the portal, pillaging and destroying towns. Dengar had been locked in war since.

News had come in the form of a Runed stone, the high priest asking the Gods for an explanation.

The stone supplied only the knowledge of a set of trials to revive Theos, as well as instructions for the Rune Choosing ceremony.

If this is the last year, I will go to classes with the Champions.

Her father had once let her see the stone tablet with the decree, but it was written entirely in Runes.

I will see them get Chosen.

"I will be enrolling Harvey and Nyx at Veritas Hall this year," the king muttered to himself.

His strong shoulders slumped momentarily.

The visitor, noticing the king's discomfort, spoke up, "Two thousand students. There's no reason the prince and princess will get Chosen. Eight go in, and you likely get to pick for four of them."

"You are right, I am being irrational. Harvey and Nyx will be fine. For now, send a message to the headmistress, Loche, to arrange a meeting. I will increase the training schedule for first-year students. They are our only shot at redemption. To think, the Gods have given such a tremendous job to the younger generation." Nyx's dad seemed to notice that he was rambling. "You are dismissed. I will be in my painting studio. Ensure no one disturbs me until dinner. Today is my day off."

"Yes, my King."

A History of Dengar

Theos Age

50 TA — Hell Portal opens

70 TA — Minotaur Wars start

82 TA — Halfblood Massacre

X — Theos dissapears

1 AT — 1st Annual Rune-Choosing Ceremony

20 AT — Blackthorns voted into power

50 AT — Prince Harvey Born

52 AT — Bastard princess Nyx born

76 AT — The Blackthorn prince and princess start school

76 AT — 75th Annual Rune-Choosing Ceremony

After Theos

CHAPTER 1: HARVEY

Welcome to Veritas Hall

Today was wondrous; it kills me not to share my joy with you. I peeked through the door when you were taking your entrance exam for Veritas Hall. I have never seen someone move the way you do. You are the perfect muse. My perfect fiancé. It almost makes it better that we can't tell anyone, our dirty little secret.

-Titan letter to Havey, 10th Day, 76 AT

The students parted like a river around rocks as Harvey Blackthorn entered the training hall. He strode confidently to the front of the assembly, taking his designated seat at the front of the room.

Titan Yarrow, his fiancé, was already sitting in the spot next to his own. Harvey sat down. The need to touch Titan nagged at him as it always did when in public. He let his leg fall to the side arrogantly, as if taking up extra room. His leg connected with Titans, and Harvey's heart sped up.

He looked over to Titan briefly, fighting the urge to stare at his perfection. Titan was beautiful, with Metallic golden hair curling into his sky-blue eyes. He smelled of warm clay and pine. Harvey closed his eyes.

Now is not the time. I need to focus. The future of the kingdom will be my responsibility one day.

Harvey wrenched his gaze away to inspect the hall better. His foot tapped with impatience before he schooled his body into stillness. The hall was large, with a high, stained-glass ceiling that lit the room.

The school is known for its stained glass.

At the front of the hall, a temporary platform had been erected. Black and white banners hung regally along the stone walls, one for each of the Elements.

"Look at all the different Elemental markers!" Titan exclaimed beside him, drawing his attention back to his fiancé.

Titan was referring to the physical signs of an Aervel's Element that were constantly on display. Even with Theos dormant in Dengar, each Aervel had a connection to one of the Elements. Elemental Markers varied in amounts and types, sometimes having to do with hair or nail colour, like Titan's Metallic gold hair and nails.

Others were dynamic, like Harvey's own Elemental Illusion Marker: eyes that changed colour with his mood. Their natural state was a soft pink, in contrast to his darker skin. When he was angry, his eyes turned crimson, most often present around his half-sister, Nyx.

Unlike Harvey, her dark hair was broken up by streaks of pink, courtesy of their father's indiscretions with a pink-haired Dyrfaldur.

I am blessed to have a beautiful, pure-blooded Aervel betrothed to be my husband. Unlike my unholy, annoying, irresponsible… Where is she anyway?

Harvey turned around to look at the hall; rows of first-year students sat chatting amiably with each other. Inconsequential to the long-lived Aervel species, the first-years ranged from twenty-one and twenty-six years of age.

Harvey looked to the back rows where the Dyrfaldur sat; they were shorter, with animalistic features. Unpredictable, and able to shift at will, the Dyrfaldur were dangerous with the Aervel's dormant Theos. A Dyrfaldur's ability to shift was a biological trait similar to Aervel's ability to fly.

Titan turned to look as well, "Gods, I wish they wouldn't let those Minotaur-kin in. It's dangerous and a disgrace to those who have lost loved ones to the Minotaur."

Not all the bodies that come back from the border are Aervel.

"Yeah, totally."

The Dyrfaldur species was often considered to be synonymous with the barbaric Minotaurs, sharing animalistic traits and a lack of a connection to the Elements.

His sister was nowhere to be seen. Her black wings were common enough, but the flash of her Electric eyes or the pink in her hair was unique enough to draw attention. Embarrassment and shame pricked at him, but Harvey kept his face neutral, slowing his heartbeat for the Dyrfaldur with superior hearing.

"Welcome, students," Headmistress Loche called for attention from the podium, drawing Harvey's focus back to the day's activities. Her pitch-black hair was pulled tight to her scalp, giving her a strict Air. A few students glanced his way, and Harvey focused on his breathing. The students in the room immediately came to attention at Loche's commanding voice. Harvey noted that her stance had opened and straightened as she addressed the audience, her eye-contact direct, confident.

Should I stop it and have someone fetch Nyx? What could she possibly be doing?

Harvey grunted softly in frustration, flexing his wings. Noticing, Titan gave him a sympathetic smile, showing both hands as if to say, 'What did you expect?'

Harvey gave him a reassuring smile.

Her antics are why I needed to get my shadows in place last week.

The Headmistress projected her voice across the ample space. Her golden nails clacked against a clipboard, the only sign of her impatience at the buzz of excitement from students. A single nail was as white as snow, the beginning signs of Theos deficiency.

"Before we start today, it is important that we give the Gods the proper respect. I call upon the Gods to witness this event: Marvos, Axios, Daelan, Elion, Harlow, Eryx, Verona, Octian. Give us your blessings." Students from around the room repeated her words, thanking the Gods in their own way. Many started with the God of their Element. Harvey imagined the Elemental Rune for Illusion when he thanked his patron God, Marvos.

Headmistress Loche clapped her hands together, transitioning from pious to charismatic in a microsecond. "First, some administrative matters. Dyrfaldur, after the ceremony is complete, you can go pick up your assignments in the administration office. After all, we can't be expected to send our ravens to the poorer parts of our country for every exception."

A few laughs came from the Aervel joining in. The Dyrfaldur half of the room was silent. The headmistress's face pinched briefly, glaring at a few of them in the back.

"The next matter of business is the Rune Choosing ceremony, will take place on the 55th Day."

I will see it this year. See who the Gods choose.

"The try-outs for being a Protector will take place on the 51st Day." Loche turned to the Dyrfaldur section to say this last part. Aervel were above being bodyguards, even in a sacred rite. All were required to be a part of the try-outs, but competing for a spot was voluntary.

Everything may change this year with the stakes, father even permitted Nyx and I to try out as Protectors. Not that the Gods give us much of a say.

The headmistress waited, letting her words sink in for everyone in the crowd. A knot of anxiety tightened at Harvey's stomach.

After letting the moment settle, the headmistress continued, "Veritas Hall is honoured this year with the presence of the prince and princess. Please give them a welcoming round of applause, and be courteous that they are here to learn. Under the Nobility Education Proclamation, injuring royalty during class is not a punishable offense."

Applause broke out around the room, eyes drawing to Harvey and the empty spot where his sister was supposed to be sitting. Harvey raised his strong chin slightly, refusing to acknowledge the unasked question of where the princess was.

Harvey stepped out into the central courtyard. It was square, with an exit leading to the training fields and halls. The area was beautifully landscaped, with wooden benches and tables artfully placed. Fighting pits had been built into the courtyard's ground, six divots filled with deep sand.

Wooden Minotaur busts stood along one stone wall; some arrows still embedded in the worn wood from lazy students. One of the older busts even had a burn mark the size of a small fireball from the age of Theos.

Minotaur, the main enemy of the Dengar Kingdom, had been ransacking their borders since 50 TA. Once, the Aervel and Dyrfaldur had been able to fight them with Elemental might, now they fought the larger beasts with fist and sword.

Harvey saw a flash of pink and black hair and sighed. His sister was sparring with another Aervel.

Harvey took off his shoes and removed the sword at his side, setting them on a bench beside the pit before dropping down to watch. The coarse sand was warm under the harsh sun, and Harvey dug his calloused feet into it, enjoying the sensation. His head came barely to the level to the courtyard.

In front of him, Nyx gripped a wooden axe and easily side-stepped the male's longsword, leaning back slightly. Titan dropped down next to

Harvey, watching as well. Nyx's eyes flashed with Electric rings, the sound of it pulsing through the courtyard.

The male was large and burly, with white hair and brown wings. *The Ice Element, if the hair is his marker,* as Harvey assumed it was. Nyx hooked the sword in the male's hands with her axe, guiding his strike into the sand.

Titan whistled in appreciation at the move, before shifting impatiently. Harvey smiled in a moment of pride for his sister before turning to Titan. "You can go," he laughed, "I'm going to watch, but I know you are dying to check out the art room."

"And the bathhouse!" Titan burst with his poorly contained excitement. His hair flopped to the side, catching the light.

"Go, it's okay, I'll catch up. I need to check on my sister first." Harvey smiled, nodding to his fiancé.

Titan smiled gratefully and lifted himself out of the pit with ease, muscles rippling. He grabbed his school map before taking off into the Air, Metallic golden wings catching the sun.

He is the top bachelor in Dengar: wealthy parents, divine beauty, and an extraordinary talent with clay. Why shouldn't I have the best the kingdom has to offer? I am the prince after all. I can't wait until Dad permits me to announce it. Then Titan will be mine in front of everyone.

Nyx swung at the male, who met the axe with his sword. He easily blocked her, but Nyx was fast and sent another two slashes at him in tandem. The male choked his hands up on his sword, muscles bulging as he was forced back; Nyx shoved herself into the space provided, unrelenting. She bent backwards to avoid a slice at her neck, just barely ducking under it. The male came with a second swing to her midriff, and Nyx stumbled back, losing her footing.

Well, there's the consequence of skipping classes in our youth.

The male swung down at her, face set in a grimace. Nyx rolled to the side, sand clouding the Air. Harvey covered his nose and mouth to avoid accidentally inhaling the particles.

A commotion outside the ring interrupted the fight. The three Aervel turned to see what was happening. An Aervel student was being dragged by guards across the courtyard towards the training fields, feral with fear.

Harvey's father was here, and Harvey quickly got out of the ring, following. The student who was being dragged thrashed and screamed, and as Harvey got closer, he noticed the claws.

Half-blood.

"You should see this, son. See the consequences of mixed blood." Harvey's father said, turning to him, waiting for Harvey to join.

Nyx went to follow as well, but their father shook his head. "You don't need to see this, not again. It's time for your brother to learn."

Again?

Harvey looked to Nyx, who looked sick, but went back to sparring.

Good.

Harvey caught up, and he and his father followed the student and guards to the edge of the cliff.

What are they…

The student was shoved to his knees, growling and thrashing in fear. His back to the cliff, battering precariously against the guards. He was incoherent as he started to shift further into his animal form.

Before the male could shift fully, Harvey's father nodded to one of the three guards. The guard to the right took his sword out and, in one clean slice, removed the Half-blood's wings.

Before he could shift and hide them.

As the Half-blood screamed in pain, the stumps on his back pouring blood, King Blackthorn held out a hand. The male was shaking, blood gushing profusely.

"Father what…"

"Give the order."

"But…"

Harvey's heartbeat pounded in his ears, his body going stiff. He tried to swallow, but he couldn't.

He couldn't breathe.

I can't

"You can"

Did I say that out loud?

Harvey's father gave him a sharp look, eyes flicking to the fighting pits. To his sister.

"Kingship doesn't come easily."

The guards were looking at him expectantly, their gaze causing his body to itch. His father didn't break his stare, expression unforgiving.

"Father I…"

Can't…

"Harvey." His father's voice hardened further, eyes boring into Harvey.

Harvey closed his eyes, teeth gnashing.

Marvos, help me.

Harvey cleared his throat.

I have to.

I need to.

This is how I protect Nyx in the future.

He couldn't bring himself to speak. Instead, he looked to one of the guards and nodded once. The guard kicked the Half-blood in the chest, sending him screaming over the edge.

Harvey rushed forward to see the male fall through the clouds. The male's red eyes met Harvey's as he fell, begging Harvey to save him. Condemning him for giving the order. He didn't break contact as he plummeted out of sight. The terror in the male's eyes shook Harvey to his core.

The screaming stopped after a minute; *he must have passed out.*

My Gods, this is brutal. I knew being a Half-blood was a death sentence, but this?

King Blackthorn waited for the guards to depart before speaking low to his son, "That is what will happen to Nyx if her heritage is discovered. Never forget this experience."

Harvey vomited off the cliff.

Feeling sick, Harvey jogged off towards the Aervel dorms. His feet slapped lightly against the marble floor. Students jumped out of the way as he rounded the corner. Thoughts raced through his head. The squelch of wings being sliced off echoed through his mind.

Stop, stop, stop.

He saw the Half-blood fall again, red eyes meeting his own with terror.

Fuck.

I want to scream.

Like the male who just screamed himself into unconsciousness, Harvey thought numbly.

My fault. My fault. My…

A small body ran into him, knocking him to the ground. A Dyrfaldur female with a pixie cut and avian eyes stared down at him.

"Don't you ever look where you are going? Do you own the hallway?" The small female glared down at him.

Harvey batted his crown out of his eyes, glaring at her. Heat flushed to his face at her proximity. As the crown prince, he did not touch others outside of training, especially not Dyrfaldur.

Her skin was a warm ivory, her eyes a sunset gold with black sclera. It was unnerving, as was her being on top of him. He suddenly realized she expected him to answer.

Just who does this female think she is? She is stopping me from getting to Titan. I bet he went straight to Kiara.

The more time he spends with Kiara, the more callous he becomes. I don't want to… touch this female. She's… Dyrfaldur.

"I would suggest you remove yourself from the crown prince's chest," his voice cracked, and he winced.

Instead of obeying, like he expected from a commoner, the female smirked in amusement. She sat up, ass on his crotch, still looking down at him.

"Why? When the crown prince seems to be enjoying it," she wiggled her ass into his length, and Harvey's mind went blank for the first time in his life.

"Because you," he sputtered, frozen under her small frame. The female watched him flounder for words, her smile growing wider. A cat with a mouse.

"You seem to have a hard…" she pursed her lips, eyebrows rising suggestively as she looked down, "time detaching yourself from me."

Did she just look at my crotch? The audacity made him even harder. He pushed her off him finally, taking control back.

This is surreal. This female has clearly gone mad. How did she even get into this school?

"Stay there. Just stay." Harvey demanded, face hot.

Harvey picked himself up off the floor, straightening his tunic and looking down at the female. "I order you to stay." He commanded, unsure of what else to do.

She laughed, "Yes, prince," she articulated mockingly.

A group of students rounded the hallway corner and stopped, looking at the situation. He felt his eyes tingle as they flared from purple to orange to red, finally landing on the sickly yellow of self-disgust. It was a weakness to have this marker. A check on the once-infinite power of Illusion.

He adjusted his tunic again, tucking his wings behind him neatly. He turned on his heels, striding through the stunned onlookers.

They will be gone by the end of the day. They saw me with a Dyrfaldur, and I am a symbol. I should do something about that female as well. Maybe… Definitely… Minotaur's balls, I have a fucking fiancé, what is going on with me?

His feet took him to the Aervel bathing room, and he used a basin to wash his face.

What is happening to me? Why am I getting hard for someone so tainted?

A Dyrfaldur.

What have I done wrong? Marvos give me a sign, is this my test?

His mind wandered back to the mysterious female. *What would it be like to let go and tangle with her in the sheets?*

Disgust bloomed in his chest, thoughts racing. He looked into the gilded mirror by the wash basin. His eyes were bright in contrast to his deep, rich complexion. They shifted between shades, highly saturated colours stark against his thick eyelashes.

She shouldn't be getting to me.

His eyes shifted to red Harvey flinched remembering the eyes of the Half-blood.

She isn't getting to me that would be ludicrous.

Harvey ran a shaking hand along the shadow of a neatly managed beard which covered his sharp jawline - *almost time to shave again.*

Appearance is everything.

Especially when I'm feeling such… confusing feelings. Maybe I am still ill from the gore of earlier. Or maybe…

The image of the female's sunset eyes filled his mind.

It wouldn't be making love like it will be with Titan on our wedding night. It would be dirty, rough, and sinful. I need to stop, or is it a challenge to my faith? Should I keep her around to accept the challenge that has been set forth?

Harvey exhaled, suddenly exhausted.

He planned to have the observers transferred… *killed?*

The image of the guard kicking the Half-blood filled his mind.

No. Just transferred.

Harvey adjusted his crown, uncomfortable with its weight.

A position in the Royal Guard at this age would be a decent bribe for them to keep their mouths shut. Good thing I haven't taken action against Kiara her father is a good male to have on my side.

Harvey clenched and unclenched his fists in pent-up lust and self-loathing. He adjusted himself in his trousers, pushed back his thick hair, and walked out of the bathing room.

CHAPTER 2: NYX

New Allies

I see you made it into Veritas Hall. Was it through a bribe? I doubt a failure like you could ever succeed. Bastards aren't welcome at this school. This won't stand. Watch your back, bastard.

-Nightmare note to Nyx, 20th Day, 76 AT

School started, and she had already read the note through enough times to have it memorized. The word "bastard" rang in her head, the itch of tears threatening to fall.

Fuck class.

Fuck this.

Fuck Nightmare.

Nyx turned towards her next class, going out to the training pits.

I just need to graduate, then I can run and leave this miserable kingdom to rot. Dad said he would have a dragon trained for me if I graduate. That's my ticket out. All I have to do is survive four years. Survive Nightmare.

Nyx had found the first note from Nightmare when she was thirteen. Now that she was twenty-four, the notes were her normal. Like clockwork, they would show up in her clothing or in her room. Nightmare always found a way. A gruesome gift sometimes came with the notes: a rotting carcass or a pile of shit.

Nyx had learned the hard way what happens if she throws them away without reading them.

I don't know how Nightmare sees everything.

The last consequence she faced was the dragon crashing through her room when she was fourteen. She still had a scar on her ear from a shard of glass.

Nyx could remember the faint whisper of a melodic whistle right before the windows broke. The torrent of sound as the glass shattered from the scaled beast slamming through it. The sound of its breathing as it stood over her. Of course, Nyx was blamed for the entire incident.

Like I would bring a fucking dragon into my room for fun! That's like saying you want to play cards with a Minotaur. Yet another instance where Astris swooped in and told my parents it was my fault. She can't be Nightmare, but she might be working with them.

Muted voices came from one of the training rings, and Nyx moved towards the sound.

Sparring will help clear my head.

"Did you see the pink in her hair?" a light female voice said from one of the rings.

"King Blackthorn doesn't seem like the type to," another female replied.

Nyx sighed, knowing who they were talking about.

No getting around it, this happens everywhere I go.

When she jumped down into the fighting pit, the whispering stopped. A female with wings white as snow stood near a softer female with lavender talons and eyes swirling with clouds.

Ice and Air.

The students looked at Nyx, dumbfounded.

"I've got the next round," Nyx declared, daring the females to quarrel.

The females nodded, cautiously starting to duel. Nyx watched as they fought.

The sound of Titan's soft, melodious laughter mixed with her brother's deeper laugh.

Ugh, he's gonna yell at me. Best to get out of here before he notices. I didn't even get a single round in.

Nyx lifted herself from the pit, walking towards her shoes. She blinked, noticing Astris next to the fine boots. She was standing above them, gloved hand reaching inside a boot. Her Icy white curly hair hung down over the boots, like fresh snow falling over her shoulder. The warm walnut hue of her skin glistened in the sun. Nyx stopped briefly, throat bobbing.

Astris.

Then she focused on her boot again, eyes narrowing in rising anger.

Nyx stormed towards Astris Archer. She and Astris had grown up together. The incident in the barn was the first offense. As the pair had matured, their animosity had grown from a spark to a wildfire.

Astris was a liar.

Nyx hated liars.

Nyx reached the cold-blooded bitch, jaw set. Astris yelped and pulled her gloved hand back out of Nyx's boot. Revealing a scorpion clamping down on her fingers. Astris flailed, trying to break free from its hold. She flung her hand out, sending the scorpion flying into Nyx's face. Nyx's squeal turned into a roar as she batted the arachnid off of her, its tail landing multiple stings. She turned to Astris, hatred boiling in her gut.

Astris stared back, too stunned to respond. Electricity snapped, as the Electric rings in Nyx's eyes crackled with energy. She snarled at Astris, anger filling her. Her face stung, and her eyes began to Water.

Nightmare. Nightmare is orchestrating this.

Nyx shut down the thought, feeling the anger in her chest.

Both of them have had an alibi, so why do I keep seeing the notes when I look at Astris?

A snarl ripped from her throat, causing Astris to take a step back. Blood bloomed on Nyx's tongue.

Nightmare sees everything.

Astris's mouth opened wide in shock. Nyx stepped towards Astris, head tilting predatorily.

Fight or flight?

Astris's long fingers came to cover her mouth as a gasp escaped from her. Her silver white eyes matched Nyx's, pupils wide in surprise.

"Nyx!" Harvey called, running to her. Nyx glanced at him. Titan and Kiara had gone now, Harvey the only other student in the courtyard.

Someone discovered me.

I should be scared.

No. This is so much larger than that.

I should be petrified.

Instead, the fury filled her with reckless abandon.

"Dorm. Now." Harvey snapped, his temper lost.

Nyx's canines snapped back into her mouth.

Nyx glared her brother down; *this isn't my fault.*

It's not like I get Half-blood lessons.

Entitled.

Arrogant.

Prick.

Fuck, calm down, Nyx felt her canines.

Harvey lowered his voice, order coating his tongue, "I said now, Nyx, don't make me bring this up with father." As she walked past, he said in a quieter tone, "mouth closed, head down."

Like I haven't done this a million times. Mouth closed, head down, breathing on a one-two pattern. I know it's saving my life, but that doesn't mean I have to like it.

Nyx did not return to her dorm, despite her brother telling her to. She stormed out with no shoes. A short way down the hallway, Nyx slipped into a classroom for privacy. The room was empty, and Nyx silently thanked Axios.

The room was small, intended for book study rather than training. The smell of books comforted her, and she slumped down by the teacher's desk. Her eyes were blurry with tears. She buried her face in her hands and let out a frustrated growl, her fangs extending again out of her control.

Damnit. Why can't I get it together? Why can't I just listen to Harvey and control myself? I am going to get myself killed. Worse than being killed, I am going to spend my last minutes in fear and pain.

Her breath came in ragged gasps as she tried to push the tears away.

Out the corner of her eye, Nyx noticed a familiar book sitting on the desk. She reached up, grabbed the novel, and held it to her chest, gritting her teeth against her past. She placed the book in her lap, running her fingers over the gold lettering embossed on the brown leather case; 'The Aervel and the Sword.'

It was a sunny day, and a nine-year-old Nyx sat reading 'The Aervel and the Sword.' She was seated above the stables, which held fine stallions and dragons her

father bred as a hobby. Her feet dangled over the edge as she turned a page, hungry to find out what would happen next.

Nyx heard a crunching of hay behind her. She tried to turn, but a hand grabbed her head from behind. Panic overtook her as she was thrown off the ledge into the pile of manure. She wiped the shit off her book desperately, tears falling down her cheeks. Bits of hay fell onto her and the pages.

She looked up, but a wooden beam blocked her view. Hay rained down, mixing with the shit as she tried to rid her body and book of the mess. The smell was rancid, causing her stomach to lurch.

Out the corner of her eye, Nyx saw Astris in the doorway. Astris watched expressionless. Embarrassment flooded Nyx's chest, warming her face. She choked down a cry and ran towards the throne room. Her parents would be there. They would make it better.

Nyx burst into the throne room, throwing the double doors wide. Tears streamed down her face as she choked, trying to catch her breath. The council was in a meeting, her father at the head of the table, a golden laurel topping his bald head. Everyone looked to her, and she froze. Astris and Astris's best friend, Kiara Marrow, watched her, amused.

"What is the meaning of this?" The king demanded, alarmed. Astris and Kiara started speaking before Nyx could.

"She was kicking rocks onto your horses and dragons. We tried to stop her, but she hit me. Then she just lost her footing and fell. Pardon, my king," a wince for emphasis as Kiara looked away touching a bruised cheek.

"I think it may have been clumsiness from Nyx missing all those lessons."

"That's not what happened!" Nyx yelled, desperation clawing at her.

"Silence," the king snapped, but Nyx was too worked up to stay calm.

"They ruined my favourite book! The one..." Nyx was cut off by King Blackthorn, "Quiet. Astris, tell us what happened."

"It happened just as Kiara stated," Astris said, eyes devoid of emotion.

Liar.

The king nodded, disappointed, "Very well then."

Nyx put the book down and reached up to grab a school map that was on the table next to her. Her eyes were puffy and itchy from crying. Nyx skimmed the locations on the map, one catching her eye. The Dyrfaldur common room. It was about one-eighth the size of the Aervel common room. Making up her mind, Nyx threw the map down and walked the long way to avoid running into her brother.

Nyx arrived at the Dyrfaldur dorms. Everything about them screamed decay. Even the stained glass was cracked and dirty. The smell of sweat and alcohol hit her nose simultaneously, as did the sounds of merriment.

Harvey never specified which dorm I had to go to, only that I had to go to the dorms.

Another thing that will royally piss Harvey off. Nyx smiled at the thought.

She found her way to the dorm lounge. It was half the size of Nyx's bedroom back at the castle. Unlike the rest of the castle where the walls were smooth, these had cracks in the stones and cobwebs in the corners. Some asshole had crossed out the symbol for Dyrfaldur and scratched the symbol for Minotaur in the wood, along with some violent sketchings of Dyrfaldur being killed by Aervel.

Nyx ignored it and grabbed a random cloak off the coat rack, draping it over her wings as she opened the door and walked through it. She walked in to find a card game in progress. The gaiety stopped when she entered. Her disguise was sloppy, but she was too exhausted to care.

Nyx was faced with stares often enough not to be phased by it. At least that's what she told herself.

A Dyrfaldur with a lion's tail and long beard excused himself from the table, avoiding eye contact with her; *so much for the king of the jungle.*

Before anyone else could get up from the table, she dropped a large bag of gold wings on the table. She tensed, a blush rising to her cheeks as she noticed that they were gambling with wooden figurines instead of wings.

"I will put up one gold wing for every figurine. Who's in?" Nyx grinned with false confidence, heart racing despite her cavalier attitude. A pair of females quickly excused themselves, Nyx's eyes pricking. She waited a second before sitting down. Only two Dyrfaldur remained. One was a male with long red hair, angular features, and a fox tail twitching under the table, the only sign of his anxiety.

The other was a female, her scent entwined with his, *lovers then.* She was petite and had tawny cat ears poking out of her unruly blonde hair.

"Triple it," the female demanded boldly.

Her partner looked at her, exasperated.

"Done." Nyx agreed before they could change their mind.

"Well, I guess we'd better win then," the male chuckled, looking at the female devotedly. "I am Skylar, and this is Freya," he introduced himself, offering her a hand.

She reached out and shook it, Freya taking her hand next. The female poured her a tankard of Severroot cider, waving off Nyx, who reached into her wings purse. The cider was fresh and sweet.

Nyx swallowed the remainder of her third cup of cider, setting the tankard down.

"So, I have to ask," Freya asked as she swept up her winnings for the third time, totalling over one hundred gold wings. "Why play with us?"

Nyx didn't mind losing the money. If she needed to buy their company, she would. She understood why they would be wary of her. Dyrfaldur were treated like trash by Aervel, seen as lesser by the Gods. Her heritage being a secret meant she needed to convince Dyrfaldur she was not a threat without disclosing too much.

She knew they were there for the money. She didn't blame them. The solution benefited all parties.

She didn't care if she never saw them again. Not really.

"Why not play a game in the Aervel dorm, where the facilities are nicer?" Skylar clarified diplomatically.

It was rare that she went a night unable to find at least one Dyrfaldur willing to risk it. It was a solution.

It was also another reason why her family disapproved of her.

She could never tell them where the money went. The only knowledge they had was that she went out nightly and came back smelling of alcohol and with an empty wings pouch.

Nyx laughed bitterly, too tired from the adrenaline of earlier and the pain of the scorpion stings that still burned her face to be anything but honest. "I may be a princess, but I am still a bastard. Spending time with me is political suicide. It is easier to find companionship where I can buy it. Now, if you will excuse me." Nyx winced.

Great, you killed that connection, good job, Nyx.

Nyx started to stand as Freya's hand shot out, grabbing her by the wrist. Freya's eyes widened as she realized what she was doing, but she did not loosen her grip. She maintained eye contact as she took a small portion of the winnings out of her wings pouch and held them out to Nyx.

That is likely a small fortune to her. The amount I gave her is one tenth of tuition. The amount she's handing back could feed her entire family for days.

"Come back tomorrow night if you want. I can get rich off you then. I'm keeping most of it because you didn't respect us enough to try."

"Next time, don't let us win; we don't care where you came from. I could use a challenge, and I think you may be the first to give me one." Skylar added.

"I give you plenty of challenges when we play!" Freya snapped at Skylar, twirling her hair around her finger.

"You cheat when it's just the two of us. At least Nyx keeps us honest. Right, Nyx?" Freya asked, grinning.

"Who's to say I won't make a deal with Skylar and help him cheat next time?" Nyx asked boldly, holding her breath.

Idiot, idiot, idiot.

Every playful barb she made was like jumping out a window with her wings bound.

"Well then, I'll just have to keep my eye on you, won't I, Aervel?" She cocked an eyebrow.

Freya met her, barb for barb, filling Nyx with unfamiliar hope.

"Don't be a stranger," Skylar smiled at her warmly as he put his arm around Freya, sauntering out.

Nyx left the wings on the broken-down table. They shifted it to the side with a clack, the table's legs uneven. The amount was minuscule to a princess.

Someone else will find it, maybe they will use some of it to fix this table.

Her mind flashed to the Aervel common area, with its luxurious couches and plump chairs. Large tables with intricate carvings along the sides were spread generously throughout the space - *the opposite of this room.*

The night Air was crisp as Nyx stepped into the courtyard, but she barely felt it. Her body hummed with the alcohol, blurring her vision slightly. *Maybe I drank a bit too much.* Nyx smiled stupidly. She had made not just one friend, but two. *I know I will have to keep it on the down-low or whatever, but there's no law against friendships -* Nyx bit her lip in barely contained excitement.

Her foot stepped into thin Air as she walked straight off the ledge of one of the fighting pits. She hit the ground hard, face pressed into the sand. She sighed, her breath blowing the grains away in a small cloud.

Scrunching her eyes closed to ward off the movement of the world around her, she pushed herself shakily to her feet. Nyx's long wings snapped out with a clap. She took off into the night, drifting from side to side as she struggled to focus on the Aervel dorms. The building was hexagonal and disappeared up into the clouds.

A door led from inside the courtyard to the dorm. She had to land to go through the door, almost slamming into the pillar.

Nyx walked through the short archway that led into the tower. The walls were a soft grey stone, the floor a galaxy of Theos infused marble. She came to a small indoor courtyard with dusty rose light falling on the floor. Nyx looked up to see a pink-stained-glass dome, hundreds of feet up.

Room... what was it?

Nyx looked down at her hand and saw a number written down: nine-hundred.

Fuck me.

Nyx looked up at the doors, watching in dread as the numbers went up by ten.

"It's not like we need to fly everywhere," Nyx muttered, voice echoing through the oversized chamber ringed with doors rising to the ceiling.

After a long and unsteady flight upwards, Nyx finally unlocked and opened the door, hovering shakily. She stepped into the dorm room, careful not to fall backwards out the door as she precariously shut it, wings tucking neatly behind her. The sounds of parties in the distance were muffled this high up.

The room was luxurious and spacious, with a view of clouds through the wall of windows. The moon reflected off the cream-colored wisps, casting a soft light into the room. The school was seamlessly built into the mountaintop, utilising the environment to its advantage.

The floor was an opulent mahogany, perfectly polished and broken up by woven rugs. Candles sat in sconces around the room, already lit. The bedding was a soft gold silk, the problem however, was that there were two beds in the room, and on one of them sat Astris *fucking* Archer.

"Oh, fuck no." Nyx snapped, glaring.

"You are drunk." Astris's face didn't falter from its usual unbothered position. *Her composure rivals even Harvey's.*

"Obviously," Nyx retorted.

"Where have you been?" Astris demanded.

"Are you my mother now? Or are you just kissing my parents' asses again?" Nyx scoffed in disgust.

"Classes start tomorrow. I need sleep, and so do you." Astris responded sluggishly.

"Say it." Nyx challenged.

If she lets out my secret before graduation… before I can…

"Say what?" Astris said blankly, running a brush through her tight curls.

"You saw," Nyx bit out, voice rising in pitch.

Why isn't she reacting?

Does she plan to turn me in?

What is she playing at?

"Saw what?" Astris raised a single eyebrow.

Nyx could hear the Electricity in her eyes sparking now. She tasted blood in her mouth as her canines elongated. Nyx refused to acknowledge her heightened sense of smell in that moment; especially as Astris always smelled like winter pines and honey with a touch of cloves. Nyx would never admit to liking this heady aroma. Even next to the rotten apple smell of Kiara.

Today was the first time Nyx smelled Astris without the scent of Kiara choking her. It was alarming, and she suddenly realized just how alone they were.

"Saw me for what I am," Nyx growled, letting her canines stay out.

"I don't know what you are talking about," Astris retorted, lying down and turning away.

Did Harvey handle it? Or is that too much for even him?

"Must have been quite a price to pay you off this time, huh? Strange, you still got stuck sharing a room with me. Is the plan to kill me in my sleep now, or will you give your best friend, Kiara, a key to do that later?"

Even if Harvey handled it, she is still… in my space. I need to figure out what her plan is.

"The rooms are decided by last name. Archer and Blackthorn, use your brain for once."

Astris adjusted her pillow for sleep. "I will remedy the room assignment tomorrow and then you will never have to sleep next to me again." Astris assured her, still not looking at her, hissing bitterly, "Won't get any sleep with you in here anyway."

"Ditto," Nyx snapped, walking to her bags that had been brought up for her.

I can't kill her in this room, too obvious. That means she can't kill me.

"Good," Astris stated.

"Good," Nyx parroted, voice scraping.

Their room fell into deep silence as the final parties wound down for the night. The silence was unbearable. She could hear Astris's even breathing, her back still facing Nyx. Nyx was suddenly conscious of every inch of her body and every sound she made. She was mindful of how Astris's smell clouded her head, mixing with the steady buzz of the alcohol that lingered. It took hours before Nyx finally fell asleep.

Nyx woke to cold liquid running down the back of her neck. She shivered, mind hazy with sleep still. It was earlier than she usually got up, the sun barely peeking through the clouds below her windows. Nyx groaned, burying her face under the covers.

I just want to sleep.

Then the smell hit her. Foul, sickly-sweet blood. Nyx opened her eyes and bit back a scream. Draped over her like a lover's embrace was a severed arm.

Fighting back vomit, Nyx jolted out of bed, blood dripping down her back.

Nyx's canines dropped, blood welling in her mouth. The suffocating fragrance of blood made her nauseous. A note lay on the bed on the pillow next to her.

There's a reason I sign off as Nightmare. Enjoy.

-Nightmare

"Fuck" Nyx gasped, holding herself tight.

Nyx looked out the window to where the school was waking up, students in the courtyard below sparring. She looked to the door of the room, panic infusing her.

It did not escape her awareness that Astris was already gone from the room.

I could tell someone? Tell them what? I woke up with an arm? That this isn't the first body part, just the first non-animal body part?

Nyx rolled the arm up in her pillowcase, double wrapping the severed end.

That when I called for help the first time, my guards had been missing from my door. That when I finally found them and brought them back, the gruesome scene had been cleaned.

The memory of clean sheets and the small army of guards that had looked at her like she was crazy kept her hands moving.

No one will believe me.

Okay, how to do this?

Fire?

No, the smell. Burying? Scent-based Dyrfaldur might find it.

Nyx's mind flashed to the execution method of Halfbloods. How the bodies likely piled at the base of the cliff.

You've got to be kidding me.

Nyx walked into the dining room an hour later, hands raw from scrubbing at them. She didn't want to eat, but her first class was strength training.

Maybe I should just skip breakfast. Nightmare likes it when I do that, but… I don't want them to win.

The room was massive, with tables of food along the far wall. Multiple long wooden tables made up the rest of the space. The ceiling was another stained-glass display, this one with shades of green.

The floor was a soft lavender marble that was infused with Illusion Theos long ago. It was faded now, a fraction of the glory it must have held during the age of Theos.

The sconces on the walls were extinguished, the light from the stained glass more than sufficient. A Rune for light, a swirl inside a circle, was on the wall next to the door. Once, that Rune would've been used to light the room at night. The sconces had been added in year 20 AT, when students and teachers could no longer activate the Runes.

At the entrance, Nyx ran into Freya and Skylar, who surprised her once again by approaching her.

"Can I buy you ladies breakfast?" Skylar asked, his arm going around Freya.

"You know it's free for students, right?" Nyx replied as they approached the two food lines.

"Oh, he knows," Freya rolled her eyes, beaming, "he just wants to feel rich for once."

They came to the two food lines, Nyx slowing. Skylar, noticing her slow pace, said, "There are two lines; this one seems to be moving faster."

"This is the Aervel line," Nyx replied, pointing to the sign hanging over the tables of food. She bit her lip, healed by her Aervel blood overnight.

Lowering her voice, she offered, "I could come with you to the Dyrfaldur line."

"You are the princess; should you not get to make exceptions?" Freya inquired. Despite her cavalier words, she looked over to the other Aervel who were now staring.

A few mutters of 'Minotaur-kin,' a slur for Dyrfaldur, reached Nyx's ears.

"Fuck it," Nyx decided, pulling her friends into the shorter line, sending a scathing glare at the Aervel ahead. Her mouth watered as she looked at the fair.

Looking back to the measly selection on the Dyrfaldur table, Nyx was glad they had chosen this line.

She forced her eyes away as a Dyrfaldur ladled herself a bowl of something Nyx could not identify.

Skylar, noticing the tension, picked up the conversation again. Wagging his eyebrows in an absurd manner, he boasted, "My pockets are brimming with my winnings from last night."

"You didn't win a single hand," Nyx quipped, shaking her head.

Freya laughed, patting Nyx awkwardly between her wings. "He will learn one of these days."

"I let you win because we are dating, and I let Nyx win because she is our friend," he said, mischief glimmering in his eyes.

Friend.

The word clanged around in her head, and Nyx slowed in line before being pulled forward by Freya. The joy from the word almost drowning out the memory of the arm.

The memory of flesh under her fingers, slick with blood, overtook her, and she tripped.

"Keep up," Freya exclaimed impatiently, grabbing her hand and dragging her toward the food.

Just like that, Nyx had not one, but two friends for the first time in her life.

They could be Nightmare. Anyone could be.

Panic shot through her briefly as her past screamed at her to run before history repeated itself.

"You will never talk to the crown princess that casually again. You will not touch her again, either," a voice bristled behind her.

Skylar stepped back, grabbing Freya a second later. Freya's eyes widened, and she backed up half a step. Realizing who was behind her, Nyx turned to look up at her brother. His dark skin and thick lashes gave him an intense look, akin to wearing eyeliner. His facial features were sharp, with stubble highlighting his sharp jaw and pitch-black hair, adorned with a silver laurel crown.

"She's my friend." The word was foreign yet freeing on her tongue. "This is none of your business."

"On the contrary, little sister, whom you fraternize with is very much my business," Harvey warned, voice low.

Nyx turned to her new friends, "Go ahead in line, I'll catch up with you later."

Nyx turned around to see that Harvey was looking at her with distaste. He grabbed her by the shoulders, forcing her to look at him, "I talked to father about you missing classes. Starting tomorrow morning, you will be attending every class."

Good luck with that

"I have transferred some of your classes over so we share every one. Now, we have eyes on us, so clean yourself up; you look a mess."

"Push me, see what happens," Nyx challenged, stepping back into line.

Four years, I just have to last four years.

Harvey was about to follow her, but stopped when Titan entered the grand dining room. Followed by Sabastian, Astris, and Kiara, the group intimidated the other students as they walked. Harvey took a minute to decide before choosing to go to his companions, leaving Nyx behind to catch up to her new friends.

"Oh no, you won't be joining us, and you aren't allowed to have friends, and oh yeah, no breathing for you either," Freya quipped sarcastically.

"Right?" Nyx asked, letting her wing brush Freya gently.

"Have you ever considered emancipation?" Skylar asked, only half-joking.

"From the throne?" Nyx laughed.

The irony.

She picked up a misshapen pink apple and added it to her plate.

The fruit's colour was faded, a result of the dormant Theos. Theos had once enhanced the plants, allowing for a big enough crop to feed the kingdom. Now food was scarce, tasteless, and held little to no nutritional value. Without Theos, sickness was spreading throughout Dengar.

"I guess I didn't think that part through. Why is your brother like that, though? I mean, he can't enjoy it, can he?" Freya jumped in.

"You would think nagging me all day, every day, would be boring for him at this point, wouldn't you? Sadly, his neurotic behaviour has not ceased since the first time I... had a breakdown."

You just had to keep talking Nyx.

"A breakdown?" Freya inquired.

Nyx's heartbeat quickened, *can she smell it on me? Smell that I'm a Half-blood?*

"It's nothing. I just have trouble... controlling my temper sometimes," Nyx said casually, breath hitching slightly.

Sabastian walked up to the line, cutting in front of Nyx and her friends. "It's no problem, is it? It's not like you go to class anyway. At least that's how it was growing up."

Skylar started to protest, but Nyx held out a hand. "No problem," she gritted out, jaw clenched. "Go ahead."

Freya looked at Nyx's face, then the back of the massive male. She squeezed Nyx's hand gratefully.

"I hope they have Severroot Cakes left," Freya changed the subject. "I have this friend who is a chef in Bexley, he's a cake genius... and he's single." Freya teased, brows raised suggestively. Nyx laughed, "I don't swing that way."

"And he has a hot sister," Skylar added, smirking.

"I can say that, you can't," Freya smacked Skylar, turning back to Nyx, "aaaand he has a hot sister," Freya said.

In front of them, Sabastian laughed condescendingly, turning around to Nyx's group. He pushed a lock of hair out of his face, the half-heart bracelet on his wrist glinting momentarily under his worn tunic sleeve.

"Now you want to fuck the Minotaur-kin? If you are looking for a release that badly, I could help. Surely a full-blooded Aervel male is far superior to some Dyrfaldur tramp." He grabbed himself suggestively. "You must be desperate to turn to the Dyrfaldur commoners. Maybe you could give Kiara a whirl again since you are only interested in female companionship."

"You get that thing near me, and I will fucking cut it off," Nyx warned quietly, "and if I hear that cunt's name again, I will cut it off regardless. Understood?"

"He's right," Astris walked over to Sabastian. "Like a Dyrfaldur could handle you."

She spat 'you' as if the word tasted foul. Nyx noted how her eyes darted to Kiara briefly for approval.

What did she mean by that?

"I doubt anyone could handle her," Sabastian quipped before loading food onto his plate.

"Her brother will likely decide who she belongs to in the end," Kiara stated as she handed a plate to Sabastian to fill for her. "With luck, no one will want her, and we can keep her around. She's not a real princess after all. Doesn't that sound fun?" Her voice indicated that it would be anything but.

"Oh, leave her alone and come play with me; I'm bored," Sabastian cut in.

Kiara sighed before pushing her way in front of them in line. She held her hand out expectantly, and on cue, Astris took it and joined Kiara, cutting in line.

Puppet.

Freya put her hand on Nyx's shoulder.

I don't have to do this alone.

The thought struck Nyx like a lightning bolt and her plans began to shift.

CHAPTER 3: HARVEY

Into the Shadows

How's that vase coming along that you were working on? I am jealous of how often you touch it when you can't touch me. When I can't touch you. Meet me after class behind Training Hall A?

-Harvey letter to Titan, 50th Day, 76 AT

Harvey Blackthorn slipped into the Aervel male bathhouse. Almost 30 days had passed since school started. He was here to meet his shadows, who spied for him regularly and were on his payroll.

They were older students, more qualified for espionage.

Keeping my sister in line is now my top priority, even if it means using subterfuge. If her secret is discovered, she will take our entire family down with her.

He went to the changing area and undressed, folding his fine clothes and placing them on a shelf. He was dirty from his dragon flight to Bexley for lunch with Titan and Sabastian.

Although he had left his dragon, Azazel, at home, the school had dragons that students could take out. The school's dragons were a more common breed, not used for war. To prevent theft, they had been trained to turn around if a student tried to take them past Bexley. If Harvey needed, he could petition to bring Azazel, but a war dragon would be uncomfortable in the small dragon stables.

In theory, Harvey could fly that far on his own, but not nearly as fast, or without getting sweaty from the exercise. Dragons were much more efficient. He had broken off from Titan and Kiara, who were going to the memorial to honour those they had lost in the Minotaur wars. Titan had lost his older cousin Ender, and Kiara had lost her mom. Harvey sometimes joined them, but he mostly left the two of them to grieve without him.

They are there for each other, that's a good thing.

He walked into the mostly empty bathhouse, wings twitching, restless. It was dinnertime, so no other students were bathing except his shadows. The bathhouse was vast, with a single large steaming pool at its centre. Runes for Water had been set into the sides of the pool, but they were now inactive. The school had connected the closest stream to the bathhouse after Theos went dormant. The bottom was a mosaic design depicting the school logo: a shield bisected by a sword, with a feather on one side and a paw print on the other. A circle of the Elemental Runes surrounded the scene.

The ceiling was stained glass, lighting up the space. This glass depicted a sunset, with warm golden rays of light, shining down on the pool. Two Aervel sat waiting patiently in the Water.

Haiden was washing his green hair and talking animatedly to Zale. Zale sat quietly as always. Haiden had green eyes and reddish-brown wings, whereas Zale had deep bronze skin, blue wings, blue eyes, and thick locks with gold beads. Harvey had chosen them to be his shadows shortly after school started.

The pair moved to sit next to him, giving him space to clean himself as they talked. Harvey took a piece of rough cloth and started meticulously grooming himself.

"Report," he ordered, not bothering to look at them.

Haiden spoke first, "Your sister has been…" a pause of hesitation followed.

"You will be honest with me. I will not punish you for any information you give." Harvey prompted.

Haiden continued, green eyes meeting Harvey's for a moment, "The princess has been spending a lot of time with… Dyrfaldur."

Zale picked up where Haiden left off, "I followed her professors. Her grades are low, but she aces every test."

"Why?" Harvey demanded.

"She has started skipping most classes," Zale intoned, quieter than before.

Harvey nodded.

She can't afford to skip in this school. Is it the companions? I will need to send a letter to Father.

"I found out information about her new Dyrfaldur companions by tracking down their families. Apologies, my prince, it took me a while to find time to take the trip to Prox and Starhollow." The male swallowed nervously, "The first, the female, is Freya Elm. Her family owns the top-rated bakery in Bexley. She is studying to be a scout for the guard. She has decent grades and has never had trouble with the law. Her other friend is Skylar Wells. He is studying to be a surgeon. He has above-average grades and has never had trouble with the law." Zale reported.

Haiden jumped in, adding to Zale's report, "The only student in your year with a record is Jordan Larkin. Her parents own the Devils Dice Den, a notorious gambling hall with deep connections to the underground criminal network. Many of the nobles, as you know, visit that Den to fulfil their more sinful desires."

"How is Nyx's emotional state?" Harvey inquired, splashing the hot Water over his face.

The two shadows looked at one another, unsure, before Haiden supplied the answer, "She seems happy around the Dyrfaldur. In classes, she clashes with all Aervel and most teachers."

"Overall, though, she has been… off." Zale added.

Harvey remained silent, taking in the information. He dipped his head back, wetting his curly black hair. Taking his time, he put Severroot scented shampoo in his hair, enjoying the smell. Breathing in the fragrant steam, he replied, "Keep an eye on the situation. We will meet again in a week. Now leave me so I may bathe in peace."

Haiden and Zale immediately got out of the Water, walking towards the changing room to give the prince the entire pool.

As Harvey was walking to Team Dynamics, he overheard Kiara's voice, followed by a lower, older voice. He would recognise the voice anywhere from his long training sessions with the male. The General, Titus Marrow, was at Veritas Hall. Harvey stopped, leaning against the wall to listen to the conversation just around the corner.

"You will be marrying a noble. It is necessary for the next step. For your future, for our family's future." General Titus's voice growled sternly.

"But I only want Harvey," Kiara pleaded.

Harvey cringed inwardly. Kiara had already been with his sister. *No thank you.* She also consistently hurt his sister. Respect for the General was the only thing that kept Harvey from punishing Kiara too severely.

General Titus sighed loudly. Harvey could imagine the man rubbing at his beard, "then make him feel something, or we will have to go to the backup plan."

"I am trying," Kiara pleaded.

"Then try something different," he growled, before sighing, "we are running out of time. The Dyrfaldur Draft Mandate failed, Blackthorn stopped it again."

For good reason.

"Why would he do that? He puts their lives above our own when it is his failure that keeps the Minotaur at our Southern borders."

"Not everyone sees everything as clearly as we do. Especially when it comes to those animals. Cut from the same foul cloth as the Minotaur."

The sound of footsteps moved toward Harvey. Harvey back peddled as quickly as he could - as far as he dared. He prayed to Marvos to help him disguise his actions. He stopped abruptly, then started walking forward at a languid pace.

General Titus rounded the corner in a fury, and Harvey raised a hand in greeting. The man who had looked furious when he first rounded the corner smiled at him. The wrath was instantly wiped from his face, replaced with something colder.

Stopping in front of Harvey, General Titus adjusted his sword, the leather of the belt creaking slightly as he did so. The General was a Venom Element, like his daughter. The Elements were not passed down through lineage, but there was usually some overlap within families. He had green eyes, green wings, and dark hair and beard.

"Good to see you settling into your studies, young prince," General Titus said, patting Harvey on the shoulder.

The man had trained all of the nobles' children from a young age. Never as vigorously as his own daughter, but Harvey winced at the memory of the bruises he had gotten over the years under his tutelage. Despite the ethics of his methods, they worked.

"Good to see you as well, General. What brings you to the school?" Harvey asked with a warm smile.

"Just checking in on my daughter; she hasn't been giving you too much trouble lately, has she?"

"No, sir," Harvey lied smoothly, "she has been getting along well in her classes, I hear."

General Titus couldn't hide his flash of anger. Interesting, Harvey thought.

"She has been doing… fine. I would have expected her to be at the top of her class by now. I will have to come by more often to train her harder. Excuse me, prince, you should not have to listen to an old male's troubles. I will let you go now; class is about to start." Just as General Titus stated, the large bell that signalled the next period clanged.

"Before you go, I will be sending you a list of recruits for the guard. I want them out of the school," Harvey instructed.

His mind flashed to the group of students that had seen him with the Dyrfaldur.

"Of course, prince, it will be done. I will be in my summer castle for the next 30 days, so send the list there instead of the castle."

"Problems in court?" Harvey hedged, trying to get more information out of him.

The older Aervel narrowed his eyes slightly before his features smoothed, "Not at all, prince, I simply have some personal matters to attend to."

"I wish you the best then, General."

"Nobilitas omnibus ante," General Titus Marrow saluted him by touching his throat with two fingers, a custom in Dengar. Fingers on the pulse of the kingdom.

Harvey waved him away, dismissing him, and the older Aervel grunted and strode off.

I don't think Marrow could train Kiara any harder.

The memory of Kiara coming into classes late, covered in bruises and cuts, filled Harvey's mind with how she would struggle through physical classes, already exhausted. It was hard to hate the female when he pitied her. It made it hard to punish her for her transgressions against his sister.

When she used to be my shadow, assignments pulled her out of those extra lessons. Maybe that's why she is so fixated on me. I was the reason she could play with the rest of the noble children. Is she using Titan to make me jealous?

Harvey walked towards Training Hall A.

Seeing Titan always makes me feel better. He is my constant in the chaos. With him by my side, everything seems more manageable.

CHAPTER 4: HARVEY

Leader

That kiss last night was... everything... Next time, let's give ourselves a bit more time. Risky? Yes. Worth it? Absolutely.

-Titan letter to Harvey, 51ˢᵗ Day, 76 AT

Harvey made his way to his first class: Intro to Venomcraft. He planned to sit next to Nyx and keep an eye on her.

Where is she? Why can't I keep her in line?

The room was humid, with shelves overcrowded with ingredients. Posters showing a variety of herbs hung on the walls. At the front of the room was a chalkboard with a list of questions on it.

- *What are the symptoms of Slumber Serums?*

- *What are the properties of Veinflare?*

The class was as monotonous as Harvey had imagined it would be. The professor was an old, crusty noble who should have retired years ago. Harvey was just glad Kiara wasn't in his class. He didn't like her looking at him, trying to ferret out his secrets. It was disconcerting and distracted him from what mattered: family.

Nyx isn't here. She should be here.

The professor started class, introducing himself as Professor Jade. He had large green wings, courtesy of his Element. His right arm was Theos deficient, looking as if it were dipped in liquid bone, with unnatural divots of eaten away flesh. Harvey noted that Jade winced whenever something touched that arm.

Focus. I need to figure out how to handle Nyx's grades.

The professor passed out vials of a clear liquid.

Focus Harvey. You can't help her if you fail yourself.

Professor Jade gave them the name of the draft: Slumber Serum. Harvey took out his inkwell and quill and wrote down the draft's name. The professor explained that they were to experience the draft for themselves, taking notes for a paper.

"Two," Harvey demanded, and the professor gave him a second draft.

If Nyx won't go to class, I will bring class to her.

Harvey looked into the clear, slightly iridescent liquid. He noted that the potion had a high viscosity, moving slower than Water when tipped. He then raised it to his nose and wafted it before tipping it into his mouth. No scent or taste came from the liquid.

He felt the draft take effect immediately and had to fight to keep his head up. Harvey grabbed the table in front of him, steadying himself.

"You are probably feeling its full effect now. This potion can be altered to change how fast it activates," the professor said, seemingly far away. "You will notice that the amounts in your textbooks have been altered. This is to account for the waning Theos in herbs. Soon, Venomcraft will be a lost art," Professor Jade sighed, covering up a cough.

Harvey swayed slightly.

"Notice how your limbs feel affected as well as your mind. As you continue, the symptoms will worsen. They will wear off eventually, but you will be unable to move after the potion has fully taken effect. Now, I will pass out the antidote."

A vial found its way into Harvey's hand. His arm was so heavy. The professor placed his hand on Harvey's arm, guiding him to drink. The drink tasted bitter and earthy, sending adrenaline through him.

"This is called Veinflare, and you probably feel some burning right about now, but that will fade. Veinflare has more than one use. Blackthorn, would you please list a few for the class?"

Harvey felt lucid again, standing with his chin high as he answered fluidly, "Veinflare has a multitude of uses, applicable both on and off the battlefield. Some uses include keeping soldiers alert for night missions, rousing individuals from unconsciousness, and even as an antidote to an allergic reaction."

"And how would one tell they have received a sleeping draught before consuming it?" the professor asked him.

"Look for iridescence and viscosity," Harvey replied, retaking his seat.

The professor showed them how to make the antidote and gave each of them a vial to fill for studying later. Harvey slipped them into his tailcoat, resmoothing the silky fabric. Tailcoats were his favourite, but during the hottest seasons, he switched to loose tunics.

"On your way out, make sure to grab a few extra Veinflare Vials. Your writing prompt is on the chalkboard."

As the class came to an end, Harvey went to the announcement board to see that somebody had posted the Protector try-out information.

It is time, Harvey thought, the weight of it settling.

It was rare to be selected, and that was a good thing. When selected, Champions and Protectors get teleported into a mysterious and deadly Labyrinth.

If they had, Harvey and the rest of the Aervel would have access to their Theos.

The Champions and Protectors were said to gain additional power from succeeding, in addition to the reinstatement of Theos for the kingdom.

That power would be a formidable tool as a future king.

It would be invaluable at the borders against the Minotaur. Being Rune-Chosen was an honour, but also a death sentence.

The Labyrinth has proven to be impossible to survive. I pity those who are Chosen. I want glory, for myself and my family, but this is better suited to someone like Kiara. Someone who trains obsessively. The top of the class. It is unsurprising that Nyx had fallen for her all those years ago.

Harvey could still picture the incident clearly.

Fourteen-year-old Harvey stood by the drinks table with Titan at the annual winter ball. The ballroom in the castle was vast, the floor a galaxy of stars, the wall windows opening onto a spacious terrace. The court waited for his sister's arrival; music was not permitted to start until the royal family had all arrived.

I hope this goes well. Kiara has treated her well thus far. Nyx has been obsessing about her dress all week as well. That isn't like her.

Nyx walked in, standing at the top of the long staircase that led into the ballroom.

She looks like a princess, Harvey thought with pride.

His happiness was short-lived as Kiara waltzed in, arm in Sabastian's. She made eye contact with Harvey, and rage welled up inside him.

She was Nyx's date for this. Not Sabastian's.

Seeing his reaction, her eyes widened in pleasure at his attention, and she put her hand on Sabastian's chest.

She wants me to be jealous, and she's using my sister to do it. Harvey's anger continued to rise, but he slowed his heart rate, forcing his body to calm.

Nyx stood, frozen. Harvey saw her hands clench, face scrunching in fury.

Her mouth is shut, but that won't help if her fangs cut through her lip. Think fast, Harvey, think.

He looked to the large windows, and the curtains rolled to each side.

Fuck. Closing his eyes for a moment, Harvey decided.

He bumped the candle on the wall next to him off the sconce; it fell to the floor next to the curtain. The fine fabric went up in flames, and Harvey ran to his sister, dragging her out of the ballroom.

Harvey rubbed his temples. *If only I could have a day where I wasn't cleaning up Nyx's messes.* Harvey had never experienced Theos since it had gone extinct before he was born. For a second, he let himself think about what it would be like to have his power.

It was short-lived as anxiety grabbed onto his stomach, wrenching it in knots. *There's no way I will get Chosen. There are thousands of students. Chances are, the people I care about will be fine as well. Especially Nyx being a Half-blood. That should protect her from the Gods' attention. Please, Marvos, don't let us be separated,* Harvey prayed.

Later in the day, Harvey walked into training hall B where the Protectors try-outs were being held. Although the school selected the Protectors, the Gods occasionally selected one themselves. It was rare, but enough to allow Dyrfaldur into both the Protector try-outs and the Rune Choosing ceremony. Otherwise, it was up to Veritas Hall and the king.

The room was cavernous, meant to train individuals in the Air as well as on the ground. Four large square rings hung from the ceiling, and smaller square rings were scattered throughout the room – all at different heights. Bars hung close to the ceiling, and on the ground was an obstacle course.

They don't mess around with the Protector selection.

In the centre of the room was a large platform with a near-impossible climbing wall. Harvey once heard some of the second-years talking about having their wings tied, forcing them to climb hundreds of feet up a mountain without flying. Harvey shuddered; wings were sensitive. He would cut off the hand of anyone who dared touch his.

Harvey took off his shoes, as was customary for training, and stepped into the deep sand. Someone had propped the door open, letting in a warm breeze smelling of pine.

Students gathered by the base of the platform, chattering among themselves. Jade stood at the centre of the group, waiting for the rest of the students. Harvey walked purposefully towards the group, his eye catching on Titan. He changed his path to move toward Titan, excited at the thought of seeing him. Harvey's elation faded as his attention snagged behind Titan to the Dyrfaldur female from the hallway.

Kiara walked up to Titan, placing a hand on Titan's shoulder. Harvey fought the jealousy that welled up. She saw his clenched fist, smiled, and continued fawning over Titan. Harvey looked away.

I need to focus on class. Titan will be mine in the end.

If he partnered with someone else, he might be able to kick Kiara's ass during whatever exercise this was. Harvey switched directions, looking for good teammates. Titan gave him a hurt look, his puppy dog eyes almost making Harvey cave.

Almost.

The promise of getting to deck Kiara in a politically acceptable way? Yes, please. Sign me up.

Harvey looked up to see that the viewer platform along the wall was filled with admin. His father and the General were also present. Harvey saw Kiara flinch as she looked up at the platform.

"Those who have submitted forms to be Protectors line up over here." Jade gestured to his right with a pained wince as his arm moved. "Those who do not wish to try-out, line up here." He motioned to his left.

Harvey went to Jade's left, noticing that Kiara and Astris had joined the Protectors line - The only Aervel. The General watched his daughter intensely, seemingly unsurprised by her choice of line.

I wouldn't have thought he would want her as a Protector; that's a Dyrfaldur job.

Harvey saw Nyx out of the corner of his eye. She was glaring at Astris with murder in her eyes.

Not again.

Harvey cut in line to stand behind his sister.

The closer I am, the faster I can react.

"Today, we will be pairing our students trying out to be Protectors with the individuals we think you will work best with. This will help us to understand how you work in a team and under the direction of a possible Champion. Before me," Jade waved his good hand at the obstacles.

"Is the obstacle course that you and your team must pass through. You will be judged on a variety of factors, from the time you finish to the way you work with a team. No results will be given today. In addition to being qualified, the Protectors will be paired based on compatibility. King

Blackthorn, General Marrow, and Headmistress Loche have decided on the teams in advance."

General Marrow dropped down off the platform, barely bothering to slow himself with his wings. He hit the ground in a dramatic cloud of sand. Students around him coughed at the dust. He ignored them, handing the list to Jade.

Jade went down the list, bone white fingers tracing the darker parchment. His long eyebrows scrunching together in concentration. Finally, he got to the names Harvey was listening for. "Princess Nyx will be pairing with Astris Archer, and Kiara Marrow."

Fuck.

Harvey barely heard the rest of the names as he watched his sister. When it came time for his name, he blinked in surprise.

"Prince Harvey will be with Skylar Wells, and Jordan Larkin." Harvey looked up to see Nyx's friend and the female he had run into walking towards him. Jordan Larkin, the female his shadows had told him about.

Turn around, don't come here, please.

The female, Skylar, and Sabastian all coalesced around him.

When the teams had all been announced, Jade introduced the challenge. "This exercise will test your teamwork as well as your adaptability. See the rings hanging from the ceiling as well as the bars? You will need to go through each ring."

A staff member flew to each square ring with a torch, lighting them on Fire.

Lovely, this is practical.

"After you go through a ring, you must fly all the way to the ceiling, over one of the bars, before coming back down for the next one. After you have completed this, you will either climb or fly up the wall behind me. Finally, you will take the zipline down to the ground level and finish the obstacle course down there. No wings after the rock wall; we want you tested on the ground as well."

Harvey looked to the obstacles on the ground: walls, beams, a short pool, and a sprint to the end.

A small body came up to his side, a smooth, small hand, intimately grabbing onto his bicep. Harvey went rigid.

Was she touching him? Again?

He looked down at the pale hand, mortified.

"We've got this," the female crooned.

"No, we don't," Harvey snapped. "I have this; you are here to support me, Dyrfaldur."

"Everyone on the starting platform," General Titus boomed.

"Minotaur's balls." Harvey cursed under his breath. He walked with his ragtag team to the start line.

The group climbed up the rope ladder, with Harvey deciding to join them rather than fly. He would need his energy for those steep climbs later.

"My name is Skylar, by the way," the Dyrfaldur male said conversationally.

"Jordan," the female chirped.

"What are your animal forms?" Harvey demanded of them, reaching up for the next rung of the ladder.

"Show us some respect, and tell us your name, Aervel," Jordan said from the rung below him.

"I am the crown prince; you know my name. Everyone knows my name. Why should I have to take the time to introduce myself to you?" Harvey put extra emphasis on the word 'you,' nose flaring in revulsion.

"Fine, darling, I can turn into a finch. Is that better?" she mocked.

"Did you seriously just?" he sputtered, "I could have you executed! No, I will have you executed. To talk to the prince-"

She cut him off, waving her hand dismissively, "If you won't bother to introduce yourself or show us an ounce of respect, then I can call you whatever I want."

He gaped at her, stupefied as she dismissed him casually.

"My form is a fox" Skylar said looking between Harvey and Jordan.

They ignored him glaring at one another. Jordan cocked a sharp brow, a smirk forming on her face. Harvey felt his skin grow hot, but he didn't take his gaze from hers. She leaned in, and he mirrored her, eyes tingling.

"Now, why don't you put those big, strong Aervel muscles to use and carry Skylar through the course? I'll guard you in the Air, and then we can be on our merry way." Jordan stated tilting her head, as if the matter was settled. Harvey could feel her soft breath on his face as he leaned in snarling.

"You won't be guarding anyone. You will not be flying yourself, and you most definitely will not be calling me 'darling.'"

"Okay, master," Jordan snarked.

"Okay, supreme overlord," Skylar added, smirking, then flinching at Harvey's glare.

Harvey never felt as powerless as he did around this female. Now, other Dyrfaldur were taking a hint from her, attempting to be equals with him. Knowing Jordan's name, would make getting rid of her easier. He made a note to have Skylar transferred as well. Perhaps execution was less threatening than losing a place at the best institution Dengar had to offer.

Skylar's family would be shamed, and the honour of training with the Aervel nobility would be squandered. Harvey's deadly silence must have scared Skylar, and the male distanced himself a bit from the problematic female, *clever lad.*

Jordan appeared to have zero sense of self-preservation. She almost scared him as much as Kiara did… almost. Harvey pulled himself up over the ledge, walking to the blunted weapons rack. Harvey grabbed a pair of twin daggers, sheathing them at his side.

"Okay, now here is the actual plan," Harvey ordered.

Jordan did not follow his plan. Upon the sound of the horn, she took off at a sprint, short hair bouncing behind her. Harvey blinked in astonishment as she leapt off the starting platform. A flash of light, and her finch took off towards the first square ring. She was ahead of the other groups, but that wouldn't last for long with her small wings. It would be impossible for her to get over the top bars.

How have I gone from having complete control over myself and everyone around me, to the idiot with his mouth hanging open and the last to leave the platform?

Harvey shut his mouth, a vein in his forehead throbbing. She would tire out within two more rings, and then he would have to change his plan to pick her up.

"Grab her as we go past," Harvey instructed, grabbing Skylar by the collar as he ran towards the platform edge.

"What if she doesn't…" Skylar started.

"Just do it." Harvey barked.

Harvey unfurled his large black wings, legs pumping. He leapt into the Air, dragging Skylar with him. The Dyrfaldur shifted, and a red fox squirmed in his arms. He let Skylar twist into position before tightening his grip and speeding through the first square. He banked right, then up and to the left. His wings snapped tight against his body as he pulled Skylar to his chest. He shot through the first ring, one of his feathers charring as it touched the Fire.

He snapped them out as soon as he was clear, pumping his wings to get to the top bar. His muscles burned as he flew up towards the bar. *Fifty more feet.*

Beside him, Nyx and Kiara were flying in tandem, occasionally bumping one another out of the way. He could hear them arguing, but couldn't make out the words with the wind rushing by his ears. His breathing grew heavy as he reached the pinnacle, flattening his body as he threaded between the ceiling and the first bar.

Keeping his wings tucked, Harvey sent them into a spinning dive towards the second ring. Skylar let out an undignified screech.

I didn't know foxes could sound that… squeaky. Is he embarrassed by it? Head in the game, Harvey; you really must be losing it if you are worried about a Dyrfaldur's feelings.

The ground sped towards them in a blur. Harvey snapped out his wings right before they reached the height of the next ring, slowing them abruptly. He flapped his wings once, digging deep into his psyche to ignore the strain. His arms were sore from holding Skylar through the flight, having to hold him tight to his chest to go through the burning rings.

The speed at which they took the plummet put a strain on his wings as he fought gravity. Harvey flapped a second time, tucking his wings to go through the ring. He went through the square ring too low, arm brushing the Fire.

Searing pain went through him, and he struggled to maintain his hold on the fox. Wings snapping out, he forced himself to continue, flying upwards once again. His arms, wings, and abs screamed as he forced his body to obey.

His body was the one thing he could always force to obey him. One thing he could always control. Harvey needed control like he needed Air. He was starving for it, and this was one way to achieve it. He could win. An idea suddenly came to him, and he smiled.

I have no time to convey the idea to my teammate. I am sick of asking. I am the prince, after all. Time to conduct these puppets. I will force Skylar's hand or let it kill him trying.

Harvey sent them over the bar, careful to avoid brushing his burned arm. Jordan had joined them, flying in the slipstream behind Harvey, allowing her to stay close behind.

I am actually impressed she is keeping up.

The dive he took this time was less steep, stopping above the teams shooting through the third ring. Harvey pounded his wings, maintaining his position slightly above the others. Skylar squirmed, seeing that they were too high for the next ring. The Fire snapped menacingly at them as they approached.

Harvey grabbed the fox by the scruff and chucked him overhand at the team that was slightly below him. Not waiting to see what happened, Harvey tucked his wings and narrowly passed through the ring.

He pushed to the front of the group as he sped up, shoving Aervel out of the way. He had forced Skylar into a position where he had to obey or fall to his death. He would have to find his way back to Harvey. Harvey risked a look back to see the fox viciously biting at another Dyrfaldur, pushing off her and jumping to the next Aervel, swiping at eyes and sensitive bits as he went.

Good. Finally, my life is going in the right direction again. The direction of control.

Four tiny paws hit his back between his wings just in time for Harvey to fly up to the final bar. Claws dug into his back, cutting into his skin as the fox clung on for dear life. The pressure eased as he went horizontally over the bar, before the claws ripped out of his flesh, the fox falling with a yowl towards the sand below.

Fuck.

Harvey dove, Jordan joining him at his side. They gained on Skylar, the fox twisting and turning desperately in the Air. They were coming up on the level of the ring, Harvey reaching out his hand for the fox. His fingers met fur, but the fox thrashed out of his hands.

"Stay still!" He yelled, snatching the fox a second time. This time, he held onto the tail, flicking the fox up into his arms. Skylar's claws dug into his fine tunic as Harvey flew them towards the next ring.

Kiara, Astris, and Nyx were flying just ahead, Nyx holding a cat that must be Freya. Kiara fished brass knuckles out of her pocket and punched another Aervel out of the Air before turning back towards Harvey and his team.

Come play, I have been looking forward to this.

The Aervel she hit flew fifty feet to the side wall, debris flying as he cracked the stone. The school spent a fortune fixing training caverns weekly, a cost that would be much lower with Theos.

Jordan cut in close to Harvey. He grunted; Kiara scared him, too. He didn't blame Jordan for wanting him to lead. Harvey slowed his pace slightly, adjusting Skylar onto his shoulder before drawing the set of twin daggers. He reached down for Jordan, hand meeting Air.

He risked a look down to see that she was indeed not there. A knife whistled through the Air, and Harvey ducked instinctively. It took a tiny tuft of hair off the top of Skylar's head, and Skylar made that high-pitched caw again.

Oops.

Harvey forgot about him. Kiara smirked at Harvey, goosebumps rising on his skin. She closed in, knife in one hand, the other clenched into a fist with brass knuckles shining.

A flash of blinding light, and a small body dropped from above onto Kiara. Jordan, now back in her main form, bear-hugged Kiara, wings and all, sending them into a plummet. Harvey looked from them to the next obstacle.

There was one more ring and then the climb to the top of the platform. Harvey grabbed Skylar, who protested loudly, and once again flung the fox. This time, he aimed through the ring and onto the platform. The fox went through the middle, and Harvey tucked his wings, diving. Skylar straightened his body into a rocket, slamming into the wall halfway up.

Oops, maybe I should've aimed a bit higher. Skylar clawed at the wall, flashing into his main form.

Ten feet below them and almost to the ground, Kiara and Jordan spun towards the sandy floor. *Not enough sand.* Harvey used his wings to propel himself faster. He was now within five feet of the pair.

He held out his hand, "Let go!"

She did not.

"Jordan!" he screamed, using her name for the first time.

Just like that, Jordan let go, taking his hand. Kiara did not release the female, but Harvey was prepared for this. He pulled Jordan into his arms as if they were in some deadly dance with gravity. Kiara was holding Jordan's arm, and Harvey could feel the click of Jordan's shoulder as it dislocated. Anger flushed through him.

How dare she mess with those under my command?

Harvey kicked out, his bare foot slamming into Kiara's face.

Let her go, he thought, sending another foot into her face.

Kiara finally let go, her vanity winning out as her nose broke under his attack. Harvey took no time to react, wings snapping out five feet from the ground. He held his wings out, pushing against the Air hard. The stroke sent them forward past Kiara as the tips of Harvey's wings brushed the ground, kicking up sand.

There was an explosion of sand behind them as Kiara slammed into the ground. Jordan's hair brushed the ground as she clung to his front, eyes never leaving his. Harvey, sweat pouring down his back and forehead, flew them up to the ring.

The three of them converged at the wall. Harvey made eye contact with Skylar, then they were racing each other. Skylar climbed with his long red hair flowing wildly. The Dyrfaldur was agile, leaping from hold to hold, finding gaps in the slick rock, never stopping.

The three of them were neck and neck as they reached the precipice, Jordan turning her head to look at the scene. As they reached the top, Jordan pushed out of his arms, leaping toward the platform.

She is a psychotic, idiotic, unpredictable fucking nuisance.

Her hand connected with the platform, and she held on.

Idiot, your shoulder is dislocated.

Her dislocated shoulder gave way, and she screamed in pain, falling. Harvey's heart skipped a beat. Skylar grabbed her, reaching the top just in time and lifting both of them onto the platform as Harvey landed.

How in the Hell is she going to make it through the second part with a dislocated shoulder?

Her arm hung limp at her side.

"*No wings includes Dyrfaldur,*" Jade shouted as the Dyrfaldur next to Harvey shifted into a hawk. Jade moved an embroidered handkerchief to his lips as he coughed.

Harvey grabbed Jordan around the waist, latching onto the zipline with one hand and leaping off the platform. He clenched his jaw against the sensation of her chest brushing against his own.

Jordan screamed at him; words lost in the wind. Her eyes were wide as they sped downward. The ground came up towards them in a blur, Harvey letting go at the last minute and tumbling down into the sand with Jordan. They were a tangle of limbs as they rolled to a stop. Harvey stood up, aware of his body on top of the female.

How does this keep happening?

General Marrow's glaring face above him helped Harvey snap out of his lustrous daze. He shoved Jordan off of him into the dirt, taking off towards the first wall. It came to the top of his head, *over six feet tall then.*

He jumped up, vaulting over with ease. Behind him, he glanced to see Skylar holding out his clasped hands for Jordan to jump up.

This will take far too long. I can't make them go faster, but I can make the others go slower.

Harvey dropped down the other side of the wall to wait.

Jordan and Skylar dropped down next. Harvey's team was in the lead.

"Keep going," he yelled, not turning to them.

Jordan and Skylar passed him without question.

Finally listening to me.

The next student barreled over. It was Sabastian. The male jumped from the wall, a war hammer raised. Harvey waited as the male fell towards him. At the last moment, he side-stepped and hit Sabastian in the back of the head with the butt of his dagger.

Sabastian fell to the sand unconscious. Harvey quickly slipped his toe under the large male's side, kicking him over so he didn't suffocate on the sand.

A flash of green, and Kiara was on him, snarling. Harvey spun, a spear piercing the sand next to him. Kiara landed in front of him, grabbing the spear. Harvey raised his two daggers, taking a brief peek behind him to see Jordan and Skylar passing the three-quarter mark.

That should be a decent head start.

Harvey threw a dagger at Kiara's foot, causing her to jump back out of the way. As she leaned forward, he swung his leg around, kicking her back. She was no Sabastian. Kiara had bested everyone in the Royal Guard twice over by now.

The female twisted like a viper, grabbing his leg and pulling him close. Nyx and Astris dropped down next to him, Nyx shoving Astris out of the way.

They are on the same team.

The distraction cost him as Kiara pulled him towards her, punching him in his nose. A crack and he grunted. Eyes unfocused, Harvey fell. Nyx turned around.

Don't do it. Just keep going. Don't pick a fight with her.

Fury filled her eyes, and the rings of Electricity in her eyes flashed, promising violence.

I need to stop this.

Harvey rolled to the side, avoiding Kiara's foot. His vision was still hazy, and his eyes stung from sweat and sand. Hands sunk deep in the sand, he kicked off in the direction of his sister. He threw the sand back in Kiara's face, an answering stream of curses causing him to smile.

Astris reached Nyx first. She grabbed Nyx, turning her away from Kiara. Harvey reached them in the blink of an eye. Grabbing Nyx's hand, he dragged her towards the next obstacle. Her eyes glanced to the viewer's platform, her face sobering. Harvey let go; *she's reckless, not stupid. Seeing our father reminded her of what is at stake.*

The three of them vaulted over the next series of walls with ease. Astris flipped over them acrobatically, Nyx forcefully threw herself up them, and Harvey used a combination of both to vault over them. The next obstacle was a series of balance beams. Harvey scrambled up the rope ladder, his body swinging violently back and forth as he climbed.

When he got to the top, he threw his arms and wings out wide, stepping onto the beam. Looking back, he saw Kiara had recovered and was gaining in on them, eyes red from the sand.

Skylar and Jordan were almost to the end of the pool, Skylar pulling at Jordan's tunic to keep her above Water.

She must be having a hard time with her shoulder.

Harvey turned his mind back to the task at hand. He ran across the beam steps light, as he kept his gaze directly ahead. The beam ended with a four-foot gap before the next one. Harvey timed his steps, *one, two, now.* He leapt. His foot slipped slightly, but he righted himself as he barrelled forward.

Jordan and Skylar passed the finish line. The entire team had to pass through. It was on Harvey now.

Another gap, and he threw himself to the penultimate beam.

Watch me, father, this is why I am your heir.

This beam was higher than the last, forcing him to put his hand down to steady himself.

Even if Nyx never had a chance.

His foot slipped again, and he skidded to the edge of the beam, backpedalling before running to the final leap. Two steps and he was on the final beam. This one was thirty feet in the Air, and below the pool started.

A scream behind him, and he turned slightly to see that Kiara had knocked a student off her beam. It was a Dyrfaldur, and he screamed as he fell. Harvey looked away. A crack as the body hit the ground, and Harvey closed his eyes in disgust. *Just a Dyrfaldur, just a…*

His sister's visage filled his mind, her fangs bared to the world. Harvey let out a frustrated sound, turning back and running to the end of the beam. He launched himself off of it. The pool below came up in a blur, his fingers hitting the Water with a cold slap. He came up, arms slashing at the Water. The sounds of screams and battle cries died every time his head went under. Four more strokes, and he grabbed the side of the pool.

Ahead of him was an empty expanse. A quick sprint to the finish line. Harvey pulled out of the pool, Nyx and Astris close on his heels. As soon as he got to his feet, Harvey broke out into a sprint. His feet pounded in the deep sand, lungs burning and arms pumping.

Ten feet.

Nine feet.

Eight.

Seven.

Almost there.

Kiara was neck and neck with him now, Astris and Nyx slightly behind.

She doesn't have her entire team. I will win even if I let her cross first.

Harvey ran the final stretch faster than he had ever run.

Princes don't come second.

Harvey regained his breath, sucking greedily at the Air. Titan finished and ran to Harvey. Titan was wearing his cousin's bracer; Ender's name engraved in the Metal. It made Harvey's heart clench to see. He had been more than a cousin to Titan, he helped raise him while Titan's dad was on the council, and his mother buried in her research. After Ender had passed, Titan had latched onto Kiara, who had lost her mom in the same battle. Harvey tried to keep his jealousy at bay, comforting himself with the knowledge that Titan had someone who could understand him. Even if that someone wasn't him.

"What was that move you pulled at the rings? Sending Kiara into the dirt, was that truly necessary?" Titan challenged breathing hard.

Yes.

"I didn't do it to…" Harvey started heart clenching, "I was just…" he glanced at Jordan.

Looking back to Titan, he explained, "This is war college, Titan. Holding back will hurt her progress. The Minotaur won't hold back, and neither will the Labyrinth."

Titan took a step back, anger flashing at the mention of the Minotaurs. A blink, and a warm smile replaced the anger, "I'm just messing with you; I know you would never do anything to hurt her. She is family."

Harvey nodded, squeezing Titan on the shoulder.

She is not family, nor will she ever be.

Titan patted a suddenly very exhausted Harvey fondly.

"A moment with the prince?" The professor hedged, looking to Titan.

Titan nodded, walking over to Kiara.

Gods, give me patience.

"If you would join me on the platform with your father, he has some things to discuss with you."

Harvey followed Jade into the Air, wings sore from the race. He landed lightly on the platform with his father, the professor, and Headmistress Loche.

King Blackthorn was fighting a smile, clearing his throat before speaking. "As the future king, it is an important skill for you to be able to lead a team. Despite winning, your team was disorganized at best, chaotic at worst."

His father's eyes met his own, holding him pinned to the platform. He was speaking as a king now, "I suggest learning more about your team and getting to know their strengths. Breaking up the team is never a viable option. There is strength in numbers. Throwing–" King Blackthorn coughed in contained amusement, the kingly mask slipping briefly.

"Throwing your teammates is not a viable solution; it breaks up the team. You did the same thing when you got to the ground obstacles."

Headmistress Loche spoke up, "If you had worked with the Dyrfaldur on each obstacle, it would have been more efficient. You got lucky, and luck should never be relied upon."

"I will work on… communicating with my team more." Harvey ground out, swallowing his pride.

His father placed a large hand on Harvey's head, ruffling his hair like he had when Harvey was a child. "Now go to your friends, I need to return to the castle after my meeting with Headmistress Loche and General Marrow to discuss the try-outs." The king walked away, calling back over his shoulder, "Good job putting family first with your sister. You make me proud, son."

CHAPTER 5: NYX

The Selection

Don't think I haven't noticed that you have been avoiding classes. Scared of me? You should be. You already know how much I crave the taste of your terror. After all, you have been receiving my presents.

-Nightmare note to Nyx, 55th Day, 76 AT

Nyx met up with her friends on the way to the Rune Choosing ceremony. It was dark out, the night quiet as if it were waiting. Nyx looked to Freya, who was walking next to her and chatting about cakes again.

I still need to figure out how to ask them to come with me after graduation. Not a lot is known about the other kingdoms. We will have to travel through Minotaur territory to leave.

Despite skipping most classes, Nyx was exhausted from dealing with Nightmare. She had started skipping classes to get extra sleep.

I just have to make it to enough classes to graduate. Nightmare wants me scared. Skipping a few classes will help with that narrative. It also gives me time to deal with the body parts. If anyone thinks they are mine, I could get expelled.

Every morning, she woke up to a different body part, and each time she had to dispose of it. This morning, she had opened her eyes to meet the gaze of a severed head.

Not the best way to wake up in the morning.

Nyx had been tempted to chuck the thing out the window, but thought better of it. Instead, she had snuck into the school's forge and burned it. The smell still invading her nostrils.

The Gods were to select the four Champions tonight. Each Champion would be marked by a sacred symbol handcrafted by the Gods. The Protectors, Chosen by the King and other important figures, would receive a tattoo of the same mark, but with a circle around it - a sign of devotion and loyalty to their Champion.

The Labyrinth would pull the Champions and Protectors into its depths to be tested at a random date within 30 days' time. The shortest time had been 6 days, the longest, 55 days.

"Who do you think will be Rune-Chosen this year?" Freya asked. "My parents will be proud if I get Chosen, but to be honest, I'm not the biggest fan of dying for the kingdom. Just not the self-sacrificing type, I guess."

"Why did you try out?" Nyx inquired, turning to look at her friend as she walked.

"It's the right thing to do. My family will starve if the crops keep failing. If my life can save everyone, it's worth it."

Nyx nodded in contemplation, the conversation dying for a few moments.

They will be hesitant to leave their families with famine taking hold of the kingdom. They are in school, likely as a way to take care of them in the future.

"We should hit the town this weekend. Go to the Devil's Dice Den. You in, Nyx?" Skylar broke the tension cheerfully.

I will have to save up enough for both families to live comfortably without Freya and Skylar.

"Let's do it," Nyx responded, grateful for the offer. "I actually have something I wanted to run by you guys later as well."

Convincing them won't be easy.

"As long as it's after a plate of food, this ceremony is cutting into my food time." Skylar joked, eyes flashing with intrigue.

They are nothing like Harvey's nasty circle of companions. I hope they agree to come with me.

"Nyx?" Freya asked, pulling Nyx from her thoughts.

"Huh?" she asked dumbly.

"I asked if you have seen the ritual before," Freya supplied.

"No, I don't think anyone is even allowed in the ritual except priests and first years. Even teachers won't be there." Nyx explained, having a more thorough education on the Gods as an Aervel noble.

"The high priest will guide the ritual, with assistance from other members of the temple. They will have us remove our clothes and swim or walk across the length of a pool to the other side. The Water is being purified now, look." Nyx pointed as they walked into Training Hall D." All you really need to know is that if the pool changes someone has been selected. The Rune that appears will tell them if they are a Champion or Protector."

Around two hundred priests lined the sides of the room. Ten priests stood around the pool, their hands in the Water. They muttered discordantly as they recited prayer after prayer for each of the Gods. Two more priests set up a series of partitions on either side of the pool. Nyx shivered at the thought of undressing and swimming naked in front of her classmates.

Nightmare could be here.

Nyx saw Harvey ahead, early as always, stepping through the doorway. He motioned to her to join the Aervel line.

"Move along, Minotaur-kin," one of the lesser priests snarled at Nyx's friends. Nyx was about to snap back, but Skylar shook his head slightly, jaw working. Nyx glowered at the priest, making note of his face.

Maybe my position can be good for something.

"For a ritual of this calibre, I'd better go to my brother," Nyx surrendered bitterly, "see you guys after!"

Nyx moved to the Aervel line, standing next to her brother. The hall was dark, with candles outlining paths throughout the space. Nyx had to hold her wings up to avoid them catching Fire.

The pool that had been blessed sat in the centre of the training cavern, inset into the ground. The candle's reflections rippled in the dark Water, the partitions now set up to either side of the pool, casting long shadows against the back wall.

Glad we will have some privacy.

The smell of Theos came from the candles, an earthy, tangy scent that was unmistakable. Even though Theos was dormant, objects imbued with Theos still existed. Only the richest nobles still had these special objects, and they were mostly reserved for ceremonies like this.

An Aervel in long white robes with a gold trim stepped onto a low pedestal.

He must be the high priest, Nyx thought, watching as he slowly raised his hands and wings to the sky.

Some of the priests lined up before him, with two priests assigned to each group of twenty. All of the lesser priests wore robes in a variety of purple shades, with Runes embroidered into the fabric.

In perfect unison, the priests began chanting in the Gods' tongue. Their voices carried eerily throughout the cavern, combining in an ethereal melody.

"Eligit propugnatores nostros. Servate animas miseras nostras. Marvos, Axios, Daelan, Elion, Harlow, Eryx, Verona, Octian."

Choose our Champions. Save our wretched souls. Marvos, Axios, Daelan, Elion, Harlow, Eryx, Verona, Octian.

The high priest beckoned, and two lesser priests jumped to respond.

The high priest's voice rose and fell with a hypnotic rhythm, carrying over the chorus of chants. Moonlight shafted through the ornate glass dome covering the cavern, causing his pale, wrinkled hands to glow with a soft luminescence as he held them high. The candlelight blurred as energy filled Nyx, and she shivered. Her hair stood on end, and goose bumps lined her skin in the low light.

Illusions of warriors' past burst to life in the Air, dancing in mock battle with one another. Students whispered in wonder at the sight, quickly silenced by the priests' hushed admonishments.

An Illusion Aervel pointed at his Fire-haired opponent in the sky, who started to spin – disoriented as he fell to the ground below. An Ice Element Aervel stomped on the ground, a Rune lighting up on her leg. Ice started to cover the Illusion wielder's leg, and his Firey opponent righted himself as the Illusion was broken. Elements shot across the space, the area momentarily an ancient battleground. Nyx was mesmerized as she watched the scene before it vanished with a *whoosh*. The Theos in the Air was thick like syrup in her lungs, the Electricity in her eyes burning brighter.

A priest came to one side of the bleachers, signalling to the first row of students. Nyx watched in fascination as, one by one, the students walked to the edge of the pool and unrobed behind the partition before walking down the stairs covered by a sheet. As instructed, the students crossed the lap pool one by one.

The priests alternated between the Dyrfaldur line and the Aervel line, and Nyx watched in mortification as the priests dumped soapy Water on Dyrfaldur before letting them in the pool.

They aren't animals. Gods, my friends are going to have to have that happen to them.

Nyx did her best to calm herself; interrupting a ritual could have dire consequences. The Gods were known to work in unpredictable ways.

The pool wasn't deep, but some of the shortest students still had to swim to keep afloat. Others waded to their necks in the dark Water. Nyx was glad for her shorter stature, not needing to wade tits-out in front of the entire school. The public nudity painfully reminded her of the time her clothes had been stolen from the lake by Kiara's friends.

Time seemed to pass imperceptibly slowly as each row went by in front of her, no sign of the Chosen. The number of remaining students began to dwindle, and no one had been selected yet.

Finally, it came to her section. She saw her brother walk straight ahead of her with his group of friends. Nyx watched as a female several spots ahead of Harvey walked behind the sheet. Nyx wished the partition was thicker, candlelight projecting shadows. She shivered at the thought of her silhouette being on display for everyone to see. She let the others pass her, hesitating with anxiety. The priest gave her a sharp look, and she slowly got back into line. Dread filled her as she stepped up the first step to the pool's deck.

The partition was made of holy fabric, stretched thin with age. Every material used in this ritual, from the candles to the towels, contained stored Theos.

It looks like it's about to give out, and something tells me they don't have a backup.

Her brother's flickering figure descended, and Nyx heard a soft splash as he dropped into the Water. Within seconds, the pool lit up with a rainbow of light, iridescent and ethereal. Her brother's silhouette in the Water wavered, appearing briefly in double.

Colours danced across his shadowed face and the floor around the pool, iridescence bathing his skin in a mirage of colours.

A wind gusted through the room, sending her two-toned hair into her eyes. The wind died, and Nyx fought her hair to see again. Her strawberry and black strands removed from her vision; Nyx blinked as the light died.

Murmuring spread throughout the room, only to be quickly silenced again by the priests. Priests who had been waiting against the far wall moved in the dark to relight the candles that had been extinguished by the phantom wind. Nyx could see one priest's hands shaking almost as much as her own.

Harvey.

Her anger towards her brother took a cold plunge, hardening her in a fragile state of shock.

Harvey finished his trek through the Water, stepping out of the pool. The pool fell dark as soon as Harvey left it. A priest guided him into a side room out of sight, quickly covering him in a towel. Blood pounded through Nyx's head with adrenaline, causing hyperawareness.

Harvey is going into the Labyrinth.

Nyx found herself cold and numb.

My brother's nomination has to be a dream, a sick joke by the heavens. Maybe it is some effect of the ritual on the mind. My brother can't be going to fucking die.

Cold awareness filled her as she understood the situation.

The pool lit up again as Titan dove in. The instant his fingers touched the Water, it transformed to liquid gold. As Titan waded through the liquified Metal, he ran his fingers along the surface in amazement.

The liquid shimmered and flowed with golden light. When Titan stepped out of the golden Water, the pool returned to its original state, but the liquid gold still poured down his body in rivulets.

Sabastian went next, the male swaggering up to the pool. He dropped in, the Water glowing blue. Around him, the Water turned into a maelstrom. It splashed violently, spilling over the edges of the pool. As soon as Sabastian stepped out, the Water went still.

Nyx's mouth hung open at his obvious nonchalance at his nudity in front of the thousands of students as he snatched the towel from the priest and threw it over his shoulder. Sabastian, who usually sauntered around like he owned the world, was stiff as he went into the side room.

He's in shock. I know all of the Chosen so far.

Kiara went next. Nyx held her breath. Nothing happened. Kiara scoffed, lifting herself out of the Water and snatching the towel from the priest.

It was time for the Dyrfaldur line to send a few students through. The priest held up an even thinner partition, the waning Theos noticeable in the enervated fabric. Freya was next, and Nyx bit her lip nervously. As she unrobed behind the partition, Nyx looked away to give her privacy. Freya went to step into the pool, but the priest dumped a bucket of cleaning solution on her before she got in, causing her to hiss in disgust.

I knew it was coming, but seeing it happen to her is awful. I need to stay calm; this would be the worst place to transition.

The Water remained unchanged, and Nyx released a breath she was holding. Freya gave Nyx a thumbs up as she got out, at odds with the serious atmosphere. Nyx chuckled tensely at her friend's antics, grateful for the brief moment of levity. She was quickly silenced with a sharp hiss by the priest closest to her.

I shouldn't have been so worried; the Gods have only ever selected a few Protectors.

Skylar snatched the bucket the priest was getting ready to dump on him, choosing to cleanse himself. He stepped lightly into the Water, long red hair hanging down his bare torso in a fiery cascade. When Skylar's foot touched the Water, it glowed softly.

Protector.

Freya, who was starting to leave out the other door for the unchosen, spun around at the light. A small keening noise came from her before she covered her mouth. Nyx fought the sensation of desperation as tears welled in her eyes.

She had only just befriended him, and now she was losing him. Losing him before their friendship could begin. Her brother, Skylar, Titan, and Sabastian would likely be dead soon. Her entire reality was being flipped upside down, the improbability of it stunning her.

Veritas Hall had approximately two thousand students per year. There was less than a one percent chance of getting Chosen, and every single one, so far, was someone she knew. The ceremony went through the first-year students with efficiency from years of repetition. The inclusion of at least two hundred priests sped the process even more.

When it was Astris's turn, Nyx watched enraptured as Astris's form disrobed behind the sheet, figure outlined. Astris descended the stairs behind the partition, her silhouette captivating Nyx; a formidable, lithe figure bewitching and commanding the room. Her long, tightly curled hair swayed with her hips as she walked down the steps, effortlessly graceful. A hand tapped Nyx, and the student behind her nudged her, pointing to the priest, who was trying to motion Nyx forward impatiently. Nyx ignored him, watching as Astris stepped into the pool. The Water lit up with a faint glow.

Protector.

Who will they place her with? Harvey?

The priest turned her head away respectfully as Nyx undressed. Her clothes fell to the floor, and the priest grabbed them to take to the other side for her. Nyx looked down at the recently darkened Water ahead, taking a deep breath and edged down the steps. Something about the liquid looked off, like oil instead of salt Water.

When her toe hit the Water, she winced at the feeling of the slippery liquid. Shuddering, Nyx stepped off the edge into the Water. Her head went under, liquid sliding across her skin unnaturally.

Blue light burst behind her closed eyelids, and she inhaled some Water. Electric blue light crackled throughout the Water, veins of Electricity flaring through the Water.

It reminded Nyx of the glowing jellyfish migration, which came with a large festival on the beach by the castle. Energy buzzed inside of her, reflecting the pulses of Electricity in the Water. Nyx was mesmerized as she watched the Electricity spider around her, skin lighting with each flash. She swam forward slowly, relishing in the magical sight, fear pumping through her being.

Nyx finished the swim, pulling herself out of the pool on the other side. She felt sick and cold, terror driving her thoughts. Decades of warriors had failed and perished before them; Nyx was all too aware of the reality of her situation.

I'm not worthy of being a Champion. Why would the Gods choose me?

A bastard.

The priest draped a thin towel over her, and she stepped to the side to don her clothes.

The Chosen were led to an antechamber, while the other students were guided out of the building. One of the lower priests brought a parchment to the high priest.

Likely the school's Protector selections and pairings.

Nyx started to walk to the room she was being ushered towards when two more rounds of luminance bathed the area. Nyx looked down at the permanent sign of her Choosing, a fresh Rune brand.

Her Aervel side winning over her Dyrfaldur heritage.

Nyx's consisted of a strong centre line that wrapped around itself like a dragon curling around a tower. Unlike Elemental Runes, this was the combination of multiple Elemental lines that represented her soul. It was beautiful. It was illegal to be a Half-blood, so this was the first time someone with Dyrfaldur blood was Chosen as a Champion.

She was to be a Champion, and she and her brother had a date
with demise.

CHAPTER 6: ASTRIS

Oath

Kiara, it has to stop. Please. The body parts have gone too far. Chicken parts are one thing, this is... messed up. Not to mention illegal. I know she didn't want to take the throne, and that angered you. Is that the reason you continue to torment her? To use me to torment her? The bond was supposed to be used for chores and political gain. That's why I agreed to exchange my freedom to eradicate my parents' debt. Helping you torture her was not a part of the bargain. Please.

-Astris letter to Kiara, 49th Day, 76 AT

Astris walked into the room with the other Protectors: Kiara and two Dyrfaldur. Kiara had been selected from the try-outs to fill the empty Protector role. Astris and the two Dyrfaldur had to wait for Kiara as she was tattooed with a Runed needle.

The Protector Rune had shown up on Astris as soon as she had gotten out of the pool. Their Champions would be revealed by a matching Rune. She looked down at the brand on her forearm, an ancient symbol inside a circle. It consisted of a curving line that looped and meandered back and forth over a straight line.

I should be a Champion. I deserve to be a Champion; I can even hold my own against Kiara. But it's a death sentence, so why do I want it so badly? It will be a chance to prove myself, maybe even a chance to separate myself from Kiara. But who is my Champion? The jagged edge of this line almost looks like... Nyx.

Astris didn't know how she made the connection; it just felt right.

She's a Half-blood, though. Nyx's partial shift on the first day of school proved that. There's no way the Gods would pick her…

Right?

Astris balled her hands into fists at her side. She looked over to Kiara, who was in the Protector line to her left.

Thank Harlow she isn't my Champion.

Astris allowed herself a half smile, feeling vindication and satisfaction.

Try acting all high and mighty despite being assigned bodyguard duty. Even the Gods want her dead.

She then glanced at Nyx. Emotions flooded her before she wrenched her gaze away.

She is the reason Kiara… Nyx is a weakness. A weakness because of how she makes me feel. What I am forced to do because of her.

Guilt, hatred, and desire threatened to drown her. Her face remained empty. Always blank, eternally stoic.

Astris learned early on that showing her emotions allowed others to manipulate her. Showing her vulnerability gave her enemies more power. She touched her chest, clutching the fabric of her tunic briefly, a nervous tic.

Her pulse thrummed; she needed to get that under control. At the castle where her family had rooms, her anxiety was rough. Somehow, it was even worse here. She had asked for the room with Nyx.

I may not have my freedom, but I can still do some things. Protect Nyx in some ways.

Astris did, however, understand why she avoided mentioning her roommate to Kiara, who had paid her way into a solo room. Astris had been careful about going to her room when Kiara wasn't around.

Then I would be a danger to Nyx, not her shield.

Astris's parents offered her a solo room, but she had refused.

I can change it, but we will be dead soon. The Labyrinth will kill us all. Maybe Kiara can make it through. Cruelty has honed her into a weapon.

The thought disgusted her. The finality of her death refused to settle in Astris's body, her mind frozen over in a haze of dissociation.

The high priest closed the door with a click. The noise was loud in the quiet chamber. The room was used for changing before and after class, smelling of damp stone and the sickly-sweet tang of towels left to mould in the corner by spoiled nobles.

The high priest cleared his throat, moving to the centre of the group, "Champions line up behind me; Protectors in front of me."

The Chosen shifted anxiously, waiting for the selection process to finish. Rustling filled the otherwise quiet room, the tension palpable in the Air. Astris walked over to the Protectors side, inhaling sharply when Nyx walked over to the Champion line.

No.

No.

No.

She is only half Aervel.

She is only half, and now she stands in a place of honour.

Guilt mixed with jealousy as she jerked her eyes to the priest again. The priest walked to the left side of the Champion line, where Titan was standing.

Figures that the golden boy Titan was Chosen as a Champion.

The priest guided Titan forward out of line then inspected the Rune on his arm. He nodded sagely to himself before walking to the Protector line.

Three other students stood in line with Astris, equal to the number of Champions. The priest went down the line, looking at each arm in tow. Astris hoped she would be Harvey's Protector. He was the most reasonable out of the Champions, and she had an amicable relationship with him.

Genuine, which was more than she could say about the majority of her relationships. Despite the treatment of his sister, he had caught her interfering in Kiara's plans to protect her more than once. *I just hate Kiara, that's why I do it.* Astris lied to herself, unwilling to face her pain.

The priest stopped in front of Kiara, guiding her to Titan. As they had practiced in simulations since grade school, Kiara dropped to her knees in front of Titan.

Bet that isn't the first time, Astris thought amusedly.

The priest brought over a bronze laurel and placed it on Titan's head. He then retrieved a sword and handed it to Titan. Titan turned the blade horizontally, holding it on either end of the flat side. The hand on the side of the blade was open, cradling the sword. The hand on the hilt grasped the leather firmly.

The priest then sprinkled a Metallic golden powder on the flat of the blade, down the fuller to keep it secure in the groove. Runes ran down the blade, glowing with the addition of the powder. Titan lowered the blade in front of Kiara, who lowered her lips to the golden powder.

Titan's hands shook with the blade, and he looked briefly to Harvey for reassurance. Kiara grabbed the blade and held it still in annoyance. Indistinguishable echoes and whispers engulfed the space as her mouth touched the powder.

The Gods are watching.

Astris's arms broke out in goosebumps.

Why do they have to be so creepy, though? Why can't they be cute and joyful?

Titan recited the words of the Champion, "**Usque ad finem huius iurisiurandi, fatum meum diis, fatum meum victori meo alligo, et vita mea illorum erit usque ad victoriam aut mortem.**"

Which translated to:

My fate, I forfeit to the Gods. My end, or Theos's beginning. Let it be written in the marrow of the world.

Kiara looked up at Titan, eyes mischievous as she replied, "**Electis virtutem meam do. Vita, voluntas, anima tua est donec iterum suspiret magia.**"

Which translated to:

Until the end of this oath, I bind my fate to the Gods, I bind my life to my Champion, and my life will be theirs until success or demise.

Kiara's eyes and veins started to glow a ghostly green then faded to nothing. With that, the first pair was united. The priest scanned the list, pairing up Champions with their Protectors. Harvey was paired with a Dyrfaldur who Astris remembered being referred to as Jordan. He was refusing to look at her; Astris hoped for his sake that he could get past his prejudices.

We will not live very long while turning on one another. This is the worst combination of individuals; the Gods must be testing us in more ways than just the obstacles we will face.

Sabastian was paired with Skylar, with whom Astris shared her morning Elements class. The silver-tongued commoner would have an interesting time managing the arrogant male. She eyed the frayed cuff of Sabastian's poorly made tunic. He hid it well, but Astris had noticed.

The male's family had a bad history of spending too many nights in the Devils Dice Den. It was like he fought extra hard to be a dick in order to distract from his own family's shame. Sabastian's father even worked with the Dyrfaldur from time to time, sharing the same wealth class. Sabastian and Skylar paired off, and Astris looked over to see that Nyx was the only available match.

No.

Out of everyone, it could not be her.

It was not possible.

The Gods are sick and twisted.

I will end up killing her.

The priest's wrinkled hand touched her wrist, and she snatched her hand back, following him reluctantly.

No, thank you, creepo.

Astris looked to Kiara, who was smiling like it was her birthday.

I have to hope Titan keeps her busy. I don't want to be her distraction. I don't want to be this close to Nyx. Too many memories. Too many disgusting memories.

The corner of her mouth turned down before she schooled it back to neutral, looking at Nyx finally.

Astris wished there was something she could do, some way to change the decision. If it were anyone but the Gods, she would think it was a mere miscommunication.

I need to distance myself from Nyx. Will that even be possible? Not with that oath in place. I will need to work overtime, like I did at the castle.

She shook her head to clear it and forced herself to keep moving. When she got to Nyx, the rest of her world faded away. She dropped to her knees unhurriedly, watching Nyx. Nyx looked at her with such loathing, a swirl of pain, disgust, and hatred.

I hate how she looks at me.

Nyx's two-toned hair fell into her eyes, black and pink strands mixing.

The pink must come from her mother's side, her brother only having black hair. Her Dyrfaldur mother, Astris realized.

"Fata mea Diis amitto. Finis meus: vel principium Theos. In medullis scribatur mundi," Nyx spat down at Astris.

The Electricity in Nyx's eyes flared, tiny zaps of neon blue spidering across a dark navy. When Astris looked deeply enough, she could pretend she was in the skies again, away from all the noise, the responsibilities, the cruelty. Looking into Nyx's eyes made Astris feel both lost and found.

The worst moments of my life have been spent looking into those hateful eyes.

The Electricity was as familiar to her as Kiara's Venomous gaze. Those eyes that spurred Kiara on in her delights. Kiara's misplaced ideas about how to get Harvey's attention.

She wants power, not him.

The priest cleared his throat impatiently. She gave him a pointed look out of the corner of her eye.

I am still a noble, and he will give me a damn minute.

Astris bowed her head, preparing herself for the next step of the ceremony. A slight shake entered her limbs as she swatted down the familiar feeling of panic.

She took in a deep breath before looking forward again. She walked up to the space in front of Nyx. Slowly, lowering herself to the ground, watching as those Electric rings pulsed.

Clearing her mind, she dipped her head, pressing her lips to the powder and tasting it. It smeared across her lips, sparkling in her mouth.

She choked on the taste, fighting to keep the tears at bay. Astris's body shivered as she tasted the concoction for the second time in her life. *The first had been…* it was too painful to think about.

Astris shut down the memory, bringing herself back into the moment. She pushed the fear down with fervour, clinging to the Electric eyes before her desperately.

I will not break.

The powder's bitter burn filled her chest before spreading throughout her body. Her eyes filled with tears, and she gritted her teeth. She wanted to escape; she wanted to be anywhere but here.

Not again, not again, not again, not again. Please just let this end.

She shoved the world back from her, disintegrating into the back of her consciousness to wait.

Help. Me.

"Electis virtutem meam do. Vita, voluntas, anima tua est donec iterum suspiret magia," she intoned, tears blinding her eyes.

She was supposed to stand. She was supposed to stand and finish the ceremony. She was numb, raw, and trapped. She wanted to run, but Nyx's gaze pierced her, pinning her to the floor. Astris's anger sputtered momentarily, Nyx holding eye contact unflinchingly, confusing Astris.

Why is Nyx still staring?

She stood stiffly, turning away from Nyx and walking back to stand next to Kiara. Every step rigid, chin tipped up slightly. The other Champions and Protectors showed no aversion to the oath.

They don't know shit about oaths.

Astris remained silent, watching as her body went through the motions. She let her mind wander, rising away from the world in her own paradigm. She daydreamed about the wind on her face, the sun on her wings; of the vast night sky and the colour of Nyx's eyes. Of rain pounding around her, drenching her with Icy awareness. Of Electricity flashing across the horizon, dancing through the thick raindrops.

Of her.

An hour later, the ceremony was complete. They had been marched in front of the other students and forced to sit through a long speech by the high priest about duty and honour. Astris did not mind; she begged the seconds to tick more slowly so she could remain in her limbo. Once the speech ended, she would have to rejoin the world. Once the speech ended, she would have to interact.

The Labyrinth's Theos would take them in its own time.

The average time given is 30 days.

Tomorrow, training would start, and they would need to prepare mentally, physically, and emotionally for the journey.

Training would consist of extra class time, private tutoring, and setting aside any classes that were irrelevant. The Labyrinth tested every facet of a person's being, but Astris doubted it would ask her about the history of Dengar. It was a common misconception that no one ever survived the Labyrinth.

Astris, who loved to lose herself in dusty old history books, knew that some Champions returned without Theos and without their minds. The temple avoided mentioning this to individuals because it sent the wrong message to the masses. The idea of the Gods leaving a husk as a reminder of their failure did not inspire confidence for the future.

Dinner was after the ceremony, and the students went silent upon their arrival. Kiara preened at the attention, but Astris hated it. Harvey wasn't having dinner with them; he had grabbed his food and muttered something about going to study. Kiara, propped in Titan's lap, complained about having to share classes with Dyrfaldur.

He looked to Kiara for approval, and she touched his face lightly. Astris moved her food around, irritated and vulnerable. Kiara looked over, noticing Astris picking at her food.

"Eat," Kiara ordered, pushing a lock of green hair out of her eyes.

Astris did not move, a familiar tingling sensation filling her limbs.

Fuck you.

Kiara raised an eyebrow at her. Astris looked her in the eye, face blank, unmoving. Her hand slowly moved on its own, picking up the fork and placing a piece of well-seasoned broccoli in her mouth. Kiara snorted softly before turning back to Titan. Astris's hands kept moving, only stopping when there was no more food in front of her.

Astris stared daggers at the back of Kiara's head, daydreaming of slamming her smug smile into the dining table. She excused herself before she did something she would regret. Something Kiara would make her regret.

Astris entered her room late that night after a long flight following the ceremony and dinner.

Nyx isn't here yet, Astris thought with relief.

She was not going to switch rooms.

All Kiara would have to do… Astris shook the thought away.

Astris walked to the floor-length mirror next to the bathroom. She stripped off her shirt, unknotting the fabric that looped under each wing to slide it over her head. Astris looked in the mirror; her eyes went straight to her chest, where her first binding Rune sat between her breasts. The first time she had tasted that disgusting substance.

"Where no one will ever see it," Kiara had told her. *She was making sure of that*, Astris thought bitterly.

Her eyes traced the Rune before pausing. She looked down at her forearm, at her Protector Rune. Looking back at her chest, she noticed that the Rune had faded slightly. She inhaled gently, thinking about her class this evening.

In 'Introduction to Runic Language Systems,' she learned that when multiple binding Runes were placed on a subject, the most recent Rune held more sway. The more visible the Rune, the more Theos was in the glyphs. Aside from a Theometer, saturation was the best way to gauge Theos.

The door opened, and Nyx walked in. Astris froze cheeks heating; Nyx's gaze was intense in a way Astris had not seen before. She blinked, and the look was gone, replaced by irritation. Astris fought the urge to touch her binding Rune on her chest, forcing her arms to remain still at her side.

"You said you would change the rooms," Nyx accused, holding Astris's gaze.

"It is polite to give someone privacy when they are in a state of undress."

"Oh, bite me."

Astris walked forward, taking Nyx by the hand. Nyx looked at her with surprise, trying to pull away. Astris's grip remained strong. She nipped Nyx's finger a little harder than the oath demanded.

"Ow, what the f…" Nyx yelped.

"Protectors have oath-binding Runes. You have the other half. Do that again, and I will make you regret it." Astris's voice increased in pitch, tears blurring her vision.

Astris brushed furiously at her eyes and dropped into bed, turning towards the wall and away from Nyx. Silent tears flowed down her cheeks, making her curls stick to her wet face. Her heart pounded rapidly.

She can control me now.

"I'm sorry," Nyx whispered. Astris opened her eyes, looking into the darkness and listening to Nyx's agitated shuffling behind her.

Nyx got into her own bed. "I will do my best not to do it to you again. That must have been scary. I have heard tales of oaths; they are no joke. I didn't think it would act like that, though."

Astris remained muted, staring into the darkness numbly.

Nyx's voice had sounded sincere, scared to control her.

Or maybe it was just a flowery statement until she wanted revenge. Astris snorted. *I hope she has me punch Kiara in her smug face.*

The more she thought about the situation, the more she was sick to her stomach.

Nyx hates me, and for good reason, yet here she is apologising to me.

Astris's mind raced long into the night before she finally drifted off into sleep. That night, Astris dreamed of open skies and a female with strawberry and black hair.

CHAPTER 7: NYX

Darkness

See that Half-blood carted away today? I did that. Second one this year. Halfbloods are easy to get rid of. A bastard princess? Give me enough time.

-Nightmare note to Nyx, 12th Day, 76 AT

Nyx woke with a hangover again. She hadn't told her friends her plan last night, too terrified to think about anything but her imminent demise.

She stretched; *why is it so dark? I must have woken up too early.*

She went to pull up the covers to realize they weren't there. The surface below her was smooth, cold, and most definitely not her bed.

Not again, Nyx thought, reliving the time she woke up in the middle of a river, courtesy of Nightmare. Suddenly, Nyx found herself caught in the terrifying grip of her past.

Nyx could feel wood under her, pressing into her wings. She dropped suddenly and yelped in surprise, panic taking hold.

I'm not in bed. I'm moving. What the fuck is happening?

Whatever this was, it was moving fast and thrashing back and forth.

Almost like I am on a boat.

The sound of Water rushing confirmed her suspicion.

Nyx took a deep breath, clearing the memory. "Minotaur's balls," she whispered.

No sound came out.

She tried to speak again. "Hello?"

Nothing came out; she could feel the vibrations in her throat, but no sound. Terror took the place of panic.

This is worse than the river.

Either a terrible dream or a Theos created sensory void.

If not for the lack of sound, I would have expected it to be Kiara or Astris. This was Theos, something neither of them can access.

Her mind shot back to her lessons; *only the Gods could have done this. This is too far beyond the realm of reality us mortals adhere to.*

Nyx pushed herself to her feet.

The Labyrinth was not of this world. Its mysterious origin and location are why Champions and their Protectors needed to be summoned. That way, no other individuals could join them to supply aid.

It can't be. We should have had more time, she thought, shaking her head.

She needed to get more information and could not rely on sight or sound.

It seems touch and smell work.

Smell!

That was the solution. Nyx steadied herself, preparing to shift.

Nothing happened.

She tried to make herself shift again, gritting her teeth and yelling ineffectually into the void. Her heart beat rapidly as she tried again, getting on all fours. Nothing happened.

The one time I need to shift, Nyx exhaled in frustration. *I don't want to be alone.*

She tried thinking of something sad, but nothing happened.

Cold sweat trickled down her back, and she shivered turning around to nothing.

She could hear the thundering of her heart in her head, the only sound in the darkness.

Alone.

Thump. Thump. Thump.

Alone.

Thump. Thump. Thump. Thump.

Alone.

Desperation clawed at her insides, fear ruling her.

I would even take Astris at this point.

She thought back to Astris in her room, the hatred she stewed in, and the other feeling that made her stomach buzz. Emotions flowed through her, and her canines dropped down.

There we go.

Nyx stood up tentatively.

She could smell Astris near her and Harvey farther away. She inhaled again, her sharpened senses allowing her a synthetic version of sight.

They must have teleported inside the maze during the night. That was why everything was off; why she didn't have her sight or hearing.

Nyx walked towards the smell of Astris.

I might as well grab my 'Protector,' who is getting off to a tremendous start needing to be rescued herself.

Nyx followed the smell of pine, honey, and cloves. She thought about making a sound to avoid startling her, but laughed silently, remembering the lack of it.

The vibrations of her throat were ineffectual; her laugh swallowed in the void.

This is a chance to pay her back for all her torments. I could kill her but then… then I would be alone.

Instead, Nyx grabbed Astris by the shoulder, finding pleasure in how she startled.

A hand grabbing her in the dark must be terrifying.

Astris pulled back, thrashing to get away.

Nyx's joy was short-lived as she came back into the reality of their situation.

I need to let her calm down and then we can go to the others.

Astris shook Nyx's hand furiously before trying to pull away again. Nyx reacted by swinging Astris, spinning her like the ballroom dancer Astris was, using her own momentum to take control. Astris bumped into her, soft curly hair bouncing into Nyx's chest, face bumping into the crook between Nyx's neck and shoulder. A soft breath forced out as Astris came flush against Nyx's sturdy frame.

Nyx held her tightly to her chest, frozen.

What now?

Astris stood stiffly, not moving. They were facing one another, and Astris carefully reached to touch Nyx to identify her. It was not a caring embrace, but an identification of body parts and locations.

Clinical.

Nyx could smell Astris, filling her nostrils as she pressed against her in the dark. Her skin was soft against Nyx's.

Nyx blinked, *pull away, pull away, pull away,* she thought angrily at herself.

Stomping down, she smiled as she felt Astris's bare toe under her foot. The situation was easier to deal with through the lens of familiar animosity.

Whoopsie.

Nyx was caught off guard as Astris rose up again from her crouch over her injured toes, getting in close and grasping her firmly. Nyx went limp, surprised at the touch; Astris's long, skinny, soft, and surprisingly cold fingers held her firmly in place. Every fibre of Nyx's being was at attention.

She became aware of the chill of Astris's hands, getting colder on her skin.

A third Element marker, that is considered lucky. A sign of powerful Theos dormant within her. I am surprised no one talks about it. Or maybe no one knows? I have never seen her touch anyone, Nyx realized, *not without gloves.*

It set her body ablaze with Icy sensation every time Astris touched her.

Today was the first time Astris and Nyx had touched, outside of combat. Nyx's body reacted to the cold, hairs rising on the back of her neck. She could feel Astris's soft breath as it puffed against her sleeping tunic. Astris reached up to Nyx's face with her other hand, feeling around, stopping suddenly.

Did she figure out who I am yet? Guess I am so unremarkable to her that she can't figure out who I am by the feeling of my body. I am the only female aside from her with curly hair. The shortest Aervel. And she saw the sleep clothes I am in. She should have figured it out instantly.

A waver and a second, equally cold hand traversed down from her neck to her chest, down her stomach. The finger shuddered slightly as it slowed, running across her hip bone. It then traced the waistband of the front of Nyx's trousers, continuing at this level around her body. Nyx imagined Astris walking around her, her wrist limp, dragging across Nyx's skin. The cold of the fingers caused her blood to heat as it went over sensitive areas. Her breath caught, heart beating faster.

Is she messing with me like Kiara? Did Kiara order her to court me? I'm not that stupid. Why now, though? In the dark, when Kiara would have wanted to see my emotions on display. See how I writhed in my own self-loathing over how much I want to touch this female.

It was a bizarre experience, the finger tracing around her body, with no indication of the female behind it. No sound of footsteps, no sound of her heartbeat pounding through her chest. The hand came to rest gently on her shoulder before Nyx snapped out of her shock.

She growled silently in frustration, grabbed Astris by the waist, and threw her over her shoulder, possibly screaming, definitely kicking. The female was much taller than her, but she was stronger.

Nyx, wrestling with Astris the entire way, making her way to the next party member. She smelled Skylar heading towards her and stopped to wait.

Astris was bumped into by another body, and she punched Nyx on the back in frustration. Nyx turned around to grab Skylar. She placed him in front of her with her right hand, Astris over her left shoulder. She then dropped Astris to the ground.

She smiled to herself. *I will hear about that later. If we make it out of this, that is.*

She reached down and grabbed Astris, who was tense with anger. Astris slapped her hand away at first before grabbing for Nyx again.

Must be really frustrating to be her right about now, Nyx thought with a smirk.

She pulled Astris into position, joining Astris's free hand with Skylar's. She then tapped Skylar on the hand twice before starting to move. She dragged the pair to Harvey, who was more manageable to grab, understanding the situation and complying.

With a single tap, they stopped at Sabastian, then Jordan, then Titan, and finally Kiara.

When they got to Kiara, a light flashed to life in the distance. A small pinprick of light ahead with a glowing Unity Rune over it. The Unity Rune was two ovals combined into a continuous figure-eight pattern. Relief and dread came in equal measure as the way forward became clear.

They walked for hours, *or was it minutes?* She started to lose track as her attention waned with exhaustion and fear. The silence ate away at Nyx, every step she took, completely silent. She felt removed from her body, unable to use two of her senses. It took every bit of courage Nyx had to not think about what could be lurking in this darkness.

If only she could ask how much longer it would be. The lack of light meant there was no way to judge distance. The small light they were following seemed almost disembodied, not illuminating any of the surrounding area.

After what Nyx assumed was a full day of walking, Harvey brought both of her hands together and to one side of her head. It was time to sleep. Nyx sent the message down the line, eventually sensing multiple snores behind her, the vibrations on the ground prevalent with the lack of other senses.

They lay in a circle, feet all touching, a precaution to avoid accidental separation. Nyx could not sleep, sitting up in the dark, heart racing. Astris's hand reached over to her as if to make sure she was still there. She was her Protector, after all.

Astris stopped when she had figured out their positions, much less sensual than the first time she touched Nyx earlier.

She discovered Nyx still sitting up and placed a hand on her, pushing down on her shoulder. Nyx fought her until Astris gave up, exasperated… or so Nyx thought, until a hand whapped lightly into the back of her head. Nyx groaned silently, lowering herself to the ground; Astris's hand remained cradling her neck.

Nyx did not care how it looked, *or was it felt? Either way, I am terrified of the group leaving me behind.*

The weight of her situation came down on her. They had no food, no Water, no shoes, and no sense of time or distance.

I am in my sleep clothes. Champions and Protectors usually are made to sleep in armour the day after the ritual. No one expected we would get pulled in within hours of the ceremony.

The odds were stacked against them, and only two members of the group gave a shit about her: her brother and Skylar. Skylar only knew her for a short time; Nyx doubted he would risk his life for her.

What will happen if Kiara or one of the others turns him against me?

They walked and walked and walked. Nyx's feet were raw and cuts peppered her legs from missteps. Their gait was hurried, eager, and driven by a hunger psychosis that only a starving person could understand.

If we don't get Water soon, we will be dead. We need to hurry.

Time stretched, and it began to feel as if the light would never arrive, but by the end of that day, they could already start to see the outlines of one another. The excitement and anticipation led to better cooperation, despite groggier minds. As they continued, the light got brighter in front of them, the group letting go of one another and ploughing towards it.

Finally, the group stepped out into the light, dirty, sweaty, and exhausted. The group fell to the rocky ground at the edge of the light, eyes adjusting to the cave.

Sound rushed back, overwhelming the group. Nyx curled in a ball on the ground, panting and holding her head, hands over her ears.

Drip.

Drip.

Drip.

Nyx got to her feet. Swaying slightly, she lifted her heavy head to look around.

She looked back the way they had come, into the dark void. Turning away from it, she inspected what was before them.

A tunnel made of smooth brown rock. A short stretch of passageway was ahead before the tunnel split off into two directions. The sides of the tunnel were dripping Water from an unknown source.

Lambent light lit the space, the source as unidentifiable as the Water dripping from the walls. Glowing mushrooms and moss also clung to the wall, and Nyx's heart leaped.

Water, and maybe even food. I've never seen food glow before though, or maybe that's just hallucinations from dehydration.

Nyx walked to the wall, lapping at the Water dripping down the surface. Soon, the others began doing the same, wincing on weary feet. Astris flapped her wings once, grabbing a few of the larger mushrooms that grew up high before touching down gracefully. She walked over to Nyx, hand outstretched. Nyx looked at her sceptically.

"For fuck's sake, I am starving, and Godssworn to protect your ass. Therefore, I must make sure you eat and don't get poisoned. Therefore, I would not poison you. Are you still with me, or should I go slower?" Astris's voice seemed to boom throughout the room, causing her heart to quicken, still unaccustomed to sound. Nyx saw red.

"What did you just say?" Nyx bristled, voice dropping low.

She stalked up to Astris's desiccated body, fighting for every movement, teeth bared. Nyx's fangs dropped down, and she covered her mouth. Astris stepped between her and the others, getting in close.

"Calm down before everyone sees. I made a promise to your brother, and I am true to my word. I will keep your secret," Astris whispered, "for Harvey, not for you."

Nyx took a deep breath, her fangs retracting, and she wiped the blood from her mouth. "I know you would never do it for me. You don't have to remind me of your... nature. I remember plenty well."

Astris opened and closed her mouth, brows pinched together slightly. The sound of Harvey grunting caused them both to turn. He got up shakily, irises now a sickly yellow. He plucked a single mushroom from Astris and popped it in his mouth, chewing before going to collect his own. Further evidence of their edibility came as Kiara placed her own into her mouth.

Nyx ignored the mushrooms in Astris's hand and instead picked her own. Sabastian handed Skylar some mushrooms, surprising Nyx. Sabastian was not one to make friends with Dyrfaldur. Then again, these circumstances were unusual at best and insane at worst. Nyx couldn't think; every breath painful, as she fought the fog that had taken over her thoughts.

Water, I need more Water.

Slow, like molasses, she struggled to grasp onto her waning thoughts like threads in the wind. Nyx looked down at the mushroom in her hand, unaware of how it had gotten there.

Minotaur's balls, I am tired.

She took a bite, and the taste of Theos covered her tongue, rich and earthy. Energy filled her in an instant, and Nyx's eyes sharpened to her surroundings.

These things have a kick.

Getting an idea, Nyx took some of the wet moss, and squeezed. A rush of Water came into her mouth. More effective than licking the walls. Sweet relief came as she drank deeply, soothing her aching throat.

The mental strain of hunger, pain, sensory deprivation, and sensory overstimulation came crashing down upon the group. The tunnel darkened, the radiant light dimming until only the mushrooms lit the way. Nyx lay down, stomach protesting at the plain mushrooms.

I hate mushrooms, Nyx thought as she was pulled into a deep and troubled sleep.

When she woke, it was to the sound of the others starting to move around, and she realized she had rolled back into Astris during the night. The soft light once again lit the tunnel to Nyx's relief. Last night the cold Air was harsh, and she had tossed and turned until she sensed something draped over her. She had nestled into it, falling asleep at last. Turns out, it was Astris's cloak… and Astris.

Astris was both Ice and warmth, her hands cold, her body balmy and soft. The contrast made Nyx's body react, her stomach clenching, hyper-aware of every body part that was touching the other female.

Astris and Nyx warmed up quickly with the shared heat, and the cloak was comforting as Nyx stirred. Astris's hand was cool on Nyx's hip, her warm breathing slow. Nyx considered pretending to be still asleep; she was so warm and comfortable, and Astris's cloak smelled of… Astris, the honey and cloves far stronger up close. Nyx breathed in the scent as quietly as she could, turning her face closer to Astris's.

Astris stirred, eyes opening to find Nyx's face staring back at her. Astris blinked before pulling back sharply, yanking the cloak off Nyx, whose head struck the stone floor with a thump. Grunting, Nyx sat up and looked around. The lighting was similar to how it had been in the evening.

The light is the same brightness as it was last night.

It would be essential to try to keep some semblance of a circadian rhythm while here. The lack of sun or a sundial made time a construct more than a guide. Nyx looked up at Astris, who dropped mushrooms on her.

"Breakfast; if you are going to sleep cuddled in my arms, you better listen to me," Astris said sharply.

"Fuck off," Nyx snapped, voice unsteady.

Nyx hoped Astris couldn't read her reaction. Embarrassment mixed with adrenaline and another emotion Nyx did not want to look at too closely. One she had felt before when Astris was searching her body. Nyx wanted to be someone else, just to get searched again.

CHAPTER 8: HARVEY

Assignments

It was. You are everything. I promise to be the best husband and King I can. I know we are bound to secrecy by my parents, rules are rules. I do think it is prudent to wait on the announcement with the stir it will create. The richest bachelor and the future king? Quite the match. Doesn't make it any easier. I crave you constantly.

-Harvey letter to Titan, 52nd Day, 76 AT

Harvey woke with Jordan at his back.

This would be so much easier if I could do this on my own.

He stiffened, her tiny body rising and falling as he peeked over his shoulder.

She's so close.

He sat up slowly, looking around. It was unsettling to wake up in the light after becoming accustomed to the pitch black and the lack of his senses. Sound assaulted his ears, his breathing a little too loud for comfort. It was similar to being hungover.

Harvey got to his feet, stretching his wings. He went over to the wall and took off a slice of moss. He grabbed a few mushrooms and headed over to Titan. He paused, looking at Jordan. Pursing his lips, he grabbed a few more and placed them by Jordan's head.

The moss and mushrooms were common in tunnel systems, but Harvey had never seen them this vibrant. Theos must be in them. He thought back to the one benefit of the Labyrinth: strength.

The boon for finishing the trials was not only the reinstatement of Theos, but supposedly an increase in an Aervel's capacity to hold Theos within them. Harvey set down the moss and started wrapping each mushroom in it; he wished he had better food to give Titan. His mind flashing to the summer when they ate by the lake every day, a feast packed by the castle staff.

This was a far cry from that luxury.

He shook Titan awake, his fingers gentle. His golden prince stirred, hair a mess, blinking sleepily through Metallic lashes. Titan's beautiful face was familiar: a comfort Harvey hung onto in the chaos.

Titan smiled, pulling the food towards himself hungrily. He took a bite and made a face; he set the mushroom in his lap before turning around to Kiara. Harvey's heart fell.

I am your fiancé.

Kiara, who was sleeping on her back, sat up, hair covering her face.

That is unsettling, Harvey thought.

Titan offered Kiara some of his mushrooms - the mushrooms Harvey found for Titan. Harvey could feel his eyes tingling and knew they had saturated red. He quickly turned away, biting the inside of his cheek.

Control, I needed to get control. I need Kiara away from my prince. She is taking the power right out of my hands and setting it ablaze. I should have seen this coming.

Titan had always been the social butterfly that lit up Harvey's garden of thorns. Now that butterfly was playing in the Venomous plants, and Harvey was stuck on the other side of the fence.

Maybe if I talk to Titan? Not until after the trials. I can't distract him. If they made it out, Harvey vowed to talk to Titan about Kiara.

It drove Harvey insane. Having their engagement secret.

Maybe Kiara wouldn't go after Titan if our engagement were made public.

His eyes changed again, likely to display the yellow of sickness and anxiety. As he looked away, a scowl coming to his face, he caught Jordan's gaze. She had one eye open and an eyebrow raised. She opened her other eye sitting up and rising to her feet. Her lips pursed as she sauntered over to him, a glint in her eye.

Not now; I cannot have this stunted, chaos demon ravaging my peace.

She swiped some moss from the wall on her way, splitting it in two, holding half out to Harvey with a bow.

"Aervel," she said with a smirk.

When had she gotten so close?

He grabbed the moss from her, overlooking her attempt to rile him. He dripped Water into his mouth from the wet fibres. It was earthy, and tasted of Theos, giving it a slight tang. It reminded him of celery - with its moisture and woody taste. This was far from the fine fare he was used to. He made a face, going to drop it. Jordan tsked at him. She handed him a mushroom this time. Their fingers brushed, and he swallowed, eyes meeting hers before looking away.

"You have to eat. We haven't eaten in days. You look even scrawnier than you did before," Jordan smirked, eyeing his well-honed muscles playfully. "Can't have my Champion dying on me."

"I'm not *your* anything," he scoffed, turning towards where Titan was now eating and talking with Kiara animatedly.

Harvey's throat tightened, and he blinked away tears before they could fall.

"The Gods say otherwise, and you just love to follow the Gods to the letter." Jordan chirped.

"You are a sacrificial lamb to keep me alive." Harvey snapped at her.

"I prefer the term saviour. Hero. Princess. Not something so bland like a lamb," she twirled around him, slender frame skinny from starvation.

He reached out instinctively.

I can remedy this. I can control the situation. This is something for me to fix.

He grabbed hold of her, putting a hand on each of her shoulders to hold her still.

"Eat," he said, pointing at the mushrooms next to her. She blinked in surprise, looking from the mushrooms to Harvey.

"Unlike your assertion that I am scrawny, you are actually scrawny."

He needed her at her finest. As much as he hated to admit it, he needed to be at his best as well. He took a bite of the mushroom, wincing. It tasted more bitter than the mushrooms he was used to. He detested the thought of eating only mushrooms for possibly months. Yet he would need to eat a plethora of them to maintain his strength. As Harvey ate, he looked around at their group consuming their breakfasts.

Astris and his sister were sitting next to each other, an arm's length away, as if they thought the other had the plague. They were doing everything to avoid looking at each other. The group wasn't going to last much longer if everyone was at each other's throats. This selection of students who despised one another must be another way the Gods were testing them.

I can fix this. I have to fix this. We need to organise. We need a leader. I was born and raised to lead. This is on me.

"Gather around everyone," Harvey called, voice firm but not loud. He didn't know if they were alone in the Labyrinth.

"Why should we listen to you?" Kiara asked, sneering. "We all need to talk. If you don't want to talk, you can go sit in the dark and wait." Harvey snapped. He had had it with her shit.

"Fine," Kiara said, snatching Titan's hand and walking off into the tunnel.

No. Please don't leave.

Harvey panicked at the thought of his fiancé going off with her. It was too late, though; they had disappeared down the tunnel. It took everything in Harvey to hold himself back.

"Idiots," Harvey snarled to himself.

I can't leave him. I should go…

Harvey started walking in the direction they had gone.

A sound came from behind them.

Harvey flipped around with the rest of the group. From the opposite direction, Kiara and Titan walked in from the dark chamber. They blinked in confusion. Harvey breathed a sigh of relief, jaw working as he glared at Kiara.

"Seems like the Gods agree with me." Harvey condescended to Kiara before waiting for them to join the others. "No splitting the group."

Astris jumped in, refusing to look at Kiara, "I agree with Harvey. We need to organise and set up our team's leadership. We have been given the gift of a safe space to organise before continuing."

Harvey smiled at her before picking up where she left off. "We have been left with nothing but the clothes we slept in. We are at a disadvantage, and fighting one another is only going to make it worse. Having set roles will limit the amount we need to… agree… with one another."

Probably not possible for Kiara.

"How far did you get before you got turned around?" Skylar queried.

Titan inspected him with disgust before answering seeing Harvey's inquisitive look. "A little over a thousand paces."

"So that's our limit" Astris muttered, brows scrunching together in concentration.

"But how will we decide on these positions?" Sabastian piped up, tugging his long hair up into a messy bun.

"Maybe we should come up with the roles available, too?" Skylar added.

"Leader, cartographers, scouts, provisioners," Harvey recited from memory as he had learned in Survival class.

"That's four, and we have four sets of Champions and Protectors," Jordan pointed out, winking at Harvey. His gaze caught on her soft mouth and lingered, hunger growing in the base of his gut. Everything about the female was a sin. Kiara's voice brought him back from his lustful thoughts and he turned to the female.

Kiara whispered something in Titan's ear, who gossiped back, giggling. "We will be provisioners," she said, smiling.

Harvey was uneasy with how easily she gave in to his leadership, choosing provisioner immediately. It was unlike Kiara to take a back seat to others. Harvey made a note to keep an eye on his meals from now on. There was no way he could deny her request without revealing his distrust of her to the group and splitting up the troop before their quest began.

"I can draw a map," Sabastian said. "I can as well," Skylar said, offering a small smile to the tall Aervel. Skylar was unusually tall for a Dyrfaldur, and both he and Sabastian towered over the rest of the group. Sabastian looked to the others, ignoring Skylar.

"Team Sabastian is on cartography," Skylar scoffed as Sabastian continued ignoring him, "that leaves scout and leadership."

"Well, Harvey has essentially declared himself in charge." Kiara snarked, twining her long green hair around one finger, sitting in Titan's lap.

Harvey's face hardened, a mix of pain, confusion, and jealousy overtaking him. Titan saw his pained look, shrinking slightly, a blush coming to his face, but he didn't remove Kiara from his lap.

Have I been blind to this? Or did it just start?

"We will take scouting," Astris said placatingly. "Nyx and I are both Aervel and the fastest fliers."

Harvey nodded, satisfied. He ignored Kiara's comment; acknowledging it would give her power. He despised this group, but taking charge was the only way to control the situation entirely. He needed control on this life-or-death journey. He needed control. He needed to be prepared.

"Right then, provisioners, why don't you collect what we will need and divide it among everyone. Cartographers, take a look at the split path and pick a direction, scouts with them," Harvey directed each team, ever the leader.

"And I'll just sit here, I guess, then," Jordan said, hands on her hips, shaking her head. "I am going with the scouts."

She looked after Nyx and Astris, who were drinking Water to prepare for the journey.

"No, you aren't," Harvey stated.

"Why, you lonely?" She said, looking up at him, eyes narrowing slightly.

"I need someone to talk plans with," he lied. In actuality, he needed to keep an eye on her.

"You mean someone to look at you and smile and nod to encourage your ego," Jordan snapped, hand on hip.

Harvey rubbed his temples in frustration. "I mean, someone to talk through my plans with. When I say something, I mean it. Now, if you will just listen to me and sit the fuck down, we can begin."

"Testy, testy," she teased, sitting down next to him, purposely letting her knee touch his.

"Are you trying to seduce me? What the fuck is your end goal, Dyrfaldur?" Harvey questioned bluntly.

Jordan brushed some dirt off his tunic before continuing nonchalantly, Harvey's blood pressure skyrocketed.

"Two questions," she raised two fingers.

"First, why the Hell do you sleep in your clothes? I usually sleep naked. Thank the Gods I chose the night clothes the night we were teleported." She smirked, biting her lip slightly, "would've been far too distracting for you."

She looked at him expectantly, and he realised he would spend a lot more energy arguing than answering her inane question.

"I stayed up late studying our group's school records and must have fallen asleep at my desk. I pulled everyone's files and studied them knowing I would need to use the information to survive. I'm glad I did." Harvey looked over at Kiara, who was pulling some mushrooms and moss off the walls. "Your second question?" His patience was wearing thin.

Jordan put down a finger before asking, "My second question is, do you have any idea what we are supposed to do in here? Like what does it mean to 'reclaim Theos'?"

"The first rule of survival is to keep moving. We need to trust in the Gods to guide us. Let me handle it and do as you are told."

Jordan raised an eyebrow at him, her silent message clear; she would not be following instructions.

Harvey needed to gain back control.

My shadows mentioned her past. The only one with a record. Given that information…

Harvey reflected; he took a steadying breath.

That's it!

Harvey was back in control. He understood the situation. He understood her. "How's your parents' gambling den doing? It is atrocious that the place is still open."

The Devil's Dice Den was the sinful stain on the pristine town of Bexley. It was hidden below respectable establishments, quite literally a den underground.

Titan once begged him to go with him to it. Harvey put a stop to that immediately.

A monopoly of sin and filth.

Jordan's mouth opened and shut, her nose flaring.

That's right, I know everything, even your dirty little secret. I wonder who got blackmailed into sending her application through.

"Gather up," he called, turning away from the silenced Jordan. The group slowly gathered, tired from the past week. He noticed Astris glancing at his sister quite often.

Interesting.

They both are single nobles, so it is not out of the realm of possibilities, except for the fact that they despise each other.

I wouldn't be surprised if they tried to kill each other while in here. I will keep an eye on that.

He dismissed the idea of their courtship. It was too ludicrous.

"Cartographers and scouts, get ready, and then move ahead." Harvey pulled a small sand hourglass out of his pocket, grateful for having fallen asleep studying with it on his person. He handed it to Sabastian.

"Turn it over when you start down the tunnel. Do not go more than one turn ahead. We can't afford to get separated. Who knows if we will find one another again." As an afterthought, he added before they could walk away, "Astris, watch my sister." Astris turned her head to meet his gaze, giving a slight nod. Nyx rolled her eyes, storming ahead. Astris followed.

"Provisioners." He waited for Titan and Kiara to stop roughhousing. He hated how she changed Titan. He gritted his teeth.

This time, he raised his voice, "Provisioners."

They finally looked up, Titan holding Kiara in a playful chokehold. "Gather as much as you can before we go, and work on weaving a bag to carry our food."

Titan saluted, smiling sillily. Kiara giggled.

He turned away from them to Jordan, who was... *what in the fuck was she doing?*

Harvey looked back at the others to see why no one else was reacting. Titan and Kiara had moved away from him. Their wings were barely visible around the corner. Titan was insisting loudly that a mushroom looked like one of their professors.

Harvey's eyes slowly turned back to Jordan. She was shirtless and was ripping the fabric of her tunic into a long strip. Her body was on full display briefly, before she started loosely binding her breasts. She leaned, bent at the waist slightly, her right hand pulling the fabric away from her left, breasts bouncing with the movement. Her eyes flicked to him, and a mischievous smile came to her lips.

Fuck. Me. Harvey stood slack-jawed.

She winked before expertly binding herself, leaving her stomach and shoulders open to the Elements.

"Can't have them swinging around in battle, now, can I?" She asked, batting her eyes at him before moving to the wall and collecting Water to splash on her face.

The Water dripped down her face, trickling off her chin. Harvey swallowed. He could feel his heart race, breathing growing heavier.

He immediately prepared to get moving, fighting the urge to watch her. Using a tiny portion of his finely spun tunic, he wrapped his bare feet. He then started stretching to warm up his muscles. He could feel Jordan's eyes on him as he stretched.

To his relief, Sabastian and Skylar strode up, Astris and Nyx in tow.

Sabastian stepped forward, all business-like, with a report. "There are two passages. The first was a dead end when the scouts searched it." He glared at Skylar. "Apparently, Dyrfaldur's noses are as useless as their kind is. Led us into a dead end."

'I have actually been doing our job.' Skylar ignored Sabastian, lifting up a flat rock with crude marks scratched on it. "I am tracking our progress so we can learn from our mistakes. Did you even pay attention in class?" Skylar asked Sabastian, who rolled his eyes.

"It's not like we had time to prepare! I thought I was studying to become a castellan, not a fucking hero!" Sabastian yelled, voice cracking.

Skylar bit his lip, glaring at Sabastian. He pushed his long red hair out of his eyes, tail twitching. Nyx put a hand on Skylar's shoulder.

Harvey waited, struggling with the desire to fix the problem, but he knew they wouldn't get very far without cooperating and delegating duties.

If it's life and death, maybe I should just take full control? Skylar is likely more capable than Sabastian. I have seen both of their grades, but I can't favour a Dyrfaldur. Does leadership mean I need to set aside social standing? Or uphold it as a sense of familiarity for everyone's psyche?

What was it that father said about my teamwork?

The words came to him after a moment. *'Even having won, your team was unorganised at best, chaotic at worst. I suggest learning more about your team beforehand, and getting to know their strengths.'*

In this situation, I need to let them work it out. I need to understand them before I can lead them properly. Best to hold off on intervening for a bit. Harvey's patience frayed as Nyx and Astris walked up, sending nasty looks at one another.

Harvey glanced at Jordan again. Her naked body flashed through his mind. He shook his head.

This distraction could get me killed. What in the fuck was she thinking, messing with me like this? Focus for the love of Marvos, focus.

She was in control, and he couldn't breathe. He couldn't think. He looked over to her; she met his eyes, golden irises stark against the black sclerae.

Beautiful.

Otherworldly.

Almost Metallic like Titan's hair.

That snapped him out of it. He looked back at Astris and Nyx, who started to talk at the same time. They glowered at one another before starting to talk again, once again interrupting each other.

Before his sister could freak out, he pointed at her. "Nyx, go."

Nyx stood at attention. "The," she stopped to glare at Astris.

This is going to be a painful journey with these two.

"The passage that is not a dead end is narrow; as far as we can see ahead, it keeps narrowing."

"Hope no one is claustrophobic," Skylar huffed a nervous laugh.

He is definitely claustrophobic.

The tunnel had a glowing Rune over it, a square. *Metal.*

This must be an Elemental trial.

Harvey thought back to the Elements and what they were known for.

Elion, the God of Metal, is known for creativity and endurance. This trial must have to do with at least one of the two.

Mushrooms and moss still covered the walls, but scarcer than where they had slept. The tunnel was warped, the sides undulating and close together. The ceiling had stalactites sharp as lances that hung at varying heights. Their tips shone slightly, Harvey looking closer to see they were Metal. As he observed them, he thought he saw the one elongate slightly.

I must be sleep-deprived.

Harvey stepped forward, "Time to get going. Since it is narrow, we will likely need to go one at a time. Let's move in order with Protectors in front of their Champions. Jordan and I will go first."

"Let's do this, prince," she said with a wink.

Nyx gave him a pointed look; she knew how much Jordan drove him crazy and found it amusing.

Bastard.

Literally, he mused.

He ignored Jordan.

The charlatan would not get the better of him.

She stepped up to the passage. As she started to walk in, Harvey's stomach tensed, panic wrenching at his gut.

Without thinking, he grabbed her by the wrist. "Not you," he looked away. She did not need to see his eye colour right now. "I don't trust a criminal to guide the group. You will be behind me."

She stepped aside, piqued at his slight.

For someone who grew up in a gambling den, she sure has a bad poker face.

He kept his gaze averted as he stepped into the passageway and started to walk. Touching the wall, Harvey noticed that it wasn't just the stalactites that were Metal, but the entire passage. He put his hand on the wall to find it was cold and unforgiving, sending shivers down his spine. Dark stains covered the walls in some spots, *blood.*

As they walked, the passageway got smaller, just as Nyx said. Harvey could hear Skylar breathing laboriously at the back of the group, Sabastian snapping at him when he slowed.

Studying to be a surgeon is not doing him any favours in the muscle department.

He likely didn't have any combat training until Veritas Hall.

The passage continued as far as Harvey could see.

This could just keep going. It could be the wrong way. We don't know anything. Pests under the Gods' feet. I wonder if they are watching us. Watching and debating ways to hurt us.

The sounds of footsteps echoed through the small space, mingling with the sounds of discordant breathing. The smell of Theos was thick in the Air, like humidity suffocating them as they walked. He could feel the stare of Jordan on his back as he moved, and his wings twitched.

Focus.

His heartbeat quickened as he squeezed sideways through the passage before it opened up slightly again. Jordan's arm brushed his sensitive wing as they slid through the space; Harvey was hyperaware of the feeling of her skin against his feathers.

Stop, she is Dyrfaldur. I need to remember her place.

She isn't worthy.

The passageway continued this way for a while. Narrowing, then opening, then narrowing again.

Something clattered behind him, and Harvey stiffened. His eyes widened, a bead of sweat coming to his forehead. He looked behind him to see Jordan equally as shaken.

Keep moving.

Roughly a mile in, they stopped for a break.

Two thousand paces for me is a mile. Four turns of the hourglass.

As the group leaned against the walls, pausing their relentless pace, Harvey reached over to gather some of the Water and bring it to his lips. His stubble brushed his hand. He would need to take the knife that was in his pocket to his beard later. He abhorred unkempt facial hair. It made him feel… common.

A soft whistling filled the room.

What was that?

It sounded like an old male wheezing.

A rumble followed it, and Harvey's eyes bulged. He looked around, finding the others equally panicked.

There was another deeper rumble, and for the second time this week, a small body crashed into him. Jordan tackled him forward into the tunnel.

How dare she? Wait… where I was just a moment ago…

The wall snapped closed like stone jaws. The sound was thunderous as the Metal clanged together. A hammer and an anvil. Harvey's heart slammed in his chest as the pair scrambled to their feet again. The wall was moving in sections, the sides undulating like a serpent. Harvey shifted from side to side, indecision crippling him. Jordan reached to feel the wall, but Harvey grabbed her wrist.

"No," he breathed, eyes not leaving the closed passage.

Our companions are on the other side.

A rumble, and Harvey jumped back, running into Jordan. The passageway reopened, revealing their friends. Harvey ran to his sister, his breathing slowing.

Had Jordan not pushed me, I would be a paste of prince right now.

This section of the passageway was big enough for two Aervel to walk side by side. Titan came to check on him. His golden hair shifted into his eyes as he looked at him, sky-blue eyes on a flawless face. Harvey's eyes traced down to his lips. Titan reached down and placed a hand on Harvey's chest.

"Are you okay?" Titan asked softly, making Harvey's heart clench.

Kiara put a gentle but firm hand on Titan, pulling him back and moving forward. Her Venom green eyes met Harvey's, and he felt bile creep to the back of his throat.

"Are you okay, Harvey?" Kiara crooned, her voice concerned, her eyes cold and calculating. Harvey didn't doubt that Kiara's concern was fabricated and strategic.

"I'm fine, thanks," Jordan said, spinning Harvey's knife through her fingers.

How did she do that? That was inside the inside pocket of my undercoat.

Harvey patted his coat in disbelief to find that his knife was indeed missing.

She interrupted him right as he was about to punch Kiara in her stupid face.

"Move," he growled at Kiara, voice low enough that no one else could hear. She took her hand away, sneering.

"I still don't think you should be leading."

"I am the prince."

A rumble, and the passageway moved. Harvey and Kiara jumped away from one another, just barely escaping getting smashed in the jaws. Harvey punched the wall in frustration, blood seeping through the cracks on his knuckles.

The passageway opened up, and he advanced on Kiara again, ready to yell at her. The passageway started to close, and Jordan once again tackled him, this time into Kiara. The three of them tumbled to the ground. The passageway behind them closed as well.

We are trapped. We need to move.

"We need to stop fighting each other!" Astris yelled from the closed-off section.

"Tell that to-" Harvey started when the passageway started to squeeze shut.

Harvey could feel his heart beating hard, blood thrumming in his veins. He swallowed, choking on his fear. He moved forward, into Kiara. The group was being pushed together slowly.

I need to get higher.

Harvey strained his wings, back muscles twinging. It was no use; the walls had them pressed to his side. He couldn't fly. His knees shook, hands clenching and unclenching.

I am going to die.

Nyx's eyes flashed, the Electricity snapping with her fear.

I have to get us out.

Harvey's mind flashed back to the try-outs.

"Breaking up the team is never a viable option. There is strength in numbers."

"We need to work together." Harvey looked up. The passageway was wider as it rose into the Air. The Metal spikes were menacing, but they had some room to climb.

"I'll pass, but thanks," Kiara replied.

The passageway rumbled, slowly closing again. Harvey tucked his wings, sending a prayer to Marvos for strength. He turned to Jordan, holding out both hands.

"Like Skylar did in the try-outs for you," Harvey explained quickly, eyes darting to the walls.

Sabastian grunted, and Harvey turned to see that he was being crushed. Sabastian had the largest shoulders.

I have to get to him, but I need to get Jordan out first.

"Now," Harvey snapped, looking into Jordan's eyes.

She leaped, using his hands to spring up, hands and feet spreading, wedging herself in place. She shuffled up the walls, holding a hand down to Harvey after she had gotten a ways up. Harvey waved her away, going to offer a hand to Nyx next, but Astris was already helping her. He grabbed Titan before Kiara could, throwing him up. Titan joined Jordan a few feet up the wall.

Kiara jumped up herself, and Harvey looked to Skylar and Sabastian. Scaling the wall, he ducked under the others, coming to the spot above Sabastian.

"Push him from the bottom while I pull," Harvey instructed Skylar.

Skylar nodded, holding his hands out for the larger male. Sabastian lifted his feet, and Skylar crawled under him and pushed up.

The walls stopped moving.

"Quick, while they are stopped," Astris yelled down.

In tandem, the two of them pushed and pulled until Sabastian was extracted with a pop. Skylar grabbed Harvey's hand, quickly scrambling up after him. The walls below them became one, the sides starting to vibrate. Harvey heard a gasp next to him. He turned to see Jordan looking at him, face pale as her eyes darted to the walls.

Harvey was thrown into the Air, the serpentine Metal undulating and spinning him up. The walls swirling and flowing below him.

Nyx ran into him in the Air, her elbow hitting Harvey in the head.

A rumble, and Harvey started to slide.

He grasped at the slick Metal with ineffectual fingers. Screams came from his companions, the clank and grind of Metal echoing in the small tunnel.

No, no, stop.

Harvey's fingers slipped as Jordan slammed into him. He spun head over heels, tumbling backwards in a tangle of limbs. The wall hit his head, causing his vision to go blurry as he was thrown to the ground. The passageway opened up in front of them.

Are we safe?

Harvey looked around to see the passageway had returned to its original width.

"Let's take a break," Nyx gasped, eyes glassy with unshed tears. "I think it's done."

Harvey nodded, going to sit down.

Another rumble, and the passageway shut near the back of the line. Sabastian screamed as his leg got pulverized between the walls, a stalactite dropped to stop the others from getting to him.

The walls moved like they were alive. Sabastian's scream echoed unnaturally, bright red blood pooling beneath him. The passageway opened, a sucking sound echoing as Sabastian's leg was freed. Skylar swore, pulling Sabastian back through his own blood as the passageway opened further, liberating him. His ankle was pulverised, but the damage went further. The Metal had left a hole through one of his calves, Skylar putting pressure on the wound immediately.

This situation makes no sense. We were fine when we were walking for the miles before this. What has changed? I can't think with the screaming.

The cries reverberated, repeating over and over again. It was preternatural and made Harvey panic.

I am not in control; I don't have all the facts. What fucking changed?

A small hand touched his arm. "It reacts when we stop," Jordan told him as he pulled her to his chest out of the way - a Metal spike shooting out at her.

That was it! He looked down at her. *She is dangerously likable. Clever and brilliant, but unpredictable in her chaos.*

His eyes met hers and held for a moment. She leaned in slightly, and he leaned in as well.

She is also a Dyrfaldur.

That thought sobered him, and he stood up rigidly.

"We need to move; we stop, we die. The passageway won't let us stop. Skylar, can you carry Sabastian?"

Skylar wrapped a piece of cloth around the wound expertly, before meeting Harvey's gaze. Sabastian was shorter by about three inches, but was much more muscular. Luckily, Skylar was abnormally tall for a Dyrfaldur. His broad shoulders were at odds with his skinny figure. Skylar tapped his toe nervously for a few precious seconds.

Think faster, Dyrfaldur.

Skylar stooped and tipped the big male across his shoulders.

Nyx pulled Astris out of the way of the wall closing again.

"Everyone else move!" Harvey ushered the group ahead of them, Jordan leading, Harvey stayed back with Sabastian and Skylar.

Skylar heaved the burly Aervel up further on his back. Sabastian situated his wings out of the way, face growing pale with pain. Harvey avoided looking at the damage.

We need to move.

Now.

Skylar started walking, and Harvey jumped back into the line behind his sister. He pushed her faster, and she did not protest.

The passageway stopped clamping shut.

As the passageway narrowed to a single file, Skylar passed Sabastian over to Harvey before slipping through himself. They found their rhythm, quickly developing an efficient system. It soothed Harvey every time they passed Sabastian. Despite the grunts of pain that came from Sabastian and the haste required, it was a routine. Harvey loved an efficient routine.

It was his haven in bedlam.

They moved like this for hours, Skylar panting from the exertion of lugging Sabastian. Harvey had to give Skylar credit; the male was robust for his stature. Sure, Skylar was tall, but he was stick thin. Harvey slung the massive male onto his shoulder the next time they came to a clearing and ushered a stunned Skylar forward.

"If you collapse, then my friend turns into mashed peas. Go." Skylar leaped ahead and took Harvey's position.

He grimaced at the change in the system but concentrated on moving quickly. The passageway began to get dark Harvey squinting.

It must be Theos connected to the outside. Theos is awe inspiring. Terrifying, but wonderful.

Sabastian was heavier than Harvey realised, and he was impressed by Skylar once again. After a few hours, he passed Sabastian back to Skylar, who took him without complaint.

"Do you see an end?" He called ahead to the others.

A few moments later, Jordan, in her finch form, flew back to them. Harvey could have sworn the finch looked smug at his surprise. He hadn't even considered her shifting in this scenario.

This will work well for a messaging system.

The finch shook her head; no.

Then we will have to endure as long as we can. That answers the question of what this test is about, endurance.

"Fly to the front and come back to inform me the moment you can see an end to this Hell. Every couple of hours, fly back as well if you have the energy, that way we can remain in communication. I want to be fully informed of the situation."

Jordan did a little loop in the Air, which Harvey took as confirmation, before she flew back to the front. Her leadership capabilities surprised him, too.

During the journey through the narrowing tunnels, there was only one decision that Jordan informed him of. The scouts decided to take the path to the right instead of continuing forward.

The light in the tunnel increased and then darkened a total of five times before Jordan flew back - five days of nonstop movement. Jordan was wavering as if drunk. They were all fatigued, and the food was running low.

Every couple of hours, one of them would collapse and need to be hauled up by those on either side of them. Their constant state of motion led to a lot of hungry party members, and a lot of snapping at one another. Despite Jordan's haggard appearance and her tired flaps, she looked excited. She turned back into her non-animal form, dropping down in line in front of Harvey.

Harvey did not stop moving as he made eye contact with Jordan; a small, hopeful smile coming to his lips. She nodded once in confirmation, walking backward. He reached out his arm over her head, narrowly stopping her head from ramming into a jagged piece of rock hanging from the ceiling.

"How far?" Harvey inquired, panting.

"A mile, and guess what?"

"I'm not in the mood to guess."

"There is a lake there, fresh Water, and fish; the bad news is it's a dead end. We will have to turn around, but… Sabastian." Jordan trailed off, a worried expression on her face as she walked backwards slowly so the tunnel wouldn't activate.

He smiled down at Jordan, Sabastian feeling lighter on his back. A break to heal would be the difference between life and death. "Lead the way, we all need to recuperate."

Jordan leaped into the Air, shifting back into her finch form. She flew ahead crookedly. Harvey smiled at Skylar before looking at Sabastian's face. He passed out an hour ago and had not stirred since. Harvey picked up his pace even more.

Fuck conserving energy.

They burst into the cavernous chamber, collapsing to the floor. Harvey looked around. He dragged Sabastian to the Water and splashed it onto his wounds. Skylar dropped to his knees, drinking the Water, before searching through the plants growing out of it.

If Harvey remembered correctly, his father worked at a relatively reputable apothecary in Star Hollow called *Thorn and Vial*. His mother was a painter, which Harvey dismissed as useless, but apothecary skills meant he could practice basic medicine if his father was teaching him the family trade.

Combined with his classes in his time at Veritas Hall, it would have to suffice.

We need a healer.

Skylar came over, a bundle of greens in his hand as well as a few sturdy branches. He looked at Harvey imploringly, "I need to set the break, and he is…"

"Say no more." Harvey positioned himself at Sabastian's head, holding him down by the shoulders.

Skylar looked apologetically at Sabastian.

"Stop Dyrfaldur," Kiara commanded Skylar. Skylar looked to Harvey for instructions.

Kiara looked to Harvey, then Skylar, "Look slightly above the ankle. He has multiple breaks, and setting them like that will make the others worse. You need to set them one by one, moving from the ankle up. His bones have also begun to heal, so you will need to break each one first before continuing."

She took Sabastian's ankle, and in one fluid moment, she set the first break. "Now you, Dyrfaldur."

"I have a name," Skylar growled back.

"Do it." Venom slipped into Kiara's voice.

"Do as she says," Harvey intervened.

Skylar pursed his lips and then set the second break.

Sabastian roared in pain, coming to consciousness in agony, biting down on one of the sticks Skylar shoved in his open mouth.

"Do I have to do everything? Go make a poultice, I'll finish." Kiara condescended, sucking at her teeth in dissatisfaction.

Kiara set the final breaks quickly, Harvey straining against the male's thrashing. When he finished helping, Harvey walked into the Water, rinsing off his sweat and other bodily fluids he cared not to think about. The pool of Water was deep, with no end in sight. Harvey hoped nothing lived down there.

Cleanliness was worth a few watery monsters. The others joined in quickly, Skylar and Nyx even dragging Sabastian into the Water to wash him. Titan managed to catch a few fish, and Kiara prepared them. Harvey bit into the fish tentatively, too tired and hungry to ask Skylar to check it for poison.

Harvey cleared his throat. "We will stay here for a few days until Sabastian has healed enough to be on his own feet with the help of a crutch. Astris and Nyx, you will be in charge of fishing; Titan and Kiara will preserve some of the fish caught and collect algae. Skylar, you will be in charge of Sabastian and his cane, and Jordan and I will craft some bags out of the reeds."

They failed to make any before, but this oasis had enough plants to make what they needed before continuing. Harvey was glad the Gods at least gave them a chance with this oasis. Even if the reprieve was a cruel joke of their impending doom throughout the trials, Harvey was grateful for the time and reluctantly grateful he wasn't alone.

CHAPTER 9: NYX

Trap

Nyx washed her hair for presumably the last time for a while, watching as a fish darted by her toes. It felt good, the cold Water against her sweat-stained skin. She appreciated Harvey taking charge of the group as she wasn't qualified to help anyone.

She scrubbed at her two-toned hair, strawberry coils darkening to red in the Water. The strands curled more dramatically, shrinking slightly as they absorbed Water.

Nyx had spent a lot of time outside before this, but not days from dawn to dusk. The Labyrinth gave her the creeps. She lamented, knowing it was their last day at the oasis before they started moving again. Sabastian was recovering quickly, his Aervel blood leading to fast healing. He was able to hobble at a decent pace with a cane made out of the only piece of flimsy wood they could find. He was lucky he was buff and balanced enough to walk on his hands if he wanted to.

Despite being more prepared this time, entering the passageway again felt like a death sentence. Nyx walked behind Astris, irritated that

Astris was taller than her. Everything seemed to irritate her about the female these days.

The way her Icy eyes lanced through Nyx's soul, the way her hips swayed as she walked, and the way Astris's voice tangled Nyx's insides.

Astris never let her emotions show - never in front of Nyx, at least. She wondered if Astris showed emotions toward Kiara. It seemed improbable. Kiara was unstable; even her friends were aware of this. Astris was many things. Dense was not one of them.

Sabastian was at the back of the group, grunting as he maneuvered through the narrow passageway with his cane. Every so often, Nyx ran her hand along the wall, capturing some Water and bringing it to her lips.

Boredom gnawed at Nyx as the hunger had done on their trek here. Starvation was preferable. Nyx always loathed boredom. It led her to make questionable decisions and feel restless and irate. She did everything possible to avoid it, even if those things got her into trouble. She started to hum a bawdy tavern song. She was sure Jordan would have joined in if she had heard, but she was far up ahead. Nyx found herself bonding with Jordan during their days at the oasis. The quick-witted and bold Dyrfaldur filled the space with energy.

If only she were my Protector.

Her humming continued for another hour before Astris's head whipped around, "If you hum that tune one more time, I swear to the Gods, I will knock out every single one of your teeth."

Astris's eyes met Nyx's and darkened as they dipped briefly to Nyx's lips. A blink and she was looking into Nyx's eyes again.

"If we keep moving, it won't close. I need to stay awake, so you are just going to have to deal with it."

Nyx started to thump out the bar tune on the stone walls, sending the beat through the passageway as she walked. Astris stopped walking, spinning to Nyx, jaw set. Nyx pursed her lips, fighting a grin. She was enjoying watching the stoic Astris squirm.

The reply to the bar tune came back through the passageway from the front of the line. It was a call-and-response-based song, and one she knew well. Nyx laughed delightedly at the returned call. Jordan must have heard the beat and taken up the call. Behind them, the beat came echoing down the chamber to them. It rang through the small space, the melodious thumps carrying through the passageway.

That has to be Skylar or Sabastian.

They fanned out more this time to avoid any accidents created by clumping together.

Their isolation meant that Nyx was alone with Astris. The wall rumbled; Nyx saw movement and grabbed Astris, pulling her into her.

"Careful there, darling," Nyx said, voice low and dripping with sarcasm. Astris was anything but darling to Nyx.

She languidly released Astris with a gentle push forward, Astris's mouth parting in surprise. Her fingers slid along Astris's hip bone as she slipped from her grasp. Adrenaline flared through Nyx. She liked this game very much. If she were going to die, she would make sure to see Astris forfeit control first. Astris started to reply, but was cut off by Nyx jerking backward to avoid the stone jaws.

"I know you enjoy checking me out, but if you wouldn't mind moving, I would rather not die."

"You dare," Astris sputtered.

"I do," Nyx said matter-of-factly, showing her teeth and a tiny bit of fang.

"What the Hell are you two doing?" Skylar ran up to the two of them. "Move!"

Astris let out an exasperated shriek before continuing. Skylar gave Nyx a questioning glance, to which Nyx gave him a thumbs-up. He shook his head, looking between them one more time before reversing to join Sabastian back at the rear. Their order would remain the same as before until they came to the next open area. Time ticked by, the group sagging with exhaustion.

Eventually, even the strongest of us will drop if this doesn't end soon.

Jordan, in finch form, flew back through the passageway. She shifted and dropped behind Nyx, joining the line behind her.

"Just got to the last fork in the passage. We will be taking a right. I'm going to tell Sabastian and Skylar. Titan and Kiara already know."

With that, she flew off, flitting through the narrow gaps with ease. An hour later, Jordan flew past them overhead with a tweet of acknowledgment. She occasionally sat on one of their shoulders to make up for the extra exercise she was doing by being a messenger. Nyx didn't mind the presence of the female, a buffer between her and Astris.

By the end of that day, as the light was fading, they came to the crossroads. Astris took a right, Nyx following. It took two more days before the passageway opened. The group was sitting in a much larger passageway as Nyx and Astris entered. A large Rune hung in this room: the Rune for unity.

This is the last bit of passageway before the narrowing walls end. Maybe the offshoots are dead ends with oases? Can we count on that? Can they even identify what would be a dead end? If I could shift, would I find out more information? Wolves have a better sense of smell than most other mammals.

"That was fast," Harvey commented.

Is he joking?

"It took two days to catch up. What do you mean?" Nyx asked cautiously.

"If you are messing with me, sister…" Harvey warned, concern etched into his features.

Astris surprised Nyx by supporting her claim, "She's right, we got too spread out. The Labyrinth has reacted to us being apart before. We need to take this seriously. We could risk getting separated and end up being alone to face each trial. The Gods want us together."

Kiara raised an eyebrow at Astris, which Nyx mirrored. Astris ignored them both, eyes on Harvey.

Interesting. Harvey shifted to a state of seriousness, nodding thoughtfully.

Asshole. You believe her over your own sister, classic Harvey.

"One turn of the hourglass from now on" Harvey concluded, "No one leaves the group without my permission."

"There's also that" Astris pointed to the Unity Rune. "It appeared as soon as we walked into this section. It seems to signify the end of this trial. It appeared after we found one another in the darkness as well."

"Let's keep an eye on all of the Runes we see. Sabastian can you ensure you mark down all Runes in each section of the map?" Harvey asked, looking at the long-haired male who nodded, scratching on the stone tablet, which was their map.

Skylar's face shifted, becoming slightly more fox-like. Dyrfaldur could change into the body of a singular type of animal and, with practice, could partially shift their features as well. Most had at least one animalistic feature that remained visible. Nyx was the exception as a Half-blood.

Nyx remembered the way Astris smelled and shivered involuntarily.

Better leave the scenting to the full-blooded Dyrfaldur.

Nyx collapsed to the floor next to Jordan, giving her shoulder a playful shove.

Astris looked at her with a peculiar look before going to sit next to Titan. "Sit next to me," Kiara said to Astris.

Astris immediately got up and walked over to sit next to Kiara.

"Puppet," Nyx coughed into her hand. She smiled as Astris stiffened.

"Enough," Harvey said, looking at them both. Astris looked murderously at Nyx. Nyx gave her a little wave before turning away. She could feel Astris's eyes on the back of her head.

The passageway split into a fork again. The right fork had the Rune for Fire, the left had Ice. Harvey chose to go left after deliberating with Sabastian and Skylar. The last choice led them to an oasis; Nyx doubted they would be that lucky again.

She was proven wrong as they approached a small cavern ripe with plants and a shallow pool in the centre.

This seems too good to be true. Titan went directly to the Water, stepping through the muddy sand into the cold pond. He stripped off his shirt, lean muscle rippling with the movement. Kiara joined immediately, cuddling up to his bare chest.

As far as Nyx was concerned, Titan and Kiara deserved each other. But it still pained Nyx to think about how her brother was feeling right now. He was gazing at Titan like a lost puppy. His natural coal-lined eyes were intense as they followed Titan's every movement.

Harvey's eyes jumped from purple, to green, to crimson. She knew that colour. Crimson was the colour his eyes turned when she pissed him off.

Jordan sat by the edge of the Water, methodically washing herself and her clothes. Astris and Nyx joined Jordan by the Water's edge. The pond was cold and refreshing. Stalactites with Ice crystals hung from the ceiling.

Theos preserved, Nyx realised with wonder.

The light in the room shone through the blueish spikes, a staggeringly beautiful sight. Nyx took a deep breath, stretching out her legs. Her muscles were strained from the constant movement of the past week. The cold Water soothed her scratched and sore feet.

Astris sat opposite her, holding eye contact with Nyx. Nyx found herself lost in Astris's eyes, incapable of looking away. They were like a frozen lake, cracks spidering like Nyx's Electricity. They drew everything and everyone in and consumed Nyx.

Sarcasm and self-loathing radiated through her as she fought to ignore the feeling in her stomach when she thought about Astris.

She's a cruel, entitled, cold sociopath. I need to stay away before I burn myself. She may be Ice cold, but she ignites me like blistering flames.

Her thoughts and eye contact with Astris were interrupted by a squeal from Kiara.

"Ack," Titan yelped, looking down at his feet.

Titan, Kiara, and Harvey were sinking in the muddy sand in the shallow Water. Titan battled it, cursing as he floundered to drag himself out. But he sank deeper, faster. The temperature dropped drastically, and the hair on the back of Nyx's neck rose.

"Stop moving! You are sinking faster!" Harvey shouted.

Titan stopped, a hurt look on his face at Harvey's raised voice.

My brother just saved your ass, you insufferable twat.

Nyx bit her tongue as she assessed the situation, stepping away from the Water's edge and pulling Astris back without thinking.

I should probably explore that.

Or I could, like, not. I like that option better. The corner of her mouth twitched up.

Fuck, wait, emergency. Okay, let's think back to the survival course I took last year. Sinking, thrashing, making her descent faster, and Harvey, who has not panicked, has stopped at his waist.

A rumble and booming crack vibrated through the cavern.

"That can't be good," Sabastian remarked from behind her.

The banks of the pool started to collapse: the Water was draining. The group began sinking again, faster this time.

Quicksand, that's what it's called; movement liquifies the sand under the individual.

The increased mass from multiple Aervel dragged them down faster. The collapsed sides caused them to sink even deeper. Movement from beneath them rippled; a long snakelike shape swam through the sand, back cresting the shallow pond. *Oh, no; I hate snakes.* A thin, short Ice-covered fin surfaced the Water behind Harvey.

Well, that's not a snake, but it is scaly.

"Don't panic," Nyx said reassuringly, "but you guys are not the only things in there. You move; you sink. Trust us, and don't thrash."

Next to her, Astris's hand flew to her mouth as she saw the monster, now behind Titan, rear up. Teeth flashed yellow, eyes red. Frost crackled at the back of its throat. The monster's scales were shards of Ice, sand running over the scales with a tinkling sound as it moved. The sound of the frost was a combination of popping and crackling. The cacophony hurt Nyx's ears.

Fuck. Well, at least it's not a snake, only an Icy sea dragon.

Astris took to the Air. "I'll draw its attention; you guys get them out!"

"I'll join you; I am of no use carrying anyone." Jordan shifted in a flash, diving at the dragon's milky white frost eyes, clawing at them before flitting away. Snow sloughed off as her finch clawed at the eyes, reforming almost instantly.

The dragon shot blue frost at Jordan out of its mouth; Astris came around behind it, kicking its head in a series of blows before rising into the Air again. Nyx paused briefly, in awe at the dragon's display of Theos she had only heard stories about.

The beast bellowed, whipping its head back and forth, nose flaring as it strained to sense them.

Its vision isn't great, Nyx realized. *It can't follow Astris's movements. It is using the quicksand and scent to see.*

Titan panicked as it got closer to him, beating at the quicksand. He started to sink again, and the dragon's head swung, pinpointing his location.

It must be using the vibrations in the sand.

The dragon breathed onto the sand, and the sand started to crystallise into Ice.

We need to get them out. Now.

Nyx leapt into the Air, Sabastian ditching the cane to join her. She was glad his wings were intact. Rocks soared past them, and Nyx glanced back to see Skylar launching them at the dragon and the quicksand surrounding it, disrupting its senses. Nyx dove for her brother first. She seized onto his outstretched forearm, adjusting her grip until she was satisfied.

"If I remember correctly from class, this will hurt like a bitch. Sorry." Nyx apologized, wincing.

Nyx slowly rose, fighting the suction and forming Ice crystals. With a pop, Harvey's shoulder dislocated, and a scream wrenched from his throat. Nyx fought back tears as she continued to pull, wings beating in mighty, elongated strokes. His wings were covered in Ice shards, and Nyx winced at the cold burn on her hands as she held him.

Harvey's foot was still stuck in the Ice. Slowly, Nyx drew Harvey out, instructing, "Kick to break up the Ice if you can; it will pull you further down, but it will stop the freezing. Trust me to fight the suction."

Harvey looked at her with hesitation for a brief moment before doing as she instructed. With one final pull, Nyx yanked her brother out, pumping her wings to get them away from the trap.

She flew him over to the rocky ground, crumpling. She couldn't rest. She had to go back. Sabastian held Kiara by the arm, Titan thrusting her up from the sand. His body was almost fully encased in Ice and sand, up to his throat now in the substance.

That did nothing but cause him to sink further; he really doesn't listen.

Sabastian dropped Kiara next to Nyx, who took to the Air again. A shout, and Nyx looked to see Astris falling from above her. Nyx switched course, pumping her wings furiously, arms pinned to her side.

She disregarded Sabastian struggling to pull Titan out; she ignored Harvey's helpless roars as he struggled to get the now frozen mud off his wings. She only saw Astris, with a deep laceration wound across one wing and the other frozen solid. She was plummeting towards the pool.

She will sink to the bottom and suffocate. That or shatter every bone in her body.

Nyx dug deep, driving herself harder than she ever had. The seconds dragged as she bolted towards Astris.

Five feet to go.

Astris was halfway to the Ice now.

Four feet.

Nyx could almost touch her.

Three.

Nyx reached her hand out, fingers stretching.

Two.

Nyx took Astris by the arm, immediately beating her wings and arching her back, willing her momentum upwards. Astris kicked at the Ice, lifting her feet as they rose, making herself small to avoid Air resistance.

The dragon's head pivoted towards them. Its mouth opened, Ice crackling in its maw.

We're dead.

A finch flew into the dragon's nostril. The dragon froze before thrashing and sneezing out Jordan. Jordan's finch shot through the Air, slamming into the wall of the cavern by where they entered. It was just enough time for Nyx to tow Astris to the shore.

Harvey took out his knife, handing it to Sabastian. When they were growing up, Sabastian was always great with throwing knives.

Good choice, Nyx thought.

One throw later, and the beast was struck solidly between the eyes, falling back with Harvey's knife in its skull. Sabastian fetched it after the beast fell, beginning his flight towards the creature before the knife even made its mark. The beast gave another shudder, but Sabastian flew at one of the stalactites, ramming into it full force with his shoulder. The stalactite fell from the ceiling, piercing the dragon.

It gave a final shudder, Sabastian snatching the half-frozen knife before the dragon could be fully enveloped in the sand. Slowly, the pool refilled with Water and the temperature rose back to how it had been before the dragon had shown itself. Another Unity Rune appeared above the cavern, glowing a soft white blue light similar to the mushrooms.

Nyx shook with exertion and dropped against Astris. Kiara walked up behind them, looking at the two of them intertwined. Kiara's frown deepened. She looked at Astris as if dissatisfied. Astris stiffened in her arms.

"Astris, come," Kiara said, and Astris jerked away from Nyx, dropping Nyx to the floor.

Astris's face was blank but strained as she limped exhausted to Kiara's side. Nyx caught herself before falling flat on her face.

I just saved her fucking life. I just saved her life, and she is just going to drop me? Literally? Fuck that. Fuck her. Fuck me for falling for it.

She glared at Kiara, who led Astris away. The female, who then dropped Astris's hand immediately, went to Titan's side, fawning over him.

Nyx limped over to Harvey, who looked back and forth between Titan and Jordan, holding his dangling arm. Nyx had set his shoulder before, as training was a full-contact activity while growing up – she was no stranger to dislodged limbs. She held out her hand. He let her grab his arm and shove it back into place, breathing laboriously. He rubbed it, inclining his head to her in thanks.

Nyx turned towards Jordan and started walking. Titan was okay, covered in dirty Ice, with his shoulder already set by Skylar. Jordan was covered in frosty dragon snot, bruised and cut from flying into the wall. She had managed to break the Ice by transforming back to her natural form. Nyx would bet wings that her ribs were cracked.

This decision between the two should not be difficult, brother.

Nyx hobbled to Jordan. The Dyrfaldur saved her life. Harvey went to Titan, Kiara, and Astris, and Nyx tensed as disappointment set in her gut.

Jordan shifted back to her regular self. She was panting on the ground, shiny from the viscous goo. Nyx flinched at the thought of being covered in dragon snot. Gashes lined every inch of Jordan's side, with bruises already developing. She held her abdomen protectively, breathing sharply and raggedly. Her face was pale, and she turned to the side and threw up. Skylar came up behind Nyx, pulling out herbs from his pockets along with some moss.

We survived another trial, just barely. I even managed to save someone. Me. I did that.

Nyx pursed her lips in contained pleasure, self-satisfaction soothing the pain of her wounds.

"I hate to say this, friend, but I think you need to roll in the sand to get the… goo off of you. I also think it is going to hurt like Hell. We need to get it off to get to the cuts. It might get in the cuts though, so be careful." Skylar said apologetically to Jordan.

Jordan nodded once, tears running down her face. She tucked her arms and rolled through the sand; Nyx used sand gently, rubbing at the frozen mud until it sloughed off. After the majority of it came off, Nyx carefully took Water from the top of the pool to rinse off the remainder. Skylar gave her a root to chew on to dull the pain. He poked at her ribs clinically, frowning.

"Nothing to do for the ribs. Only pain management. Let's dress these cuts."

Nyx helped him apply a poultice and a section of moss to each wound. They sat there for hours, administering the paste, as the rest of the group bathed the wings of Titan, Kiara, and Harvey.

Such bullshit.

Nyx shook her head in disgust, making eye contact with Skylar, who conveyed the same sentiment.

They decided to set camp for the night as the light started to fade in the cavern. Jordan insisted on sleeping next to Harvey as his Protector, ignoring Nyx's protests.

That idiot needs to learn to get over himself and to stop treating Dyrfaldur like shit. Astris lay down beside her, Kiara and Titan on her other side. *Great. Now, I have to lie near Kiara. I will be lucky if my throat isn't slit in the middle of the night.*

Nyx woke in the middle of the night, needing to pee. She thought about telling Astris, but dismissed the idea out of stupidity. Instead, she tapped Jordan to come with her. Jordan looked to Harvey, who was fast asleep, before looking back at Nyx.

"He wasn't there for you," Nyx whispered.

That did it.

Jordan nodded in the almost pitch-black night. The two females stepped gingerly over the other party members, going around the same bend in the corridor they had taken to get here. As they turned the corner, they overheard noises.

Was there a new obstacle that just appeared? The Labyrinth has not created obstacles out of thin Air before.

The Labyrinth, as far as Nyx could tell, was predictably sectioned.

This is probably a bad idea. Maybe we should turn around.

She took Jordan's hand, who squeezed back in acknowledgment.

The two of them walked towards the disturbance. Nyx winced as her foot cracked a rib bone on the path the *click* echoing slightly.

They paused, but when the sounds continued unfettered, they started moving again.

They tiptoed forward, holding their breath, careful not to step on any more bones. The noises clarified: grunts, panting, and repeated slaps. Jordan paused, realizing what the sound was at the same time as Nyx.

The two of them crept forward when a voice said behind them, "What the fuck are you two doing?"

Both females shushed Harvey, Nyx shoving her hands over his mouth.

"Listen," Nyx said, holding still.

Harvey struggled but stopped as he, too, noticed the sound. Nyx let go of him when she was sure he wouldn't give away their presence.

A feathery gasp and a female's voice called out in pleasure before being stifled.

"Kiara," Nyx whispered, feeling sick to her stomach.

It brought back memories that caused bile to fill her mouth. She shoved it down before seeing her brother freeze next to them.

Harvey went still as death for a second, then shoved past them towards the sound. Nyx chased him, Jordan trailing behind her.

"Let's just go," Nyx pleaded, looking at her brother.

He ignored her, continuing ahead and forcing Nyx and Jordan to jog to catch up. The three of them rounded a slight curve in the path, a blue light coming through the tunnel. They slowed their steps before rounding the corner. Glowing mushrooms lined the ceiling, casting an eerie blue light down on the scene.

Titan held Kiara under her thighs, her back against the wall. His hands dug into her skin, forearm muscles highlighted in the glow.

They were both naked, sweat trickling down their backs. Kiara clawed at his back, moaning and moving her hips into him, the sound of slapping increased in ferocity as Metallic golden hair fell away from the male's face. His strong cheekbones were elegant in the limited lighting.

Titan was positioned with Kiara's legs to either side of him, pumping in and out of her aggressively. She met him with every stroke, encouraging him to go deeper, faster. Titan growled as he buried his head into her neck. He pressed Kiara forcefully into the wall, kissing her as he panted. His muscular back rippled as his ass clenched with each movement.

Kiara opened her eyes over his shoulder, gaze catching on the three spectators. Delight lit in her eyes as she realized the situation. She held eye contact with Harvey as Titan pounded into her. Her moans echoed through the chamber, louder than before. Titan grew louder as well.

"That's it, keep going; you know just how I like it," Kiara crooned in Titan's ear, loud enough for them to hear as well.

"Mmm, yes, I do," he murmured into her hair.

She threw her head back, possessive, as she held Titan's head against her neck, moving her hips faster. She let out little moans with every thrust now; a satisfied, vicious smile plastered across her face. Nyx grabbed Harvey's trembling hand, drawing the group away from the cavern. Her brother needed her.

CHAPTER 10: HARVEY

Hallucinations

For an arranged engagement, we are the perfect pair. There is no one I would rather be with. You deserve the world.

-Titan letter to Harvey, 1ˢᵗ Day, 75 AT

Jordan and Nyx led Harvey back to the cavern, Jordan holding onto Harvey's elbow softly, Nyx holding his other arm tentatively. Harvey ignored Jordan, focusing on his sister. His Protector couldn't help him with this one.

The pair of females guided him to his sleeping spot, waiting until Harvey was seated before sitting down themselves. He was numb, surveying the world from afar. Tears started cascading down his cheeks, his hands clenching tight. He could feel his fingernails biting into his palms. The sound of wet slapping filled his head.

I am going to be ill.

A silent sob racked his throat, his body convulsing. Jordan's hand ran slow circles down his back, soothing him. He closed his eyes, tears pouring down his face harder now, dropping onto his arm as he curled up. He was too tired to fight her. Jordan continued to rub his back until he fell asleep.

The morning arrived, and Harvey flinched at the light on his sensitive eyes. Titan and Kiara laughed against the wall, and it all came

back to him. Bile rose, and he swallowed painfully. Harvey's eyes were dry and swollen from crying.

Titan hummed and said, 'Yes, I do.' Their relationship has been going on for a while. While I have been pining for Titan, he was fucking her. How was I so clueless? He doesn't want our engagement. He doesn't want me.

Kiara had changed Titan while Harvey had been preoccupied with his princely duties and keeping everyone alive. Kiara had closed in on his relationship with Titan.

Titan is changing. Becoming someone else when he is around her. Someone I am not in love with. He thought ruefully.

His world was falling out from under him. Harvey's breathing quickened, and he gagged in tears.

Stop, stop, stop, stop, stop, stop, stop, that is enough. He begged his tears, his body, and his heart to hide his pain. To hide the evidence.

Kiara knew I wanted him, but she didn't know about the engagement. Titan knew. He knew, and he didn't care.

Harvey looked to his sister.

Oh my Gods I… Nyx… Fuck, I'm a monster. Our family motto of 'family first'? I have never truly meant it, picking and choosing how to help. Now I will. I am done pleasing the nobles at the expense of my family.

He looked to Nyx, who looked back at him with concern.

Guilt bubbled inside him, mixing with his misery.

Kiara may have played me, but I played my own sister. I blamed her because it was easier and just… not right now. Too much. I need control. You are spinning out, Harvey; get your shit together.

He gulped in Air, feeling the humiliation and betrayal like a blade piercing his abdomen.

Jordan squatted down by him, holding out a mushroom and some moss. Sickness overwhelmed Harvey and he shook his head sharply. She examined him, not with pity, but with an assessing eye. After a few moments of maintaining eye contact with him, her golden irises filled his tear-blurred vision.

"You don't have to talk, not with them. Not until you are ready. Stay with me today," Jordan said, standing and holding out a hand to help him up.

He took it, rising and brushing the dirt off. He tried to talk but found himself choking every time he tried. She nodded in understanding, placing a hand on his shoulder. With the height difference, it was a pointless attempt, but she didn't pull her hand away. Aervel were typically taller than Dyrfaldur, especially Aervel males and Dyrfaldur females.

Harvey and Jordan walked at the back of the group, Nyx and Astris taking the lead with Skylar and Sabastian. Sabastian's leg was healed, and he discarded the cane, which was cracked from his weight. Titan and Kiara bantered ahead of them, and a bitter taste permeated Harvey's mouth. He glanced away, down to Jordan. Two small blocks of wood danced across her fingers. He looked closer to see that they were dice.

Where had she gotten those? Whatever. He was too fatigued to care.

They walked in silence for the morning, maintaining the silence through their break for lunch. The dice clacked across Jordan's knuckles in a display of skill.

Clack, clack, click, clack.

The dice clicked against one another as they danced through her fingers in a calming pattern. She switched up the rhythms randomly, not needing to pay attention to the dice.

The group came up on the fork where they branched off and turned left a few days ago. This pathway was significantly wider, enough for them to walk side by side easily.

"Four gold wings, both of them are even," Jordan bet, pitching the dice up and capturing them in her hands, obscuring the result.

"That's quite a sum. Not copper or silver wings? Do you even have that much?"

"Princes are rich. I know an opportunity when I see one," she sniggered, face begging him to play along. "No need for the funds if I win."

Finances won't matter if we are dead. Harvey shrugged off the dark thought, focusing back on Jordan.

"We are stuck in a Labyrinth and have been for over a month, according to the cartographers. What are you going to spend it on? I don't even have any wings on me." Harvey replied incredulously.

"Exactly, you have nothing to lose. Or is it that you are scared? Scared to lose to a Dyrfaldur," she taunted, gnawing on her lip.

Harvey swallowed at the motion, captivated. He turned away sharply, collecting himself.

"Make it ten gold wings," he grunted, stopping and waiting.

She beamed and opened her hands. A two and a four. Harvey grabbed the dice, weighing it in his hands. His fingers brushed hers and his skin ignited where they connected. He looked down to her, his gaze lingering, before handing the dice back. She raised a single eyebrow. Harvey scoffed, a smile coming to his lips.

"They aren't weighted," she snapped at him.

Harvey smirked, handing the dice back, "again."

After he lost a significant amount of the crown's money to her, she showed him some dice tricks. Apparently, she had convinced Skylar to carve her some from roots coming out of the sides of the cave.

I wonder if they have a history of…

Harvey's eyes darted to the skinny male who was with a block of wood that Harvey couldn't make out as he followed Sabastian. Harvey's gaze then flicked to Jordan, his eyes tearing up again.

Why do I care if she sleeps with someone? Skylar has a partner; I am being irrational.

Wet slapping sounds came unbidden to his mind, Kiara's feminine grunts mixed with Titan's deeper ones. Kiara's vibrant green eyes penetrated the dark as she held eye contact with him. Harvey flinched involuntarily.

I don't want this. Not really. This is because of Titan.

"What transpired last night probably destroyed you. Don't let it get us killed, okay? The best vengeance is living through this Hell, reclaiming our kingdom's Theos, and then getting even," Jordan consoled.

"Why do you even care?" Harvey whispered, feeling vulnerable.

"I care because we are a team. That means if one of us goes down, we all go down." She took a pause, looking away.

Her fingers danced faster, the wooden dice clacking a tense beat. "I care because I know what it is like to love someone unattainable," her voice lowered as she said it, eyes downcast.

They walked in silence for a few more minutes before Harvey spoke up.

"Who was it? The one who you can never have." Harvey finally gave in to his inquisitiveness.

He did not know a lot about being a commoner, but he thought they had more freedom. Freedom to love who they wanted. His brow creased in thought.

"His name is Francis, and he is now a member of the temple," she replied after a silence. "The month before he announced his decision to join the temple, I professed my love for him. I asked him to stay with me, to find a different profession. He refused, calling me blasphemous."

Jordan took a deep breath before continuing, "Villagers said he loved the Gods more than he loved me, and that I should accept his faith. I could have followed him and served the temple with him. I couldn't do it, though." She looked at Harvey, eyes imploring him to understand. "I couldn't give up my life and join him with the Gods. So, I told him that. I told him I wanted to be free. Not in service to anyone, even the Gods."

The temples in Dengar, although available to the public, hold many secrets. Old scriptures contain accounts of interactions with the Gods along with all the phenomena surrounding the Choosing Ceremony and Labyrinth. Guarding the Gods' secrets was paramount. Priests were unable to date or wed outside of the temple.

Jordan would have been his mistress if she had followed him. It was ironic that she was now trapped in the Labyrinth created and governed by the Gods, the very thing her old lover had left her to study.

"I bet Francis would be envious of you being selected by the Gods." Harvey said as he raised an eyebrow.

Jordan cracked a smile. "Oh, you have no idea. Now, I think it's only fair that I pay it forward. Help a fellow citizen… Er, are you a citizen as the prince, or is there a higher tier than citizenship allotted only to rulers?"

"Still a citizen," he chuckled.

"Right, anyways," she pivoted to him, "I got my revenge by being here. I'm not giving it up by dying before I get to see his face when he finds out."

Harvey let out a booming laugh, forgetting his melancholy for a moment. It had been a while since he had laughed.

"I lost my freedom by getting selected, but I also gained some. If we don't die, we will be seen as the Gods Chosen. Status and freedom go hand in hand. Also, I am leaving rich with the," she calculated on her fingers, making a show of it, "hundred gold wings you owe me, thirty Sabastian owes me, and later tonight I was thinking about going for a record with how much I can swindle out of Titan."

At the mention of Titan's name, Harvey wilted again. A flash of Titan's muscles flexing as he held Kiara against the wall. Her fingernails were clawing into his back. Harvey shook his head, willing the image away.

"Do you think we will make it out of here?" Jordan questioned, breaking the quietude.

"I don't know," he whispered, not looking at her.

An hour later, Harvey and Jordan came up on the group, which had come to a stop, staring at the dead end in front of them.

That makes no sense, though.

There were no other options; the other way was the quicksand. The group shifted to allow him to see in front of them, and Harvey saw the reason.

The passageway did not end. In the centre of the wall that obstructed the way forward, there was an entrance to a tunnel, crawling size.

Above the tunnel was the sign for Venom. The four-pointed star throbbed with green Theos. The tunnel looked like a mouth with a million teeth. The inside had thorns of various sizes lining the sides. Dried blood from past Champions and Protectors tipped the thorns. The entrance was barely the size of an Aervel male.

Sabastian groaned, kicking the wall. "Do the Gods hate my stature? Are they punishing me for my massive biceps? The Metal trial almost took me out."

"Shut up," Kiara snapped at him, reaching inside the tunnel.

She pulled her hand back quickly, flinching. "The walls of the tunnel have thorns. Looking at the colouring and smell, these contain the poison Dreamrot. It causes extreme pain and is known to be the most painful of the root-based poisons. In high doses, it can cause hallucinations."

Kiara looked at the tunnel disdainfully. "I would say this is going to be a high dose. What do you say, leader?" she asked, emphasising the word 'leader.' She turned to Harvey.

"We have no other way to go. This trial is to test us as representatives of the kingdom. We push forward," Harvey said, hoping he sounded confident and leader-like despite his desire to shove Kiara's face into the wall. Patience was never his strong suit. He could control this situation, though. The group shuffled around, no one wanting to experience what was going to come next.

They needed someone to rally behind. And someone to kick them in the ass if the promise of glory wasn't enough. He couldn't be in the front and the back at once. He wasn't alone, though, was he?

He looked to Jordan. "Evens, you go first, odds, you go last."

"Seems like both options are pretty shit."

He waited, patience coming easier than usual. He was dreading what happened next. The dice flew into the Air, tiny divots marking the number on each side. She caught them with a flair, holding them up for his inspection.

"Jordan will take the lead."

"The Dyrfaldur?" Titan questioned, face crunching.

Harvey's temper flared before he shoved it down.

You say that word like you just stepped on Minotaur crap.

"Jordan will take the lead," Harvey repeated himself. "I will take the rear and ensure everyone makes it through okay. Any questions?"

Tension filled the Air as he looked around the circle.

"Okay then," he declared.

Jordan ripped a length of fabric off what was binding her breasts.

Does she keep doing that on purpose?

She used the fabric to wrap her hands.

"What are you doing?" he asked.

"Um, protecting my hands."

She bound the remainder back around her chest, showing more cleavage than before. Harvey swallowed, keeping his eyes locked on hers. He would not violate her by staring. She wasn't doing this for attention; she was doing it for practical reasons.

She is a Dyrfaldur. There is no future with her; we would get executed if ever seen so much as kissing. Her changing in front of me was on purpose. She knows I want her, or at least expects it. There is no future with her. There can't be.

"You are shifting and staying in that form until we reach the end." Harvey ordered.

"It is an ordeal; you just said so. I am just as Chosen as you. I will make it through on my own." Jordan snapped.

"For the Champions! It is an ordeal for us! You don't have to do this. Here, take my jacket at least."

"No, give it to someone else in the group. I can always shift if it gets too bad. I refuse to believe I am just your glorified bodyguard."

I like the idea of you being my bodyguard. I like the idea of you being mine.

"We need someone leading us who isn't hallucinating," he said, gentler. He wanted to protect Jordan, but she made it hard. "Please," he added.

It's normal to be have strong feelings for comrades in arms. This is a reaction to our shared experiences not... her.

Nyx looked at him curiously. He was one to demand, not ask. Harvey was the prince; he said something, and it became a reality. This Dyrfaldur female was the only one who ever made him doubt this.

She looked at him a beat before huffing, "All right, we will do this your way."

She entered the tunnel, and one by one, the group followed. His sister started to enter, but he grabbed her by the arm. Without a word, he draped his undercoat around her. She looked at him open-mouthed, which made him feel dirty.

She shouldn't be surprised at me helping her. What does that say about me?

"I'm doing it for our parents." Harvey lied, begging the universe for Nyx to believe him. He didn't deserve her forgiveness, not yet.

She narrowed her eyes, thinking, before nodding and entering the tunnel. Yelps came first from everyone as they entered the tunnel. As the group got deeper into the tunnel, the yelps turned into cries. When the rest of the party entered, he ducked his head inside and pulled himself forward through the small space.

Thorns lined the walls of the tunnel. They snagged on his skin, his hair, his clothes, and his sensitive wings. He could feel some feathers get yanked out, but he ignored it as he pushed on.

Directly in front of him, Skylar cried out. Harvey could see a thorn poking out of the male's hand, skewering it. It was one of the larger needles, approximately four inches long.

Harvey put a comforting hand on the male's back, "I know it hurts, but you need to pull yourself loose. The more we stop, the longer this goes on. You've got this."

"Think of Freya," Sabastian called back. "Don't want her thinking you're a baby who got stopped by a tiny thorn."

"It is through my fucking hand!" Skylar said, losing his composure.

"Pull loose now, Skylar. That is an order," Harvey barked.

Skylar was losing his head; he needed authority in the chaos. Harvey was an expert in order. Skylar cried out, pulling his hand upwards slowly. Blood dripped down as the thorn clung to the wound, refusing to budge. The male's gaze met Harvey's. Skylar looked like he was going to pass out.

The male was already pale, and he still had half of his hand stuck on the thorn - new *plan*.

"New plan, hold still," Harvey said to Skylar.

He was too long for Harvey to reach behind him, so he had to be next to him. The only problem was that the tunnel was too small for two. Harvey gritted his teeth, dragging himself against the side of the tunnel to squeeze past the male. Thorns bit into him, blood dripping under his now-torn tunic.

We will all be nude by the end of this tunnel. He thought with a spark of amusement.

He finally reached a spot where he could grab onto the male's wrist. Harvey took a breath and leaned forward on his stomach, wings flared to hold him in place. Thorns dug into his wings, and he ignored them, using them to push himself the last couple of inches to hover over Skylar's hand.

"Tell me about Freya," he said to the male as he examined the hand, placing his body between the male and his hand.

The less he saw, the better.

"She is my girlfriend," he said, perking up.

Harvey pretended to listen as he examined the hand. The thorn was coming out the other side and was soaked in blood. The first thing to look for in a piercing wound is barbs left from the perforating object. He looked closer at the needle, leaning forward. The thorns dug into him, burrowing under the skin. The thorn had barbs that kept it lodged in the skin, making extraction challenging.

"You have hair," Skylar babbled.

Kiara must not have lied about the poison.

Harvey needed to keep them moving. He would need to free Skylar quickly.

Not all the thorns were long like this one. Most were short enough that they only sank a quarter of an inch into the skin, still enough to administer poison and initiate bleeding, especially when they were all being pricked constantly in the narrow tunnel. Barbs caught on their skin, ripping out the flesh.

This trap is meant to keep you locked mentally in hallucinations while you bleed out. The long thorns are intended to stop or slow us as we become disoriented. I need to focus.

Harvey's vision got fuzzy, and he suddenly forgot why he was there.

Why was there so much blood?

Why was this male screaming? His tail is fluffy, Harvey thought, giggling.

Would it be rude to ask to touch it?

He isn't an animal, so yes, that would be incredibly rude, Harvey.

Focus.

Self-reflection later.

He had to move, but something flashed in the corner of his vision.

He looked down. The thorn in front of him seemed to throb with a beat only he could hear. The sight reminded him of a course he took in his youth. He had done arrow removal training many times when his father brought him to Veritas Hall as a child to help in the training exercises as a healer.

Never with this much blood, though, it is so glossy.

Instincts took over, and Harvey noticed the barbs.

What am I doing? Where am I?

There was a fox skewered in front of him. A purple fox that swirled in and out of his vision.

Focus.

I need to get control.

Control and discipline. I should start with this soldier. The arrow went clean through. Screams filled his ears, but he ignored them.

There are barbs on both sides.

He chuckled.

My instructor will be so pleased if I can do this. If I can perform one of the most complicated emergency procedures.

He looked to the side to see no one was next to him. Instead, a swirling fox sat patiently.

Where did Titan go? Why is there a fox in the classroom?

Harvey could feel himself holding a surgical instrument.

Where is everyone?

He looked down and saw a hand. Something was through it.

The extraction!

Both ends will tear through the flesh. There are barbs on either side of the hand. Both ends will tear through the flesh. I need to snap the thorn in two places to get it out.

"Stay still" Harvey told the male; eyes fixated on the hand as he worked.

Harvey snapped it off the wall first.

This wall looks silly. When did it get so velvety? Maybe I should take a nap. He was holding something. *Fuck, the extraction!*

Skylar was passed out, body zooming in and out of focus, a pool of blood spread around the male below Harvey.

Focus. Control. Focus. Fuck, the room is spinning. Why was the room so fucking small? I am a prince, dammit! I will talk with the castellan. This has to be a joke!

He huffed in frustration; *oh, wait, what was this?* He was holding something. The extraction was half done. The extraction was his examination.

My father must be mad at me, teaching me a lesson by giving me such an intense test. I will have to complete it to get my room back, or was it Nyx's room? I didn't mean to let Nyx bring that dragon into the castle.

Focus, Harvey.

For the second time, Harvey snapped the thorn. This time, he snapped it inside the hand with a slight, precise movement. Not hard enough to tear through the entire hand, but enough to snap the thorn.

The thorn slipped, pink blood on it.

Wait, pink? Why is the blood pink? The medical procedure is an unusual task from father. It is a cutting-edge medical procedure.

He attempted to free the hand again, bloody hands clamping onto the slippery needle. He used the ground as leverage, trying to push it through.

Why was it so spikey? The floor was sharp. Why was the floor sharp, and my hands warm and sticky, and... oh fuck. Harvey breathed in, closing his eyes.

The world shifted, colours pulsating around him. He needed to focus. With precision, he pulled both halves out at the same time without dragging any barbs through the skin, a successful extraction.

"Harvey, we need to move; keep following me," Sabastian yelled ahead of him.

He didn't understand why everyone was in such a hurry. He dragged himself through the tunnel.

Crawling through something, what a bizarre exercise. Harvey giggled, the sound of his voice echoing loudly.

Sabastian was next to him. *Why am I next to Sabastian? I typically went in line with Titan.* His hand brushed a male passed out on the ground. Harvey slapped the male's face lightly until he woke up.

Why am I waking him? The male looked around before moving forward. He was winning the race. I need to follow. Why am I going so slow? Why am I so wet and sticky? Not Water, something less... fuck I forgot. Why can't I think?

"Static leads to being stuck," Harvey repeated one of his father's phrases in his head.

"Yes, Gods, now fucking move Harvey," a voice cried, begging.

He looked around, and the Venom became less potent. He looked at his blood-soaked clothes, his hand pouring blood in thick rivulets down his arm.

He was alone in the tunnel; *how long had it been?*

Harvey looked down his hand. A hole went through it, clogged with sticky blood.

It was my hand I extracted the barb from.

Harvey put a hand over the wound, desperate to stop the flow.

Oh Gods, is that where it went through?

Blood squished between his fingers as he fought the unstoppable flood.

I was hallucinating. Fuck I almost died.

A wave of sluggishness hit him, making his limbs heavy. Panic spiked in him, giving him a small boost.

I still might if I don't move, now!

He began to drag himself forward. Little prickers snagged onto him. His right hand was throbbing. He looked down. A large hole was through his hand. He slumped to the side, the world blurring by him.

Help.

His vision went black.

CHAPTER 11: NYX

Forced Proximity

Did you talk to your dad about taking the throne after Harvey? You, my love, would be a much better ruler than your brother. I know you think you don't want it, but you said you would think about it. You have failed me in the past; it's okay. I expect it at this point.

-Kiara letter to Nyx, 360th Day, 65 AT

Nyx pulled herself out of the tunnel, tears streaming down her face; images of Kiara and her past haunted her. Her clothes were in tatters, revealing more skin than she was comfortable with. She blew her hair out of her face as she lay on the floor. The ceiling was tall and dark, like black obsidian, identical to the floor. Nyx laughed maniacally, watching the mushrooms dance.

They were dancing just for her.

A face came above her, *such a beautiful face.*

"The Venom will wear off for you in a few minutes. Hang in there," the beautiful female soothed.

Her hair brushed Nyx's face. It tickled. She smiled up at the face.

The female looks confused, amused, and is that desire? Who is this breathtaking goddess?

She reached up to touch the female's face. The female pulled back, looking away, sorrow flickering across her face. Instead, a hand guided her up and over a wall, pulling her down to sit. She leaned against the stranger, the female tucking her hand behind Nyx's back.

Fuck, she is gorgeous.

The poison wore off after a few minutes, and Nyx jolted to her feet. "I am so sorry," she said to Astris.

"It is fine," Astris replied, glancing at Kiara.

Nyx nodded, biting her bottom lip, unsure what to say. She turned to go before stopping herself. She ran an assessing eye over Astris. She was injured just as severely as Nyx was. Her feet moved before she could comprehend her actions.

She sat Astris down, capturing Water in her hands and washing Astris's cuts. Astris protested, claiming she should be washing Nyx's cuts, but Nyx glowered at her silently until she stopped resisting.

"Glad you finally learned who's in charge," Nyx said jokingly.

Astris turned red, pursing her lips. She looked around before standing and walking past Nyx.

As she passed, she whispered in Nyx's ear. "You may have the bond to control me, but we both know you would drop to your knees for me if I asked."

Nyx's stomach lit on Fire, her knees going weak. She could feel the wetness between her thighs as she took a moment to collect herself.

What the fuck is happening? This was Astris fucking Archer. What is happening to Astris? What changed?

She looked over to the tunnel, all thoughts of Astris leaving her head. Sabastian came out, dragging Skylar, who shifted into a fox. He was trying to bite Sabastian, who was holding him by the scruff, wings a mess of blood and feathers. Sabastian threw the fox to the ground, leaping away from its bite.

Her brother was supposed to come next. The group was spread out a few minutes apart. Nyx held her side; a thorn had torn through her abdomen, causing her to stumble occasionally. One minute went by, then two, three, four, five, she started to panic.

Sabastian, finally coming off the hallucinations, spoke up, panting, "Harvey was stuck the last time I saw him. Skylar got a nasty cut to the head and was shifting back and forth with his hallucinations in front of Harvey. The bastard bit me the entire way. I don't know if Harvey got free. I can go back in there to find out."

"No," Jordan said, "I am his Protector. I am also the only one who can turn around in the tunnel by shifting."

With that, Jordan jumped into the Air, a flash, and she flew down the tunnel. Nyx stumbled to the tunnel's opening, watching the finch as it flew down and out of sight. She didn't know how long Jordan had been in the tunnel and was unable to estimate how long she would take.

I wish I had an hourglass like Harvey.

Agitation bubbled under her skin as she counted the seconds.

Astris stood beside her, looking into the tunnel as well. Her hand brushed Nyx's as she waited with her. Nyx swallowed, goosebumps forming on her arms at the contact. A few minutes later, Jordan, shifted out of her finch, was visible. She was dragging Harvey, slamming her forearm on the floor of the tunnel, ignoring the needles, as she pulled herself and Harvey towards the exit.

Was the female actually using the thorns through her flesh as a way to move faster? So much blood… that is too much, way too much. Skylar had better get over his hallucinations soon, or Harvey will bleed out.

When Jordan pushed Harvey out of the tunnel and crawled out herself, her arms were a mangled mess, grated like cheese. Blood drenched the fabric binding her and slices down her stomach. Her thighs weren't much better, having thin lines so dense they appeared as if they were one wound. Jordan had placed herself under Harvey in the overly small tunnel, taking most of his weight on her, on the thorns. The female had saved her brother. A Unity Rune flared to life in the Air as soon as the pair hit the ground of the chamber.

Astris and Nyx ran to Harvey. He was mumbling nonsense, a large hole was through his hand, spurting blood at a rapid rate. The rest of his body was just as bad, since he had given his jacket to Nyx. Despite Jordan's efforts, Harvey was far too big for her to do much more than drag him. He was passed out, limp, and a dead weight.

Skylar came over, assessing both Harvey and Jordan.

He began dressing Harvey's hand first, deeming it more immediate. "The thorn looks like it was in him for a while; it also managed to do a great deal of damage to the bones. The continuous stream of Venom must have made him hallucinate more, and then the blood loss finally caused him to pass out." Skylar rubbed the back of his head in thought.

He turned to address Nyx. "There isn't much we can do; we have no string to sew the wound. I will stop the bleeding now with this plant. It's from Kiara, but I checked it myself to ensure its…" he trailed off, peeking nervously at Kiara, who was tending to Titan's wounds.

"He is not in danger of dying or any permanent damage, but he will be weaker for a while until he heals. Let's leave him to rest for a bit before we wake him. All of us are too injured to endure any more challenges tonight."

Jordan kneeled down next to Harvey, attempting to adjust him. Nyx kneeled, moving her brother with the Dyrfaldur female onto his jacket that Nyx was placing down for him, guilt stabbing through her.

Harvey whistled a unique tune, "let's go Azazel, father is asking for you." Harvey's dragon. Nyx had been jealous for weeks when he had whistle-bonded the ruby dragon. Nyx filed away the whistle in case she ever needed to borrow Azazel. It would've been helpful to know Nightmare's dragon's whistle.

Dragons are feral until they hear it, each dragon's whistle trained into the creature since birth.

Not that I would ever be allowed one.

Once Harvey was on his back and his head was in Jordan's lap, Nyx finally moved to sit down. The passageway opened up to a long corridor ahead of them. The path seemed endless, stretching into the distance like a twisted welcoming mat.

"I think we should consider scouting the next location while Harvey recovers," Astris said.

"We should stay together; you don't need to go galivanting off." Kiara snorted in haughty indignation. "You don't want to leave me, do you, Astris?"

"Scouting is actually a good idea," Sabastian cut in, "I could use a nap."

Skylar threw the hourglass to Astris, "Harvey said only two turns."

"Ugh, you are all incorrigible," Kiara squealed, storming off, Titan following.

Nyx ignored them. None of this made sense.

Astris wants to scout with me… alone? If she wanted to kill me, she would have done it already. It seems, for now, that she and Kiara still wish to get their entertainment out of tormenting me. The real question is why haven't I tried to kill her recently? Why can't I bring myself to even attempt it? I will deal with it later. I could use this chance to stretch my wings.

The corridor ahead was open and cavernous. Perfect for flying. Her wings unfurled, stretching wide.

"Let's go," Nyx said to Astris, ignoring Kiara.

"Astris," Kiara said, looking at her over her shoulder with a mocking grin. "Don't have too much fun with our little friend while I'm not there," she crooned.

Astris looked at her for a minute before walking out into the corridor, Nyx following.

"Let's fly," Astris said before Nyx could say anything.

She leaped into the Air, wings unfurling. Nyx followed her, wings stretching wide. It had been a while since she was able to spread them fully. The Labyrinth did not favour those with wings.

It's ironic, since the Aervel were the Chosen Champions.

Her wings were sore from confinement, and the ability to stretch them was precious in this underground nightmare. Even the cuts across her from the thorns did not take away from the joy of flying.

Nyx's night-kissed wings were slightly larger than Astris's snow-white wings. She quickly caught up, falling into step with Astris. They flew in silence through the empty and unending tunnel, only stopping when the light had finally faded.

The pair landed, catching their breath.

Astris looked down at the hourglass. "We flew for one turn. We should camp here for the night."

Nyx grunted in agreement, drinking some Water from the wall.

They split a massive glowing mushroom to eat, more bitter than the regular ones at the start. Having choked down the entirety of their portions, the pair lay down to sleep. Their wings touched, reassurance in the quietude. A wind blew through the corridor and Nyx shivered, feeling vulnerable. She couldn't sleep in the cold. Astris turned over, curling herself around Nyx.

Nyx froze, confused.

"It's my job as your Protector. If you make it awkward, I'll leave you to freeze to death."

Astris's cold hands shook on Nyx's skin despite her bravado. The heat from her body warmed Nyx, and the cold of her hands ignited her. The smell of pine and honey washed over her. Nyx couldn't think.

Astris Archer is holding me. Astris Archer is holding me, and I…

I like it.

The warmth of Astris's arms was intended to help her sleep and keep her warm. Instead, it caused her to be wide awake, burning with desire. Hyper-aware of every part of her touching Astris. Her silky wing draped over Nyx and brushed her cheek with a soft white feather.

I can feel desire building inside me. Last time I felt this way… No. She will always side with Kiara. Get a grip Nyx.

Nyx shook her head to clear it, unwilling to examine the emotion.

This display of affection has to be a trap. Wait… What had Kiara said before we left?

'Don't have too much fun with our little friend while I'm not there,' Nyx remembered with a shudder. She tried to roll away, but Astris held her there.

"Sleep," Astris said, voice husky.

"Why are you doing this?" Nyx writhed in her arms, Astris's wings now encasing them from both sides. The space warmed quickly as the two females faced one another.

"I am trying to sleep. I am trying to keep my Champion alive. Suck it up, you know we don't have options."

"Don't have too much fun with our little friend while I'm not there," Nyx bit out, body tense.

"I won't hurt you. Not while we are… I won't hurt you."

"Not while we are what? Without an audience?"

"What do you want me to say? It doesn't matter!"

Astris swallowed uncomfortably.

"It doesn't matter? Are you serious?" Nyx's voice rose in hysterics. "If you want to help me understand, you can start by explaining why you are so fucking two-faced," Nyx demanded, fangs on full display while she maintained eye contact with Astris.

"Go to sleep," Astris stared blankly, eyes darting to the fangs before closing them.

She is vulnerable. I hesitated too long; I have a chance; I should kill her here. Before she kills me, I should strike first… right?

Instead, Nyx growled at Astris, eyes filled with fury.

"No," Nyx snapped. "Don't treat me like a child."

"I know you aren't a child, Nyx," Astris sighed before adjusting, "I'm going to bed."

"I don't understand you, and I don't trust you," Nyx ground out, frustrated.

Why can't I do it? I should kill her now that we have no witnesses. Why is she being so vulnerable? Closing her eyes when I could attack. Why was she so… bold since entering the Labyrinth? Was it the danger? The distance from Kiara? It doesn't matter; I will try to stay awake.

Nyx turned back away from Astris, scooting a few feet away. Astris didn't try to follow this time, but Nyx could hear her teeth chattering as soon as Nyx moved away. The cold hit Nyx immediately. It took every bit of her willpower to continue staying away from Astris's embrace. She tossed and turned, the cold making her writhe in discomfort. Finally, after a few hours, she fell into a fitful sleep.

The light rose, signifying morning. Nyx stood up with a grumble, going to drink some Water from the cave wall. Goosebumps lined her skin still, as she closed her eyes, imagining a cup of tea.

Fuck, I would kill for a hot tea right now.

"You're too cold," Astris said, coming up behind her, cold hand touching her.

Astris grabbed her parchment-thin overcoat. With a practiced motion, Astris undid the buttons, the fabric beneath her wings coming free from the front of her garment. She took the thin overcoat and tried to place it on Nyx. Nyx tried to bat her hand away.

"I don't know what sort of fucked up game," Nyx started.

"I'm not playing," Astris pleaded, cutting her off.

"You are always playing. Now let's go before we lose the light," Nyx cut her off, taking off, leaving Astris's next words to float away on the wind.

I don't owe her anything. I don't need to listen to a word she says.

Nyx's wings pumped in the Air, rocketing her forward.

I have no reason to go slow enough for her to keep up. Nyx smiled, readying herself. *I will just fly until I come to a fork, then spend my time alone; instead of spending the day with Astris.*

Astris came up behind her, making up the distance and keeping pace. Her wings pounded powerfully at the Air, an expert in the sky.

It has been a while since we've flown together. She must have gotten faster. No matter, I will just have to speed up.

Nyx let her wings stretch out as she flew, dragging at the Air in long strokes. Each stroke of her wings shot her ahead of Astris into the empty corridor. She picked up the pace, pounding her wings down in time to her racing heart.

The flight will be a good exercise at this pace. I haven't been able to use my wings in a while, she thought, breathing heavily.

White caught in the corner of her vision as Astris's wing clipped her own.

You have got to be fucking kidding me.

Nyx dug deeper, speeding up. Astris kept pace, her slightly smaller wings beating hard. Nyx looked over in disbelief, fighting the twitch at the corner of her mouth.

I don't remember anyone being able to come close to my speed, especially Astris, who was a slow flyer growing up. Astris turned her head to look at Nyx.

Astris's silver eyes were vibrant, and her dark skin was warm, inviting, and silky. Nyx wavered in the Air, scowling.

Nyx was taking her seriously now, paying attention to the length of her wing strokes, the aerodynamics of her body position, her breathing techniques, and her environment. Her mind buzzed as she revelled in the challenge. Her muscles burned, firing on pure willpower.

Astris must be tiring now.

Nyx looked over to Astris, who was beaming.

Her smile lit up her face, eyes sparkling and teeth flashing. Astris's laugh rang through the corridor, joyous and unbridled. It was contagious. A smile broke through Nyx's scowl as she pushed deeper, glancing over at Astris as she pulled forward.

An eyebrow raised, her gaze challenged Astris to keep up. Astris did not disappoint. A laugh escaped Nyx as she forgot their situation briefly. They were going so quickly that they almost missed the first fork in the path, landing in a skid and backtracking.

"Which one?" Astris asked, turning to Nyx expectantly.

"Why would I know? Just pick one."

"You're the Champion."

"Shut up about the Champion bullshit."

"It's not bullshit. The Gods chose you. Do you know how many times I dreamt about being a Champion as a kid? Being *the* Aervel to bring back the Theos. Then *you* were Chosen as the Champion." Astris's expression soured. "You aren't even fully Aervel. You don't even care, do you?"

"So, you dreamed about dying since you were a child. I didn't peg you for an idiot. You place far too much faith in the Gods if you are eager to die for them. If you really want to please them, why don't you just expose me so I am executed?" Nyx snapped.

"I wouldn't do that to you! The Gods have tied me to you. I will put everything into protecting you because I believe in our Gods. Don't you dare minimise the honour, you are a disgrace to our Kingdom! It was supposed to be me!" Astris's voice cracked on her next words, "everyone expected it of me. Everyone. You don't know what it's like to have expectations like that on you."

"I'm the fucking princess," Nyx said, spitting out the word princess. "You don't think I don't have expectations?"

"Not like I do! You're not the primary heir! You don't understand what sort of pressure it entails. You don't have to work hard, and you just are good at things, no matter how much you half-ass it. You are exceptional, and you don't care!"

"I'm a bastard. Bastards don't impress, they meet expectations," Nyx scoffed. "I can succeed all I want. You and Kiara will just destroy my reputation again."

"You already do that yourself!" Guilt filled Astris's voice, causing it to waver uncertainly.

"Well," Nyx felt the Fire drain out of her, "I guess we are at an impasse."

The two of them stood in silence, assessing one another.

"Let's just call a truce. We should only be out another day before going back. They will worry, and our battling to the death would leave us vulnerable to the Labyrinth."

"For once, we agree, make sure you stay out of my way," Nyx said. "And while you're at it, wipe that look off your face."

"What look?" Astris's brows pulled together in confusion.

"That blank look you get, it makes you look unintelligent, and that isn't you," Nyx snapped before blushing, realising the compliment she had unintentionally given Astris.

She liked seeing Astris show emotion, any emotion; she hated the walls Astris put up.

If I could, I would melt the Ice mask Astris has crafted for herself…

I like seeing her smile, she thought to herself, swallowing hard.

This cave business was bringing out her honesty, and she was not a fan. Maybe Kiara was poisoning her. It would explain why her gaze was now locked onto Astris's lips. Nyx wanted to lean forward. Her body begged her to. Instead, she let her wings snap out again, taking the path to the right without discussion. Astris followed, giving her some space.

"Not everything is as it seems. My relationship with Kiara," Astris paused, face going taut as if fighting something. "Just be careful, okay?"

"Is that a threat?"

"If you want to take it as that. I am not the true threat, though. Not even close."

"Then tell me what it is."

"I cannot."

"Nightmare," Nyx accused, pulling back.

"Not a Nightmare, merely trapped in one."

Maybe she is more like me than I realise.

CHAPTER 12: NYX

Alone

Everyone who befriends you leaves you. Why would that be? You are unlovable.

-Nightmare note to Nyx, 152nd Day, 74 AT

Nyx landed, coming to a sliding stop by the group. She had interrogated Astris more about Nightmare, but she didn't get anywhere. The female was as cryptic as ever, not giving an inch. Frankness was not in Astris's vocabulary.

She has to at least know about Nightmare. She didn't react in confusion when I mentioned the name. What was that with being trapped in it? Does that mean she is a victim of Nightmare as well? Or an accomplice?

Harvey was up and walking, which gave Nyx relief. Seeing him laid out, blood pooling around him, frightened her. He glanced over to her, giving her a rare smile.

Nyx and Astris had been stopped by a fork in the road which needed to be investigated and recorded by the cartographers.

The group set out at dawn; Nyx was relieved to be back with the group. She couldn't breathe when alone with Astris, couldn't think.

She would hang out with Skylar today. *His nonchalant attitude will cheer me up.*

Nyx dropped back to Skylar, falling into pace with him. Ahead, Astris looked over her shoulder at her, face a mask.

Nyx looked away. Skylar was eager to talk. It seems he and Sabastian also were having problems. The mild-mannered, optimistic Skylar was having a hard time bonding with an arrogant idealist. Sabastian enjoyed tormenting him, too. Not in the way Kiara tormented Nyx. Sabastian enjoyed antagonising Skylar like one would a younger brother: rough, but without malice. Meanwhile, Kiara had no qualms about excessive cruelty.

They continued down the passageway for a week, camping along the way before coming to a cavern. A large chasm spanned the room, too deep to see the bottom.

Is this a challenge for Aervel to help their Dyrfaldur across?

She didn't understand why it would be this easy.

Her stomach buzzed with anticipation.

Something is missing, she thought. Looking to the ground before the ledge, she saw the Rune for Air: a spiral.

This has to be a trial.

Sabastian sauntered up to the chasm, looking down over the edge.

Maybe we should…

Titan ran up behind him, abruptly grabbing Sabastian in a jump scare.

Idiot.

Sabastian feigned fear, hand over heart, mouth ajar as he faked a swoon off the ledge. The half-heart charm on his bracelet swung with the movement. Nyx held her breath as Sabastian dove into the chasm. Moments later, he came careening upwards, cresting the side of the chasm and continuing towards the ceiling.

Titan laughed harder.

Too fast. He has no control!

"Something is wrong with him!" Nyx yelled. "You idiot, this is a trial," she snapped at Titan.

Titan stopped laughing, looking over the edge. Sabastian stopped flapping his wings, seeming to fall towards the ceiling fifty feet above.

"What in the fuck is happening? Titan, I am going to string your twig neck if I make it out of this." Sabastian called out.

"It's not my fault; you chose to let yourself fall; there was totally time to catch yourself!"

"Shut up, Titan," Jordan snapped.

She's showing some teeth.

Harvey ran to the edge, Astris following from beside Nyx. Sabastian was in more immediate danger. Nyx snapped herself out of her fantasy to assess the scene before her. Sabastian was in the Air, wings limp as he was thrown in different directions: left, right, down, up.

"I am going to be fucking sick," he shouted, hands over his mouth.

By the colour of his skin, he wasn't bluffing. The male's skin was turning greener by the second. As Sabastian was getting flung around, she studied how his body was moving; instead of moving backward as if being dragged, he appeared to be shoved in different directions.

A few times, he came dangerously close to colliding with the rocky sides of the cavern. At one point, he plummeted, and she counted the seconds, waiting for him to come up again. She needed to gauge how far he was being dragged down, but the cavern was dark, the visibility low.

The cavern has to have a unique wind field, Nyx realised with a start.

"Harvey!" she yelled.

"I know! The problem is getting him out without getting caught in it ourselves. It doesn't look like he can fly against the gale with the constant change."

"I can't!" Sabastian cried, long black hair whipping against the wind.

"He is going to have so many knots in his hair," Skylar whispered, absently touching his long red hair.

Nyx started to reply when suddenly, she saw Titan jump off the edge, a rope of clothes tied to him. Kiara held the other end.

"What are you doing?" Nyx yelled, Harvey turning with her gaze.

"Quiet, Bastard," Kiara snapped, bending her legs and leaning back as Titan swung wildly. "We don't need your help."

The rope pulled tight, and Kiara screamed as she was dragged over the edge.

Nyx looked down, getting as close to the edge as she dared. The rope had wrapped itself around the three Aervel, binding them awkwardly.

"Shift," Harvey ordered Skylar and Jordan.

Skylar shifted, but Jordan just raised an eyebrow. Harvey growled, scruffing the fox and handing him to Nyx before grabbing Jordan.

"They are going to die, suck up your unearned pride and shift!"

"You think this is pride?" Jordan challenged.

A scream that was cut off in a gurgle came from below. The group looked down to where the rope was now choking Titan.

"Shift!" Harvey roared, moving towards Jordan.

She bared her teeth at him before flashing into a finch. Jordan came to sit on his shoulder, pecking at him. Harvey grabbed the finch, tucking her in his tunic.

"Stay together and link hands as soon as we hit the rest of the group," Harvey called as he leaped off the ledge.

Nyx started running, jumping off the ledge with Skylar's fox on her right and Astris on his left. The trio hit the wind field, and Nyx's body itched at the Theos as they were flung to the side. Nyx grabbed Skylar's fox before he could plummet away from the group. Astris grabbed him from the other side, anchoring the three of them together.

They swung towards the other group, which was careening towards the far wall. The group was fighting, their words muffled in the howling wind. The group slammed into the wall, Harvey pulling at the rope around Titan's neck, as Nyx collided with him.

He dropped the rope, starting to fall away from the group. Sabastian grabbed him, bulging muscles straining as he dragged her brother back into the tangle of limbs and wings. A crack, and they hit the wall, Kiara's head snapping to the side.

"Get the rope, we can use it," Sabastian offered up, pulling at the makeshift rope that was still around Titan's neck.

Nyx reached to help, left hand still holding Skylar by the scruff. Kiara slapped her hand away from Titan, eyes narrowing.

A gust of Air howled through the chasm, the wind changing abruptly again. The wall behind Nyx collided with her head, surprising her. Her hands loosened, the fox and rope slipping from her grasp as she was wrenched from the group.

Harvey reached for her, but he was in the centre of the group, holding the entire mass together. His eyes went wide as he watched her fall, eyes filled with undisguised terror. She reached up towards him as if she could still save herself.

Nyx tumbled away from the group. She could hear her brother screaming her name after her.

Don't let go, brother, Nyx begged the universe.

The darkness enveloped her as she was thrown through the Air. Fear filled her as she slammed into the far wall, her head ringing.

She was dizzy, unable to get her bearings with the Theos forcing them towards their demise.

That's the catch, she thought. *We are blown longer in each direction now, increasing our velocity. Too bad I will die before I can share that information.*

She did not doubt that the last hundred feet would only consist of a single direction: down. The Aervel would be too disoriented to stop the descent with their wings.

She choked on bile, feeling adrift from changing directions in the dark. The dark around her was empty; the only sound that of Air rushing through her ears.

I am going to die. There is no correcting my descent without another body.

Everything she smashed into only muddled her further.

I don't want this to be the end.

Tears streamed from her eyes, hitting different parts of her as she was flung around. The chasm was getting darker as she fell, and she could no longer see the light at the top.

I am so pathetic. Get it together, get it together, get it… Her heart raced, breathing stuttering as she sobbed. The wall struck her again, and she cried out in pain.

I can't take much more of this. I can't right myself, and even if I could, there is no way I would be able to find the wall. I can only watch one direction, and every time, I am wrong. What if this never ends? What if I keep falling until I die of blood loss?

Smack.

Warm liquid ran down her head, coating her body in splatters as she hit another rock.

Panic poisoned her thoughts, and Nyx let out a blood-curdling, terror-filled scream. All of her pride going out the window, she cried out into the void as she smashed into a wall, crumpling. She had been falling for minutes now since she detached from the group.

Another scream escaped her throat, choked and primal. She tried to get her wings out to slow herself as she had in the group, but the Air's force was too much for her to handle alone, and her wings crushed, feathers tearing out painfully. Tears clogged her throat, choking her. At this point, Nyx was sobbing harder than she had since she was a child. The dread of the void and the erratic beatings overwhelmed her.

She grasped at the wall as she hit it next, but her fingernails scraped against the uneven rock, and she cried out as one of her nails pulled off. Pain demanded her attention as she pulled the hand close to her body. Another hit from behind, and Nyx bent forward, spine stinging from the impact.

Please let there be a bottom. I don't want to die slowly like this.

A thin body slammed into her, wrapping around her protectively. The smell of Astris filled Nyx's nose. She sobbed harder, too emotional to think about how it looked.

"Hey, stay with me," Astris said, hand petting the back of her head.

A smack and Nyx flinched, but the pain didn't come. Astris took the hit by surrounding her.

Nyx cried harder, unable to pull herself together. Her heart pounded through her body, in her ears.

"Shh, angel," Astris tugged her closer, "it's okay, everything is okay now."

Did she just call me… I must have hit my head hard to be imagining something that ludicrous.

Nyx tried to reply but choked on her tears, eyes crackling loudly. She gagged, the fear thick in her throat. Her mind was racing, adrenaline shooting like Electricity in her veins.

"Hey, stay with me, angel; everything is going to be okay. It's going to be okay; I am here. I will make it better."

Another smack as they hit the wall again. Once again, Astris took the hit, a soft grunt escaping her this time.

"Stop!" Nyx cried out, lowering her voice to a cracked whisper. "It's no use; stop shielding me; let me take some of the hits."

"Mm, not until you have calmed down, angel. I need you to believe in me, to trust me. If you can do that, I can get you out of here."

Nyx's breathing hitched as she attempted to swallow her scream. A cry broke out of her. She buried her face in Astris's neck. Astris's smell washed over her, soothing her nerves. Nyx closed her eyes, focusing on slowing her breathing. Slowly, she calmed down. Astris held her until she relaxed, patiently despite the danger.

"Good, now you are going to shift for me. I am going to hold you in front of me, taking the damage from all other sides, so you can focus. Grab onto the wall. Then you need to get yourself out of here."

"No," Nyx stated, gripping Astris tighter.

"What?" Astris asked, confusion overtaking her features.

"I said no. I'm not fucking leaving you." Nyx insisted, knuckles white from holding on.

"I don't have claws," Astris explained, eyebrows drawing together as she tried unsuccessfully to push her away.

"I'll carry you." Nyx insisted.

"Not against the wind," Astris stated sadly.

"Yes, against the wind. Fear isn't a good look on you, Astris." Nyx hoped that pissing her off would work. "You and I know I am only as scared as you are. I am not leaving you." There was a pause, Nyx swallowing. "Please"

Astris's body stiffened before relaxing.

Astris murmured her agreement, and Nyx adjusted herself so that Astris was behind her. She was hyper-aware of Astris's chest against her back, of her hands on Nyx's waist. She arched back into Astris imperceptibly, enjoying the touch in the safety of the dark. Her heart raced for an entirely new reason now.

"Shift," Astris said.

Nyx tried to focus. She only ever shifted on accident. She had no fucking control.

How am I supposed to do this? Why am I so fucking useless?

She was in the arms of the enemy. She knew she shouldn't be enjoying it. She knew it was wrong. She knew this was her bully, the best friend of someone who had ruined Nyx's life for years. Anger flared through her, causing her eyes to change, Electric rings still crackling in them.

She could see better in the dark now.

"You feel emotions, and you shift, yeah? Not to rush you, but I'm not feeling fur." Astris rambled, voice rising in pitch.

"I have never done it on purpose, okay?" Nyx retorted.

Astris froze for a moment. "I guess I will have to take this into my own hands."

"What are you doing?"

Cold fingers ran along her jaw, setting her skin on Fire. She wanted more. She wanted everything this female had to offer.

Nyx leaned into the touch, hating herself.

We are going to die if it is up to me. A bastard and a Half-blood.

One of Astris's hands traced her jaw, the other roaming across her hip. It travelled up her side, dancing around her breasts, much to Nyx's disappointment. Instead, it went to her throat.

That's much less disappointing.

Nyx bit her tongue to keep a moan in. The cold hand tightened, ensuring to stay away from the windpipe, restricting blood flow, not Air. She pressed, slowly increasing the pressure.

Nyx tried to ignore the insistent throbbing in her core, begging for release. This wasn't working. Astris pushed Nyx into the next wall, hard; surprising and angering Nyx. Nyx tasted blood as her fangs began to drop.

"See, the problem is you seem to change at the beginning of an emotion. Since lust isn't working, that must mean its only anger."

Astris leaned in close, and Nyx's breathing hitched. Astris laughed seductively. "We will have to talk about that later, angel. Or maybe I'll get Kiara for you."

Nyx's stomach tightened, loathing taking over.

"Shut up!" Nyx growled.

They slammed into the wall once again.

"Now would be great."

Nyx shrieked in frustration, fangs slicing into her lip.

Get it together, Nyx; you can think about how close Astris is later.

Nyx tasted a drop of blood.

Pain, pain works. I just have to give in to it.

Nyx opened her mouth wide, willing her fangs out as she bit down on her lip as hard as she could. Her right fang pierced her lip, pain waking Nyx's senses. Tears pooled in her eyes, and she could feel the shift start. This time, she didn't fight it.

Her eyes and mouth changed first, a tail, then the paws and fur. The only time she had ever fully shifted was when the dragon was crashing into her room. Nyx lay limp in Astris's arms, feeling powerless without her arms or hands. A blow and she almost lost the shift as they hit the wall again. Astris was taking the brunt of the damage, but it still shook her. Nyx held out her claws like some sort of puppy crampon. The situation was embarrassing, to say the least.

The wall slammed into them, hitting Nyx's paws. She clawed at it, losing her grip. They tried again, and the next time, the hit came from the front. Her paws stuck this time, and she dug them deep into the wall. Her claws were strong enough to go against swords, sharp enough to pierce rock. Astris clung to her back, arms around Nyx's wolf's neck.

Nyx ran up the wall, legs burning. She had never exercised in her wolf form before. She never shifted. It was coming back to bite her now. She never in her wildest dreams could have imagined her Dyrfaldur side saving her life.

I need to pay attention. If I lose the shift, we are dead.

Astris did her best to cling as close to Nyx's back as possible, avoiding Air resistance, with Nyx's claws holding them to the wall. She was frozen still as they climbed, which Nyx was grateful for.

For someone so thin, she is as strong as a Minotaur, Nyx thought.

They climbed for hours, Astris putting her chilled hands-on Nyx's wolf's ears to cool her down as she climbed. The light filled the chasm again, and they could hear the group above. They had formed a circle now, Jordan and Skylar back in their main forms. Harvey was in the centre, holding the group together.

Nyx stopped; they couldn't see her like this. Astris, sensing her hesitation, looked up to the group. She bent her head by Nyx's ear. The soft warmth of her breath caused Nyx to shiver.

"Just the nails now, I will join you on the wall. We can keep this hidden."

"Why are you helping me?"

Astris ignored her question, shifting to the wall beside her, hand gripping Nyx's still. Nyx focused, taking a few breaths before shifting back. Her grip instantly lessened, and she grasped at the wall. Her pinkie finger was bloody, the claw missing.

That must have been where I lost the fingernail.

Slowly, Astris and Nyx climbed up toward the group. Harvey caught her gaze, and a look of relief crossed over his pinched features. He nodded to Astris, motioning for Sabastian to turn around. The male twisted, facing Nyx now. He held out a hand to the pair of them.

"Shift your hands back when we jump," Astris instructed, not bothering to wait for her opinion before counting down.

So much for the kind female who saved me; the Ice queen has once again taken her throne.

"Two, one!"

The pair pushed off as Sabastian swung towards them on the pinwheel of bodies. They jumped, Astris grabbing Sabastian's hand with her own, her other hand in Nyx's.

Harvey and Sabastian worked together, passing everyone around until they were in a large circle, all holding hands, Harvey and Sabastian in the middle.

Everyone was attached now. Jordan and Skylar had shifted back while they had been apart from the group. The wall came up behind Titan and Kiara, who kicked off, angling their feet lower to gain height.

They rose slightly before the tempest changed, dragged them in the wrong direction, smashing them against the side wall. Harvey squeezed Nyx's wrist; the wall was coming up. He kept looking at her, as if to make sure she was real. His attention made her uncomfortable.

I know what to do with asshole Harvey, but I don't know how to handle worried brother Harvey.

She prepared for the wall, bending her legs slightly to take the impact. Nyx and Astris used their legs to push off the wall, a gale pulling the group down immediately after. They plummeted for a full minute before changing direction violently. The group was silent, fixated on the task at hand. Bickering had ceased, allowing the group to work together.

The next time they hit the wall, Titan, Kiara, and Nyx pushed at the same time. It worked; three was just enough to push against the Theos.

We can do this! A few more good pushes and we will be out.

"Three is the lucky number, keep that up," Sabastian encouraged, face lighting up with hope.

This time, the wall came up behind Jordan. Kiara and Skylar helped as she kicked off, the group rising to the level of the cliff.

Almost there.

One more push from Nyx, Astris, and Titan, and they rose above ground level. Sabastian tensed in the centre, swinging Harvey at the edge with one hand. Harvey tumbled to the ground, immediately throwing the rope to Sabastian.

Pulling hard, Nyx sensed the moment she left the wind trap. Her body fell to the ground, and she choked on a relieved sob, focusing her eyes on a glowing mushroom as the world continued to sway around her. The Unity Rune that appeared seemed to spin as well.

Sabastian threw up, Skylar moving to hold back the male's hair. Sabastian, to Nyx's surprise, let the male help. It was weird to look at Astris now, after all that happened in the chasm.

Astris was back to her stone mask, taking the leather offered by Kiara. She pulled her tight curls back in a loose ponytail. Nyx was elated, touching her lip where she had bitten it. She had shifted, and it wasn't… bad. It felt right, like putting on an old and time-worn tunic.

I actually did it.

The group got ready to leave the chamber. Harvey put his hand on Astris's shoulder, giving her a nod. Nyx stared at Astris, sighing. It was hard to forget what Astris felt like when she touched her. She wished she were unshifted when Astris was clinging to her back.

She wished Astris were closer.

Closer to kill her maybe.

Being in her wolf form was like looking through a lens. The body both belonged to her, and did not, simultaneously. She was disembodied in her wolf form, her senses both stronger and weaker.

I could talk to Skylar or Jordan. How would I even do that, though?

Astris bumped into her as she filed out of the cavern in front of her, whispering in her ear.

"No dying on my watch, an-gel," Astris said the new pet-name slowly, enjoying each syllable before turning and walking away to join Kiara.

My Gods, I didn't imagine that. What has happened to Astris Archer?

CHAPTER 13: HARVEY

Drowning

I took your advice and tightened up my stance with the longsword. Thank you for the custom sword you sent. Void Metal is precious even if it no longer works. I will make you proud. I have not forgotten the guidance you gave at the try-outs. I will strive to be a better leader. One that our family can be proud of.

-Harvey letter to King Blackthorn, 30th Day, 76 AT

Harvey walked at the front of the group again, Jordan taking a turn at the back. Their separation meant Harvey was left to stew in his thoughts.

Maybe I can trust Astris to handle Nyx.

After such a harrowing challenge, the group was broken up into Champion-Protector pairs again, with the exception of Harvey and Jordan.

The Protectors must be feeling a lot of pressure right now, especially Astris. Nyx gets into trouble even when she's trying not to.

Nyx gave him a look when he asked her about what happened. He couldn't believe she got out relatively unscathed. Just as he couldn't begin to fathom that Astris let go of the group. She handed him a wriggling fox, then propelled off of him in the direction of Nyx.

He still had a foot-sized bruise on his stomach from her kick. The only thing that had kept him from following was his position holding the entire group together.

Should I have chosen her over the lives of the group? I could have shifted the others to Sabastian. I should have...

Astris had a plan, right?

She had to.

She would never jump without a plan, without having a solid chance of success.

That just wasn't Astris.

Neither was kicking me in the stomach.

He was the crown prince. She was usually hyperaware of that fact. Even as children, she avoided being aggressive with him on the playing field.

He made a note to ask the two of them about what occurred in the chasm. He touched his stomach again and laughed; a bruise for his sister's life.

Done. A thousand times, done.

Jordan flew up, doing the hourly check-in she insisted upon making. As she dropped down, flashing out of her shift, she looked him up and down. Harvey sighed, "Look, Sabastian's leg and my hand are almost healed. With the navigators good to go, and Nyx and Astris happy to scout... just stay up here."

"Mmm, you miss me," she said, circling him as they walked.

"I miss my flesh shield for the next obstacle we face," Harvey grunted, eyes lingering on her dimple as she smirked at him.

"Flesh shield, I like that," she paused, hand on her chin as if thinking, "I expect to be rubbed down with oil every night."

"Can you go even an hour without saying something vulgar?" Harvey questioned annoyedly.

"Let's see…. no," she chirped. "I enjoy making you squirm too much to stop."

"I would say I can't believe you have energy after that last challenge, but you were tucked in my shirt for half of it."

"I enjoyed every moment of it."

"Don't get used to it," he murmured, face heating.

It was getting easier to talk to her. Somehow, through all the danger and pain, they grew comfortable with one another. Or at least as comfortable as Harvey was with anyone.

Too much unpredictability in others.

With her, though, he was just starting to understand.

She deflects with sex and is trying to use it to get in my head… and trousers.

He was unclear on whether she actually was attracted to him, or just enjoyed how he reacted. Knowing this fact did nothing to help him.

The group came to their next obstacle. What looked like a wall of Water stood in their way. Looking closer, Harvey realised the entire tunnel was filled with Water. Visibility was a bit murky, but Harvey didn't see any monsters. The ground before the Water had another Rune on it, a droplet: The Water trial.

Honestly, this might be a good thing; everyone is starting to smell a bit.

A concoction of blood, sweat, tears, and mushrooms surrounded the group.

"Sabastian and Skylar," Harvey called while inspecting the wall.

It was as if there was glass holding the Water in, but when he touched it, his hand went straight into the Water without resistance. Harvey marvelled at the Theos holding the Water back. The liquid was cold against his skin, and he watched as rays of light came from the top of the Water.

Looking up, glowing mushrooms hung from the ceiling. The whole scene was awe-inspiring, and Harvey burned the sight into his mind. The rays of light highlighted the edges of coral across the bottom; the bright colours muted in the Water that darkened towards the bottom. A jellyfish danced by his face, and Harvey reached out to touch it, the tiny creature floating just out of reach. Harvey turned back to Sabastian and Skylar.

"You two scout with the others this time. I have a bad feeling about this one. Too calm"

Sabastian looked like he wanted to say something, opening and closing his mouth like a fish. Harvey was about to ask when the male shook his head and dove in, taking away Harvey's chance. Skylar jumped in right after, tail flowing behind.

Harvey sat down by the wall, dipping his hands in it and washing himself. The others followed suit as they waited for Sabastian and Skylar.

Half a turn of an hourglass later, the four of them appeared in the Watery wall, bursting through the barrier onto the ground. Sabastian's long black hair stuck to his face, and he brushed the mess out of his eyes, coming to sit by Harvey.

"There are several sections of Water; each section gets slightly longer. We do not know how far it goes, but the first one is only about ten feet." Sabastian informed him, showing him the flat rock they had been using to map the Labyrinth.

"Sounds good," Harvey said before Jordan cut him off.

"Why don't you guys go ahead? We will hold back like before; gotta make sure you get back for the next decision." She was talking quickly, wringing her hands absentmindedly.

"Sure thing, bosses," Sabastian said, whistling to Skylar, who scoffed but followed.

Plural, that means that he is warming up to the Dyrfaldur. Everyone is. Even Kiara held Jordan's hand in the Air trial.

The two of them went through the wall. Harvey watched as they swam off, Skylar's fox tail waving behind him. The others followed, leaving Jordan and Harvey last.

"Alright, let's do this!" Harvey was eager at the thought of bathing.

Finally, it's time to scrub this dirt off; a bath will feel divine. It won't be as fun as that, but whatever. A bath is a bath, even if it might kill us.

Harvey dove in without a second thought, swimming a few feet before realising Jordan wasn't following. He began to swim back, but Jordan jumped in. He watched in utter astonishment as the female proceeded to drown, not even a partial swim.

Has she even seen someone swim before? How did I not know this?

Seeing a bubble come out of her mouth, Harvey got over his utter stupefaction. He dove lower, feet touching the ground of the tunnel. Harvey lunged, kicking off the floor and tackling her, torpedoing through the Water to the other side. They slammed on the ground, Harvey on top of Jordan. He immediately checked her vitals. Nothing.

Fuck.

Harvey pinched her nose, taking a deep breath before touching his lips to hers and blowing into her open mouth. In between each breath, Harvey shoved down on her chest hard. One second breath, one-second recovery breath.

One.

Breath.

Two.

Breath.

By the time he got to four, he began to panic, but on the sixth breath, she shot up. Her forehead slammed into Harvey's, and she immediately evacuated all the Water from her lungs directly next to him.

Harvey patted her back firmly until she coughed up the last of it. She slowly recovered her breathing, short hair sticking to her forehead, and golden eyes regaining focus. Those sunset eyes met his own, and his breath left him. After she had fully recovered, the pair realised their position and quickly stood. Harvey stabilised her as she wobbled a bit.

"So, when were you going to tell me you can't swim?" Harvey was furious, clamping his teeth shut, lips pursed in worry. Panic and mania overtook his thinking, drowning him.

"I thought it would be easy. I didn't want to be the only one who needed help." Jordan replied weakly. "I managed in the try-outs with Skylar's help."

"But you can't swim, and you just… drowned. You didn't even move your arms. You just dove, then… nothing." A manic laugh came from him, and he covered his mouth.

"Sorry," he bit his tongue, "I just" breath. "It was so bad, and you almost died, and I was,"

Harvey was hysterical now, emotion causing tears to prickle at the corners of his eyes, fogging his vision. His laughs were strained, the fear of losing her turning to incredulity and humour.

"I'm glad you find my almost death funny," she said, arms crossed, but a smile pulled at the corner of her mouth.

"Okay, so I won't have time to teach you, especially when we don't know what is ahead. I am a strong swimmer; if you ride on my back, it might work." He put a hand to his chin in thought, rubbing the stubble that was growing.

The memory of his father's words filled Harvey with shame, *'I suggest learning more about your team and getting to know their strengths.'*

"What would that entail?" she asked nervously, starting to shiver a bit. Harvey wished he had a jacket for her.

"Hold onto my shoulders. Lay between my wings as we start swimming." He said with a shit-eating grin, "Probably want to hold your breath this time too."

She smacked his arm playfully, and Harvey rubbed his elbow dramatically.

"Did you just strike the crown prince?" Harvey said coyly.

"Yes, yes, I did. Don't think I won't do it again." To his hands raised in supplication, she said, "Now squat down because, for a short prince, you are still an Aervel."

"Short prince," Harvey snorted, squatting down.

Am I really lowering myself for a Dyrfaldur?

He looked over his shoulder at her, meeting her gaze.

She is more than her species. They all are. Maybe the laws should be re-examined.

Harvey looked back at the wall of Water, a fish darting by his nose. Feeling hands clasped around his shoulders, he stood slowly. Her feet left the ground, and she clung to his back with her knees as well, shaking slightly.

He put his hand on her knee, looking back at her. "All you have to do is take a deep breath, then hold it until I tell you otherwise."

She nodded nervously, pulling closer to him. "I'm ready." she said.

"Okay, hold your breath on three. One. Two. Three."

She took a deep breath, and Harvey followed, filling his lungs deeply. With another glance back to make sure she was still there, he jumped into the Water, arms extended.

The Water was lukewarm and clear, unassuming in its normalcy. Fish swam around, and Jordan tensed. A fat fish with a glowing bulb on its head passed below them, maw closing around a smaller fish that had swam too close.

We are halfway through. She better not panic now. He thought anxiously.

She managed to hold it together, though, and they collapsed through the Theos barrier to the ground. Jordan rolled off his back, making sure to miss his wings, before lying on her back, breathing hard.

She looked over at him again and smacked him.

"Ow, what the?" he started, but she held up a single finger.

"You didn't tell me about the fucking monsters in there."

"Those were fish. Just the larger kind."

"Like the to-eat kind or the eating-you kind."

"The to-eat kind," he smiled.

"You just," she was sputtering now and hit his arm again.

"Ow," he laughed, pinning her to the ground.

He looked down at her, noticing how her eyes shimmered. Instead, they were like liquid gold. Not like Titan's cold Metal, no, these were inviting.

She is beautiful.

Realising what he was doing, his eyes widened, and he jumped up.

"I'm sorry. I don't know what came over me." Harvey pleaded. Guilt filled him as he thought of Titan.

She laughed, "You don't have to hide how I make you feel. None of your judgmental friends are here now."

He didn't bother to correct her, pursing his lips. Instead of replying, he held out his hand for her, squatting down.

"I wish it were that simple," he muttered, starting the countdown so she couldn't reply.

I don't know what this female is doing to me. I need to shut this down before it kills me. Sleeping with a Dyrfaldur as an Aervel is punishable by death.

With that thought, he took off into the Water. It was murky, the visibility worsening as he swam. Coral and other sea life grew on the bottom, an entire ecosystem fit into just one section of the tunnel. They went through two more sections of Water, each longer than the last.

Harvey estimated each section was doubling, the first ten feet, twenty feet, forty feet, and the next one should be eighty feet. The max Harvey had done back in training in one breath was three hundred feet. His father used Water exercises to increase his breathwork for battle. On top of that, visibility had been reduced to a few feet in front of them at a time.

I'll have to thank the old man later; his trainers were brutal but effective.

Two more sections, and they were at one hundred and sixty feet for the last section. Harvey and Jordan were starting to take longer breaks between each section. They hoarded each breath, wholly focused. Gasping every time, they slid through the barrier onto the cave ground, wet rock scraping like a whetstone. Jordan was pale from holding her breath. Despite being well-trained and fit, she didn't have any breath training. She was also, well…

Tiny.

The next tunnel of Water was massive. The tunnels were growing wider, the Water longer. Plants and fish thrived in these deeper caverns, unafraid of their presence. Jordan was clinging to him, talons out in mid-shift, starting to convulse in trembling spasms. Panic filled Harvey as he glanced at her palling face.

Still at least one hundred feet to go, fuck we are so screwed if this keeps getting worse. I have to hurry; no time to conserve my Air by swimming slower. I need to get her out. Now. She needs Air. Control, get control. Ground yourself, Harv.

Harvey started counting; with each stroke, he counted.

One, two, three, he counted like it was a prayer. His mouth opened involuntarily, sucking in Water and causing panic.

Everything else faded away: the burning in his lungs, the small grasp weakening on his shoulders. He altered the length of each stroke, pulling at the Water with all of his strength. The muscles in every part of his body activated as he shoved them the final couple of feet.

They fell out the other side, both retching. Water splashed over the rock, the sounds of spluttering and dry heaving filling Harvey's ears. He threw up again, the sound making his stomach turn more. Harvey, finally expelling the last drop of Water and mushrooms, looked up.

The rest of the group was spread throughout the cavern, covered in blood and soaking wet. Titan looked up at him, managing a tired salute. Kiara lay on his shoulder.

Titan looked weak, his perfect Metallic hair plastered to his head, mixed with blood. Harvey's heart clenched at the golden strands-stained red. His mind flashed to all of the times he wished he could run his fingers through that hair. The Metallic strands like liquid gold.

Throughout all of the life-and-death scenarios, it was becoming easier to ignore Titan and Kiara. It was easier to shove the images of them together away.

I was too tired to stay awake before. After I saw them fucking, I didn't process it.

Astris rose to her feet, coming over to give a report. She wobbled as she got up, Nyx steadying her.

That's a first.

Harvey looked over to Jordan; she was sitting up now, dazed but okay. His breathing calmed; *she is okay, everything is okay.*

"Report," he said as Astris walked up to him, standing at attention above him.

Water dripped off her, splashing Harvey in the face.

Something really fucked up happened since we saw everyone last.

"There is something in the next Water tunnel. It attacked us."

"Come again?" Harvey said, hoping he had heard her wrong.

Nyx walked over, holding one arm. "It is fast, unrealistically too fast. It overtook us in a second."

I shouldn't have let her get out of my sight.

"It's some kind of gatekeeper. We all went in at different times, but ended up getting stuck together and getting stopped by it. Sabastian had to go back in to get Kiara." Astris's face twitched, but no emotion broke through.

It's a shame Sabastian had to mess with the natural selection process in action.

CHAPTER 14: NYX

Breathless

It seems you have given up on classes. Just in time for the try-outs. Oops. Guess you should've trained.

-Nightmare note to Nyx, 52nd Day, 76 AT

Nyx cast the note into the Water angrily. The notes had thankfully stopped when she had entered the Labyrinth. This one had teleported with her, having been slipped in her pocket while she was asleep.

Nightmare was right, I should have trained. I am behind everyone; I can't keep up.

Astris was standing by Harvey, reporting to him.

She is the only noble I have ever met who puts duty over her own hide. Astris has a lot more… guts than I gave her credit for.

Nyx stumbled to her feet, walking over in time to hear her brother say, "Come again?"

"It is fast, unrealistically fast. It overtook us in a second." Astris fought the waver in her voice.

The image of the beast came unbidden to her mind, anxiety surfacing.

Just as I was…

Her thoughts digressed to how much her relationship with her brother had improved while in the Labyrinth. She bit her lip in frustration, brows drawing together.

"It's some sort of gatekeeper. We all went in at separate times, but ended up getting stuck together and being stopped by it. Sabastian had to go back in to get Kiara. It barely fits in the tunnel, it's so large. From what I can tell, it's serpentine." Astris relayed. She looked to Kiara, who raised an eyebrow at her.

Was that a flinch? What is going on between Astris and Kiara?

Nyx shook her head to clear it.

Her mind flashed to Astris, years younger, lying through her teeth, the panic and hopelessness she caused. Recently, Nyx was seeing a different Astris, both fragile and bold.

Astris stood in the dark, body quivering uncontrollably. Nyx had never seen her frightened, vulnerable, or undone. She looked as delicate as freshly formed Ice as she yelled at Nyx, voice cracking,

"Protectors have oath-binding Runes. You have the other half. Do that again, and I will make you regret it. You do not fucking control me."

Astris lashed out; a wounded animal, someone in agonising pain, who had been that way for a long while.

Then, in the wind chamber, away from the group. Astris held me. She was nurturing. She called me... Nyx choked at the memory, eyes darting to Astris, who was finishing up the report.

"The cavern runs about three hundred and twenty feet long, ten feet deep, and ten feet wide," Astris reported.

"Who can still fight?" Harvey asked the group.

Nyx spoke up this time, "Skylar isn't a good enough swimmer. He shouldn't fight with us. I vote we have him and Jordan make their way along the sidewall as we fight the thing."

"Agreed," Harvey said quickly with a half glance at Jordan. Then he glanced at Titan.

"Titan will ensure you three make it through while the rest of us fight." Harvey declared, ignoring his sister's protestations.

Titan interrupted, "Why do I have to work with the Dyrfaldur? Do I have to shuttle them across like some pack mule?"

"Because I said so." Harvey snapped, turning away from the golden-haired male. Titan went silent, face paling as he turned to stand next to Kiara. Harvey's eyes briefly flashed to a green-yellow mix: *jealousy and nausea.*

Poor Harv, Nyx thought.

Even after picking Titan time and time again, Titan would never choose him first. Not truly. He would have done so years ago if he had any interest.

Harvey nodded, "Okay, so we have Titan escorting Jordan and Skylar through the Water along the wall. Titan, check in with those two to figure out how you will get them across."

"Now I have to take orders from them?" Titan whined petulantly.

"This isn't a joke, Titan. We could all die, and this fit you are throwing will get everyone killed," Harvey snarled.

Titan looked at him, mouth open. Kiara grabbed Titan's hand, comforting him.

Real mature.

Nyx turned away from the spoiled noble to look at her brother.

I'm glad he's not nearly as snobby as the others. He's still got a stick up his ass, though.

"Everyone else over here, line up," Harvey commanded, motioning to the area in front of him.

Sabastian and Kiara came over, joining their huddle. Kiara stood next to Nyx, and Nyx flinched instinctively. Astris's fingers brush Nyx's in comfort.

Was her touch in my imagination?

"How are we supposed to beat something so fast? If we can't keep up with it, we can't hit it." Nyx spoke up, meeting her brother's eyes. "We have to go around it somehow."

"The trials are all meant to be passable. Even if it's a near impossible chance." Harvey replied.

"Every test can be passed; that does not mean we need to fight. We don't even have any weapons, only a stupid pocket knife," Nyx argued.

"Um, guys," Sabastian said tentatively.

Nyx and Harvey turned to him in sync, snapping, "What?"

"I noticed some wood on the bottom of the last tunnel of Water. Maybe that could be of some help." Sabastian rubbed the back of his head sheepishly.

"I didn't see anything," Nyx said, confused.

"Neither did I," Harvey confirmed.

A haughty laugh came from Kiara. They looked at her, and she rolled her eyes, "Do you really have to ask?"

Nyx turned to Sabastian, looking into his deep blue eyes. His long hair hung wet, framing his angular face.

Water. She realised. *His Element is Water.*

"He can see it because his Element is Water," Nyx said with confidence. The assertion felt right, a preternatural sign of her accuracy.

"We haven't finished the Labyrinth. There is no Theos. Otherwise, we could just…" Kiara wiggled her fingers in the Air.

"Or maybe it's only starting to wake up, coming out of its dormant state inside us," Astris said.

"Sabastian, can you go back and retrieve the wood?" Harvey asked.

"How much?" Sabastian asked.

"Two long shafts for each of us," Harvey said, in prince mode once again.

"We can sharpen them with the pocket knife," Nyx offered.

A spark of hope kindled in her gut as the possibility of a plan began to form.

"Hey, Harv," Nyx said, a wide smile plastered on her face. "Remember that battle game dad used to play with us? The tower?"

"Now's really not the time for reminiscing," Harvey said, patience strained.

"Harvey!" Nyx snapped, pointing a look at him

Think, you dolt.

"What?" He yelled back, annoyed. His eyes shifted from orange to blue as he understood.

There we go, brother, Nyx thought with a smile on her face.

"Anyone gonna fill us in?" Kiara said, checking her nails.

"Sabastian, get that wood," Harvey said, grinning at Nyx.

The king jumped into the Air, wings beating.

'Get me to touch the ground. I touch the ground once, and you can skip lessons for the entire week.'

Considering how many lessons the prince and princess had, they jumped at this opportunity.

The observatory was a large room at the top of a massive spiral staircase. It stood in the centre of the castle courtyard, unused and forgotten. The stairs themselves were tightly compact and meant for one Aervel at a time. The structure itself was entirely stone.

With Harvey at the top of the stairs and Nyx at the bottom, their father hovered in the middle. His feet were only a few feet off the ground, but previous attempts to drop down on him failed.

Everything failed.

Nyx was finding herself getting more and more frustrated, but Harvey assessed the situation. Assessed it and led them to victory.

Young Harvey and even younger Nyx bounced off the walls of the staircase, utilising every surface to increase their speed. Finally, using a pincer move, the royal siblings managed to tackle their father down the stairs. Their father more than made good on his word, giving them not only the week off but also bringing them sweets from a bakery in Bexley. They had a chef in the castle, but Hearth & Crumb was made with all of the unhealthy ingredients the castle chef would never deign to use.

Half an hour later, they each held two spears, everyone in a line in front of the barrier of Water. Skylar spent the time while everyone else recovered from their swim to hone the wood into spears. Spears with barbs.

Harvey looked at her and nodded before taking a deep breath and diving in on the left of the tunnel, swimming low and fast to the wall. A shadowy shape started moving towards him, scales scraping the ground. A flash of red eyes as it turned towards Harvey.

The monster clocked him instantly. Nyx's turn now; she penetrated the Water in the middle, diving straight ahead. The beast was up ahead, shooting straight for Harvey. Its green scales rippled in the unnatural light that lit the Labyrinth. It was as girthy as Sabastian was tall, and as long as the vast dining tables back at Veritas Hall. The monster had multiple layers of teeth that shone menacingly in the dark Water.

Nyx threw her first spear. The subtle vibrations in the Water from her body and her first spear driving the creature to change targets. The spear bounced off harmlessly, thrown from too far back and weakened by Water resistance.

Yeah, that's right, I'm the weak one. Come over this way.

Nyx splashed through the Water recklessly, using her extra movement to distort the liquid around her.

We need to pass the monster between us. Without getting eaten in the process.

Her lungs were already strained from the movement.

Sabastian, Titan, Skylar, and Jordan will be entering about now. I need to buy them time to get into position.

Nyx looked at the monster as it barrelled down toward her. It was massive. The closer she got, the more she realized that she may have made a terrible mistake.

The beast vibrated when it detected her, the Water around her undulating with its tail. A caudal lure to draw in its prey.

She swam forward, the monster speeding to meet her. As she swam, it opened its mouth wide. Wider than Nyx was tall. As if it planned on swallowing her whole.

Two seconds until it reached her.

She swam down and forward to meet it. The remaining staff in her hand was slimy with plant growth and hard to grip.

Just as it was close enough to touch, another spear hit it from the right side.

She let the monster get a bit close, Nyx thought, glaring at Astris. Astris winked at her, raising an eyebrow.

The spear skewered the monster directly in the eye, enraging it. The barbs Skylar whittled into the spear caught. Blue blood spilled into the Water, muddying it. Nyx's vision went dark, blood clouding the Water. Nyx swiped at the Water, the scene revealing with each swipe. The thrashing creature bit at the Water, the mouth snapping next to her wing. Nyx pulled back, but was hit by the tail.

Caught in a vortex, Nyx fought to swim to the bottom to get under the monster. Every time she made some progress, she was thrown to the side.

The tail hit her, and Nyx let out some of her precious Air with a gasp. Nyx pulled at the Water again; she was almost there.

Her feet hit the bottom, and she grabbed for her extra spear. It was missing, she looked back to see it had fallen when she had gotten hit.

New plan.

The spear she had thrown first was lodged under a rock in front of her. She swam towards the weapon.

The barbs held the spear deep in the mud, and she dug in as her feet started to slip on the ground. She hooked a foot under a big rock, teeth gritting at the strain. The monster noticed her, its remaining eye turning to her. The red surface shone in the dark Water, teeth flashing as it dove for her.

Come on Sabastian.

She looked up to see the male above the monster's head, back to the ceiling, as he looked down on the scene. His arms working to keep him pressed against the tunnel's ceiling.

The monster was almost on her now, and Nyx gritted her teeth, yanking hard.

The spear came loose, and Nyx flipped it around.

The monster slammed into her, skewering itself on the spear. The wriggling caused the spear to shake, the wood threatening to break.

Come on, come on, come on, Sabastian.

The monster thrashed again, the spear cracking in Nyx's hands. She held it together as best she could, spreading her hands. Her right hand was now inches from the monster's teeth.

Above her, Sabastian kicked off, shooting down towards the monster like a falling star. His hair streamed behind him, Watery eyes matching his surroundings. He proffered the spear ahead of him.

A crack, and Nyx's spear broke; the monster surged forward.

This is the end.

Sabastian's spear lanced into the top of the beast's head, powerful thighs clamping around its neck. The monster writhed, shooting upwards.

He is going to slam Sabastian into the ceiling Nyx realized.

Her spear pulled loose as the monster swam upwards, Sabastian riding its head.

Now!

She shot forward with the splintering spear, swimming under the beast. Rotating, she planted her bare feet firmly on the tunnel floor. Her foot crunched on a skull but she ignored it. Nyx kicked off the bottom, broken spear held forward.

Sabastian was at the ceiling now; his legs coiled under him as he fought the monster's attempt to smash him into the ceiling. With a look of determination, Sabastian's muscles strained. The monster jolted downwards, and Nyx speared the beast as she met it.

Its momentum caused her to rocket down, feet slamming against the tunnel floor. Her lungs burned. Nyx felt her legs tremble as she pushed against the monster. Sabastian was on top, his own spear holding the monster in place, skewered between him and Nyx.

Nyx's arm creaked with effort, and she used her body to compensate, bracing and pushing with her legs. The spear threatened to crack again, but she held it close to the monster.

Even if I can help kill this thing, it will be worth it. I can't let go. They are counting on me.

The scales brushed her hands, and she pushed harder, feeling the flesh give slightly.

The beast began turning, and Harvey shot from his place on the left, pushing off the wall. The third spear stuck in the beast, who was still stuck between the ceiling and floor by Nyx and Sabastian.

As it tried to turn, Astris hit it from the right. Finally, the beast tried to back up; Kiara stabbed from the back, holding it in place.

Nyx could feel her lungs start to burn.

We won't make it if we don't end this before running out of breath.

Trapped on all sides, spears stuck in its flesh, the monster continued to thrash. Nyx felt dizzy from lack of oxygen. She clamped her mouth shut to avoid taking in more Water. Still, she held on, gritting her teeth.

I will not break. I cannot break.

Shards of the wood stuck into her hands painfully, the beast pushing it in further. The pain in her hands mixed with the burning in her lungs. Nyx's vision started to go fuzzy at the corners, and she pushed to stay alert.

I will be everything they think I am incapable of.

Nyx pushed harder, teeth clamped hard against the Water, fighting to get in as she strained. Her wrist gave a jolt of pain, and she tensed at the shooting sensation.

She noted with alarm that the beast was dragging them to the middle of the section of Water.

So much for going back to take a breath; this is the worst place to be. On top of that, I think I just fractured my wrist.

The beast was flailing more slowly now. Every time it dragged them a little bit away from position, it rammed itself harder into another spear. Blood filled the Water, deepening them to zero visibility as the monster finished its death throes. Nyx couldn't see any of her companions, but she needed to move. She was almost out of Air.

I can't do this, I just. I didn't train for this, I skipped so many lessons, I am behind everyone.

Water threatened to choke her as she held her breath, biting against the unpleasant sensation. She caught her brother's eyes through the murky Water. He looked back at her, and fear laced his expression as he noticed she wasn't moving.

I have to move. I need to survive, even if it's for him.

Nyx dropped the spear and swam hard. She had used the majority of her Air in the fight. Every fibre of her being trembled with the burn of oxygen deprivation. Her wrist bit at her every time she took a stroke.

Five more feet.

Four more feet.

Nyx could see the shapes of her companions on the other side of the wall. She reached out desperate to grab onto something, someone.

Sabastian, who was directly ahead of her out of the Water, watched her stop and reached out his hand. With the last bit of energy she could muster, Nyx grasped onto his large hand.

Sabastian dragged her out of the Water, the two of them falling to the ground next to the others. Sweet Air filled her as she coughed against the burn, eyes itchy as they watered.

The light of a Unity Rune came from above, but Nyx didn't bother to look, instead closing her eyes. Slowly, Nyx's breathing came slower, the fresh Air tickling her insides as she sucked hungrily at it. After catching her breath, Nyx opened her eyes to see that everyone was there. They had done the impossible. The Unity Rune shone brightly in the Air to prove it.

She looked over to Harvey, who was lying on the ground a few feet from her. He smiled at her, pride filling his vision. Nyx smiled back, closing her eyes and enjoying the sensation of Air filling her lungs. The pain from her wrist was overshadowed by her success.

I did it.

Shackled

Don't think my presents stopping means my generosity is done. The Labyrinth will not save you. It will kill you as surely as I had planned to. Poetic justice for someone born out of unholy indiscretions. Your father was just barely able to maintain the throne after you were born. Hurting your family from birth. Typical.

**Unopened* Nightmare note to Nyx, 55th Day, 76 AT*

Nyx took an extra helping of the mushrooms, emboldened by her success in the Water trial. It was her idea that saved them. Sabastian moved next to Nyx, surprising her. "Can we talk?" he asked solemnly. Nyx looked around, momentarily confused. He never talked to her. He was also never this serious.

Cautiously, Nyx nodded and followed Sabastian around the corner. The male shifted from foot to foot, running a hand through his thick hair.

"I should probably start by apologising for how I have treated you. Being a bastard? It doesn't matter. The Gods chose you as surely as they chose me. I am sorry for how I acted and… talked about your friends." The male turned beet red, eyes darting away.

She liked this version of him, his soft features had hardened, and his goofy smile had been replaced with a thoughtful frown. She could see herself becoming friends with this version of Sabastian.

"Thank you," Nyx uttered, unable to come up with a more eloquent response. Heat came to her face, and she glanced at her scraped-up feet, then looked up to see that he was still shuffling uncomfortably. "What is it?"

Nyx waited while the male mustered up the courage to speak. Finally, he took a deep breath, "I don't want to get in the middle of things, I just can't not tell you. I was going to tell Harvey, but he has been so busy. It's still your family, so I thought you should... Ya know?"

"It's okay, whatever it is, you can tell me," Nyx encouraged.

Sabastian blew out a breath, a lock of his hair blowing with the exhale. Closing his eyes, he started again, "It's about Kiara and her father. I overheard her and Titan talking. They were talking about a plan to..."

"Everything alright in here?" Kiara stepped around the corner, grinning at them both. Nyx's stomach dropped.

"Nothing, just asking Nyx about her hair routine."

"She has different hair than you," Kiara pointed out, one eyebrow raised.

"Well, you said I shouldn't take advice from my Protector on my hair, only following instructions." Sabastian snapped as he pushed past her. Kiara smiled, holding a hand out to Nyx.

Nyx ignored the hand, pushing past the female as well.

The group spent the night by the last tunnel of Water, deciding to wait until the morning to venture further. When the artificial light rose in the tunnel gradually, Nyx groaned. Sighing, Nyx sat up and looked around.

Sabastian and Skylar had caught a few fish in the Water before she woke, both favouring the morning over the night. She overheard them whispering about a shop in Bexley that sold custom bone combs.

Males, Nyx thought with amusement.

By the time they started moving, the light entirely filled the tunnel. Skylar and Sabastian stood, bickering over the map's orientation. Astris and Nyx let them take the lead, not wanting to deal with their disagreement directly.

Nyx took the time to wrap her feet. The wraps cut into the wounds, but would help prevent more. It was difficult to do with her wrist screaming at her with every movement.

"I am the Aervel, the Champion! The Gods meant for me to decide." Sabastian argued.

"And I am your Pro-tec-tor." Skylar enunciated slowly, "That means I make sure you don't do anything stupid." Skylar put himself face-to-face with the other male, teeth flashing. He looked skinny next to the bulky Aervel.

Nyx laughed, ignoring them as she adjusted her makeshift foot wraps.

Finally, Sabastian overruled Skylar, deciding to take the tunnel to the right.

I would trust it more if Skylar had chosen, but it's not my job to lead.

Nyx walked to join the group at the crossroads.

The tunnel got slightly dimmer as they walked, goosebumps covering her skin.

That can't be a good sign. I should...

Just as Nyx was about to speak up, a cold heavy sensation circled her wrist. Looking down, Nyx watched a handcuff materialising on her right wrist. A blur, and she was yanked violently to the left, watching her world move unbidden around her. Nyx collided with Astris, falling in a tangle of limbs and wings.

"What the actual…" Astris started, rounding on her.

Nyx held up their joined wrists solemnly, hissing at the pain.

"Not me," Nyx insisted.

"Minotaur's balls," Astris swore.

"Yeah," Nyx agreed, holding up the magical cuffs.

Around them, the other Champion and Protector pairs were shackled together, those not next to each other had teleported instantaneously to their partner.

Nyx turned around, pulling Astris with her mangled wrist. "We need to get out before this gets worse. We could use a rock to get them off?"

"They are imbued with Theos, there's no way a rock will work," Astris replied.

A wall slid down from the ceiling, trapping them from going back; a large glowing Rune in the centre: *Electricity*. Nyx had a feeling they would not like what was going to happen next.

The room's floor was comprised of large white tiles, and in the middle, a series of rods criss-crossed across the width of the room, blocking the way forward. Skeletons lay around the room all in pairs. Anxiety roiled in her gut, Nyx forcing her eyes away from the bodies.

I have a bad feeling about this.

Nyx estimated that the section blocked off by rods was at least fifteen feet in length. She looked up to the ceiling to see it was lit up with Elemental Runes from end to end in an intricate web.

At their feet, more Runes and Elemental Lines spread across the floor. These had been used before the disappearance of Theos to imbue objects with power. They gave intention, while the Elemental Runes served as a symbol of the God and the Element associated with it. The Rune for Electricity shone above the others. Astris stepped forward, jerking Nyx towards the Runes on the floor. Nyx growled, her wrist twinging.

"Wait, let's think about this first!" Nyx yelled, fighting her.

"I can read these," Astris said, tugging on her and ignoring her protests.

"She was in Advanced History; her father is a historian who works with Titan's mother. Back off." Harvey ordered, and Nyx reluctantly conceded the point.

Nyx let Astris pull her forward, squatting down next to her. Their wings brushed, and Astris glared at her before going back to her task.

Jeez.

"It says unlock here, and then *this* is the symbol for 'self.'" Astris's hand traced the glyphs as she spoke. "This symbol I don't recognise, but it says it will unlock the bands. My interpretation of this would be that we need to touch the shackles to the symbol on that far wall there." Astris pointed ahead past a series of Metal rods and pillars blocking the way.

The group gathered around, Skylar grabbing Sabastian roughly and pulling him over. The male has been in a bad mood since last night.

What could Kiara and Titan be planning that would have the male this worked up?

Enough to make him scared of her.

"Only one way to go," Titan said, pulling Kiara towards the rods.

This dynamic couldn't possibly end well. The idiot is leading the monster. Or was the monster leading the idiot?

Suddenly, the tile under Titan and Kiara dropped straight down. They fell into one another, unprepared. Water began filling the hole, covering them to their mid calves. Goosebumps covered Nyx's arm: *Water, and Electricity.*

"Yuck, now we are wet again," Titan said, lifting his feet and shaking them before jumping back out of the Water. Kiara joined him on the tile behind the hole. The group all held their breath. Nothing happened.

"We should continue," Harvey said, cautiously making his way forward, chained to Jordan.

It looked funny, the tiny Dyrfaldur female on his arm. Every step almost lifted the female clean off the floor with the short chain. Nyx and Astris had an advantage, both Aervel, allowing for less of a height difference.

Well, technically only half…

I am a special kind of bastard. I can't forget that, forget what I am. But maybe… maybe I can become something more by finishing the Labyrinth.

Within moments, the party was soaked through. Some of the tiles triggered Water to fall from the ceiling, and others dropped to various depths into pools of Water. Nyx's hair dripped onto her wet wings, and she flapped them to try to get some of the moisture out.

Why Water? We just did a Water challenge, so what's the catch?

Astris halted abruptly. Nyx, who was watching her feet, looked up. The tangle of bars had enough gaps for them to slip through in some locations.

This is labelled as an Electricity obstacle, and I don't see a single spark of it.

A wall slid into place, the rock closing the exit behind them. Harvey caught her gaze, his eyes orange with anxiety.

As they stepped onto the final tile before the rods, a crackle went through the room. A blue flash, and sparks of Electricity pulsed down each of the bars.

There's the Electricity.

Nyx watched as the row in front of her lit up. In quick succession, different sections of rods lit up with blue Electricity, crackling violently. Astris stood, stock still, watching the wild sparks.

Is she scared? No, she looks focused. What, is she going to make the Electricity stop with pure willpower?

It seemed to be pulsing in a pattern, but Nyx couldn't follow it.

They would have better luck breaking down the wall behind them. Nyx looked back at the wall blocking their way out.

No, the Gods wouldn't let us skip a trial.

Astris pulled her closer to the collection of rods, Nyx digging her heels in. She was forced for follow, wrist weak from the fracture.

"Oh yeah, get near the Electricity while wet; great idea. Now fucking stop before you get us killed!" Nyx yelped, fighting her.

Astris shushed her before turning to her, a small smile gracing her lips. It was a look Nyx had never seen before, and she knew she would not enjoy the consequences.

"That is the catch, we will need to go between the top and bottom rods. We will also have to be aware of two patterns and use a combination of flying and acrobatics to get through them." Astris explained.

Harvey jumped in, adding, "we will need to count exactly. The gaps are small, and the pattern moves quickly."

Astris nodded at him. "We will have to move fast."

"The top and bottom patterns are the same, just reversed." Nyx added, "We need to track both patterns."

Astris breathed out a sigh. "It's pointless to keep talking. Time to go," Astris stated gruffly, bending her legs, readying to jump to the first rod.

Nyx copied Astris, watching for her signal.

Fighting her will kill us both.

The pair moved in tandem, wings beating hard. Their wings clashed as they flew, forcing them to veer apart. The shackles pulled them back together with a sharp yank, and they were diving again to avoid the rod above them as it lit up. Nyx grunted at the flash of hot pain that radiated up her arm, gritting her teeth. Their hands hit the next rod, and they hung on, legs dangling.

"Wings tucked," Nyx said as they swung under the first rod.

"Agreed," Astris replied, focusing on the rods. They both tucked their wings, using only their arms and legs to move.

"Now!" Astris exclaimed, and they both swung to the next row of poles, clamping onto the ones above them before dropping down to stand on another cluster. The rods above them electrified, Nyx's eyes matching the pulse.

"Feet," Nyx yelped, and the two of them jumped to avoid the surge. Nyx's foot wrap caught the Electricity, the combination of the Water and fabric caused the wrap to catch Fire.

Nyx kicked her feet desperately, and Astris batted the fabric away with her wing.

Astris chanced a look behind them.

Behind them, the others followed, staying close and following their movements. Harvey and Jordan made up the back of the line, and

Kiara and Titan were in-between. As Nyx looked back, Titan and Kiara dove through a gap, arms stretched forward. Nyx focused back on the task at hand.

"Bottom row, one forward," Astris said, shorthand as they were taught in small unit tactics.

The pair skipped over one of the rods, Electricity zapping under their feet. A droplet of Water fell off of Nyx onto the rod as she jumped, sizzling and cracking. Nyx's heart was beating in time to the zaps now, body reacting to the Electricity. The bars were slippery under her; Nyx adjusted her feet before their next move.

Astris and Nyx were perfectly in sync as they dropped onto a lower bar on the other side. Immediately after, Astris jumped up to the bar ten feet above them. Nyx reacted instantly, her reflexes heightened with adrenaline. She followed without question, hands hitting the bar with a slap. The bar under them lit up, and Nyx held her breath, her fingers slippery on the wet Metal. Her wrist demanded her attention, but Nyx forced it out of her mind.

"Down," Nyx instructed, Astris following swiftly. Her fingers slipped slightly, and she fell awkwardly, her ankle twisting. Nyx gritted against the pain, ignoring Astris's worried gaze. They had come up on the next big section of bars.

Nyx looked, but there were no gaps big enough for them. They would have to use the small gap under the bottom rod, crawling on elbows and knees to slip through the tight space. A tile was under the rods, meaning they would be underwater as well.

Nyx and Astris got on their stomachs, Nyx's left black wing on top of Astris's right white wing. The pair crawled arm over arm, skin scraping on the ground. The rods electrified, and Nyx pushed Astris down with her wing, dropping to her stomach as well.

The tile started to fill, and the pair struggled across the short expanse.

The Electricity snapped at them menacingly as the Water rose around them. Nyx ducked under the next rod, chin dipping under the Water. One more tile to go, then they would be able to stand.

As they got on the next tile, it dipped lower than the last, Water rapidly filling the hole. Nyx took a sharp deep breath, going under the cold Water with Astris. The Electricity lit up the Water in a blue-white glow, shifting in a disorienting pattern.

Astris's wing got too close to the rod above them, and it zapped. Nyx pulled Astris further down. The female hadn't managed to get a breath in before she had gone under. She was choking, body shaking. Nyx held her down, panic filling her.

Just a few more seconds, then she could let them up.

Astris's eyes met hers underwater, and Nyx reached forward, grabbing Astris by the chin. The female was pale, the whites of her eyes showing in fear. Nyx leaned forward, careful to keep her wings pressing down on them, and pressed her mouth to Astris, giving her some of her Air.

The female's eyes went wide, but she nodded in thanks. Finally, the Electric flow stopped, allowing them to crawl to the next gap.

"Almost there," Nyx coaxed.

Astris bent her legs, and Nyx copied, the pair grabbing onto the next bar.

Astris lost her grip and started to fall. Nyx used the shackle to pull her up, screaming in pain. Her wrist almost gave out, joints creaking in protest.

Gods, my wrist. I need to keep pushing. I stop, and it's not just me who gets fried. I can do this. Dig deep, Nyx.

Astris grabbed onto the bar, fingers slipping as she gripped. Once Astris had regained her grip, the pair swung forward. Nyx let her feet go first, snapping her knees up and bending slightly back. Her hands hit the bar, and she threaded her legs through her two hands. Nyx could feel the Electricity barely brush her skin as she went through. Astris grunted in pain as her chin met the same fate.

Even getting near the Electrified bars hurts.

Nyx's legs kicked through her spread arms; letting go of the bar she held, and bending her back in a painful arch to avoid another rod. The shackles went taut briefly.

We need to stay in sync.

Five more moves and they would be through.

Methodically, Nyx and Astris operated their way through the tangle of Electricity, sensitive to every body part. Astris led them through, timing their jumps to the pattern. Nyx didn't dare look ahead to see how far they had to go, instead focusing on only their next move. She had risked enough by looking back earlier. It surprised Nyx when they finally dropped down onto the rock at the end of the web by the unlocking Rune. Quickly, the pair moved out of the way for the other pairs coming through.

Kiara and Titan came next, Kiara pushing Titan's golden head down before he could get electrified.

She is the reason that pair is succeeding.

Two more leaps, and the second pair joined them. The groups that had finished watched with bated breath as the final two pairs continued through the obstacle.

Sabastian dragged Skylar towards the end, impatient. It would have been funny in any other circumstance. The larger Aervel male dragged the slender Dyrfaldur male along by his wrist. It was only made possible by Sabastian's enormous muscle mass.

"Slow down," Skylar begged, fighting the male's careless movements. Two more rods to go.

Sabastian jumped to the next rod, Skylar's eyes going wide, "It's about to light up, move!"

"Shut up Dyrfal—" the rod lit up with Electricity, Sabastian's retort turning into a scream. Skylar cried out in pain, his wrist charring from the cuff.

The sound was loud and jarring, primal to its core.

Sabastian's body was stiff, eyes starting to glow as the Electrical charge surged through him.

The whites of his eyes shone in the crackling flashes, his limbs jerking. The smell of burning flesh filled the room as his skin blistered, charring from the inside out.

No.

Nyx jumped forward, as if she could stop it.

The male's hands curled into unnatural balls, blood pouring from his eyes. The crimson tears stark against his pale skin as he turned his eyes to her. Nyx held his gaze in horror, barely able to breathe. She could feel her pulse pumping through her limbs, her throat constricting in a scream.

Am I screaming?

Nyx couldn't tell. All she knew was that his eyes and his hair flowing around him were infused with Electrical threads. Sabastian's scream turned to a strangled gurgle, and he crumpled forward onto the rod as it went dark. Skylar was pulled onto the next rod as Sabastian's body fell.

Silence filled the space as the shock of what had happened flooded everyone. Nyx observed as the cuff hooking Sabastian to Skylar disintegrated. The large Aervel male, unmoving.

His body was bent over the bar, long hair smoking as it brushed the ground. Harvey roared behind Sabastian, and Nyx's world disappeared around her. The breath she had been holding came out in a choked whimper.

Past images of the male flashed behind her eyes as her mind raced to grasp reality.

Sabastian's smile as he threw a knife behind his back at the apple on her head. Sabastian, as he wrapped his hair up into a bun, telling a raucous story, eyes alight.

His face, full of life, vanished from her memory; replaced by the one she just witnessed as he died. All she could see was the bloodied tears. All she could hear was the gurgle as he choked on his own blood. All she could smell was the burnt flesh, sickeningly sweet as it seasoned the Air. Skylar jumped forward to check the male's vitals, leaning over precariously to check his pulse. Shaking his head, he straddled Sabastian. Skylar's red hair dangled down as he pumped at the Aervel's chest.

Sabastian's dead. Skylar is in shock, but he needs to move. The rod will light up again. It isn't in him to give up on a patient.

Two more seconds, he needs to go now!

"Move, Skylar," Nyx screamed. The male was in shock, unmoving.

One second.

"Please," she yelled, terror lacing her words.

Skylar looked to her, face twisting in agony. He grabbed the half-heart bracelet off Sabastian, before throwing himself to the next rod. He glanced at Sabastian's body one last time before working the rest of the way through the rods, moving freely without being cuffed.

Harvey and Jordan came through last. They had to jump over Sabastian's body to finish. They landed on the rocky ground hard, stumbling briefly. Harvey turned to the side, vomiting violently. Tears wracked his body as he screamed in frustration, slapping the wall with the hand unattached to Jordan. His hand cracked against the rock, debris shaking loose where his palm connected.

Nyx quickly tapped her wrist to the unlock Rune, which was a circle with two parallel lines intersecting it. The cuff dissolved instantly, but Nyx didn't watch. Instead, she ran to her brother, pulling him into an embrace. The pair cried, Jordan standing quietly next to the siblings, allowing them their moment. They stayed like that for a while, until Harvey's sobs subsided.

Harvey let go of his sister, leading Jordan gently to the unlock the Rune. Tapping it, he patted Skylar on the back gently. "You made the right decision. He was dead the moment the rod lit up."

Raising his voice, Harvey addressed the group, "We can't stop here. We can grieve later. Let's get out of this hellish place first."

Kiara and Titan undid their shackles, the final pair to do so. As soon as they dissolved, the wall closing them in the tunnel opened up behind them. They would have to go through the Electricity again, this time without shackles. Nyx didn't know if she could go on. It was her Element that had done this. The one flashing in her eyes. Guilt bit into her, making her tremble.

CHAPTER 16: HARVEY

Goodbye

I acquired the cow for the "mission". I will meet you with Titan at the back entrance. We will all have to ride the same one... the brutes are faster than I expected. I suddenly understand why the Minotaur have been such a problem at our borders. We go to school tomorrow, tonight is our last night for this.

-Sabastian note to Harvey 18th Day, 76 AT

Harvey waited at the end of the cavern by the now-open door with Jordan. His body was heavy, his bones buzzing. Tears ran down his face, but he brushed them back. *I should have paid more attention and taken charge more. Something. Anything.* He had been passive, trusting. Now Sabastian was dead.

Nyx and Astris would go first through the Metal bars. Harvey looked up to the ceiling, tears pouring as he begged the Gods to protect his sister. This obstacle had already killed one of them.

"Astris," Harvey started, catching her eye. She looked to Nyx and nodded slightly. Nyx raised an eyebrow, but he kept his face serious, "focus. This isn't a game."

She didn't fight him, eyes red from crying. The pair then turned and took off through the obstacle.

His sister bobbed under a rod above her head, dipping down beyond his vision. Harvey clenched and unclenched his hands as he watched with bated breath. He coughed, throat tightening and eyes unblinking.

Astris and Nyx leaped into the Air onto the next rod, two more to go. Relief pushed at the edges of his subconscious, but he pushed it back.

This isn't over.

Astris counted, fingers twitching as she and Nyx waited. A three-second gap, then the upper rods would light up, and the bottom rods would be safe.

A flash, and the rod went out.

Too early! The rhythm has changed, and they haven't noticed.

Harvey observed, frozen, the panic in him spiking. They stepped onto the bars early, ducking under the upper rods.

"The rhythm changed!" Harvey cried out, panicked.

Too late.

Not Nyx, not her, please Marvos, Axios,

anyone.

As the second zap came, Nyx realised a second before Astris. He watched in horror as she pushed Astris off the bar, hitting the rod with her abdomen. The Electricity filled his sister's body, blue brilliance running through her veins. Her back arched at an unnatural bow, the smell of burned flesh invading Harvey's nostrils. Her hair rising into the Air as Sabastian's had.

"No!" Harvey and Astris screamed at the same time.

Astris's scream combined with Harvey's. The sound was one of pure agony and fear. Tears blurred his eyes, and Harvey's tooth chipped as he slammed his teeth together, swallowing his next tormented cry.

Titan and Kiara watched from the other end of the cavern, the last to go.

Hold it together, hold it together, hold it together, hold it...

Harvey choked on a sob, lunging towards the rods, blind to the danger. Jordan tried to stop him, but he overpowered her easily. Heedless of the pattern, unaware of anything that wasn't his sister. Harvey moved on pure instinct, acrobatically throwing himself through the obstacles at a rapid velocity.

His sister, who was still caught in the current, had her head thrown back, the whites of her eyes visible. The strike finished, and Nyx's body went limp on the rod, Astris grabbed her by the waist, pulling her off the rod. Tears poured down Astris's face. Harvey ignoring the final rods, diving between them and hitting the rock hard, cracking the ground. A small crater punched into the floor below him. Ignoring the sting from the landing, he dashed to his sister.

His sister, who was...

Fine...

Clothes burnt... but fine.

She had a burn line across her stomach, but other than that, the Electricity hadn't hurt her. Smoke rose from her clothes, and Harvey patted a flame out softly.

He then touched Nyx's neck, checking her pulse. It was fine. Nothing, aside from the burn, had happened. His mouth opened in astonishment as Nyx sat up. Astris let out a pained cry; her eyes checking every inch of Nyx for damage. Electricity zapped around him, but Harvey ignored it, looking at his sister.

"What?" Nyx asked.

"You're... you're alive," Harvey stammered.

"I don't know how."

Astris pulled Nyx to her feet, "Electricity is your Element. Similar to…"

Astris trailed off at the memory of Sabastian. Kiara and Titan dropped down next to the rest of the group from the entrance, likely having heard the commotion. Titan put his hand on Harvey's shoulder. Harvey flinched away, stepping closer to Jordan.

Jordan joined them at his sister's side, bumping his shoulder before checking on Nyx. She lightly traced under the burn mark across Nyx's stomach.

"Did it not shock her?" Jordan asked, confused.

"I'm okay, guys." Nyx's eyebrows came together as a hurricane of emotions flashed in her eyes.

"No, you are not," Harvey insisted, inspecting her over and over.

"Actually," Skylar said, joining as well. He still looked pale from losing Sabastian. Checking Nyx's vitals, he looked to Harvey, "Actually, I think she might be."

"Amateurs," Kiara scoffed.

Kiara went to inspect Nyx, who glared at her, guarding her stomach subconsciously. Kiara smirked, noticing the move. Astris turned away, swiping at her face.

"Have some information to add?" Harvey challenged; he was the prince, and she couldn't touch him.

I am so close to not giving a damn about her status. So close to punching her in her ridiculous, green face.

Kiara lifted her chin in a condescending manner, "Didn't you study the Elements? What they can do with Theos?" Kiara tilted her head predatorily.

Kiara continued speaking as if she were talking to children, "She got hit by an unnatural amount. Actual Electricity is likely less powerful, considering how far her back arched and how quickly Sabastian perished. With Nyx's full powers, she could likely sit on the bar without consequences. We are Aervel. Unlike…" Kiara implied, looking to the Dyrfaldur in the group. Shaking her head in disgust she continued, "The first rule of the Elements is that Aervel cannot be hurt by their Element. With my full powers I could jump into a pond of poison and be unaffected."

The group stayed silent, taking in the new information, Skylar clenched his fists at his side. Harvey smiled at Kiara coldly, "If you want to be my general, you will treat your team with respect. We have already seen what happens when we don't work together." Harvey turned his back on Kiara in a show of power.

Try it, I fucking dare you, bitch. My sister, my family, my reputation. Mess with one of us, and we will destroy you.

"I think she is right. I have heard tales of Fire Element Aervel being immune to burns." Jordan assuaged, cutting the tension.

"She is a monster, but a smart one." Nyx snarled, not bothering to keep her voice low.

Harvey had to give it to Kiara, though. She knew a lot about Theos.

I just have to work with her until we are done. If we ever cease this dance with death that is. I didn't think we would make it this far.

The hope was almost too sweet to indulge in. He looked at Jordan, who was looking at him with worry. He realised with a pang of fear that he would miss her; if they made it out of this, he would miss her.

She has become a part of me.

The group carefully finished the obstacle, walking through the open door back to the main tunnel. A Unity Rune hung above the now smaller group.

The path had changed slightly while they were inside; a new pathway opened for them to explore. They ignored the fork in the tunnel, following the newly opened path. Harvey caught Skylar looking down at the map he had made with Sabastian.

He must feel guilty for surviving, Nyx as well.

The group moved in silence, still in shock from Sabastian's death. The new tunnel they went down looked much like the last, but it had denser vegetation on the walls. Skylar and Kiara stopped regularly to collect plants.

Harvey stopped the group in the tunnel, grabbing some mushrooms and flowers. Without a word, he organised the flowers, bringing over the biggest, flattest rock he could find. It was about the size of his forearm, perfect for what he needed it for. Catching on to what he was doing, Skylar crouched down and scratched Sabastian's name into the stone.

Under his name, he put the symbol for Water. It was a far cry from the memorial ceremonies held in Dengar, but they did their best to honour the memory of Sabastian. Even Kiara collected some flowers, surrounding the rock with a variety of colours. Skylar set down the small bracelet that had been on Sabastain's wrist, the half heart charm clinking softly against the stone.

Whoever held the other half…

Harvey grabbed the wall to steady himself. Nyx put her hand on Harvey's shoulder in consolation; he had been closer to Sabastian than she had.

Harvey looked at the stone with the name of his friend, swallowing hard to avoid breaking into sobs again.

"Daelan, God of Water, accept this male into your realm," Harvey whispered.

"Vale et Vale," the others responded in unison. Farewell and goodbye.

A phantom breeze blew through the tunnel, smelling like the sea.

The Gods had accepted him.

"Does anyone have any words or stories they want to share?" Harvey asked the group.

Titan stepped forward, and Harvey's nose flared, but he stayed silent.

"The day before school, Sabastian pulled off the biggest prank of his long career of debauchery."

Harvey laughed, closing his eyes as another tear slipped out.

It was the night before his first day of college. Harvey crept down the corridor towards the back entrance to the castle. Most of the castle had gone to bed for the night. His job in this mission would be to open the back door for the others.

He approached the door to find two Aervel guarding the door: Blake and Caitlin. Harvey pulled the bottle of wine out of his tunic, holding it out to the guards. Caitlin lowered her brows at the offer, "And what is this bribe for, huh?" Her wrinkled face twisted in amusement.

"A bribe for us to leave the back door open." Blake guessed, raising their brows at Harvey.

Harvey shrugged sheepishly, rubbing the back of his head. "If I said it wasn't, would you believe me?"

"No," Caitlin supplied, unamused, the beads in her locks clanking.

"Come on, Cait, it's his last night in the castle. Our young prince is going to college tomorrow. Let's take our break early."

The older female snorted at them, "You will be taking the blame if this blows back in our faces."

Blake turned to Harvey with a mischievous smile, offering an arm to Caitlin. The female took it with a huff, following the younger Aervel down the side corridor. Blake snagged the expensive bottle of wine on their way past him, "trouble tax."

Harvey chuckled, pulling the door open for Titan and Sabastian. Sabastian had his hair up in a bun and was holding onto a cow's halter. Titan was sitting on the animal, a bottle of wine in his hand.

"Ready?" Sabastian asked, handing him a flute.

Harvey sighed. This was not what his father had intended when he ordered Harvey to take lessons. Sabastian looped the strap of a small drum over his shoulder. He jumped up on the cow behind Titan. The beast shifted, uncomfortable with their weight.

"This won't work," Sabastian complained, hand around his chin. His eyes lit up, and Harvey bit his lip, ready for the chaos about to follow. He knew that look. "To the stables!"

When the group had reached the stables, cow in hand, Sabastian walked over to the pen holding the fine stallions and dragons that Harvey's father bred. He stopped, looking first to the beautiful dragons, which were behind thick Metal instead of wood. He reached out to one of the dragons, a deep ruby red with a spiked head. The beast snapped at him, and Sabastian pulled his hand back.

"No chance you will tell me their whistle?" Sabastian asked, referring to the whistle that would turn the beasts docile for riding.

"You wish, not even Nyx knows it," Harvey raised an eyebrow at the male who sighed, turning to the stallions. Sabastian selected two, passing one lead rope to Harvey.

"I get the cow," Sabastian said, dragging Titan off and handing him the horse's lead.

"Let's do this."

"We were so loud we woke up the castle. The king came out in," Titan was laughing and crying now, "he was in his sleep clothes. I have never seen a king so… dishevelled. Then…" Titan gulped, trying to get his emotions under control.

Harvey finished the story for him, "Sabastian walked to my father, the king of Dengar, and offered him the cow and a bottle of wine. Against all odds, Father joined us. Sabastian had convinced the king of Dengar to ride a cow around his own castle while playing tavern songs with us."

The group sat in their thoughts, the smell of Theos thick in the Air by the grave marker.

After Harvey's muscles had stiffened, and his throat had grown dry from crying, he took a deep breath and started moving again. The rest of the group followed him, stuck in thoughts of their lost friend.

A couple of hours later, the tunnel widened. White sand covered the rock, their feet sinking deep until it was up to their calves. The stretch of sand covered their path as far as Harvey could see. The terrain mimicked that of a desert. Heat permeated the cavern, the visibility low. The ceiling was impossibly high, a glowing Rune hanging in the Air: Illusion.

There were no walls to follow this time. The temperature was boiling, with no Water in sight and sand reflecting the heat onto their bodies. After collecting and drinking as much Water as possible from the tunnel walls, Skylar found some large roots to carve into capless bottles.

He handed them to Kiara and Titan, who filled them and tucked them into a bag they had fashioned from the bottom half of Titan's shirt. Skylar joined them, assisting in gathering food as well.

The group set off. Harvey estimated that they had around a week before running out of Water.

Here's to hoping this chamber ends sometime before then.

They trekked in silence, exhaustion quickly taking hold of the group, the heat slowing their limbs. Harvey regularly found himself pulling party members back into line.

Titan pointed out an oasis in the distance, the entire group following excitedly. Harvey did not see it, but figured the group outweighed the individual. He had been relieved at the idea of another oasis. When they ranged a few miles, and the 'oasis' never got any closer, Harvey redirected the group back on the path. Headed straight for the Rune in the sky.

How am I supposed to get everyone through this? I am the only one who can see through the mirages, and they keep wandering off like drunken toddlers.

Skylar startled him by matching his stride, joining him at the front. The male was the only one with some sense of direction. Jordan walked close, and Harvey regularly reached out to check her location.

"I see the mirages too," Skylar said, not looking at Harvey as he walked.

The male's eyes were bloodshot from crying over Sabastian. His death had been especially hard on the male as Sabastian's Protector.

"Do your best to help me keep the others in line. Losing someone now could mean we never find them again. How is it that you can see through them?"

"My sense of smell has kept me from being tricked. To some Dyrfaldur, smell is as powerful as sight." Skylar explained, voice scratchy from dehydration. Kiara and Titan were rationing the group's Water.

"I am lucky the mushrooms and moss have such a distinctive smell. Your aptitude at identifying mirages is saving us; it is nearly impossible to navigate in this. Even with my sense of smell, I would be lost without you. Theos really is awakening."

Harvey considered the male anew; there was more to him than Harvey gave him credit for.

Maybe I was too judgmental of him.

At the start of the Labyrinth, Harvey had dismissed Skylar as an eventual casualty. His healing gift was helpful, but Kiara could heal as well. Now Harvey reconsidered this.

He has been of more use than I realised, especially when I don't trust Kiara.

We can rely on his abilities in this challenge, in any challenge, really. I am starting to trust him…

"I want you in front for this one; if anyone gives you a hard time, come to me," Harvey whispered to preserve his strength. "I need to stay in the back so I can stop others from wandering. I can see them clearly."

Skylar looked at him, surprised, but he nodded in recognition. Jordan walked over, touching Harvey on the arm. She gave him a small smile. His heart sped up. He forced the feeling down with all his willpower.

It must be the exercise. Harvey allowed his delusion to comfort him. *As soon as we leave, everything will go back to normal. I won't feel this… connection to her.*

All of a sudden, the ground in front of them started to move; a subsurface ripple that grew to a bulge. The sand was loose, shifting forward as something beneath the surface moved slowly towards them.

What is that?

Skylar stopped moving, dancing backwards towards the group, away from it. The movement stopped for a moment, then the sand began to swirl, a whirlpool of sediment. Particles flew up into the Air, Harvey covering his eyes.

The sand went still again.

Flat.

Where is it?

"Where…"

A burst of sand, and pinchers the length of an arm latched onto Skylar's leg. Skylar yelped, reaching out for Titan, who grabbed him by the forearm, looking as surprised at his reaction as Skylar did.

A pit opened, and the layer of sand covering it was thrown off.

Skylar was being pulled down, yanked by his leg.

Skylar managed to slow his descent, hand catching on one of the ridges, screwing down in a spiral pattern.

"He has it! Pull now!" Harvey yelled to Titan, staying away from the edge.

Titan struggled, muscles tense and his soft features drew into a determined scowl. Skylar started to rise, pulling with Titan. Harvey moved to grab the male's other hand. He latched on and heaved.

We've got him!

Harvey and Titan pulled, Skylar's foot finding the edge of the pit.

Sand flew in the Air, blocking Harvey's view. The side of the pit began to shift again; a landslide was dragging the three males in. Harvey fell, hitting the bottom of the pit hard.

Harvey saw the monster for the first time as he got to his feet. It was hairy and insectoid. The creature blended in with the sand, only visible from close up.

It looked like a tick, back covered in a protective shield.

It moved slowly, patiently.

Harvey's eyes darted to the sides of the pit desperately.

Looking up, he saw the others standing on the edge.

"Stand back!"

Too late.

Sand flew again, causing Harvey to fall back and blink furiously.

Screams echoed as the others fell, Nyx falling on Harvey, knocking the wind out of him.

"My leg is on Fire," Skylar whimpered from beside him.

Harvey swiped at his eyes and spat out the sand in his mouth.

"Did it pierce the skin?" Harvey asked hoarsely, watching the beast as it started to vibrate menacingly.

"Its mandible went through my leg," Skylar panted.

The insect lunged toward them, and Harvey jumped away.

It snatched Skylar again, who screamed.

Harvey dove towards the male, but Astris got there first. She kicked out, shin connecting with its jaw. The insect reared back, diving under the sand again.

"G-g-gods, it burns," Skylar stuttered, his speech muddied.

"Kiara!" Harvey prompted.

"Oh yeah, I would love to help the Dyrfaldur." Kiara's pupils narrowed as she licked her lower lip.

A rumble, and the sands shifted under them again.

"Now, Kiara!" Harvey ordered.

Kiara scoffed, grabbing the injured Skylar and taking off into the Air.

The sand exploded again, the insect lunging from behind Harvey. He ducked, but it grabbed Jordan around the waist.

No.

Fear filled him as he dove after her.

I shouldn't have ducked.

Before she could get dragged under, he grabbed her arm.

She will be ripped in half if I don't let go.

Nyx and Astris joined, scooping at the sand to uncover the beast and victim. It fought them, burrowing backwards, hissing. The hair on the back of Harvey's neck stood on end. A choking sound from Jordan caused the adrenaline in him to spike.

If I let go, she will go under.

Jordan screamed, the wounds deepening as it dragged.

Harvey let go, diving at the beast. It opened its jaws to intercept his lunge.

The beast was thrown to the side, Jordan dropping as Nyx punched the insect's head. Blood poured from her hand, and she swore.

"It's too hard," Nyx called. "We have to go! Get Jordan!"

"It has an exoskeleton for a reason," Harvey fumed.

Jordan's eyes met his own. Harvey stepped between her and the insect. She was holding her side, face pale with pain.

"Nyx," Harvey met her eyes, the message clear.

Her jaw set, grinding down, before she scooped Jordan into her arms.

It was just Harvey, Titan, and Astris in the pit now.

Kiara had better be working on healing them.

A knife flew through the Air, dropping right next to his foot.

Skylar had the knife. He must be stable.

"Get it flipped over," Harvey instructed, circling it with Titan. It began burrowing down again.

Oh no, you don't.

Harvey skipped behind the beast, blocking its retreat. It turned, charging towards him, on the offensive now. Harvey waited until the last minute. The jaws snapped close to his face, and Harvey let his body fall back, foot redirecting the beast upwards with a mighty kick. Harvey's bones shook with the impact.

Astris and Titan came to either side, grabbing the shell and propelling the beast up and backwards.

Harvey ran forward, pushing himself up from where he had fallen, knife proffered.

He leaped on its underbelly with a war cry, blade sinking into the soft flesh, dragging a line through its abdomen.

Nyx carried Skylar in fox form. The male had tried to get them to leave him, but Nyx had shut that down. She finally mentioned the male's lover to get him to stop fighting them. Five days went by. Skylar consulted with Harvey at every mirage. Every time they saw a bulge in the sand, they moved off course, risking getting lost. Thus far, they had been managing to keep the group together.

Harvey was intrigued by this whisper of his power, regularly stopping the group from walking off. He had finally been able to put Jordan down this morning, her wounds mostly closed. Nyx letting Skylar walk himself as well now. Kiara had been able to come up with an antidote to the Venom using the insect's own parts she had harvested.

The mirages looked like a hazy version of what the others described to Harvey, easily identified as fakes. A day ago, he insisted upon the Champions and Protectors tying themselves together. They had to use some clothing to do so, tying their wrists to the person in front of them.

We are running low on clothing by continually ripping parts off, Harvey mused. *Especially…* Harvey looked at Jordan. He swallowed, forcing his gaze away.

The order they landed on was Skylar at the front, Nyx and Astris, Titan and Kiara, and finally Jordan and Harvey.

Harvey extracted his eyes from Jordan's pale skin, her slight frame camouflaged naturally by the white sand.

I almost lost her.

Every couple of hours, a sandstorm blew through the cavern. The group huddled together, wings and backs to the Elements. The sand pierced their skin, and Harvey closed his eyes against the onslaught of sharp particles. It felt like being pricked all over his body, his skin chafing. His feathers were caked in sand, making them itchy.

It will take weeks to get this much sand out of my feathers, he lamented.

There isn't much to do on the walks; talking takes up too much energy.

Similar to the Metal trial, the group fell into a rhythm.

I am grateful for the monotony; it means we aren't facing danger.

They would wake with the artificial sun and walk in an awkward line until midday, taking a break to have a small ration of mushrooms and Water.

This morning, Nyx and Astris had to wake him and Jordan vigorously, by shaking them until they stirred. Harvey felt sluggish, his body slowed, and his mind foggy. The dehydration and heat were taking their toll.

Kiara dropped back, handing Harvey and Jordan their Water rations for the day with disdain.

She saved Skylar. She deserves a little trust.

Harvey drank deeply, swallowing his ration in one greedy swallow. The Water moved more slowly than seemed normal, slightly iridescent.

I wonder if Kiara spit in it.

Kiara snatched the bottle out of his hand, grabbing Jordan's as well, before moving ahead again.

The day ticked by, and Harvey started to feel his limbs grow heavier. It was different from the dehydration, muddying Harvey's thoughts.

The sand looks really comfortable right now.

Harvey grinned at the ground stupidly, the sandy hills looking inviting.

Sit down now, and you die; keep walking, just another step, everyone else is still going. I am a weakling; everything is just so heavy.

Maybe a short break could help?

Harvey looked to Jordan. She looked sluggish as well, walking more slowly.

Repeatedly, Harvey and Jordan tripped on the sand, falling behind at the back of the group.

Why are we the only ones? Is this some sort of Theos? What is going on?

Harvey felt himself canting sideways, vision sliding out of focus. Blackness overtook him.

Harvey blinked up to see Titan looking down at him. Jordan was passed out on his chest.

"What's going on with you, man? Stop cuddling up to that..." Titan made a disgusting sound. "If you want to fuck that badly, I can find you an Aervel female, or male to tumble with. Gods, that's nasty."

When did we fall? Why is there sand in my mouth? I am on my back... but my tongue is covered.

Every time Harvey blinked, darkness soothed him.

Something is on top of me... I can catch up, can't I? Wait, what the Hell had Titan said? I'm not cuddling anyone... Wait... What was I thinking about?

He needed a moment. He pinched himself to try to wake up, debating rubbing sand in his eyes.

No Water, bad idea. Why am I so foggy? Titan, wait...

Harvey looked up again, Titan and now Kiara standing above him.

Is Titan... disgusted with me?

Why?

"Yeah, what is going on with you? Didn't know you had a commoner fetish," Kiara smirked in a voice filled with disdain.

She turned to Titan, "the prince needs time to think about his position. Time to think about the creature plastered to his chest and where it came from. How much the Hell portal has destroyed. How many Aervel have…" Kiara's voice caught, and she snarled.

Titan put a consoling hand on her shoulder. "Let's keep going. They can catch up when they're done."

Titan spit on the ground next to them before taking Kaira's hand and walking away.

Harvey watched helplessly as Titan and Kiara faded into the distance. The group was moving ahead unknowingly without them.

Fuck, something isn't right. They are leaving us. If I just close my eyes for a moment, maybe I can refresh. Reset, and be good to go. Then I can catch up to them.

Harvey's vision went black again.

He woke up abruptly, throwing a body off of him in the process.

Jordan.

Is that why Titan called me nasty?

Maybe I can catch one more nap? Just a few moments.

Jordan opened her mouth to talk, wincing at her dry throat. She tipped her bottle up, still having it on her.

A single drop dripped onto her lips.

The liquid was moving… slower. It reminds me of… Minotaur's balls. What was I thinking?

Harvey jolted, smacking the bottle out of her hands before rummaging through his pockets desperately. *There has to be something to help.* Jordan looked at him, too tired to fight, her head again on his chest.

That's not a good sign, but she has the right idea. It is smart to relax. Maybe if we just let ourselves...

Harvey passed out for the third time.

Harvey woke up with sand starting to cover his nose. He snorted and choked, inhaling more sand. On his chest, Jordan's head was getting covered by the ever-shifting particles. He lifted her head, doing his best to sit up and hold her upright.

Please stay awake, please stay awake.

Harvey repeated the words over and over in his brain. He begged his body to stay awake, opening his eyes wide. Harvey then gently set Jordan into his lap.

"Happy to see me?" She muttered, giggling.

"What?" Harvey asked, confusion made worse by his mental fog.

"That hard thing poking into my ass." The corner of her mouth lifted, her lips cracked and bleeding.

Hard... thing?

Harvey reached under her, feeling a hard cylindrical shape poking out of his jacket.

What is this?

He lifted a vial.

Veinflare!

How had it survived this long? I must have fallen asleep with some, the night we were taken into the Labyrinth.

As soon as she was securely in his lap, he grabbed the Veinflare, tipping it into his mouth. Half of the bottle he left for Jordan. The drop hit his tongue, bitter, earthy, and tingling. Harvey's heart rate sped up, his vision growing less fuzzy.

This has more of a kick than it did in class. The Theos in the place must have infused it.

Hurriedly, Harvey tipped the remainder of the Veinflare into Jordan's mouth, closing her jaw for her.

"Please just swallow; it will be okay if you just swallow. I can't carry you, please." He begged, massaging her throat carefully.

Every moment he waited was longer than the last, the sands shifting restlessly.

How did this happen? The last thing I remember was… Kiara… the Water. My Gods, she poisoned us.

Slumber Serum.

Jordan's throat moved nearly imperceptivity, eyes fluttering. "I've never had a prince beg me before."

She smirked up at him. "Now let me get up," she said, pushing at him weakly.

Harvey removed himself immediately, watching her intently. She looked up, catching the intensity of his stare.

"What?" She laughed, a brow raised tentatively.

She looked up into his eyes, golden iris's sparkling in the light.

He lifted a hand to her face, cupping it. He ran his finger across her strong lips, her face small in his hands.

Beautiful.

"Never mind, it is nothing," Harvey said, smiling at her before dropping his hand.

She scowled at him, beginning to protest, "No, tell me."

He cut her off, "Let's go. We shouldn't waste Water."

He could swear he caught her mimicking him as he turned towards the direction the others had gone, or at least his best guess at their direction. They must not have noticed them missing. Titan and Kiara were the only ones to see them fall behind.

Had Jordan really fallen on me like that? It was too… perfect.

She had been settled comfortably on him the first time he woke, her hand over his heart, face nestled against his neck. It was intimate, unlike a fall.

Why did I have so much sand in my mouth? The sand wasn't covering my face, but it was in my mouth. Also, how would she have fallen on me face-first?

We were going in the same direction and kept wavering apart like drunk sailors.

The makeshift rope holding them had been broken. It sat half covered on the ground next to them. Harvey spat out the remaining sand that he hadn't swallowed. He had to fight the bile that threatened to follow. He called out for the group; voice lost in the wind.

No communication with the group means I am lacking information. On top of that, Nyx and Skylar are the only ones able to navigate in this mess with their superior senses of smell.

Harvey slowed his breathing.

I can see through the Illusions, but that doesn't tell me where to go. I need something to orient me. I need to find the Rune, but the sand is blowing too much.

"What was that earlier, while you were touching my face?" Jordan asked again, shoving him lightly.

"It was nothing. Just leave it," Harvey implored, still marching toward where he thought they should go. His jaw clenched as a blush heated his face.

"Or you could just tell me," She tried, challenging him.

"Just leave it," he exclaimed, coughing from the slight rise in his voice.

"You're going the wrong way," she murmured.

"What? How do you know?" Harvey asked, turning to her, irritated.

"Why did you touch my face like that?" she asked, slowly enunciating the words, eyes crinkling.

"You are incorrigible, ill-mannered, insolent. Just answer my question, how do you know we are going the wrong way?" he ranted.

"You forgot intoxicating," she teased.

Yes, I did.

"No, I didn't," he groused.

She looks particularly pleased with herself.

"Beg," she stated her terms.

"Absolutely the Hell not." Harvey scoffed. "I am the prince."

"Hmm," she hummed, lowering herself into the sand.

"What the Hell are you doing?" Harvey sighed.

Jordan shrugged, "Waiting for you to stop throwing a tantrum."

He couldn't control her, not like he did with the rest of the world. He couldn't force her to help him. She was the only individual who regularly defied him. The only one he couldn't bring himself to punish.

I should have executed her five times over by now. She has disrespected the crown time and time again.

She has also saved my life. Also…

she has started to…

mean something to me.

"Please," he finally caved, turning to her.

"Please, what?" she prompted.

She is going to make me say it. She is going to make the prince of Dengar beg. Beg for her. As if I don't already burn for her, my self-disgust is the only thing keeping me faithful to the Gods.

"Please, tell me how you know we are going the wrong way," he growled low in his throat.

"You are the prince. Doesn't that mean you know best?" The taunt in her voice made his stomach clench. He narrowed his eyes at her.

"I am the one who can see through Illusions," Harvey begged the Gods for patience. Jordan was unlike anyone he had ever met.

"Each Dyrfaldur has their animal form, correct?" She lectured.

"Gods give me strength, yes." He didn't need a lesson; he learned as a child repeated.

"Well, we don't have to be fully shifted to get some of our animal's abilities. Especially when our animal marker is our eyes." Jordan explained.

"Like yours," Harvey said, suddenly interested.

"Finches can see more colours than Aervel, more shades of each colour." She met his eyes, "The Illusions get to me, but sweat shows up in UV light… which I can see. Your vision helps you see past Illusions, but not the way to go."

"What are you getting at?" he asked, patience wearing thin.

"We are going to follow the trail of dried sweat, Prince," Jordan smirked, walking away from him. "They're less than a mile off based on evaporation."

Looking at the expanse of sand, Harvey stepped to the side, allowing her to pass.

CHAPTER 17: NYX

Breaking Point

The ball is tomorrow. Is your dress ready? I am sure you will look resplendent in it. I have to say, I am still disappointed in you for your lack of ambition. It is embarrassing to be with a princess who has no desire for the throne. Think about it.

-Kiara note to Nyx, 201st Day, 65 AT

The group broke through the sand line days ago, and Harvey and Jordan were nowhere to be found. She fingered her wrist, which was mostly healed now, stiff but no longer painful. Just as Nyx began to walk back into the shifting sands, she stopped when her brother and Jordan appeared out of the haze. She immediately attempted to go back in, but Astris and Skylar stopped her. She had been about to try again, when her brother and Jordan arrived, the Unity Rune appearing. Finally, everyone was safe and together.

"How did you get so far behind? It's been two days! How could you do that to us?" Nyx started as soon as Harvey and Jordan's tired frames stumbled to the rocky ground.

I know I am being irrational; there was no way he was choosing to worry me.

To stay behind to be with Jordan would be dangerous and reckless.

That just isn't Harvey.

Still, Nyx couldn't let go of her anger.

I was scared for him. She realised, looking at her brother.

"We were drugged," Harvey said, shocking everyone into silence. That was the last thing Nyx expected him to say.

"How? Who?" Nyx asked.

There were no other Aervel or Dyrfaldur in the Labyrinth, only the members of their small troop.

Harvey is implying that there is a traitor in our midst.

"Are you sure you didn't just want some time with the Dyrfaldur?" Titan snarked.

"Oh, come off it, Titan. You fucking watched us drop. Right after you and Kiara gave us Water. Do you seriously think I would take a break in the middle of a fucking desert?" Harvey was in Titan's face now.

Harvey has never stood against Titan.

Her brother's stature was significantly shorter than Titan, his black hair coming to just below Titan's eyes.

Titan steeled himself, snarling, "All I saw was you and your little Dyrfaldur whore cuddling and getting left behind. I told you to keep up, and that animal," he pointed a finger at Jordan, "was all over you. Maybe if you stayed with your kind, you wouldn't get lost on a mission."

Silence filled the space; the only sound was the wind whistling softly. Nyx licked her lips, looking at the scene.

The Unity Rune flickered, *or was that my imagination?*

I should stop this. We can't be fighting here and now. Not on a life-or-death mission. Of all times for Harvey and Titan to have a falling out, did it have to be on this deadly quest?

"My kind," Harvey tasted the words as if he found them bitter. "Why don't you believe me? Is it Kiara? What is happening between you two?" Everything was coming out now.

He will pull himself together.

"I saw you two together. I know you are fucking. I know you are fucking her while engaged to me. If you want to talk about morality, let's talk about that."

Or not. Wait… engaged?

"You two are engaged?" Nyx asked, mouth opening in shock.

That's why he has refused to let go of him. Why Harvey has been obsessed with him, because he thinks they will marry.

Nyx glanced at Jordan, who had gone pale, staring at Harvey with a look Nyx couldn't identify.

Harvey turned to her, "Father made me keep it secret. I can't anymore, though. I can't be locked in this situation. I won't be with someone who fucks another behind my back. Did you seriously not consider it could be staged Titan?"

Titan stood stock still before responding, "You have become a Dyrfaldur sympathiser. I never wanted you; I only wanted the position you had to offer. Now, you are tainted by that," he pointed at Jordan again, "animal."

Harvey's eyes turned a dark crimson. "We are done. You and I? After this Labyrinth, you will never talk to me again. The engagement is off. Your beauty is the only value you hold; too bad it doesn't extend to your personality."

"Take that back," Kiara snarled, coming to Titan's rescue.

"Back off, Kiara," Harvey warned.

"I don't think so. See, all we have to do is tell the nobles that you have become attached to the Dyrfaldur. Even princes can be executed."

"You dare," Harvey growled.

"Titan, why don't we show the prince what we do to Dyrfaldur?"

"You touch them, you die." Harvey's voice dropped, threat dripping from every syllable. "Now get on your knees. Bow to your prince."

Old Harvey would never have done this.

The harsh reality of their situation quickly extinguished the swell of pride that washed through Nyx.

Now isn't the time. I should stop this.

Kiara and Titan's claims wouldn't go without being investigated; all it would take is Harvey reacting the wrong way in front of the court.

Now that he is becoming an ally to the Dyrfaldur, Kiara will stop at nothing to prove it.

Titan smiled maliciously, "Going to order me around? Use your princely status to lower me to her level? Make me bow to some Dyrfaldur slut? I would rather jump in the Hell portal."

Titan will stop at nothing.

Nyx's feet were frozen to the ground as she watched.

Harvey ignored his words, continuing with a frightening calm, "What's going to happen is you are going to apologise to Jordan and Skylar. You are going to fall to your knees and beg."

"I will not…" Titan sputtered.

My Gods. Harvey isn't playing.

Harvey cut him off coldly, "You will, and here is why." Harvey barked a dry, merciless laugh, taking a steadying breath, eyes closed.

He might kill him.

"If you don't, I will break every bone in your body. I will break every fucking bone in your body, and I will leave you here. Alone. Now. Beg." Harvey growled, stalking towards Titan.

"Don't listen to him," Kiara drawled to Titan, inspecting her nails. "You know he won't hurt you. Let's kill the Dyrfaldur and get it over with. No one will know what happened in here. Not without survivors."

Kiara moved like a viper towards Jordan. Harvey jumped between them. Within seconds, he was on her, shoving Kiara into the tunnel wall. She hit the rock hard, tunnel shuddering from the impact of a full-blooded Aervel's shove. Harvey was holding his forearm across her throat, snarling in her face.

Titan came up behind him, grabbing Harvey by the shoulder and shoving him. Harvey skidded back a few feet, looking murderous.

Time to step in before they bring down the fucking Labyrinth.

Nyx saw Jordan beginning to walk over and she shook her head at her.

It is best not to aggravate the situation further.

The female looked frustrated, but backed off. Then, without a second for Nyx to comprehend what was happening, Harvey's fist connected with Titan's face with a crack. Titan's head snapped back, blood gushing from the wound as he grabbed his nose.

The two Aervel stood face-to-face, their muscles primed for battle. Nyx, Astris, and Skylar all started moving at the same time. Nyx and Jordan went to stop Harvey, and Skylar and Astris grabbed Titan. Kiara was laughing wildly in amusement. Nyx fought to keep calm.

It's my time to be the mature one.

Harvey tugged on Nyx and Jordan, pushing towards Kiara and snarling.

The group staying together won't work; we will kill each other.

"You will regret it if you kill him. I promise we won't let anything happen to Jordan or Skylar." Nyx said, pulling on her brother. "We are camping separately tonight."

Jordan whispered something in his ear, and Harvey stopped fighting.

Good.

"Astris with me," Kiara said. Astris walked over, eyes meeting Nyx's briefly.

I don't understand where her allegiances lie.

"Astris, you will be with us," Harvey ordered, glaring at Kiara.

Kiara pursed her lips, pausing and touching her chin. "On second thought, I no longer need you, Astris."

Fear flashed through Astris's eyes as she looked between the two groups. Tentatively, she walked back to Nyx, glancing nervously at Kiara. Kiara smiled at her maliciously, teeth flashing with the promise of retribution.

We will protect her. I won't let Kiara get to her.

In silence, Nyx, Astris, Harvey, Skylar, and Jordan went further into the tunnel, away from Titan and Kiara. By the end of the day, they came to the next challenge.

Looks like this is as far as we can get away from them. Let's hope it is enough.

Nyx looked at the others worriedly. Her eyes met her brother's, his eyes dancing between colours.

I have never seen him like this. Everyone is changing. Even Astris chose to leave Kiara's side.

Nyx's eyes went to Astris. Silent, ethereal, and observant, Astris was the only one of the group who scared her. She was unpredictable. A puppet of Kiara, or so Nyx had thought. Now… Nyx didn't know what to think.

Maybe her time on this journey has changed her. Even Harvey is changing. As much as I am proud of him for standing up for the Dyrfaldur, he is still unstable from the Titan situation. The Gods want us united, but everyone knows, picking up something that has shattered is how you get cut.

CHAPTER 18: JORDAN

Desire and Fire

We miss you, little Devil. The den's patrons miss you as well. Old Willy says hi, and that he expects a rematch. Are you staying safe? I know you have a tendency to take on challenges bigger than yourself. The mention of the prince in your last letter was worrisome. When we said you should use school as a way to rise in station, we didn't mean for you to put yourself in danger. Isn't there a nice Dyrfaldur you can approach? Your dad and I cannot condone this dangerous behaviour. Seducing the prince is not a challenge; it is suicide. Not to mention the danger of you falling for him. No matter how much you claim to hate him, love has a funny way of taking us by surprise.

Note to Jordan, 40th Day, 76 AT

The next challenge lay before them, heating the entire tunnel and making it uncomfortably hot. The walls reflected a warm orange glow; the group's shadows moving like flames. Magma spanned the tunnel ahead, a river of heat and Fire. Jordan noted that the ceiling gradually lowered as the tunnel stretched on. The Fire Rune glowed above the river: a single flame.

They clearly don't want us flying our way out of this one. Harvey walked to the wall, warm with heat, and lay down against it.

Jordan sat down next to him, Nyx on the other side with Astris. The five of them agreed to strategize in the morning, huddling in for sleep. Nyx and Astris fell asleep against one another immediately.

Jordan looked over to Harvey, who was getting ready for bed.

He is quite nice to look at, she thought absently.

Impossible, uptight, asshole, but gorgeous.

I want him.

Jordan looked down to her abdomen where the scar from the insectoid monster curved around her body.

This wasn't in my plan. I wasn't supposed to care. I don't matter to him. So why can't I get him out of my head?

She watched hungrily as he took off his tunic, chucking it to the side. The heat kissed his skin, sweat shining on his obnoxiously muscled torso.

How many abs is that? Twenty?

"He was about to kill Titan for you," Astris said next to her. Jordan hadn't realized the female was awake.

Jordan glanced at Harvey; *this journey is changing everyone.*

"He has grown, hasn't he?" Jordan remarked, looking at the prince.

"We all have," Astris said, standing up and walking away.

Okay… conversation over then.

He was engaged to Titan. Why am I… jealous knowing that?

Jordan remembered Harvey touching her face in the desert.

I can't read him. I don't understand why he defended us, defended Dyrfaldur. Coal-lined eyes flashed to her, a clever smile following. *I am in some real trouble.*

had calmed significantly since leaving Titan and Kiara behind. A smirk graced his face as he noticed her looking at his muscles.

Cocky Aervel.

She turned away from him, face heating. She sensed a presence behind her, and Jordan fought a shiver. She did not turn around.

Let's see what he does.

A warm hand fell on her shoulder, strong and calloused from sword work.

"Come with me?" Harvey requested gently, his voice pleading.

Jordan nodded, following him into an alcove away from the eyes and ears of the others. He stopped in front of her face, expression blank, eyes a deep purple, ringed in gold. She only noticed this colour ignite when he was turned towards her and Titan.

I know what it means now.

His hand came up to cup her face, tilting her chin up to him. His eyes met hers, gaze intense. He blinked and stepped away, hands clasping behind his back.

"I am sorry," he started. "Titan should never have talked that way, he…" Harvey brushed the hair out of his eyes, "wasn't always like this."

"Are you sure it isn't *you* that has changed?" She challenged, meeting his gaze. She stepped into him. He did not move, gaze dropping to her mouth.

"No," he replied honestly. "I always had hatred in my heart for your kind, but something tells me I was wrong. Why would the Gods select both Dyrfaldur and Aervel for the trials? I don't think…" Harvey took a deep breath before continuing, "I don't think Dyrfaldur are lesser or unholy. It's simply not possible, not when you make me feel…"

Open up. Please.

"Tell me," Jordan whispered. "How do I make you feel?"

Harvey shook his head, throat bobbing, "Once I tell you, there's no going back. You won't want what happens next. I have already put your life at risk."

"I can handle it. Trust me to handle it."

I decide what I can handle.

"I can't let you get hurt," he insisted, hand roving to her face as if he couldn't help but touch her.

Jordan's body burned with desire.

Fuck me.

I want this.

I want him.

I want the prince of Dengar.

"You don't get to decide that for me," she warned.

He studied her, "What is it you want, exactly?"

"Exactly?" She faltered at his blunt inquiry.

"Every. Single. Detail." He rasped out each syllable, eyes flicking to her lips.

Is he actually considering this?

Harvey backed Jordan against the wall. His arms caged her, holding her in place.

Am I considering this?

His head tilted predatorily as he leaned in. Warmth bloomed in her, a Fire that could not be quenched. Desire flooded her thoughts, his scent heady.

The law can go to Hell.

Harvey's body was hard against her, his attraction evident.

I want this.

She swallowed. His eyes darted to her throat, the corner of his mouth twitching. Her body shook with need.

Fuck it.

"I want you to take me against this wall. Hard, rough, and with every ounce of that Aervel swagger you carry. I want you to mark me, to claim me. I want you to own me. Tonight, I want to be yours." Jordan raised her chin, gathering every ounce of courage she had. "The law can go to Hell. I need you inside me."

His eyes flashed with indecision, before she met his gaze.

"Fuck it" He growled, echoing her thoughts and pulling her close.

He hummed with pleasure and desire, deep vibrations traveling up her body. She shivered, leaning into him. He grunted at her closeness, eyes going distant for a moment. Jordan smirked.

I'm not alone in this. He wants me too.

"What I was going to say before is…" his lips brushed against her own.

She leaned in to chase it, but he pulled away, holding her at bay with a single finger still beneath her chin, pushing up. He was in control now, and for the first time since meeting him, she surrendered to him.

He tsked at her, gently seizing her chin now, "Patience, princess." His voice was so decadent, resonant, and passionate that it took her off guard.

Princess.

He stepped closer to her, and she let out a soft gasp. He hummed, the sound of it resonating through her, causing her body to burn with need. A small gasp escaped her as his hand snaked around her waist, pulling her to him. He was hard against her, his impressive length becoming evident. Jordan swallowed.

Gods I want to feel him inside me. Jordan's hand brushed over his chis sled chest, fingers dipping with his muscular curves.

"What I was going to say before, is that every time I look into your eyes, I feel my breathing cease, and my body plummets…" He was so close now she could smell old books and rich tea leaves.

She breathed in the scent, desperate to bathe in it.

He will be mine. I won't accept any reality where he isn't mine.

He captured her attention again, the hand behind her back dragging across the waistband of her pants around to her hipbone; she shivered.

"…I plummet out of the world I understand, out of my very reality. I keep falling until it is only you and me. Until we are the only ones in existence. Until you are all I can see. Your voice is all I hear, and it is in that darkness that you become my prayer, my hope, my Goddess."

My Goddess. He said "my".

His fingers were gentle on her chin, urging her to keep looking at him.

I could look at him forever. He looks like he was carved out of stone, sculpted by the Gods themselves.

A beat, and his leg was between hers, hand closing around her throat. His mouth met hers, and Jordan melted. He tasted good. Like pear and Severroot.

More.

Harvey tightened the grip on her throat, and she let out an involuntary moan. He pulled back, smirking at her devilishly.

"Patience," he crooned, leaning in to nip at her lip.

No.

"Fuck me," she retorted, eyes narrowing in challenge.

"Beg," he rumbled, maintaining her eye contact.

His taste was intoxicating, the rich flavour of him still in her mouth.

"Please," Jordan breathed.

"Please, what, Goddess?" he coaxed.

I need him. Now.

"Please fuck me. Fuck me until I forget my name. Fuck me until I join you in the darkness you plummet into." She begged, losing her composure.

A flash of teeth, and his hand tightened further around her throat, mouth at her ear. "With pleasure, princess," he purred, nipping her ear lightly before finding her mouth.

Fuck.

His mouth explored hers languidly, luxuriously. She groaned as his tongue flicked across her own, opening up for him more. One hand went to her ass, lifting her off the ground with ease, the other releasing her neck and pinning her arm above her head.

"Mmm, if only we had a bed, I suppose we will have to make do with the wall… for now." Harvey mused, inspecting her in front of him.

He's implying he wants more than just right now. More than just a release. Something deeper with me.

His hardness pressed into her as he kissed her deeply, taking his time. Her moans rose as he explored her mouth, then trailed down her neck. Nimble fingers slid behind her back, undoing the makeshift knot on the cloth binding her breasts. The long strip of fabric unravelled onto the floor with a tug. He stepped back, smiling, inspecting her with desire.

Does he like what he sees? Gods his eyes! I have never seen them this rich a purple.

He walked a half circle around her slowly, stopping and raising an eyebrow when she tried to turn with him. Her back pressed against the wall of the cave still.

"I have been waiting a very long time to see you," he purred appreciatively.

"And?" she whispered.

She could feel her heart beating wildly.

"You are more gorgeous than even my wildest dreams could have conjured, than they *did* conjure." His eyes traced her breasts, dipping lower, then up to her mouth again.

This time, when he kissed her, it was not the lazy, slow strokes he started with. He was feral, hand cupping her breast as he kissed down her neck, fingers trailing across her exposed skin. She pushed her body into him, desperate for more contact.

"Fuck," he groaned, deep in his throat. The sound filled her body, and Jordan ran her fingers down his hard stomach. His muscles tightened instinctively at the touch. A flash of his smile caused her own stomach to clench.

He is so painfully, attractive.

His fingers dug into her hips as he kissed her without restraint. His hands tugged at her trousers, and he dropped to his knees before her, pulling her trousers as he went. He looked up at her as if she were his God, her name a prayer primed on his lips.

This is sacrilege.

The prince of Dengar, was on his knees before her; shirtless and looking at her as if she were his entire world.

Good thing, I am a sinner.

A hand traced up the inside of her leg, lifting it to rest over his shoulder.

What is he…

He huffed a laugh, his breath warm against her wet thighs. "Now, be my good princess and stay very still for me. I want to take my time as I feast on you."

Jordan stood above him, lips parted slightly, breasts heavy. A light sheen of sweat covered them both, the heated rock reflecting on their skin. Harvey's tongue dipped between her legs, tasting.

Fuck.

He hummed in pleasure, grabbing her ass and pulling her into his mouth.

He started slowly, tongue dipping inside her, tracing slow circles around her entrance. "Fuck, you taste amazing," he murmured before dragging his tongue up her centre, flicking the sensitive bundle of nerves.

She laced her hands in his thick black hair, holding on as he devoured her.

Jordan cried out as he focused on her clit, dragging his tongue across it slowly. She closed her eyes, head tilting back as his fingers teased her entrance.

"Sooo wet for me," he murmured.

Only for you.

"Please don't stop," she pleaded.

I need more. I need him.

"I like it when you beg," Harvey hummed in pleasure.

"I like it when you make me beg," she teased, voice catching as he slipped a finger inside her.

He laughed softly, pleased with himself, as he added a second finger.

"Let's play a game then." Harvey's eyes shone with mischief.

I like games.

"Does it end with your cock inside me?" Jordan asked. The corner of her mouth lifted wickedly.

"That all depends on you; the rules are simple," he pumped his fingers in and out of her slowly as he spoke.

If he keeps doing that I am going to cum.

"Oh, fuck," Jordan said, tension building in her body. She gripped him as she shuddered.

"Mmmm, not yet," he reprimanded. "The only rule is that if you say anything other than my name, I will stop. Any sound, any gasp, any noise other than my name, and I will stop."

I can feel him through his trousers.

"And what do I get if I win?" Jordan gasped, attempting to compose herself.

I know what I want to win.

A knowing smile graced his lips, and he ignored her question, dipping between her thighs with his mouth. His tongue swirled tight circles around her clit, before taking it in his mouth and sucking.

Jordan cried out in pleasure, body tensing. The sensation immediately stopped. She looked down at him, annoyed.

I have been wanting this since we met.

He raised a flawlessly sculpted eyebrow at her. She pursed her lips, glaring at him.

I will give anything to make him start again. Harvey's eyes shone, *he knows how badly I need him right now.* Not releasing her gaze, he took her clit in his mouth again.

She tensed, "Harvey, Harvey, Harvey!" She was rocking against him now, unable to control herself.

Harvey's fingers coaxed her from the inside as he feasted focused on her clit. Relentless strokes of his tongue barraged her, overwhelming her senses.

"Harvey, Harvey, Harvey." His name on her lips became a prayer, his tongue between her legs the answer.

His soft black wings brushed her thighs, feathers trailing across her bare skin. The sensations combined in an intoxicating mixture, his right hand at her sex, his left trailing to her throat, his nails digging in with a delicious bite.

After a final series of strokes, she reached a climax, screaming his name as she crashed over the edge. He continued licking the sensitive area, holding her still as she bucked. She came to a second climax and whimpered as her prince devoured her sex, long fingers pumping inside her vigorously.

"Harvey," she begged; he stood, trailing kisses up her stomach as he did so.

I want more. I want to see him undone. Unleashed.

His mouth met hers, and she could taste herself on his tongue. She pulled at the strings of his trousers, desperate to free him. He helped her, nimbly undoing the strings with his fingers and pulling them down.

Gods, now that I know what he can do with them.

The wetness between her thighs increased, causing her legs to slide against one another.

He sprang free, cock fully hard and huge in both length and girth. Jordan figured there might be a proportionate difference in Aervel males. They were a significantly larger species than the Dyrfaldur. Now Jordan knew it extended… below the belt as well. Jordan swallowed, admiring him standing there, his hair mussed from her hands, a hungry look in his eyes.

So big. He is so much bigger than I have ever had.

He pumped himself in his hand a few times, watching her. Her body clenched, wetness dripping down her thighs, her clit throbbing.

I want him.

She bit her lip, exposing her throat to him with a grin. It was a dare.

"Play a bit rougher with me," she begged with her eyes.

Show me what you look like undone.

His grin turned feral as he approached her slowly, head cocking to the side as he examined her. A tongue ran up her throat, and then a sharp pain as he nipped her. She gasped at the sensation, thighs tightening together. He kicked her feet apart with another tsk.

Jordan felt him at her entrance as he situated himself. His mouth found her neck again, kissing and nipping as he slowly pushed inside her.

Fuck he is massive. Does this thing have no end?

Eventually, Harvey entered her fully, halting to give her time to adjust. Slowly, he started to pump in and out of her at the same speed as he had with his fingers. She met him with every stroke, begging for him to go harder.

He obliged, her bare ass pressing into the warm, smooth stone as he lifted her up his length. He kept her in the Air a moment before lowering her back onto his cock. She buried her face in his neck, kissing the warm skin, running her tongue along his vein as a panther shifter had once done to her. He shivered.

Good prince.

"Fuck, princess, you are so tight," he crooned with pleasure.

I never wanted to be a princess.

He pushed into her. She moaned, closing her eyes to the sensation as he filled her. He started pumping into her, pinning her to the wall harder.

I just wanted to blackmail him. Now?

Tension coiled tight inside her again, as Jordan's body shook.

I will be anything he wants.

He took his left hand, flicking nimble fingers across her clit as he fucked her, the other hand holding her wrists in place above her head. She stood on tiptoes to match his height.

I will be everything he wants.

"I'm going to cum again," she gasped.

His mouth found her neck, and he started kissing again.

I will be his queen.

He bit down hard as he sped up. He was pounding into her now, control shattered at last. His teeth dug into the sensitive skin of her neck. Pain mixed with the feeling of him filling her in a delectable mix.

Harvey roared, movements becoming jerky as he got close to his release. A droplet of warm blood dripped from his teeth, and Jordan cried out in pleasure, senses in overload. This time, it was her name that was chanted repeatedly. Harvey found his release, her name a prayer, her his Goddess.

CHAPTER 19: NYX

Oath

I had to order the execution of a noble today. It pains me every time I have to... Even without taking the throne, you are in a position to campaign to be on the High Council. Think about it.

-King Blackthorn to Nyx. 42nd Day, 76 AT

Nyx plugged her ears, facing Astris as night fell. The female was calm and unshaken, like always. The sounds of Nyx's brother and Jordan fucking filled the cavern. Skylar was in his fox form, curled up against the wall. Another sound of pleasure, and Nyx closed her eyes briefly, cringing at the sounds from down the tunnel.

Not like closing my eyes will help with the sound. Why can't he wait until we get out of here? I guess I know the answer to that. I need to make sure this never gets out. It's my turn to protect my brother.

"I suppose I don't have to tell you that I will kill you if you tell anyone about what he's doing," Nyx warned Astris.

"I haven't told anyone anything about your secret. I won't tell anyone your brother's secret either," Astris snapped back. "He's your brother, but he's my friend too."

Nyx went still at the mention of her being a Half-blood. Astris held her gaze, silver eyes intense. Her hand came to rest on Nyx's shoulder softly. She reached up to run her hands through Nyx's two-toned hair. Nyx leaned into the touch, losing herself in the moment.

Fuck it, fuck it, fuck it, fuck it.

Another moan filled the tunnel, and they pulled away from one another.

Never fucking mind. Though, that interruption was probably a good thing.

Astris Archer was the last Aervel that Nyx needed to involve herself with. She was still Kiara's friend.

But she didn't turn me in for being a Half-blood.

Astris blinked, mask slipping into place. Nyx hated that mask. Astris then ripped off two small pieces of cloth from her frayed shirt and handed them to her.

"For your ears," she stated.

Nyx huffed a surprised laugh, "Thanks."

Nyx woke to the sound of steps in the dark. The smell of rotten apples filled her nose, and she froze. Staying still, eyes closed, Nyx listened. Feet stepped lightly over her brother and Jordan, approaching Nyx and Astris. Nyx prepared herself to fight, holding still, looking through her lashes. Instead of an attack, Nyx heard Kiara's voice.

"Come, now," Kiara's voice demanded.

Nyx heard Astris get up.

Why is she listening to her? Is she going to betray us as well? Should I get Harvey? Wait. Patience. Remember father's lessons. I am at an advantage; don't squander it.

Nyx opened her eyes when the footsteps sounded far enough away. Slowly, she lifted her head, looking around. Kiara and Astris were walking towards the lava.

Are they moving ahead without the group?

Nyx crept closer, keeping to the shadows, away from the light of the lava.

Kiara stopped ten feet from the lava. "You should have stayed loyal. I am about to become one of the most powerful females in all of Dengar. I can have anyone I want. Use anyone I want. Now you are nothing but a loose end."

Astris started to reply, but Kiara cut her off. "Quiet," Kiara ordered.

Astris shut her mouth immediately.

Coward. What the fuck? This isn't the Astris I have seen recently. This is the Astris I saw back at school, at the castle.

"As I was saying, I have no need for you, not after we leave here. Everything is finally coming together, now it is up to father. I have evolved to bigger machinations than the games we have played together. Now, do me a favour and walk straight ahead into the lava without stopping."

Astris's head whipped to Kiara, and Nyx's stomach dropped.

What is happening? She wouldn't...

Astris started walking, haltingly, painfully, towards the lava.

She was going to do it.

Why the Hell would she?

The bond.

I can stop this.

She promised not to use it, but fuck that. She would not let Astris kill herself. Nyx stood, running forward.

"Astris, stop!" Nyx screamed across the cavern, voice breaking with fear.

Astris's head whipped to her; fear, confusion, pain, panic, and relief filled her eyes. Tears poured down her face, silver eyes wild. Nyx's heart wrenched at the sight, tears pricking the corners of her own eyes. Kiara looked at Nyx, scowling.

Astris doesn't have control of herself, Nyx realised with a start.

"Astris, sprint into the lava," Kiara barked at Astris.

Astris turned on her heels, sprinting. Nyx was Airborne in a second. Harvey, Jordan, and Skylar were on their feet now, standing behind her, woken by Nyx's scream.

"Astris, come to me, run and plug your ears! Don't listen to what she has to say!" Nyx screamed again, wings pounding the Air.

Too far, too far! I need to move faster.

Astris stopped.

Thank the Gods.

She plugged her ears, sprinting towards Nyx, who dove low, holding out her hand. She had to get her in the Air, now. There, she could clamp her wings down and carry her. Astris was taller than Nyx, but she would still be light enough to carry.

Nyx dove, arm extended as she passed. Astris took her hand without hesitation, swinging into the Air as Nyx pulled up. Astris tucked in her wings immediately, grabbing Nyx's other hand dangling below her.

"Let go, Astris dear," Kiara called, and Astris's hands loosened.

Nyx used all her strength to hold on, using her arms to swing Astris in the Air, flipping her up. Her arms stung with the effort. Astris, kept her wings tucked.

She trusts me.

Nyx tucked her wings for a second, dropping a foot below Astris. Arms out, she grabbed Astris around the middle, cocooning her in her wings.

Below, Harvey, Jordan, and Skylar reached Kiara. Kiara met Harvey's first strike, arms crossed in front of her. Harvey's blow shoved her back, and Kiara tilted forward at the waist, hand grabbing the rock below her as she slid back towards the lava. She stopped a few feet from the lava, sprinting back towards Harvey, who was charging at her.

A roundhouse from Kiara to Harvey's face, which he barely blocked. A vial of something flew from her hand, crashing at Harvey's feet. As he blocked the kick, the vial shattered, breaking over his legs. Harvey screamed, legs boiling with acid, dropping his guard. The second kick came as Kiara was still in midair. Her leg arced towards his other side. This time, he couldn't block it and went sprawling to the side, dangerously close to the lava.

Nyx's wingbeats stuttered, but looking down at Astris, she forced herself to fly away. Skylar leapt at Kiara, latching onto her arm before getting thrown to the ground violently. He tried to get up again, but Kiara kicked him in the head, knocking him out cold.

I need to help him, but I can't let Astris get near Kiara.

Nyx plummeted again, diving down into the tunnel, back towards the sand cavern. Her hands loosened, Astris's weight too much to continue bearing. She dropped Astris below her, letting her feet hit the ground first. The pair hit the ground, tumbling across the stone before both turned to see Jordan bashing Kiara in the face with her fist.

Nice.

Kiara dodged her next punch, ducking low and sweeping Jordan's legs out from under her. The female hit the ground hard. Harvey stepped in front of her protectively, snarling.

Skylar came to consciousness, and launched himself towards Kiara with a snarl.

Kiara looked around, sucking at her teeth in annoyance.

She is outnumbered, and will struggle to beat us all, even if she is a better fighter.

Nyx looked to the vial Kiara was spinning in her hand as she deliberated.

Especially when she fights dirty, Nyx thought bitterly.

Kiara jumped into the Air, taking flight; she soared above them, shooting in the direction of the sand cavern. Nyx tried to catch her as she left, throwing herself into the Air as the female flew past. The effort was in vain as Kiara easily outmanoeuvred her, disappearing down the tunnel.

Nyx turned to look at Astris; Astris grabbed her by the front of her shirt, dragging Nyx into her. Astris kissed Nyx fiercely, without reservation. Tears streamed down her cheeks, and Nyx pulled away to brush them away.

She… We…

"You're okay now, you're okay, you're going to be okay," Nyx whispered to her, holding Astris against her chest.

I can protect her with our bond.

"Shhh it's okay. I will kill her; I won't let her hurt you again. It will all be okay. Until then, we have our bond to override hers. I can give you orders too, so I will continue to countermand her commands. I promise"

Nyx choked on her next words, "I am so sorry you have been alone for all this time through this. I am sorry I treated you like the enemy when you were suffering with me."

Astris replied in a whisper, dejected. "Our bond will break if we get out of here. It was conditional on the Labyrinth."

"We need a contingency plan," Harvey commented, cutting into their conversation, Jordan on his arm. Nyx smiled at their linked arms. "Why did she want to control you specifically?" Harvey asked.

Astris took a deep breath, meeting their gazes, "She wants to be queen. My parents owed her a debt. I didn't think…" Astris looked to Nyx, face crumpling. "Kiara is *Nightmare*. She was mad at you for not fighting Harvey for the throne. If you had, she would have asked for your hand. When it was clear you didn't want the throne, she changed to Harvey. Titan and her are planning something, along with the General. That's all I know. I wish I could tell you more."

"Nightmare?" Skylar asked, looking between Astris and Nyx.

Nyx bit her cheek, not wanting to say the next part. Astris watched her, giving Nyx time to collect herself.

Taking a deep breath, Nyx explained, "Nightmare is the name my tormenter has used in her letters. She has been putting body parts in my bed for… years. Along with little notes."

Guilt clenched at Nyx. *Why do I feel guilty? I tried to tell them. I tried.*

"Excuse me?" Harvey growled, hands clenching and eyes shifting to crimson. "Why didn't you tell me? I could've handled it."

"Because she wouldn't let her," Astris supplied, Icy eyes meeting Nyx's.

Relief filled Nyx at Astris's intervention.

Nyx nodded, "When I didn't do what she wanted, she would punish me. That's how the dragon got into my room. Why I missed so many classes."

Harvey's mouth dropped open, "That's how that… it was her dragon. I thought you had just… you were so jealous…" Harvey took a breath before meeting her eyes, "we will have her executed. She is a danger to the kingdom, to us."

"We can't just kill her, you know that. Not with the General. Even if we did it in here, we would have to kill Titan too," Nyx said, looking at Harvey.

"What about Astris's bond, though? We can't leave her like this." Skylar insisted, looking to Harvey.

"I can stop her from controlling you with the bond we have," Nyx explained again, touching Astris softly.

Astris shook her head, "That bond will end when we leave. As soon as we are out of here, I am hers again."

"There is one way," Nyx started, the insane idea taking hold.

"You could bind yourself to one of us in the old way. It is the only way we can do it without Aurum Devotum," Nyx said in a solemn tone.

"That's illegal," Harvey exclaimed.

"We are way past that point already, brother," Nyx looked pointedly at Harvey and Jordan's linked arms.

"It is dangerous," Skylar argued, jumping into the conversation.

"It is our only option." Nyx insisted, making eye contact with Skylar, then her brother.

Astris started to tremble again in her arms. Nyx pulled her closer, soothing the female, "We won't force you, but you need to counteract Kiara's power; my ability to do so likely won't last outside the trial. There's a way for you to remain free."

Nyx didn't question her decision; she dropped to her knees in front of Astris.

"What are you…" Harvey started, but Nyx held up a hand.

Her mind flashed to all the times Astris watched her.

The look in her eyes wasn't nonchalance; it was isolation. I was too trapped in my own self-loathing to notice.

Nyx sank her teeth into her own flesh, drawing blood. The taste of copper burst onto her tongue as she started chanting.
"Theon evoco ut hanc animam liget."

I call forth Theos to bind this soul.

The group went still, Harvey paling, and Astris's mouth parting in shock.

Nyx held out her hand to Astris. "You won't be alone in this. We will share the bond. I will have control over you, and you will have control over me. A double bond."

Harvey interrupted, "That has never been done before. Are you insane?"

"I don't want you to get hurt, Nyx," Astris implored her, looking to Harvey.

"It's my choice, Astris. I am choosing to be bound to you, regardless of the risk. You deserve your freedom. Don't take my choice away," Nyx begged.

Astris's eyes flashed in understanding.

"Why?" Astris met her gaze, vulnerable. The word hung in the Air between them.

Why? Because we are the same.

"You have protected me with your life. You dove into the abyss for me. Let me protect you. Even if it is a risk, I want to be the one. I will respect what you decide," Nyx said, holding Astris's gaze.

"We don't know what a double bond will do," Harvey warned. "Just do a single bond, or better yet, bond Astris to me!"

Astris looked to Harvey voice softening. "It wasn't my choice the first time. The double bond will let me be free. I haven't been free since…"

Tears filled her eyes before her face hardened.

"This time, I choose Nyx." Astris didn't look at Harvey, her gaze solely on Nyx.

Harvey shook with uncertainty, and Astris and Nyx took advantage of his internal war. It was clear he wanted to stop them but was hesitant to control Astris after learning about Kiara. Jordan put a calming hand on his bicep.

Astris touched her lips to Nyx's bleeding wrist. She looked up, pulling away with blood on her lips. Astris did the same, biting into her arm with more difficulty than Nyx had. Nyx lowered her head to Astris's blood, warm against her tongue.

This bond was deeper than Kiara's bond with Astris. Created the ancient way instead of with Aurum Devotum. More powerful and more dangerous.

Unlike Aurum Devotum, this oath was all-encompassing. The power of the Labyrinth cemented the bond in place, and Nyx wondered if their bond would be stronger.

While Aurum Devotum required the body to comply, the ritual Runes created with this bond went deeper. It affected not only the individual's body, but also their mind. Aurum Devotum caused the body to move without the consent of the individual.

This ritual gave the Runes user the power to control their bonded partner's mind in addition to their body. In theory, this provided the individual with full control, even over the individual's personality.

"*Sint duo unum,*" the pair chanted in unison.

Let two become one.

Nyx and Astris said the final words in the old language, the ancient bond sinking into their souls. Light flashed between them, their Champion and Protector Runes lighting up. The light grew, whiting out Nyx's world briefly. Pain lanced through her wrist, and both Astris and Nyx cried out in pain.

A Rune appeared on Nyx's left arm, mirroring the one that appeared on Astris. Their previous Runes remained, still located on the arm opposite the new Rune. Astris held her hand out to Nyx, who took it and rose. Nyx looked down at her new Rune, a Unity Rune within a circle. Nyx looked to Astris who was inspecting it, her eyebrows drawn together in thought.

Nyx's world shifted, everything intensifying. Her vision doubled briefly. Emotions of fear and uncertainty flashed through her in a flurry, and she grabbed onto Harvey to steady herself.

"What have I done? Why did I let her do this for me? Why did I ignore Harvey?" A flurry of thoughts, not her own, filled her mind.

Panic filled Nyx as her eyes widened.

Am I going crazy? She thought, as Astris jumped in shock at the same time.

Nyx's vision blurred, and suddenly, she was looking at herself through Astris's eyes. A blink and she was back to herself. Nyx swayed, Harvey steadying her.

"Our minds," Astris started.

Nyx nodded in agreement, eyes wide. Harvey looked between the two of them.

"What is happening? Are you two okay? I should have stopped you," Harvey agonized, panic straining his features.

"We are okay, it's okay," Astris and Nyx spoke at the same time.

"Fuck," Jordan intoned into the shocked silence that followed.

Five minutes later, Nyx and Astris were fighting off the confusion of their minds, fighting the meld. Nyx fought her own thoughts, embarrassed at the idea of Astris having unfettered access. Astris blushed as well.

Get your shit under control. Nyx thought to herself fiercely.

Astris giggled, surprising Nyx.

"We might just lose our minds," she winked.

"Who's to say we haven't already?" Nyx replied, face splitting in a smile.

"It's really, really, not funny," Harvey sighed, exasperated. "Well, minds-intact or not, we need to move. Kiara is a danger to us."

That sobered them, and within minutes, the group was ready to proceed.

Nyx wobbled as her vision switched once again.

I should really think more before acting.

Astris's voice cut in, *"but that would be far less fun — I want you impulsive. I am done following rules."*

"Stop grinning at one another and move," Harvey barked at them, stepping up to the edge of the lava field. "I'll go first."

Harvey took a deep breath, leaping onto the first stone. A yelp, and he was Airborne.

"Hot! That is scalding!" Harvey exclaimed.

"Let me see your feet," Jordan said worriedly.

Harvey landed with a wince, raising his foot. In addition to the acid burns from the vials leaving deep holes in his flesh, he now had blistering burns across the bottoms of his feet.

"I have a theory," Astris said, leaping to the first rock. Nyx reached out to grab her, but it was too late.

"My powers are awakening too; they must come out as a protective measure naturally," she said in amazement; standing on the scalding surface, her feet covered in frost.

She hopped a little bit, "Still toasty, though."

Nyx could feel the warmth coming through her own feet, "Cut that out. I feel it, too, and you aren't coping as well as you're letting on."

"This bond is killing my badass reputation," Astris lamented dramatically, hopping back.

"We could have Astris piggyback Nyx across, and I could fly. I'm not sure Astris can carry me, even if she makes two trips. I will have to risk injury on this," Harvey reasoned.

Astris winced, nodding. "Sorry, I don't think I can carry you."

Harvey was on the shorter side for an Aervel, but he was still a pure-blooded Aervel. He was a block of muscle and the same height as Astris.

"You could fly low, but you wouldn't be able to stop. No matter how far this goes, none of us will be able to stop moving," Harvey informed them.

"We need to wrap our feet," Skylar suggested. "Wet the fabric first to combat the heat." Skylar, using the last of his shirt, pressed it into some moss on the wall. Slowly, the shirt saturated with the Water, and Skylar started binding his feet.

Jordan shifted uncomfortably, looking back at the tunnel behind them. "Whatever we do, we should leave now."

Minutes later, the group were all wrapping their feet in rags. Nyx climbed onto Astris's back as Jordan shifted with a flash. With that, the group set off. Astris hopping quickly between stones.

The first time their perspective changed, they almost fell into the lava. If not for a correction from Harvey's wing, they would have descended into it.

Nyx looked at her brother; he was flying low, wings barely moving as he slotted under the low ceiling. Jordan had shifted and was at his shoulder, keeping pace with him. Astris bent low as they walked; Nyx could feel her thighs start to burn through the bond.

This is weird, Nyx thought at Astris.

"*You think?*" Astris somehow managed to sound sarcastic in her mind. Then quieter, "*I'm so sorry for how I treated you.*"

I had companionship I paid for; you were alone, Nyx stated.

"*So were you.*"

I had drinking buddies, Nyx mused.

Astris looked over her shoulder, glaring at her briefly.

"*That doesn't count, not when I know you paid for it.*"

How did you know that?

Astris's mind went quiet, but unbidden, an image flashed into Nyx's mind. A memory of Astris's, Nyx realised.

Nyx sat at the table, drink in hand, with a group of Dyrfaldur. She was covered in cuts still from the dragon attack. Agonising pain gripped Astris's chest, pain and desire. She wanted to join. She wanted to laugh with her.

Gods, she is gorgeous.

The memory went blank, Astris shifted under her.

"I didn't mean to show you that," Astris spoke into her mind.

I know, Nyx thought, pouring emotion into it.

Nyx closed her eyes, calling to mind her own memory.

Astris's long legs ate up the marble dance floor, and she dipped the other female, whose head nearly touched the floor.

The female is nothing next to Astris; how she moves is unreal. If I am the Hermes Fire lighting up a blade in a tempest, Astris is the permafrost coating a sword in the early morning, shining like tiny crystals.

Astris stopped moving, caught in the memory.

"What's going on?" Harvey yelled over his shoulder, a few yards ahead already.

"This mind-combining shit is hard," Nyx snapped at him.

Fucking cock block.

Astris's surprise and embarrassment filled her mind.

Whoops, that was out loud. Or is it out minded?

Whatever.

The cavern ceiling dipped lower and lower, forcing them to focus. Nyx kept her wings tucked, Astris tucking hers around herself. While Astris crouched through the tunnel, Nyx could feel her feet heating up.

Skylar's fox was in front of them, paws wrapped in wet fabric. He danced from rock to rock, agility allowing him to avoid catching Fire.

"Fuck, fuck, fuck." Astris started to panic.

Nyx could feel pain mixing with the burn of her thighs.

There has to be something I can do! We could switch off. Nyx thought.

"No," Astris insisted

Yes, Nyx argued

"No," Astris declared, sending an image of her teeth bared.

Nyx grinned, face hurting.

That has been happening a lot recently.

Nyx closed her eyes, focusing on the feeling of each step, leaning into the pain coming from Astris's thighs and feet.

Maybe I can…

They switched bodies, Nyx opening her eyes to see the cavern ahead. Astris's feet burned despite the frost, and Nyx hopped, feeling her body bounce on top of herself.

Thank fuck, I'm not as heavy as I thought. Still, this is like strength training on steroids.

"Give me back my fucking body. You can't just hijack it!" Astris called into her mind.

Nyx ignored her, pushing Astris's body through the exercise, taking on the mental strain.

I am already letting you ruin your physical body for me. Let me help. I said I would only use the bond to protect you. This is me doing that.

Ahead, Harvey's wings started to brush against the sides of the tunnel. He started beating his wings short and fast, like a hummingbird. Nyx could smell burning feathers and flesh.

The stones kept getting further and further apart as the tunnel narrowed. It forced Harvey to land, using his wings in combination with his legs. Soon, he was lunging across the rocks, wings flapping over each gap.

Nyx watched as his wing hit the side of the cave, Harvey cringed away instinctively. His instinctual flinch, sent him into a free fall, wings no longer holding his weight. His face was inches from the lava when Jordan darted to the top of the tunnel and shifted. Her hand snatched Harvey by the collar, and she yanked him up.

His movement stopped just long enough for Harvey to use his wings again. Nyx's breath caught as she watched Jordan fall, wingless. Just before she hit the lava, she shifted again. The finch flew low by the lava before returning to Harvey's side.

She keeps saving his life. If Harvey doesn't try to give her a title after this, I will.

Nyx's stomach dropped, the dread doubling as she and Astris looked at the challenge ahead. They would have to dip low as well; the problem was they had two bodies and twice the height. Harvey was alone, and Jordan had shifted to pass through this obstacle.

Nyx blinked, still in Astris's body.

What if?

She reflected, focusing on the sensation of panic she felt when Astris had been in peril.

She could feel her fangs drop, but which body is that? Instead of fighting the transition, she leaned into it, using the pain from the hot stones to transition.

"You just shifted my body. Nyx. Nyx!"

I know, Nyx thought in astonishment. *Now hang on.*

Astris sent Nyx an image of her grinning before grabbing hard onto thick fur with Nyx's hands. Nyx guided Astris's wolf across the stones, using Astris's heat resistance to leap across the expansive gaps.

There were four more to go, the distance getting wider and wider between rocks. Nyx pounced to the next one, back paw barely hitting the stone. On the next stone, Astris used Nyx's wings to give them more lift. Two more to go. The next jump had Astris's wolf tumbling almost to the lava. Fire bit at them, the heat causing exhaustion.

One more to go.

The final jump had the pair tumbling to the ground, rolling to a stop at Harvey's feet. Harvey and Jordan were sitting, gaping at them as they arrived in wolf form, Skylar standing in disbelief and shock.

Nyx switched their bodies, shifting Astris back. When Nyx met Skylar's gaze she flinched.

I could have trusted him with the truth.

A Unity Rune flickered to life above them, but its light kept dimming, losing its brilliance.

It must not be full power with only some of us having passed.

Nyx's triumph at making it through the challenge with Astris died as she spotted her brother. Pain wrenched through her chest as she saw the blistering and bleeding soles of his feet. He did not have the protections Astris and Nyx offered each other. Jordan squeezed some moss Water onto Harvey's feet, gaze meeting Nyx's.

He likely won't be able to walk for a while. How are we supposed to make it through while carrying him? We could wait, but... Kiara.

Nyx's determined gaze met Astris's fearful one, and they shared a moment of understanding. They would survive this, together.

CHAPTER 20: HARVEY

Riddle Me This

I sent you a puzzle lock for your birthday. When you open it, you will find your actual gift inside. Good luck.

-Queen Blackthorn letter to Harvey, 8th Day 50 AT

The group walked through the night, Nyx carrying Harvey on her back. His sister refused to let anyone else take him. She began fussing over him from the moment she saw his feet.

Swallow your pride, Harvey, he thought. *You know damn well how much it hurts to stand, let alone walk.*

Still, he hoped the cavern would open up soon so he could fly. The tips of his wings were singed as well, and he cringed at the thought of them brushing against the walls again.

"We have to be almost done," Astris stated from beside Nyx.

"What makes you say that?" Harvey asked her.

"Every obstacle has had an Element attached to it. Fire was the last of the eight Elements," Astris explained.

"I hate to ask, but do we need to wait for Kiara and Titan? There is a chance the final trial won't be accessible without them." Skylar asked.

Harvey's thoughts went to his ex-fiancé.

Being pulled away from our usual environment was the conduit to our change. I let Titan and Kiara torment Nyx.

Harvey closed his eyes.

All because I was obsessed with Titan. I was thinking of my position and power instead of my family.

I told myself I did what I could, but did I truly?

Or was I blind to my own reality?

I was a monster just like him; I discriminated against all I deemed below me. I ignored my own sister's plight for the promise of the General's favour. I ignored the signs of Titan changing… ignored Kiara's influence.

Harvey's rumination was interrupted when Nyx stopped at the next trial. The tunnel opened into a large chamber. Above the doorway, all of the Elemental Runes glowed. The chamber was a grey stone flecked with purple and gold. The floor was slick to match the walls and high ceiling. At the centre of the space was a glowing crystal on a tall pedestal. Light reflected from it in a prismatic display of the Elements. As Harvey looked at it, he watched a wave crash inside the crystal.

That must be it. The end. Where the Theos has been stored all these years.

Around the room was a ring of monstrous statues in aggressive stances, as if ready to fight. Each one was taller than Harvey, and a darker grey than the rest of the room.

The crystal is the end; it's almost over. We are going to get out of here.

Nyx rushed forward before Harvey could caution her.

As soon as she stepped into the room, the two statues on either side of the entrance lowered their axes with a *clack*. One statue was an Aervel, the other was a Dyrfaldur. Each held an axe and a buckler.

The statues looked at them lifelessly before opening their mouths in tandem to speak: "Eight statues surround the crystal. Eight guardians." They spoke in complete unison. Their voices filled the room with a thousand echoes, a growl entering the low timbre of their voices as they finished. "Fight them through wit or grit, the end result is the same. Only then, the crystal you may claim."

"That can't be good," Nyx whispered, wiggling her fingers up at him.

"No, it cannot," Harvey replied, dropping down off her back.

He winced as his feet hit the cool, slick floor. They were still raw and burned. It took everything in his power not to give in to the pain and sink to his knees, cradling his feet like a child.

Harvey mastered his mind, stepping past the statues, which now raised their axes to let them pass. He stepped to the centre where the crystal sat, inspecting it and the surrounding room.

The crystal was mounted on a pedestal that sat at shoulder height to Harvey. Harvey tried to pull the crystal off, but it was locked in place.

It was worth a shot.

Around him, the statues loomed, depicting a variety of monsters. Each one stood on a short platform with words engraved on the bottom. Harvey inspected the words under the first creature. It was a Hydra, heads tall and looming.

The words are a riddle, Harvey realised.

"Fight through wit or grit; the end result is the same," he muttered to himself.

Harvey stepped back to the centre of the room, taking stock of the creatures. Starting at the Hydra, he went around, listing the creatures.

"Hydra, Ettin, Cyclops, Chimera, Golem, Basilisk, Skeleton, and a Minotaur."

"Eight Elements; check them for any Elemental Runes," Astris said.

"You're right," Jordan yelled from the Golem statue, "there are handprints with Runes in them for the Elements; each monster has assigned Elements."

"Multiple?" Harvey asked

"I have a feeling anyone else who jumps in to help won't like the result," Astris remarked. "Nyx is Electricity, Harvey is Illusion, and I am Ice. We are limited by that."

"Agreed," Harvey confirmed.

"Except their Protectors, that is," Jordan corrected, grinning at Harvey.

"We don't know that," Harvey replied. "Dyrfaldur aren't connected to the Elements. You won't be able to activate any of them."

"Why else would we be here? I may not be able to activate them, but I can still fight," Jordan argued.

"Let's deal with that afterwards. I don't want to risk anyone." Harvey's eyes met Jordan's, and he felt a warmth creep up his neck.

"What about any monsters with an Element we don't have?" Nyx asked.

"It looks like every statue has at least two Elements. We should avoid fighting regardless. They gave us an option for no bloodshed. Let's take it."

"Alright, everyone, go around and look at the riddles on the pedestals under the statues. Check with the group before taking action," Harvey warned.

Harvey walked forward to the first monster: a Hydra. It stood tall, wrought out of stone, overly sized, and hissing. Its powerful claws gripped the stone pedestal, where two handprints were sunken into the stone.

Water and Fire, Harvey thought, looking at the symbol in each handprint.

The pain of renewed grief bit at Harvey's psyche, but he forced the feelings away.

I can't afford to get distracted; too much is at stake. The riddle was scrawled into the stone before them:

I burn, but am held

Take me out for a lark

Or put me in a room, dark

Contained, my sides weld

Harvey started working through the riddle.

Something that burns narrows it down to three options: Fireplace, lantern, or something living. With the sides welded and the ability to carry the Fire? It has to be a lantern.

Harvey looked to his team, who were wandering from statue to statue.

This is far too important to do on my own. I need to trust my team, as they have trusted me.

"Over here," Harvey called, motioning the group to join him at the next statue. The next statue was the Ettin, a two-headed giant that lived in the mountainous regions of Dengar. Harvey moved to stand in front of it. The riddle below it was:

Hearts I cut

Eyes I shut

I may be short in height

But that doesn't affect my bite

Weapons, sharp, not bludgeoning-based. Something short…

"Dagger," Nyx spoke up, surprising Harvey. She noticed his surprise and gave him a small smirk, pointing at the dagger in the Ettin's belt. Harvey's mouth dropped open.

"One down," Jordan cheered, pumping a fist.

"Well, that was convenient," Skylar remarked merrily.

"The Gods don't do convenient," Harvey replied, sobering the group again.

"Lantern, for the Hydra," Astris concluded, looking at the beast thoughtfully.

Harvey nodded, "That's what I was thinking as well."

"Let's read all of them before answering. The light is dimming, and we can sleep on some of the riddles." Harvey suggested, and the others agreed.

Harvey moved on to the Cyclops. It was taller than Harvey and twice as wide.

Its bicep is as large as my thigh.

He looked at the riddle and read:

I sing a breathy song

Sleepy or vivacious

Soft or strong

Pores and keys efficacious

Next, the group walked to the Chimera. It had the body of a lion, with two heads on its shoulders. One head was a lion, and the other head was a nasty-looking goat with wickedly sharp horns. Finally, a snake served as the monstrosity's tail. Under this monster was the riddle:

A shadow of an escort

An exchange of support

I walk with you

Strides true

The Golem came after the Chimera. It appeared melted and uneven; its body slumped slightly to one side. Drops of mud sloughed off of it, now frozen in stone. The Runes showed Metal and Air.

"We shouldn't count on any fights. I get the sense we need to complete all of these challenges before the crystal will be accessible," Jordan replied with an edge to her voice.

Harvey cleared his throat and read the next riddle:

I drain while dampening

I sweeten and bite the tongue

I befuddle yet prompt candour

I may blush red or pale

Or prompt a boisterous tale

I drain while dampening, does that refer to the act of Water falling down a drain, or a more abstract version of drain?

Dampening refers to moisture, so possibly something that both hydrates and dehydrates. That, in combination with the boisterous tale, leads me to believe alcohol is the answer.

"It has to be some type of alcohol," Harvey answered, and the rest of the group nodded in agreement. "Basilisk next." Harvey walked to the giant serpent. It sat curled on the pedestal; head reared back in an aggressive stance. Its fangs were as long as Harvey's forearm. "This one looks difficult to fight; let's hope we can solve it."

Harvey read the Basilisk's riddle:

I offer shelter or comfort

Cradled in my domain

I offer assistance in sickness or health

"The next one is the Skeleton."

The Skeleton stood on the pedestal above the riddle. It was the same height as Astris and had wings made of bone. In its hands, it held a longsword, ready to fight.

"Jordan, you read this one," Harvey offered, looking to the female.

I have no clue how I ignored her beauty this long; she is captivating.

Jordan caught his look and blushed. She turned away slightly, reading the next riddle out loud:

Keep me warm

Sunshine or storm

I dance with you

Your journey true

The final statue was a Minotaur. With the head of a bull, it looked like a half-shifted bull-Dyrfaldur, but twice the size and bulging with muscle. Harvey took an involuntary step back as he looked up its massive body to its beady eyes. It was twice Harvey's height, with powerful corded muscles along its arms and legs. Its horns were as long as daggers, curved slightly. Harvey wrenched his eyes away from the beast that had ravaged his kingdom since the Hell portal. The riddle below it read:

Unwanted, but sometimes needed

Wrists become impeded

Freedom, I grip

Skin raw, I strip

After studying all the statues, Harvey turned to the group.

"Has anyone come up with any answers to the riddles? So far, we have the Hydra and the Ettin figured out. I don't know how we will solve the Hydra without Sabastian, though. It is activated by Water and Fire. We have neither in our party."

"I'll do it," Skylar said firmly, "I was his Protector."

Harvey was about to protest, but he recognised determination in the male. He watched as Skylar walked over to the pedestal with the Hydra. Looking from one hand print to another, he put one hand on each. The beast reared up, its body turning to flesh.

"Lantern," Skylar said, and Harvey held his breath.

The Hydra dipped its long neck to inspect him. After considering the male for a moment, it tipped its head in a small bow, rearing its head back, and solidifying to stone. Skylar looked over to them and gave a small thumbs-up.

"I have been waiting a long time to see Freya. I didn't think we would succeed, but now I will do anything to make that happen," Skylar stated, tears welling in the corners of his eyes.

Harvey nodded at the male in acknowledgement. "We will get home; I will get us home."

"We will get us home," Nyx corrected, walking to Skylar and placing a hand on him. "I miss her too," her voice softened.

Harvey walked to the Ettin. "This one is Illusion; I will solve it. Everyone is in agreement that the answer is 'dagger'?"

The others nodded, and Harvey placed his hand down. The Ettin brandished a large cudgel, bottom fangs stained red from blood. Harvey made eye contact with the monster and spoke clearly, "dagger."

The Ettin inclined his heads, solidifying. Harvey let out the breath he had been holding. He removed his hand, joining the others who had moved to the next statue.

It was the Cyclops "I don't know the answer to this riddle," Harvey admitted. He read the riddle again:

I sing a breathy song

Sleepy or vivacious

Soft or strong

Pores and keys efficacious

"I've got nothing," Astris said, reading the riddle as well.

"Its Elements are Metal and Water. I don't feel comfortable guessing. As much as I hate it, I think we need to wait for Titan and Kiara."

"Minotaur's balls" Nyx growled.

"The best we can do for now is to knock out as many of the riddles as we can before the light has fully subsided," Astris offered up, but she looked shaken by the idea of Kiara and Titan returning. Nyx put a comforting hand on her lower back.

They have gotten… intimate.

Harvey raised an eyebrow at Nyx, who refused to look at him.

I guess she hasn't come to terms with it yet.

"The remaining statues are the Chimera, Golem, Basilisk, Skeleton, and Minotaur. Does anyone know the answers to any of those riddles?"

"I think the Golem's is 'wine', but we will have to wait for Titan and Kiara on that one as well," Jordan sighed in frustration.

"That makes sense, something that can be either pale or red, and causes one to become boisterous," Skylar jumped in.

"I know the Minotaur's," Astris's voice was soft, pained. She swallowed before continuing:

"The answer is shackles," Astris spat out the word, fury slipping into her tone. "I'm sure Kiara will be able to answer that one. It's her Element."

"I want to fight," Astris said, frost covering her arms.

"Look down," Harvey said. She scowled, but looked down in amazement at the Theos. Her body relaxed visibly. "Nyx and I will fight first; you can fight the next one if you calm down enough to have a clear head. For this first one, no Protectors, we need to conserve our strength."

Astris let out a frustrated growl before walking to the entrance of the cavern with Skylar and Jordan.

Harvey walked around the circle, selecting the Chimera. Harvey and Nyx placed their hands in their respective positions for Illusion and Electricity. As they touched the pedestal, the beast came to life. It was the size of a large horse, its stone disintegrating into flesh as the Theos took hold. The Chimera shook out its mane, its other head swiping the Air with its horns. Behind it, the tail hissed, and the snake tasted the Air menacingly as it swung around to face them. The Chimera crouched, ready to fight.

Harvey felt uncertain as he realised, he didn't know how to activate it.

"Um… battle?" Nothing happened. "Let's try… fight?" Harvey intoned, and the Chimera came to life, a rack of weapons appearing behind it.

Thank you, Marvos, for not making us fight without one.

Harvey and Nyx circled around the Chimera. They moved in tandem without thinking. The Chimera's muscles bunched as it prepared to leap. The beast bound towards them before disappearing into thin Air.

They waited, Harvey and Nyx spinning around, looking for the creature. It appeared right next to Nyx.

"Watch out," Harvey roared, and Nyx jumped back, flipping away as the Chimera appeared behind her.

Another Chimera appeared, this one hazy at the edges.

An Illusion! Harvey realised as the second Chimera lunged at him. He turned away from it, stabbing at the real one. Nyx yelped as one of the Chimeras went through him.

Electricity speared towards Nyx from the Chimera. Nyx ducked. Harvey ran around behind the Chimera, grabbing a longsword and a pair of throwing axes, their weapons of choice. He threw the axes next to Nyx, who was circling and dodging the Chimera. Nyx dove forward, grabbing one axe in each hand then jumping back away again.

The Chimera swiped a paw at her, claws flashing. Nyx threw an axe at the left side of the beast, kicking off the ground toward the right. A swing at the beast's side opened up a gash. It snarled at her, mouth opening. Electricity crackled in its throat as it faced her, teeth bared.

I need to get its attention away from Nyx. Harvey gritted his teeth in determination.

"Don't ignore me!" Harvey roared at the beast, jumping off the pedestal, sword raised high. The beast met him in the Air, teeth clamping on his sword, claws slashing at him. The Chimera easily overpowered him, shoving him into the rock. The ground split around him at the impact, blood spraying from the claws embedded in his chest. Harvey screamed. Coughing blood, he looked into the eyes of the lion. It started to rip at him, claws sharp as knives. His vision blurred as the pain overwhelmed him. Nausea rushed through him as he watched the snarling lion's head open its mouth and lunge.

Nyx slammed into the Chimera, ripping it off of Harvey. He screamed as the claws popped out of his skin, gushing crimson blood. Nyx and the Chimera tumbled to the floor, Nyx's black feathers flying in the Air.

Harvey pushed himself to his feet, coughing blood. His feet burned, and he tripped before catching himself. Jordan was in front of him as he rose, her body between him and the Chimera.

She shouldn't be here! I told her to hold back.

She had managed to get her hands on a bow and was tracking the Chimera as it rolled with Nyx. She let one loose, and the Chimera's heads let out a combination of screams and growls as the arrow pierced its flank. The Chimera and Nyx separated, Nyx running to join Jordan and Harvey.

"So much for keeping Protectors out of it! You could have gotten yourself killed," Harvey snapped at Jordan.

"You're welcome," she snapped back at him.

Harvey took to the Air, wings pumping as he became Airborne. Blood poured from his side, dripping onto the ground as he took off. He held a hand over the wound, awake with the pain.

Nyx faced the monster, her teeth bared, matching the Chimera. She brandished her axe, swinging at the lion's head. The lion took the axe slash to the skull, roaring. The goat head swung towards her, horn skewering Nyx's side. Nyx screamed, and Harvey dropped down from the Air towards the Chimera.

I won't let this end here. We are so close.

His massive sword swung in a large arc, wings shooting him forward with one enormous beat. Metal flashed as it swiped down and lopped off the goat's head. At the last minute, Harvey's vision doubled, the sword cloning as he swung. The beast reacted to the Illusion.

I must have lost a lot of blood to be seeing double.

The snake tail struck at him, and he caught it on his blade. The oversized fangs clashed against the Metal. Electricity flowed the blade, and Harvey yelped, dropping it. His hands smoked, and he dodged the snake again, ducking under its fangs. The goat head's stump was bleeding profusely, but the lion head was still fighting alongside the snake. Nyx spun away from the decapitated goat head, body coming free. Blood covered the ground, from both Aervel and the Chimera. Astris jumped in, pulling Nyx away from the Chimera's snapping jaws. Nyx fell to the ground, eyes rolling back as she held her side.

Jordan shot another arrow into the monster, slotting the arrow through the serpent's eye. The tail went limp.

Just the lion now, Harvey thought, bolstered. He winced at his feet, the burn blisters opening. His bare feet were slippery on the floor with the open blisters and blood. The pain and nausea swept through him again, and he fought to stay upright.

Harvey rolled, snagging his sword.

Almost there.

The Chimera, with two stumps bleeding, lunged at Harvey. Harvey leapt back, flipping away and blocking a fang with the blade. A blister opened with the movement, and he grunted.

Nyx kicked the beast's flank, drawing its attention. Jordan sent another arrow flying, shooting it through the lion's eye as the creature turned. The Chimera shuddered once before collapsing to the ground.

Gods, she is an amazing shot.

Harvey fell to the floor, exhausted. He ignored the blood on the floor and put a hand to his side. His Aervel healing had already started closing the wound. The dismantled Chimera disintegrated, reappearing whole and stonified in a bow on the pedestal.

"We won't be able to make it through all of them today," Harvey sighed.

"The other group is likely to catch up with us soon," Astris warned. "We can only hope that they take a while to cross the magma."

"There's still light to clear another monster. I don't want to jinx it, but if we succeed, does anyone have any clue where we will end up?" Nyx asked, Skylar binding her wounds. She shook off her shoulders, a look of determination in her eyes.

Astris jumped into the conversation. "The priests and philosophers don't agree on the subject, but all agree that the Champions and Protectors will teleport to where the 'seat of power' is. This leads me to believe it is the castle, a popular theory among the priests. That's where the husks of failed Champions show up anyway," Astris grabbed a long whip off the weapons rack. "Nyx, I'd ask if you were still good to fight, but I can feel your pent-up energy. You guys break; we will take the next one."

Harvey walked to the entrance, sitting up against the two statues that guard the door, Jordan joining him. Nyx grabbed her axe that had fallen to the floor. Harvey watched as Nyx and Astris put their hands on the pedestal under the Aervel Skeleton, having decided the riddle was unsolvable.

"Fight," They intoned, completely in sync, each placing a hand on their respective Element.

The Aervel monstrosity came to life, brandishing a short axe in one hand and a buckler in the other arm. Astris and Nyx backed up to the centre of the room, each going to a different side of the creature. It cocked its head at them, stone eyes tracking them in a predatory fashion.

Nyx lunged, axes slashing in tandem. The Skeleton met her blow for blow, sparks lighting up the cavern as the two faced off. Astris unfurled the whip, letting the barbed tail hang down. She snapped it at the Skeleton, and an Ice shield blocked the strike, appearing in mid-Air.

"Fuck," Harvey said, sitting up straighter. "I should have seen this coming. The Chimera used Theos as well." Havey raised his voice, "It has Theos!"

Astris sent a flurry of strikes at the Aervel, who turned to meet her. It raised its shield, coating it in Electricity. The hairs on Astris's neck stood up. She stopped, eyes narrowing; the Aervel maintained dead eye contact with her as it blocked a strike from Nyx.

With the back of its hand, it struck Nyx in a dismissive blow. His sister flew backward, rolling and skidding across the rock. Her black bloody feathers coated the ground. Harvey could smell the sickly-sweet blood the scent thick in the room. He could taste the copper on his tongue as he watched with bated breath. A drop of cold sweat dripped down his back, and he shivered slightly.

The Skeleton grabbed onto Astris, frost covering its bony hand. Astris shrugged off the Icy embrace, unaffected, leaping back.

Her Theos is continuing to come back as well, Harvey noted, eyes tracking the fight.

The blood on the floor splashed under her feet, covering her legs in a spray of gore.

The 'Blood Chamber', that's what I will call this place if we ever get out. I wonder, if I try to intervene, what will this place do to me? I'm not a Protector or one of the Elements required.

Struck with an idea, Harvey turned to the statue sentries that guarded the door.

"Hey, boneheads, what would happen if I interfered right now?" he held the gaze of the hollowed eye sockets.

The statues considered him, and Harvey wondered if they would even bother to respond. In unison, they answered his query, "Interference leads to the loss of your mind."

"Great, so if I try to interfere, I become half a version of myself," Harvey cringed, turning to watch Nyx and Astris again. "That must be how Champions came back as husks, mindless with their bodies desiccated, unable to build muscle."

Kiara strutted in and took in the scene. She hummed in pleasure as Nyx screamed, and Harvey lost it. He turned to Kiara, lashing out. A punch, and she fell to the ground.

Gods that felt good.

The Skeleton pulled its sword free, immediately moving to strike Nyx down. Astris and Nyx dove to opposite sides, hitting the rock hard. The Skeleton chased after Astris, continually striking at her with Ice and a blade. Astris danced out of the way, body agile.

Kiara got to her feet behind Harvey, wiping the blood off her mouth. She curled into Titan's side, whispering something to him. Titan looked at Harvey murderously. Harvey glared back at him, fury overtaking him. He forced himself to turn away. His sister needed him, and this time he was choosing her.

Kiara won't take a cheap shot with Titan here. He still thinks she is honourable. Nyx is the priority... she has been the second choice for too long.

Nyx approached from the other side of the Skeleton, axes brandished. The cut to her abdomen was deep, causing her to lilt to one side.

Our lineage values family above all else. I have never embodied our values. I am not worthy of the crown... Nyx is.

Nyx's body lit with Electricity as she let out a battle cry. Two steps, and she leapt on top of the Aervel's back, axes coming around each side of the Aervel's neck. It Electrified, but Nyx was immune.

She used the axes to hook and snap the spine. Each axe head pulled vertebrae in a different direction, and the spine was ripped in half like fresh bread. The Skeleton dissolved, appearing on the pedestal in a deep bow.

Nyx and Astris limped over to Harvey and the others. Astris's eyes met Kiara's, the temperature dropping in the room. Nyx positioned herself between the two, Electricity still dancing across her skin.

"We're done for the day," Nyx commanded, glaring at the group.

Blood dripped down her side and arm, and she clutched it. Astris, noticing her wound, placed a hand on Nyx's lower back, guiding her out of the blood-soaked chamber. Skylar followed, going to work immediately, ignoring the drama and binding everyone's wounds expertly.

Harvey looked one last time to his sister as Astris led her out of the chamber, pride filling him.

She has come a long way.

CHAPTER 21: ASTRIS

Tempest and Ice

My beautiful daughter, I hope you are doing well at Veritas Hall. I have included money for your school supplies in this letter. General Titus saving us from debt has truly changed our lives. Now we can finally give you more of what you deserve. The Gods have blessed our family.

*-Kayleen Archer letter to Astris, 20*th *Day, 76 AT*

Nyx and Astris walked silently past Kiara and the others, Nyx brushing her wing against Astris. They walked down the hallway, far away from the others, delving into a false path to be alone.

Always alone. Astris thought as they walked, unintentionally transmitting the thought to Nyx.

"No," Nyx transmitted into Astris's mind. *"I will always be here."*

Astris looked at her, startled by the vulnerability and conviction in the words.

I don't understand. Why are you okay with how I treated you? Astris's regret echoing in the words.

"I am not okay with the actions you took, but us... this, I like," Nyx said this out loud, blushing and motioning between them.

Wait blushing? She should hate me; she should despise me. Why is she looking at me that way?

"Is it really that surprising?" Nyx thought back.

Nyx took Astris's hand, and Astris froze. She stared down at Nyx's hand in hers. Nyx pulled her in, catching her at the waist.

"What?" Astris breathed.

"Want to do something crazy?" Nyx said huskily.

"Yes," Astris whispered, Nyx up close now.

Astris watched the Electricity flash, pulsing through Nyx's irises. She could hear the crackle of the power, static Electricity gathering in her hair.

You aren't an Electrified blade like I thought. Astris reflected, *you are the product of a powerful earthquake, the explosion of Electrical coruscation. You light up the world around you.*

Astris remembered the one time she had witnessed the rare sight. She was up in the Air to avoid the quakes, and her vision flashed white as the sky Electrified with the earth's friction. She imagined the sight and the wonder it had brought. Unlike lightning, it came in a single explosion, like Nyx's spontaneous and intense nature.

Nyx smirked, *"Gods, you are cheesy… Thank you for showing me that, it was beautiful… like you."*

Astris could feel the evidence of her embarrassment rise to her face, eliciting a wider smile from Nyx. Nyx leaned in slowly, eyes darting to Astris's lips. Astris's mind went blank as she closed the distance, crashing into the kiss. It was better than she remembered from the Fire trial. Nyx's lips were soft, hands tentatively holding her by the waist.

Astris smiled into the kiss, unable to help herself. Teeth flashed, and Astris could see Nyx fighting her own smile.

"It's pretty inconvenient to be this happy with what I want to do to you." Astris sent her thought into Nyx's mind, and Nyx giggled. Nyx's laugh was the most exquisite sound Astris had ever heard her make. The sound felt precious, a vulnerability vocalised in a display of trust.

The kiss deepened, smiles fading as their lust took over. Astris trailed her hands across Nyx's body, hands brushing over her hip bones, tight core, and muscular back. Nyx trembled under Astris's touch.

I want you, Astris begged mentally, too engulfed in the kiss to break free.

"You have me," Nyx vowed, pressing her body flush against Astris.

Astris's mind went blank, her body reacting with double the intensity. Every movement, every touch, every observation, doubled. Desire filled Astris until she was drunk on it. She growled deep in her throat, sucking at Nyx's bottom lip. Astris ran her tongue gently over it, holding it between her teeth, before slowly dragging her teeth back. Nyx gasped, voice like honey in Astris's ears.

"My turn," Nyx growled in her mind.

Astris's heart raced at the challenge. She leaned forward, eyes narrowing slightly, gaze locking hers in place.

Astris felt Nyx's leg sweep before she saw it. Somehow, Nyx hid her intentions from her, catching Astris off guard.

With a hand behind her neck and the other at her waist, Nyx dipped her. Slowly, she lowered Astris to the floor.

Nyx was poised above her, hand under Astris's head to protect it from the ground. Her body was muscled from training, her shoulders broad. Nyx's strawberry strands, soft in the darkening tunnel, tickled Astris's skin.

She set Astris down, standing up. "What?" Astris asked, starting to sit up.

Nyx pulled clumps of moss off the wall, surprising a laugh out of Astris as dirt clods fell on her. Nyx placed the moss under Astris's head for extra comfort, pushing the hair out of her face. Nyx's hand dragging along Astris's midriff.

Kisses trailed up her neck, soft in contrast to Nyx's lean muscles. Nyx took Astris's earlobe in her mouth, dragging it through her teeth. Astris shivered, goosebumps running down her skin. Electric desire filled them both as Nyx's knee slid between Astris's thighs.

Her leg dragged luxuriously against her centre, friction gathering. She rolled her eyes back, groaning at the touch.

"Fuck, angel," Astris's breath caught, capturing Nyx's mouth again.

More. I want more.

"Mmm, I love the sounds you make for me," Nyx crooned into the kiss.

Astris's body reacted, tension building. She growled, raising a knee and flipping herself on top. Nyx's eyes widened in shock, then relaxed with pleasure, her eyes settling on a dare. Astris took the dare, never one to back down from a challenge.

Astris pinned Nyx, arms above her head. Nyx's gaze held Astris's unblinkingly. Her eyes were intense, desire swirling, causing the Electricity to zap violently, eyelashes lighting up briefly. A slight crackle came from her Electric-ringed eyes, and Astris could feel the hairs on the back of her neck rise.

The power surged below her like a live wire. Electricity danced down Nyx's face, crackling loudly now. Astris traced the path of the sparks, adrenaline shooting through her veins and mingling with pleasure. Astris could feel her hair rise with the dancing energy. She pulled at Nyx's shirt, undoing the buttons under each wing, slipping it off to expose Nyx. The fabric dropped, exposing her bare chest. Cold Air nipped at her exposed skin.

Gorgeous, so entirely, and brilliantly stunning, Astris thought.

Nyx swallowed, lips parting slightly. Her skin was pebbled with goosebumps, her chest pushing up towards her in an arch, as if her body was subconsciously fighting to be closer to Astris. A frustrated sound, and Nyx flipped them back expertly, ensuring Astris's head found the moss again.

"Now, now, I have been waiting for this for too long for you to try to dominate me. I have been picturing this for years, hating myself for it. Now, be my good angel and listen," Nyx chided.

Surprise filled Astris, and Nyx's eyes sparked.

She said my, Astris thought, shocked into silence.

Nyx's hands slowly trailed across her skin teasingly. Nyx gently pulled at her shirt, a request. Astris pulled off her torn shirt, sitting up briefly. As soon as Astris had taken it off, cold Air kissed her skin. Astris looked to Nyx.

I need to be close to you. Astris thought, pleading with Nyx. *I don't want anything between us. That has been the case for far too long.*

Nyx obliged her, maintaining eye contact as she took off her own tunic, weight pinning Astris's hips to the ground. Kisses trailed down her neck, tracing her collarbone, and Astris closed her eyes. Nyx's breasts brushed her own, the nipples pebbling against her sensitive skin.

Every touch was doubled, every sensation shared. Talking stopped, and Nyx kissed Astris, exploring her body. Her knee went between where her thighs met, a question. Astris parted for her, an answer. She pulled at Nyx's hips desperately, grinding into her. Nyx huffed a low laugh.

Please, Astris begged mentally.

Nyx crashed into her, pressing into Astris's sex as she slowly traced her teeth with her tongue.

Fuck.

Fingers came to rest on her hips, pulling Astris closer, lifting her slightly off the ground. Nyx's lips found her throat, trailing kisses down the centre, pinning Astris down.

The kisses continued, soft yet demanding. Down between Astris's breasts, hands pulling at her pants. Astris helped, kicking her pants off and pulling Nyx back to her. Skin brushed on skin, and Nyx's lips drifted downwards. Astris plunged her hands into Nyx's hair, feeling the soft strands running through her fingers.

Nyx kissed down past her sex and down her thigh, stopping at her knee. Slowly, the kisses trailed back up, following the inside of her thigh.

Astris trembled, wetness increasing, Nyx's breath warm against her skin. Two more kisses and Nyx blew gently on her, cold Air prompting her body to clench before Nyx's tongue plunged into her. Astris cried out, Nyx grabbing her by the hips. Nyx lifted Astris by her ass, using her hands to rock her against her mouth. Astris felt the pressure increase and ebb, lighting her on Fire.

More, more, more. Astris begged.

Astris's toes curled, soft wet sounds filling the corridor as Nyx lapped at her lavishly, short nails digging into her skin. Nyx's tongue dipped into her again, going deeper and deeper, before curling up. Astris bit her lip, eyes rolling back. Nyx's tongue teased Astris's G-spot, coaxing her before pulling out and latching onto her clit.

Cool Air touched the slick wetness between her thighs, and Astris projected her desires into Nyx's mind, too wrapped in the sensation to talk. Nyx obliged her.

Nyx dropped back between her legs.

Tongue dragging languidly across Astris's clit, swirling around it twice before sucking it into her mouth. Astris gasped, moving her shin up between Nyx's. Astris lay below Nyx, one shin angled up, pressing into Nyx's pussy. Wetness pooled there, and Astris pushed against her as Nyx feasted on her, short enough to make the position work.

Soft, warm, and wet, Astris explored Nyx, thigh rubbing through Nyx's legs, pressing up. Nyx came alive, pushing her down and going back to Astris's body, frustrated at the interruption. Astris smirked, feeling Nyx's impatience.

"You taste how I always imagined," Nyx breathed into her.

Astris blushed at the lust that laced through Nyx's voice. Fingers traced up her thigh, teasing her at first. With one hand, Nyx intertwined her fingers with Astris's own. Her other hand between Astris's legs.

Slowly, Nyx filled her with two fingers, thrumming her fingers up, creating friction and pushing Astris closer to climax.

"You are so beautiful, laid out for me." Nyx whispered, her eyes flashing.

Nyx captured Astris's clit in her mouth, careful with the sensitive bundle of nerves. Astris clenched around Nyx's fingers, whimpering involuntarily. Nyx's tongue lapped at her clit, top teeth creating a barrier that trapped her clit between teeth and tongue.

The pressure was rougher, more direct now, Nyx lightly nipping at her clit. Astris yelped, and Nyx's laugh reverberated through her sensually.

Gods, her voice could make me cum alone, Astris thought.

Pleased laughter filled her mind as Nyx increased her pace. She dipped her head down, gently running her tongue up and down Astris's slit. Another finger and Astris felt herself stretch luxuriously, pressure building through her as she arched into Nyx's mouth.

Nyx pulled away, Astris reaching for her. Nyx's left hand, still entwined in her own, pulled her up into a kiss. Astris groaned into it, pushing into Nyx.

"I want you to sit on my face," Nyx said, pulling at Astris insistently, "I want you to ride my tongue until you are trembling for me."

I am far too heavy for that, Astris started to protest mentally, but Nyx silenced her anxieties.

"You are tiny, and I am far from breakable. What do you say, darling?" Astris considered her before biting her lip. She tilted her head in consent, projecting her desires mentally. She allowed Nyx to lie down and guide her. Astris positioned herself above Nyx, nervously looking into her Electric eyes.

Nyx, sensing her insecurities, grabbed her, pulling her into her face. Astris gasped as Nyx consumed her from below, dragging her across her face. Astris's knees settled on either side of Nyx. She closed her eyes, tilting her head back, lips parting slightly. Tension built in her body, lighting up her very soul.

I can't hold myself back any longer, Astris thought, breathing rapidly.

Nyx pulled her in, ushering Astris to climax. Astris shook as the pleasure rolled through her body, toes curling involuntarily. Nyx didn't stop, holding her tightly, controlling Astris's bucking hips. Nyx shook as she went through the orgasm with Astris, Astris's senses slipping into Nyx's. Astris could feel Nyx's desire mingling with her own.

Sensations overloaded her, and Nyx's tongue slowed for a few seconds to let her adjust. Her body relaxed, feeling raw. Nyx sped up again.

"Oh Gods," Astris moaned, body singing for Nyx. Astris's body stiffened and shook, crying out as she shattered again. Nyx lapped up her cum greedily. Fingers pressed into Astris's thighs, bruising slightly as she was held into place, pleasure blinding Astris. Stars danced across her vision as she tilted her head back, body bucking for a second time.

Thoughts exited her mind as pure sensation took over. Electricity danced through Nyx's tongue, lightly zapping her clit, the light shock sensations sending Astris over the edge again.

"Fuck angel," Astris breathed, Nyx's tongue slowing.

"Stop," Astris said, and Nyx immediately did so, looking up at her, confused. "Now I get to taste you."

Nyx's confusion turned to desire as she let Astris up, kissing her. Lust coursed through Astris, leaving her sore and soaking. Nyx's desire matched her own, running through her body like a tempest.

Astris swallowed at the sight of Nyx spread out in front of her. Vulnerable and Electrified by her lust. Astris could feel the buzz surge through her, matching the Electricity dancing across Nyx's skin.

This is surreal.

Longing gnawed through Astris, but she didn't rush, shaking fingers coming to rest on Nyx's hip. Astris leaned down, pressing a kiss on her hip. Methodically and lustfully, Astris kissed Nyx. Nyx's lips were soft, her mouth tasting like Astris. Astris continued kissing her, meandering down her body.

The light in the corridor was dimmed now, but Astris could still see Nyx in the soft glow remaining. Her skin was silky, contrasting with her athletic frame and intense eyes. Nyx watched her hungrily, shuddering at the soft kisses.

When Astris reached her core, she took her time. She dipped her head between Nyx's legs, relishing how Nyx tasted. She tasted sweet, like pomegranate juice. Astris smiled, noticing how Nyx twitched under her. Astris put her hand in Nyx's, fingers laced in Nyx's as she devoured her sex. Nyx cried out in pleasure, Astris feeling Nyx's adrenaline and lust pump through her veins. She took a finger, dragging it down Nyx's stomach, admiring the way her warm, chestnut brown skin pebbled.

I do this to her. She thought, amazed as Nyx gasped.

"You always have." Nyx asserted.

Astris dipped her head down again, licking up Nyx's centre slowly, flicking the bundle of nerves. It tasted like lemons, honey and pomegranate. Astris sighed into Nyx, relishing in the sensations. She took her left hand off of Nyx's hip, sliding it down to her entrance. Nyx gasped, making Astris smile in satisfaction.

Astris teased her, dancing on the edge of her entrance, sucking at the bundle of nerves. Nyx moaned, hands grasping at the rock below her. Her fingers dug into the ground, knuckles white. The ground cracked under Nyx's grasp.

Astris's eyes met Nyx's, and Nyx gasped soft breath tickling Astris. Her vision shifted, switching with Nyx's and leaving her looking into her own eyes. Each iris held an Icy snowstorm, swirling crystals alive. Astris gasped at the sight, her vision switching back.

Astris looked down at Nyx. At the female who had changed everything.

I want her trembling for me.

Astris lowered her mouth again, finger trailing Nyx's thigh softly. Her tongue swirled around Nyx's clit, sucking hard. Nyx bit her lip, throat bobbing as she breathed heavily. Astris smiled, curling her fingers downward, sliding her finger around the edges of Nyx's entrance.

Every centimetre caused Nyx to shiver as Astris circled back to curl her fingers upwards inside of Nyx. When Nyx stopped shaking, Astris pumped her fingers in and out, her thumb brushing against Nyx's clit.

Nyx gasped, tightening around her fingers. Astris relished in Nyx's ecstasy, traces of it shooting through her own body. Astris used her tongue to bring Nyx to release. Feeling the warmth pour over her hand and into her mouth. Sweetness covered her tongue, and she licked faster, diving her fingers deeper and deeper.

I have wanted this for so long.

Astris thought, relishing in Nyx's reactions.

Nyx came again, harder this time, back arching in the Air and her eyes rolling back. Nyx breathed heavily, looking into Astris's eyes. She pushed herself up, eyes soft as she pulled Astris in for a gentle kiss.

Astris and Nyx spent the entire night, back and forth, bringing one another to exquisite pleasure. Sleep was impossible when Astris had been waiting for Nyx for so long.

Even if I didn't know it, I was waiting for her. Waiting for this.

Only when the light was starting to fill the corridor did they stop, satiated in each other's arms.

CHAPTER 22: HARVEY

Reawakening

Sometimes I torture myself with thoughts of the revival of Theos. What would it be like? What would I do with it? How would Veritas Hall change? I hope I get to experience it in my lifetime. I doubt I will.

-Harvey's journal 15th Day, 68 AT

Gathering at first light, Harvey, Skylar and Jordan waited for Nyx and Astris. He didn't know what to think about the implications of them being off together all night.

They were enemies for so long, but I suppose that was Kiara's influence.

The pair walked up, bumping each other's shoulders playfully. Nyx's cheeks were flushed, her eyes bright.

"How's that all-nighter treating you?" he smirked at Nyx, who rolled her eyes at him, joining him.

"It's payback for you," Nyx held up one hand in an O shape. With her other hand, she stuck her pointer into the O, dramatically slamming it in and out of it.

Harvey's brows rose in amusement before moving to the task at hand. Steeling himself, he walked to Titan, who was standing by the crystal, looking into it. The Elements played across his face, colours dancing off his Metallic hair.

I used to be crippled by his beauty, now… nothing. I feel absolutely nothing but disgust for him.

The revelation slammed into Harvey, and he blinked before getting Titan's attention.

"We figured out the riddles for the Golem and the Minotaur. You are the only one in our group who can activate the Cyclops and Golem. Kiara will need to do the Minotaur and Basilisk," Harvey stated, face neutral.

"Why you?" Titan snarled at him.

"What do you mean?" Harvey asked, brows drawing together.

"Why is it you whom Kiara fixated on? Why is it that no matter what I do, she is watching you? You treat her like trash, choosing Dyrfaldur over both of us. You don't deserve her."

"You're right, I deserve better." Harvey fought the urge to look at Jordan. Their romance was still forbidden. "I will never be with someone who tries to manipulate me for attention. You don't know what you are doing, Titan. You don't know who she really is, what she wants." Harvey's words were loud in the space, the others silent.

"I will be everything Kiara wants. I don't care about the cost. She told me her plan; unlike you, I have the balls to give her what she desires. I have the balls to stand up and demand the Dyrfaldur finally be treated as the war criminals they are. You failed, and now it's my turn." Titan showed his teeth in a feral flash of white. "Once she and I are wed, I will destroy you."

Harvey bit his cheek. His eyes shifted with an itch. He knew subconsciously he could stop the change if he wanted, but he knew how intimidating his red eyes could be.

I want Titan to see exactly how I feel about him. Exactly what I think about his pathetic threat.

"Dyrfaldur have no connection to the Minotaur! They didn't kill Ender or Kiara's mother!" Harvey seethed as he took a step towards Titan ready to fight again. "You are hanging on to what helps you feel better in an attempt to block out your own pain. It won't work. Your cousin and Kiara's mom, they are already gone. It has been decades since the war."

"They look like them, Harvey. They look like them and they have no Theos, just like the Minotaur. Ever seen a bull-Dyrfaldur? I have, and it looks just like that monster." Titan pointed a Metallic fingernail at the Minotaur statue.

Astris walked over, saving Harvey from himself. She looked to Titan, stepping slightly in front of Harvey, "The answer for the Golem is wine, the Minotaur's answer is shackles. Go to Kiara if you want her so badly."

Titan looked like he was about to argue. A glance at Kiara, and he went to her side instead. Harvey monitored as the pair went to the Golem and then the Minotaur, deactivating the statues. Titan spit on the Minotaur statue before walking away. Kiara smirked as she watched.

The Cyclops and Basilisk are the only ones left. We are so close. So close to going home.

Titan went up to the Cyclops. He read the riddle out loud.

"I sing a breathy song

Sleepy or vivacious

Soft or strong

Pores and keys efficacious"

Titan tapped his finger to his chin before putting his hand down without consulting the group. The Cyclops brandished its weapon.

"Flute" Titan answered the riddle, voice confident.

The Cyclops bowed to him, and Titan turned back to the group. Harvey ignored how Titan's self-satisfied smile grated at him.

Harvey pointed to the Basilisk, turning to Kiara. "Any ideas on the riddle?"

Harvey could feel Titan's stare boring into his back. Kiara looked pleased at his attention, moving closer. He held out a hand to keep her away, stepping back with his hands balled at his sides. She noticed and raised an eyebrow, disappointment evident. Kiara sighed and moved to touch the pedestal. After a moment, she turned and shook her head, "It seems this one is actually difficult. I also don't know the correct answer."

"Then we will have to fight; it's Ice and Venom and a Protector each. So Astris and Kiara," Harvey instructed.

"You should let their Champions join" Skylar suggested.

Nyx and Astris nodded in agreement, perfectly in sync.

We need to find out more about the double bond. I don't think they can control it yet, or even realise that they are acting as one. Just like the statues.

"How do we know that Champions can join outside of their Element?" Kiara questioned Harvey.

"I activated the Hydra," Skylar spoke up from the entrance where he was laying out a makeshift infirmary. "We didn't have Water because we… because I lost Sabastian. Since I activated it in his name, it stands to reason that your bonded partner is able to join."

Kiara considered him, nodding to herself before silently walking towards the Basilisk. Kiara and Astris walked up to the pedestal. Astris's body was tense as she rigidly stepped up next to the female. Nyx stepped closer to Astris instinctively, as Harvey surveyed the scene. She put her hand on Astris, and Titan put his hand on Kiara. The Basilisk towered over them, long fangs tapering to sharp points. It was reared up, ready to strike, its head brushing the ceiling around fifty feet tall.

"Saying the word 'fight' will activate it," Harvey explained to Kiara and Titan.

"Fight," Kiara and Astris said as one.

As soon as they said the words, Kiara's blade flashed, and Astris cried out, pulling away. A shallow cut appeared on her shoulder.

What is she doing? Not working together got Sabastian killed.

The basilisk unfolded itself, fangs the height of Nyx. It stretched out, scales pitch black, tinted with green as it moved in the light. The basilisk was by far the most dangerous monster in here, aside from the Skeleton. Nyx swallowed, eyes wide with fear at the serpent.

Harvey yelled at Kiara, breaking his sister's trance, "Cut it out! Fight the monster, and we will deal with each other later!"

Kiara ignored him, cutting at Astris again. This time, Nyx was there, axe flashing to meet the small dagger Kiara was hiding. Kiara danced over to the weapons rack, retrieving a spear and dropping her daggers. She flipped the spear end over end, advancing on his sister.

"Fuck, fuck, fuck," Harvey muttered, panicking.

This Labyrinth has taken every scrap of control I thought unassailable.

Jordan put a hand on his shoulder, eyes intent on the fight. He relaxed slightly at the touch. Titan joined the battle, pulling the attention of the serpent from the others.

Thank fuck he is thinking. He can't fight it on his own, though.

Kiara sent a kick at Nyx's stomach, sending her backward. She exhaled loudly as she flew backward into Astris. Astris caught her, pushing her to the side as Kiara struck again at Astris. Astris leaned back under the blade. Nyx dropped and swung her leg at Kiara's, toppling her to the ground.

"This is how Sabastian died! Kiara, think!" Harvey was pacing now.

I can't do anything!

The Basilisk struck Kiara and Nyx with its powerful tail, sending both into a pedestal with a plume of dust. Rocks crashed to the ground around them, dust covering them from view. Astris cried out in pain at the same time as Nyx.

I hope Kiara didn't clock that. Get up, sister.

Kiara and Nyx rose to their feet, and the basilisk snapped at Astris. Astris used her whip to encircle a fang, pulling the beast's head into the ground with a mighty snap.

The beast hit the ground, and Harvey watched Titan look between Kiara and Nyx, then to Astris.

Don't do it, man, don't fucking do it.

Titan seemed to make up his mind, calling to Harvey, "You didn't think I would settle for just one taste of revenge? I will take away everyone you care about, finishing with your precious sister."

Titan charged at Astris in a flash of gold.

"Titan!" Harvey roared, pulling forward. Skylar tackled him to the ground, wrenching his arm behind his back.

"Trust them!" Skylar yelled at him, grunting with the strain. "Remember what happens if we interfere."

Harvey watched from the ground, helpless. Nyx and Kiara collided, Nyx using her axe to hook Kiara's spear to redirect the attack.

Nyx doesn't have the practice time Kiara has. She won't be able to keep up, Harvey thought with horror.

A turn, and Nyx swung the axe backward at Kiara's head. Kiara ducked, flipping the butt of her spear into Nyx's stomach. Nyx crumpled briefly, giving Kiara an opening.

No, no, no, please, Gods no!

The Basilisk rammed into both of them, knocking them away from one another again. Harvey watched with bated breath as Kiara stood up, stabbing at the serpent's eye. She made contact, taking out one of the monster's eyes with a vicious stab. A sucking sound as the eye's liquid sloshed, the beast rearing back. Viscous liquid seeped from the eye, the large sphere deflating slightly. A spark of hope kindled inside him.

"Nyx!" Harvey yelled to his sister, who met his gaze, blood dripping into one eye. "You are the charge that will Electrify this kingdom. Don't you dare give in."

A blow came towards Nyx from Kiara, and she grabbed the shaft of the spear with her hand, throwing it to the side and kicking out. Her movements were faster now, her confidence bolstered. Harvey could hear the faint cracking as her eyes sparked. Kiara barely blocked the kick, on the defensive now.

Titan and Astris started exchanging blows. Titan wielded a short sword and shield, and Astris expertly redirected the blows with her whip slashes. With ferocious dexterity she flipped and turned, dodging blow after blow. Her whip snaked around Titan's ankles, pulling him off his feet.

That's it!

The sound of the whip combined with the tinkling and scraping of scales as the basilisk moved. A cacophony that was reached a crescendo as the fight intensified.

The Basilisk snapped at Nyx and Kiara, and they turned to face the beast. It was bleeding from its right eye and stood tall next to the females. It bit at Kiara, who sidestepped, stabbing at it.

The scales scraped along the ground as it lashed out again. Kiara ducked back, green hair touching the bloody ground. Nyx responded by swinging a combination of axe strikes at its exposed flank.

Kiara, seeing that Nyx was distracted, stabbed sideways at Nyx. Nyx took the spear to the calf, dropping to her knees in front of the Basilisk. A nasty wound opened on her calf, Nyx grunting as she hit the ground.

"Watch out," Harvey cried as Kiara advanced on Nyx.

How dare she, while Nyx is down?

Nyx barely got her axes up in time for the barrage of strikes Kiara sent at her. The wood clacked as it hit the Metal, a beat to their deadly dance. She fell back, blocking each blow narrowly, as Kiara slashed at her from above. Titan jumped in, stopping a fang from cutting into Kiara while dodging Astris's whip.

Titan is dead. So Gods damned dead. I will kill him myself. No one fucks with my sister.

Harvey's body shook violently, and Skylar leaned down, ready to stop him. Jordan dropped down beside them, leg brushing against Harvey. Even her touch did nothing to assuage the torment of his powerlessness.

Kiara's spear slashed across Nyx's cheek, blood welling and dripping down Nyx's face. Another slash, deeper, went across the diagonal of her face, opening up a large gash by her mouth. Jordan looked between the two, flashing into a bird. Skylar tried to catch the finch, but Jordan flew over the battle. She dove down, passing Kiara's face tauntingly.

No!

"Don't engage," Harvey yelled, terrified.

He could deal with the consequences himself, but he couldn't deal with Jordan getting hurt. He just couldn't.

Kiara made a disgusted noise, swinging at the finch in a wide arc. Her spear barely missed.

I am so glad Jordan is a skilled flyer.

Nyx kicked up into Kiara's crotch, and Kiara fumbled, giving Nyx time to scramble up again. She blocked a blow from the Basilisk, ducking low as Astris and Titan flew over her head into the wall. The beast hissed menacingly, mad at their inattention.

Good job, Astris. You two might have a chance against her.

Titan hit the wall, cracking it and falling to the floor. He spat out blood, eyes murderous, and a vibrant blue. The gold of his nails contrasted with the blood on his hands.

"Bitch," he snarled, wiping the blood away from his face.

Astris didn't give him a chance to take a break. She sent a series of whip strikes at him; fury incarnate. The sound was thunderous as the whip cleaved the Air with a powerful slap. Titan dodged from side to side, twisting to avoid the deadly arcs.

The serpent slithered between Nyx and the others, isolating her. Harvey couldn't see what was happening behind it. His heart raced, and he pulled at Skylar. Jordan's finch dove again, targeting the Basilisk's other eye. A tail flick, and she went flying into the ground. Harvey screamed as Jordan dropped, tears pricking at his eyes.

Nyx ran past, scooping up the finch and running across the serpent's body, jumping down the other side to Astris. The serpent moved to attack, turning away from Harvey. He could still see Astris's whip still swinging above it.

That's a good sign, at least.

Astris rocketed, flying into the ceiling, jaw back as if she was receiving a powerful uppercut. Debris fell from the ceiling as she fell on top of the Basilisk. The Basilisk snapped at her, fang piercing her forearm. Astris dropped her whip as the beast impaled her.

It shook her around like a rag doll, smashing her into the ground again and again. Nyx screamed in pain in tandem with Astris. The sound was terrible, gurgling cries mixed with the sound of a body snapping back and forth. Tears poured down Harvey's face. Gritting his teeth, Harvey panted through them, eyes wide, tracking the scene. Skylar held him down, Harvey pinned to the ground now. He fought the male, struggling to gain leverage.

I am helpless!

Titan approached the scene, blade bared.

He wouldn't, Harvey thought, but the words felt hollow. Harvey's hand gripped the rock in anticipation as he roared in frustration from his position on the ground.

Harvey watched in horror as Titan swung his sword down. The world slowed, his focus only on the scene before him as it played out in front of him. Astris moved at the last moment, and the blade hit her shoulder, continuing until the hiss of the slice turned into the scrape of bone on Metal.

The blade continued its path through the flesh to the other side of the arm, freeing itself in a spray of crimson. Her arm thudded to the floor, the flesh squelching as it slapped into the pools of blood. Harvey's blood thrummed with his speeding heart rate as he stopped breathing momentarily, disbelief drowning him.

Released, she flipped through the Air, landing next to Harvey in a heap. Blood splashed on his face, and he blinked furiously. Harvey looked up into Astris's pain-filled eyes in horror. The blood from her missing arm spread under her and Harvey. He snorted in some of the liquid, gagging on bile as his head swam.

His heart beat loudly in his head, hammering at his chest like a prisoner in a cell. Red on white as her hair spread in the puddle, soft curls darkening. Blood seeped into her right eye, causing the sclera to darken as her hair had. A gasp escaped her lips, rippling the puddle under her chin. Harvey gagged again, the concentrated smell assaulting his nose. Warm, sticky liquid covered his chin and chest. Skylar yelped, jumping back and pulling Harvey up and away.

"We have to stop the bleeding," Harvey urged Skylar.

"How can I trust you not to join the fight?" Skylar yelled, still holding onto him while standing.

A scream from Astris as her shock broke into pure terror. The sound was unlike anything Harvey had ever experienced, the female wild and primal. Her movements caused the bleeding stump that was her forearm to spurt more blood.

She needs to stay still, or she will bleed out.

"Because she means something to Nyx now. Nyx is still up and fighting; if Astris dies, it will break her! We don't know what the… what will happen," Harvey begged, choking on his tears.

I can't talk about the bond with Kiara and Titan around.

Quieter, he begged, "Please."

Skylar let go, Harvey falling out of his arms to the floor. Harvey scrambled to Astris, dragging himself through her blood, stripping off his tunic. He wrapped it around her upper arm, creating a tourniquet. He finished the bandage off by covering the entire stump with the remainder of his shirt. It bloomed with red spots as the blood continued flowing.

It's not working.

Harvey's throat constricted with a stifled scream.

Fire. We need Fire or something to cauterise the wound. We don't have anyone here with that Element. Maybe Ice? It won't last long.

"Astris, cover your arm in Ice. We need to stop the bleeding," Harvey ordered.

Astris looked at him, pale with pain. She looked down at her arm, stupefied.

She's in shock. She can't do it. We have no training with Theos.

Skylar ran over with handfuls of moss from the stash he had prepared, pressing them into the stump. They wouldn't do a lot, but they would help staunch the bleeding. Skylar rebounded Harvey's tourniquet tighter, taking his place at Astris's side. Astris's eyes widened, looking down at her arm on the ground.

She started screaming. Pain, fear, and loss lacing every cry. Nyx screamed in tandem as she fought Kiara, Titan, and the Basilisk.

We need to end this. Now.

"Go for the Basilisk, Nyx; then we can help! I've got Astris! Focus!" Harvey called out to his sister.

Nyx turned to him, tears streaming down her face, loud sobs wracking her body. She shook in the shared pain, swaying slightly. She nodded solemnly, ducking under Titan's sword strike without looking. Then pivoting, she flipped forward over Kiara's lunging spear. She kicked Kiara as she passed, using Kiara's shoulder as a launch pad towards the monster.

Three against one now, and Kiara is the strongest fighter.

Nyx charged at a full sprint towards the beast, dodging Titan. The serpent was blind in one eye, small slashes covering its body, bleeding green blood. Its eye was bruising now, purple and misshapen, the lid half closed.

Nyx screamed a battle cry, and Harvey watched as Electricity coated her entire body. The light of the Electricity played across her skin and lit up the area as she moved. She was a live wire as she buried her axes into the side of the serpent. Running towards its tail, she dragged her blades through the thick skin.

The smell of burning flesh filled the cavern, mingling with the blood coating the floor, making it slick and slippery. Her axes were heating from the Electricity and burning through the flesh. A hissing exhale whooshed through the room as the snake exhaled a roar like a cobra. Harvey shook with the sound as it rushed through him, the vibrations in the Air hitting him.

"Titan, please," Harvey screamed, begging now.

Titan pursed his lips and made a disgusted sound. He looked to Nyx, then to Kiara, sighing. Titan flew over before Kiara could stop him. He dove, flipping onto his back and sliding across the blood-covered ground under the serpent's head.

Titan stabbed upwards, then released the sword as the beast started its death throes, rolling to the side. Nyx leapt on top, strawberry and black hair flying as she made the final blow to the back of its skull.

The beast shuddered and collapsed, disappearing. Nyx fell to the ground next to her axes. The Basilisk reappeared in stone form, head bowed on the pedestal. The group sat for a moment, taking in the monumental achievement. They had done the impossible. They had succeeded where so many had failed. The crystal flashed, rising into the Air – ready to be claimed. A Unity Rune sat above it, this one blood red and dim.

A soft click came from the crystal, the Elements a maelstrom of contained power.

His kingdom would be safe now.

Our kingdom, Harvey thought, looking to his sister.

Nyx stepped into his vision, and Harvey choked out a laugh, emotions swirling.

"We did it," he whispered.

"We get to go home now," she responded.

The kingdom would be his someday, and he had saved it before taking the throne.

Saved it… *and gained something more valuable than the entire kingdom.*

Harvey let out a breath he had been holding as Jordan rose from behind the beast. She had a black eye and was clutching her ribs, but otherwise, she was okay. Relief flooded through him. Jordan's sunset eyes held his as the world disappeared around them.

His skin itched, and Harvey looked down to see more minor cuts; as he focused on them, they stitched back together.

Theos is making me heal faster.

Their amazement at their achievement was short-lived, as Astris screamed again in pain. Skylar elevated the severed limb. Nyx clutched at her own arm in shared pain.

That's her dominant arm, Harvey thought in horror.

"Titan, you will pay for this. When we get back to the kingdom, you will be held accountable."

The Elements in the crystal were swirling brighter now. Along the side of the pedestal, a small hole opened, a tiny note dropping out and onto the bloody floor. Jordan started moving slowly around the side of the room, eyes darting to the paper on the ground.

Titan and Kiara haven't noticed yet. Titan was about to respond when he stopped, looking down at himself in confusion.

What is he…

Harvey started to feel his body hum with power. It began as a whisper, rising in intensity by the second. Nyx's eyes flashed with Electricity, moving down her face until her entire body was sparking. She held her hands out, examining them in wonder.

Harvey looked to see Kiara's veins changing, now shining luminescent through her pale skin, a vibrant green series of channels branching across her skin.

Titan was changing next to her, liquid gold coating his hands and creeping up his arms. Harvey looked down to his own arms.

Harvey's nails were each a different colour now, his skin seeming to shimmer in a slight iridescence.

Looking to Astris, Harvey noted that she had changed as well. Her feathers had hardened to crystalline Ice, semi-transparent and sparkling.

This is the power of Theos. Just barely the surface of what it can do. What I can now do. Theos is as awe inspiring as the stories claim.

Harvey looked down at the bloody ground. Astris's arm lay there, a reminder of the loss. Harvey picked it up and carried it away from her. He cringed at the feeling of cooling flesh as he placed it behind the Minotaur statue.

She doesn't need that reminder.

As Harvey walked to discard the limb, he noticed Kiara yelling at Titan, who stood cringing away from her.

I'm glad I see them for who they truly are now.

Kiara lowered her voice, caressing Titan's face. Titan instantly brightened.

Jordan reached the pedestal, snagging the paper and slipping it between her breasts.

Why would there be a paper with the crystal? What could be the significance?

Kiara turned around, seeing Jordan by the crystal.

"Hey," Kiara barked, stalking over.

Jordan left the crystal, keeping her body facing towards Kiara as she came to Harvey's side. He brushed his body against her in comfort, too scared to risk Kiara catching them.

I am protecting her by acting indifferent towards her. I can't show more emotion. My connection to her will get her killed. The amount I showed was already too much. I can't be the reason Jordan is in danger. We should kill Kiara before we leave…

Kiara walked with Titan to the pedestal. The pair circled the crystal, faces alight with the glow of the Elements shifting within. Titan had changed as well. He looked as if he had dipped both hands in pure gold, the material covering his hands all the way to his elbows.

Kiara touched the crystal, and the ground trembled. Harvey's vision went black momentarily, power burning through his veins. He gritted his teeth against the sensation as his power came fully into his being, overwhelming his senses.

Kiara flashed away, disappearing from the chamber after touching the crystal. Titan looked surprised before following her lead, touching the crystal and sneering at Harvey one last time before leaving. The crystal remained, still flashing with power.

Now it was just Harvey, Jordan, Nyx, Skylar, and Astris who remained in the chamber. Harvey turned to Skylar. "Skylar, you take Astris. Once we are back home, Kiara and Titan won't dare attack us. We will follow shortly. I need to talk to my sister and Jordan before we return."

Skylar complied quickly, ever the healer, lifting Astris and touching them both to the crystal. They disappeared in another flash of light.

"What's going on?" Nyx asked. She was breathing hard, face pale. "Why aren't you racing for the crystal?" Her face pinched in pain.

She must be feeling a portion of Astris's pain.

"Kiara missed something when we finished the trial." Jordan held out the paper for her inspection, looking to Harvey for guidance. He held his hand out, accepting it from her solemnly.

I have worshiped the Gods my whole life, and now I get to read something from them. Maybe it will even tell us why Theos was lost in the first place.

Slowly, fingers shaking, Harvey unrolled the weathered page. It unfurled slowly to reveal a map. More specifically, it was a map of the kingdom, but it included one thing their maps did not.

Another kingdom to the north of the mountain range, in which Veritas Hall was located. Harvey ran his finger over the marker for their school before inspecting the new icon. There, within a large series of buildings nestled in the forest, was another symbol. Above it, the words made Harvey's blood run cold. It read: Veritas Hall War College.

Two?

Harvey furrowed his brow, running his hand down to where their school was located again. It was also on the map labelled the same thing: Veritas Hall. The final thing on the map was a small poem.

Working hand in hand

The reparations from Theos banned

None of our creations abominable

Deciding rank, mortals playing at being Gods

Watch, listen, learn

Mortals playing at being Gods. Being asked to learn. Being given a map to another school, this isn't over. We have Theos, but we aren't done pleasing the Gods yet.

"We should get Astris to look at this when we get back. She has always excelled in history and Rune classes," Nyx suggested, looking at the crystal. She was worried about Astris, Harvey noticed. "Go, Nyx," Harvey whispered, "go to her." Nyx nodded, turning to leave.

She jogged towards the crystal before stopping and turning back. "The laws haven't changed. You should say your goodbyes before you leave. You two will be separated and killed if they find out. Kiara is probably already spreading rumours. I'll see you two in a minute."

She turned back and walked over to the crystal, touching it and flashing away. Harvey turned to Jordan, stomach sinking, heart beating fast. "I will talk to my father. I will fix this, and we will be together. I vow it." Harvey handed the paper back to her, and she raised her eyebrows. "I don't want others to get their hands on this before we have a chance to study it. I have a weird feeling about this note. I also have a bad feeling about Kiara and what she will do when confronted about her behaviour in the Labyrinth. They wouldn't expect you to have it. Hide it well."

Jordan slipped the paper away, expertly slipping it between her breasts as if it were contraband. Harvey lifted a hand to her face, pushing the short hair out of her eyes softly. He lowered his mouth to hers and kissed her deeply, pulling her in tight to his body.

He sucked at her lower lip, hands dragging her hips into him. He needed her closer. Needed to feel every inch of her. He pulled away slightly, moving to run his lips down the column of her throat. Claiming her. He went to lower her to the ground, but blood splashed underfoot. They broke apart, Harvey offering his hand silently.

This isn't the end of our story.

The pair walked to the crystal, holding hands, before reluctantly releasing the hold.

"Together," Jordan said, looking to the prince.

"Always," he replied, and they touched the crystal together, victorious and hopeful.

CHAPTER 23: HARVEY

Crown

I am so very proud of you and your sister for getting into Veritas Hall. I am glad I made you apply as the other students do; I think it is important that you both learn to earn things for yourselves. Take care of your sister; she hasn't always gotten along with her peers as you have. My hope is that after we give the throne to the next elected family, we will be able to have more time with one another.

-King Blackthorn letter to Harvey 12th Day, 76 AT

A flash, and they were all in the throne room, bleeding on the marble floors. *We arrived at the same time.* Relief filled Harvey at the sight of the familiar room. The cold marble under his fingers was familiar, and Harvey's heart soared.

Home.

Clapping filled Harvey's ears as he looked up to see the room full of the nobility. The area was big enough to fit hundreds of Aervel, the largest room in the kingdom.

The newly acquired Theos in Harvey surged, disorienting him. His vision doubled, and he closed his eyes against it. When the disorientation subsided, Harvey looked around. It was night-time, the sconces lit. The ceiling was clear glass, showing the stars above.

The floor matched the night sky. The surface was like a galaxy with a deep purple base and flecks of silver, mimicking the stars above.

Harvey watched as the blood on his torso and legs smeared across the pristine surface.

The familiar floor, desecrated by his blood. Astris was next to him, on the ground with Skylar. Skylar was propping himself up and holding the remainder of his shirt to the wound.

Something is wrong. Why aren't they helping? Why is Astris on the floor? Stop clapping and help us.

Nyx was on the floor, spasming from the bolts of energy that ran through her. The other Electricity Aervel in the room were shaking, but she was convulsing. Over and over again, her back arched into the Air, caught by the current.

We have more power since we completed the trials, Harvey realised.

Harvey crawled over to her, going to touch her, but pausing. He whispered to her instead, "It's going to be okay, I promise you will be okay. I will make sure you are okay."

Harvey looked around in bewilderment, but his vision kept shifting, forcing him to stop moving.

I am feeling the extra power as well.

Nausea threatened to overtake him, and he clenched his jaw and closed his eyes, shoving the unpleasant sensation aside.

Aervel stood around, drinks in hand. Elemental markers were different now. Harvey recognised his old history tutor, a Fire Element Aervel. His once red hair was now a living flame. The Venom Element Aervel who stood next to him opened her mouth to show green fangs.

"Why aren't you helping us?" Harvey shouted at his old tutor. No one responded, but the clapping died down.

Adrenaline pumped through his veins from the fight, making him unstable. He shook his head, acclimating to his new powers. It muddied his mind, out of his control. Throbbing filled his head as he fought the pounding in his skull.

His vision kept changing, and he opened his mouth in horror. He could see through each courtier's skin now. Veins lit up like golden rivers, faintly glowing under the skin. He shook his head, and his vision went back to normal, the veins disappearing under the skin.

Illusion is rare. It seems I am having the worst symptoms aside from Nyx.

Harvey pushed to his feet, swaying. The world swirled around him, and he fell to one knee before shoving himself back to his feet.

I need to talk to Father, Harvey thought, wavering. *This is unacceptable.*

Vision clearing slightly, he immediately understood what was wrong. He looked over to see Nyx staring open-mouthed at their parents and the entire council in chains next to the throne.

On the throne sat Kiara's father. The male now had poisonous-looking mushrooms growing on his green wings. On his neck was a ring of green skin.

Is it sizzling, or am I still disoriented?

Did I fail the trials? Am I imagining this?

Did we even leave?

Am I dead?

Stop.

Stop Harvey.

Focus.

The council members consisted of eight Aervel. One for each Element. Titan's parents were the only ones missing, his father a Fire

Element, and his mom a Metal Element. They were all old and wrinkled, some having held the throne in the past.

Are those… Void Metal shackles? They have our parents in Void Metal restraints.

Harvey had heard about the old method of blocking Theos in his History classes. A rare Metal that stopped the flow of power. It sucked in light, sucked at his Theos. They pulled him in, his body drawn towards their anti-Theos.

The restraints would prevent the use of Theos, or the shifting of Dyrfaldur.

"Take Harvey, Nyx, Astris, and that Dyrfaldur there," Kiara said to a guard, pointing a long finger at Jordan. "I want that Dyrfaldur as my personal pet. Can I have her father?"

Harvey opened his mouth. Then closed it.

Pet is better than dead for being affiliated with me.

Pure willpower kept Harvey from reacting, but his body trembled with rage.

The General waved his hand in dismissal. "You can have any Dyrfaldur you want. We will be changing things around anyway. While you were gone, a group of Dyrfaldur raided a food store in Bexley. Crime is rampant, and we will deal with it swiftly and harshly."

They were probably starving. The food was dwindling, and we hoarded it. That is hardly rampant; it's just an excuse to punish them.

Kiara smiled, making eye contact with Harvey. She turned to the wall, which once held ancient swords, but now held collars. She selected a smaller Void Metal collar, with a small red gem embedded in the front.

"Collars for animals," Kiara hummed, looking to the heavens, and handing it to a guard.

Fury filled Harvey. As his anger rose, his vision spun, the room warping around him. Some of the nobles around him stepped back.

My Theos is reacting to my emotions.

The warp disoriented him as well, and Harvey vomited as the spinning subsided. Kiara laughed from the pedestal before snapping at the guards. Multiple guards broke off from their posts, advancing on the group.

Jordan looked to Harvey, eyes widening before running and hugging Skylar, who was on the floor next to Astris, still frantically fighting the flow of blood. Skylar, surprised, was knocked over by Jordan. She fell on top of him, face moving next to his ear, whispering something. Harvey caught a brief glimpse of the map being transferred to Skylar's pocket.

Kiara can't get that map. She will destroy the evidence. She cares about power, not the Gods. Good job, Jordan.

Skylar's face, which was pale with shock, hardened in determination.

Jordan was grabbed by two guards and pulled away from Skylar violently. Skylar ignored the guards, trying to go back to Astris. They pulled her out of his grasp, the guards struggling to figure out how to cuff her with her missing arm. What remained of her arm was pouring blood.

She needs medical attention.

A guard grabbed a collar, clamping it around her neck. A Fire Aervel soldier lit up his hand with Fire and grabbed the open wound, cauterising it. Without any potions for pain. Astris and Nyx screamed. Tears poured down Harvey's face as he bawled like a child for the first time in decades. His insides lurched again, but he had already emptied his stomach. He spat bile onto the floor, the guards stepping back from the splash.

I know them. They helped raise me. They sparred with me as a child and escorted me on trips to town.

The guards who approached Nyx hesitated. Nyx was still convulsing.

Why is she not able to accept her power? Is it harder for Halfbloods?

Harvey jumped up, looking around for a weapon. Their weapons in the trial hadn't followed their teleport back. Harvey tried to call up his new powers. He stepped to the side, imagining a copy of himself stepping the other way. The Fire Element guard moved to grab the clone, but the Illusion Element guard stopped him.

They advanced on Harvey, and he backed up, looking around frantically.

I could fly, but I would be leaving Nyx and Astris behind. I can't do it. I can't leave them.

His sister finally stopped convulsing. She was curled up, eyes zapping with power. The guards dragged her to her feet, causing her to cry out. She tried to bite one, but he backhanded her.

The guards surrounded Harvey, and he swung at one. His fist connected with the male's nose, breaking it. Hands grabbed him from behind, pulling him backwards off his feet. The guards held him up, clamping the Metal on him and grabbing the chain of iron. The cuffs were cold, and his body slumped, energy draining. Everything moved slowly, and he felt drugged.

So this is the power of Void Metal.

Harvey looked at the guard to his right. It was Blake, the guard who had stood by Harvey's door every night. They were a Metal Element, with silver wings. The guard on his other side, Caitlin, was one who regaled Harvey with stories at the dinner table. He remembered her kind face in the Firelight, animated with her tales.

Two more guards stood behind him, but when he tried to look at them, a blast of Ice hit the left side of his face. The cold crystals cut into his cheek, leaving tiny cuts, and threatening to get into his eyes. Harvey closed his eyes, turning his head forward again. He could feel his tears frozen on the left side of his face.

Harvey instead looked at Blake to his right.

"How's your little sister, Elise, I believe? We will have to have you two over for dinner again soon." Harvey snarled at Blake. Quieter, he asked them both, "How could you do this?"

"It's nothing personal," Blake whispered, jaw clenched. "Sometimes a better deal is just too good to pass up. Now be quiet."

The guards dragged them towards their parents and the council. They approached the throne and were pushed to their knees in front of the general.

Titus Marrow stood above them, his green eyes toxic, "I have been waiting for this for a very long time. Welcome to the new age. Nobilitas omnibus ante."

He nodded to the guards holding their parents and the council. In unison, the guards drew their swords.

No.

The swords raised.

No.

Time slowed for Harvey as he watched in abject terror as the swords swung down. His muscles tensed, irrationally moving to stop the impossible.

The guards' hold on him stopped him short as he screamed, Nyx screaming with him. He barely heard it, the sound drowned out by his panic.

The swords finished their descent, sharp blades neatly slicing off the heads of the entire council. The heads of Harvey and Nyx's parents. Eight spheres thudded to the marble, splatting against the fine floors. Harvey looked around to see Dyrfaldur in chains in the corners of the room.

Kiara walked up to him, getting in his face. He pulled at the guards to get to her, rage driving him to madness. She snatched something from another guard, showing it to Harvey. It was his Laurel crown. They must have taken it from his dorm. Slowly, eyes watching Harvey, she placed the crown on her head.

"Should have joined me when you had the chance. Welcome to the New Age. Monarchy looks good on Dengar, don't you think?"

CHAPTER 24: NYX

Worthy

A ruler isn't someone who wears the crown. They aren't the richest in the kingdom, or even the most popular. We elect our ruling families because they earn it. Someday, it will be your turn to earn the position we have been granted.

-King Blackthorn letter to Harvey 34th Day, 76 AT

Nyx felt the moment her newly acquired Theos went dark again. It was like falling asleep again after having woken from a coma. It was all wrong. She closed her eyes against the cold Metal as she was marched from the throne room next to the others.

All of it was for nothing. We had just succeeded. I had just succeeded. For the first time I was worthy. Now I am chained up. A failure.

Harvey was being escorted ahead of her, and Jordan and Astris were behind. Astris had her head bent, eyes distant as she followed her guards. Nyx had never seen her that dejected.

Dead. They were all dead.

Her legs shook uncontrollably, each step precarious as her emotions threatened to bring her to her knees. The faces of the council and her father flashed in her mind.

Gone.

Sobs wracked her body as she was dragged, half feral, through the halls she had once called home. Her wings were bound in rope, the rest of her trussed up like an animal. Nyx had a Void Metal collar on, and her wrists were bound in regular shackles. The collar itched her throat, the cold, slimy Metal making it hard to breathe. She looked over to Astris, eyes catching on her cauterised wound.

No. We gave up too much to lose here.

Sabastian's face filled her mind, and Nyx stopped walking. The guard to her left dragged her forward, and Nyx started walking again, the beginnings of a plan forming. The corner of her mouth twitched up, but she trained it down, keeping her composure. She dropped her gaze, letting her muscles go weak as she gave in to the guards.

Thank you, Kiara. You have hardened me. Tempered me in your forge of cruelty.

Her legs stopped shaking as her plan gave her hope.

You may have been my Nightmare, but you forgot one detail.

Nyx slowed her steps further, dragging her body dejectedly.

You forced me to adapt.

To learn.

To fight.

She would only get one shot at this. Failure was not an option.

Once we are underground, there will be no saving us.

The hallway up ahead ended in a right turn leading to the dungeons. Large windows stood to their left, letting in light. Surprise would be her biggest weapon. This meant she wouldn't be able to clue the others into her plan.

She couldn't communicate through the bond; the Theos binding them had gone silent once more. Nyx looked desperately at Astris, but she still had her head down.

The windows up ahead came into view.

This could kill me.

Another step forward.

This is a bad idea.

Their steps echoed across the floor, Nyx's bare feet raw. *Five more feet.*

Nyx tried to get her brother's attention, but he was ahead of her. He and his guards turned the corner, heading towards the stairs that would lead them into the prison. Nyx took a deep breath, fighting to keep her head down, fake lethargy slowing her movements.

I should reconsider; this is madness.

Two more steps, the light filled the hallway, and Nyx stepped into it as she approached the window.

Now!

Nyx threw an elbow in the face of the guard to her right, simultaneously stomping on the other guard's foot. Harvey turned around, dragging his startled guards as they also turned. The guard to her right let out a curse as she surged forward.

I won't be her prisoner.

Nyx closed her eyes, turning her face as she barrelled into the window, crashing through the glass into thin Air. Moonlight lit the lake ahead, and next to it, the stables.

The ground sped up towards her, hundreds of feet below.

Here's to hoping they haven't moved them.

Nyx whistled as loudly as she could, the three-note melody that would summon Azazel.

Dragons were in the stables, and I am such an idiot.

Harvey had been hallucinating when he had whistled the tune, and even if it worked, they would have to break out. Her wings strained against the ropes, the fibres dragging across the sensitive skin and pulling out feathers.

What if they moved them?

What if they had them moved to the front lines?

What if they aren't even here?

Nyx whistled again, tears streaming up her face as she fell. The ground got closer as she hurtled towards her death. A scream wrenched from her throat.

This was the end.

Commotion came from above her.

I hope I gave them enough of a distraction to get loose. At least then my death will count for something.

Harvey's eyes filled her mind as he had urged her to fight. *'You are the charge that will Electrify this kingdom. Don't you dare give in.'*

Urged her to be strong.

Fifty feet until the ground.

They are all relying on me. This has to work.

Nyx bit her scream off, taking a deep breath and giving a final loud whistle. She would go down fighting. The ground was close now, and Nyx could almost make out the texture of stones on the pathway below.

Thump.

Thump.

Thump.

Her heart pounded, her fangs now bared at her impending death.

A flash of red, and scales hit her in a crash. The ruby dragon collided into her with full force as Nyx grabbed onto its neck spikes. It pulled up, wings pounding as the pair flew up the side of the castle. She struggled with her hands bound to hold on, extending her claws to latch onto the beast as it soared up.

It worked!

Glass protruded from the back of her hand, but Nyx grit her teeth against it. Wind whipped at Nyx as the dragon flew up the side of the castle, stones falling as they collided again and again.

Astris's face came into view as she rose to the level of the window she had jumped out of. Astris was being dragged down the set of stairs to the dungeon, but she pulled away from the guards briefly. One of them grabbed her before she could get far, but she was able to call out to Nyx.

"Go!"

EPILOGUE

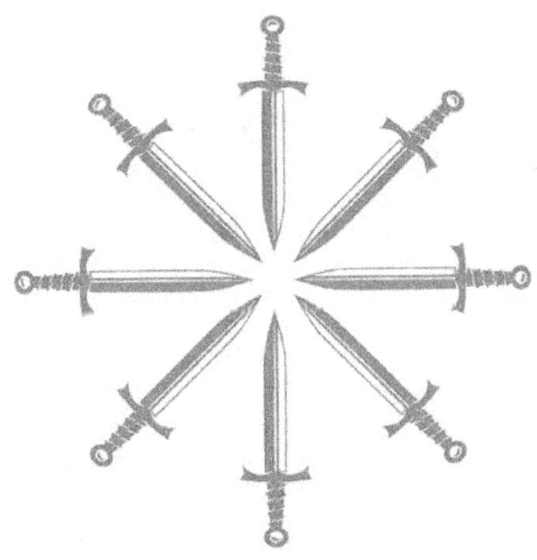

MIKO THE LOST GOD OF THE DYRFALDUR:

Sometimes, I get stuck in a loop.

Loops, I get stuck in.

No way out.

No way in.

No way out.

Mortals are like that.

That is like mortals.

Hatred makes portals.

Mortals make portals.

Portals make hatred.

Loops, I get stuck in.

Sometimes, I get stuck in a loop.

GLOSSARY:

Aervel *(er-VEHL)- A winged race of celestials*

Axios *(AK-see-ohs)- God of Electricity*

Daelan *(DAY-len)- God of Water*

Dengar *(den-GAR)- The kingdom*

Dyrfaldur *(Dur-fahl-DER)- A race of animal shifters*

Elion *(EL-ee-on)- God of Metal*

Eryx *(AIR-iks)- God of Fire*

Harlow *(HAR-loh)- God of Ice*

Hell Portal- *The portal to Hell that opened in 50 TA*

Marvos *(MAR-fohs)- God of Illusion*

Rune-Chosen- *Those selected to go into the Labyrinth*

Octian *(OCT-ee-uhn)- God of Air*

Veritas Hall *(VER-eh-tas hall)- Dengar's official war college*

Verona *(vuh-ROH-nuh)- God of Venom*

ACKNOWLEDGEMENTS-

This book has developed into something much darker and grittier than I had originally planned. I would like to thank everyone who has taken this journey with me, delving into difficult topics that resonate through today's society. From editors to readers, this book is here because of you.

The story isn't over yet...

Follow the author at:

Instagram: @q_christina_w_author

TikTok: @q.c.b.wauthor

Website and about the author:

https://q-christina-byrnes-wampler-author.com

Have some feedback?

Email: q.christina.author@gmail.com

www.ingramcontent.com/pod-product-compliance
Lightning Source LLC
Chambersburg PA
CBHW071343300726
48976CB00006B/1756